Writing Woman, Writing Place

Writing Woman, Writing Place analyses the ways in which contemporary women writers in the two 'settler' colonies of Australia and South Africa explore notions of self, identity and place in their fiction.

Both Australian and South African societies are undergoing the process of coming to terms with their often violent colonial pasts and, in doing so, are also re-evaluating and re-examining the history of white privilege and indigenous dispossession. Contemporary women writers in these two societies are still addressing similar issues as did earlier generations of women writers, such as exclusions from discourses of nation, a problematic relationship to place and belonging, relations with indigenous people and the way in which women's subjectivity has been constructed through national stereotypes and representations. This book describes and analyses some contemporary responses to 'writing woman, writing place' through close readings of particular texts that explore these issues.

Three main strands run through the readings offered in *Writing Woman, Writing Place* – the theme of violence and the violence of representational practice itself, the revisioning of history, and the writers' consciousness of their own paradoxical subject-position within the nation as both privileged and excluded. Texts by established writers from both Australia and South Africa are examined in this context, including international prize-winning novelists Kate Grenville and Thea Astley from Australia and Nadine Gordimer from South Africa, as well as those by newly emerging and younger writers. The readings are offered not so much as comparative but as cross-cultural, taking into account both similarities and differences, inviting the reader to find links and connections across these cultures.

Writing Woman, Writing Place will be of essential interest to students and academics within the fields of postcolonial literature and women's writing.

Sue Kossew was born in South Africa and spent her childhood in Zambia. She lived and taught in England and has been in Australia since 1987. She is a senior lecturer in the School of English at the University of New South Wales. Her previous publications have been in the field of South African and Australian literature, notably on J. M. Coetzee, André Brink and Nadine Gordimer.

Postcolonial literatures

Edited in collaboration with the Centre for Colonial and Postcolonial Studies, University of Kent at Canterbury

This series aims to present a wide range of scholarly and innovative research into postcolonial literatures by specialists in the field. Volumes will concentrate on writers and writing originating in previously (or presently) colonised areas, and will include material from non-anglophone as well as anglophone colonies and literatures. The series will also include collections of important essays from older journals, and re-issues of classic texts on postcolonial subjects. Routledge is pleased to invite proposals for new books in the series. Interested authors should contact either Lyn Innes and Rod Edmond at the Centre for Colonial and Postcolonial Studies, University of Kent at Canterbury, or Joe Whiting, Commissioning Editor for Routledge Research.

The series comprises two strands:

Routledge Research in Postcolonial Literatures is a forum for innovative new research intended for a high-level specialist readership, and titles will be available in hardback only. Titles include:

Readings in Postcolonial Literatures aims to address the needs of students and teachers, and the titles will be published in hardback and paperback. Titles include:

Writing Woman, Writing Place

Contemporary Australian and South African fiction

Sue Kossew

Routledge
Taylor & Francis Group

LONDON AND NEW YORK

First published 2004
by Routledge
11 New Fetter Lane, London EC4P 4EE

Simultaneously published in the USA and Canada
by Routledge
29 West 35th Street, New York, NY 10001

Routledge is an imprint of the Taylor & Francis Group

© 2004 Sue Kossew

Typeset in Baskerville by
Florence Production Ltd, Stoodleigh, Devon
Printed and bound in Malta by Gutenberg Press Ltd

British Library Cataloguing in Publication Data
A catalogue record for this book is available from the British Library

Library of Congress Cataloging in Publication Data
A catalog record for this book has been requested

ISBN 0–415–28649–2

In memory of my parents, Doris and Philip

Contents

     Anne Landsman's *The Devil's Chimney*

7   Revisioning history   135
     Elleke Boehmer's *Bloodlines* and Anne Harries' *Manly Pursuits*

8   A state of violence: the politics of truth and
     reconciliation   150
     Gillian Slovo's *Red Dust* and Nadine Gordimer's
     The House Gun

PART 3
Beyond the national   **163**

9   Exile and belonging   165
     Nadine Gordimer's *The Pickup* and Eva Sallis'
     The City of Sealions

     Notes   178
     Bibliography   183
     Index   197

Acknowledgements

There are many people to thank for their help and support during the research and writing of this book. I could not have completed the project without the support of a UNSW Faculty of Arts and Social Sciences Teaching Release Fellowship. Two successive Australian Research Council Small Grant awards enabled me to carry out research in South Africa and in Australia. I gratefully acknowledge this support.

Others to thank include those who have provided me with research assistance at various stages: Penny Ingram, Fiona Probyn, Luisa Webb and Elizabeth McMahon; and those who have provided helpful advice and suggestions when it was most needed, including Lyn Innes, Dorothy Driver, Kay Schaffer, Dianne Schwerdt, Leon de Kock, Jenny Noble and Barbara Nicholson; and Lynne Schey for her friendship and support.

Some of the work that makes up this book has been presented in the form of conference papers and/or published previously. Thanks to the copyright holders and/or editors for permission to reprint here. These include:

'The Politics of Exile and Belonging in Nadine Gordimer's *The Pickup*', *scrutiny2: issues in english studies in southern africa*, 8.1 (2003).
'Something Terrible Happened: Nadine Gordimer's *The House Gun* and the Politics of Violence and Recovery', *Mots Pluriels*, 13 (2000). Online. Available: http://www.arts.uwa.edu.au/MotsPluriels/MP1300sk.html. Reprinted in Sue Kossew and Dianne Schwerdt (eds) (2001) *Re-imagining Africa: New Critical Perspectives*, New York: Nova Science.
' "The Voice of the Times": *Fin-de-siecle* and the Voice of Doom in Thea Astley's *Drylands*', *CRNLE Journal 2000*: 177–183.

Finally, thanks to my family for their patience during the writing of this book.

Introduction
Place, space and gender

It has been suggested that it is 'deeply unfashionable' (Whitlock 2000: 41) to engage with the notion of the settler subject and that little has been done to theorise this aspect of colonial and postcolonial identity. Indeed, Gillian Whitlock goes further in suggesting that there is 'active hostility' to the 'inclusion of Australian, Canadian, South African and New Zealand colonial settlements in the framework of the postcolonial' (Whitlock 2000: 41). Yet, it seems to me to be a crucial project of post-colonial theory to examine the ways in which such 'unsettled settlers' (in J. M. Coetzee's memorable phrase) inscribe, through their literary practices, their shifting and ambivalent identities and subjectivities, illuminating as it does the complex nature of resistance, complicity and representation.

Even more intricate, and presumably then more risky to examine, is the position within settler identities of the white or 'post-colonising' woman who can be seen to have an 'in-between' subjectivity, often caught between masculinist discourses of nationalism and a kind of maternal role involving compassion and reconciliation. At the same time, these women often share a history of violence with the indigenous colonised peoples, whether it be through exclusionary practices (being written out of history), through 'domestic' violence, or through entrenched attitudes of discrimination. Susan Sheridan, at the end of her study of Australian colonial women writers, suggests that 'postcolonial feminists' should explore those areas 'on the faultlines where tensions and collusions between "sex", "race" and "nation" become visible' (Sheridan 1995: 169). It is on this 'faultline' that this study is situated.

It is, indeed, these very concerns and issues, expressed in different ways, that often still surface in the writing of contemporary 'white' or non-indigenous women in the settler colonies. Such women writers are concerned to explore their relationship to place and to environmental issues, their relationships with indigenous people, and to respond to the often violent ways in which their subjectivity is, and has been, constructed. This book is an attempt to analyse and describe some of these contemporary responses to 'writing woman, writing place' through analyses of particular texts that explore these issues at an historical moment when both nations are undergoing radical self-examination and redefinition. There is both a thematic and theoretical dimension to this process in that I am attempting to look at the particular types of complicity, resistance and representation that these women writers engage with in their texts. Often, this involves an ironic refiguring of gender and race relations. Sometimes, it involves a rewriting of history to bring into focus women who have been ignored. Other texts focus on the kinds of violence experienced by women in settler colonies, either directly or indirectly. This particular book addresses only South African and Australian 'white' women writers, as to include those from Canada and New Zealand would have made the scope too wide – this is a future project.

In selecting contemporary writers and texts, I have included both well-known and newer writers. Thea Astley and Kate Grenville, for example, are both long-established and award-winning Australian women novelists. Astley's fiction has always taken risks in its engagement with the darker underside of white settlement in Australia, paying particular regard to racial and gender injustices, and the award of the Miles Franklin literary prize in 2000 for her novel *Drylands*, marking the fourth time she has won this prestigious national prize, speaks of her importance within Australian national literary culture. Kate Grenville was awarded the Orange Prize for Fiction in 2001 for her novel, *The Idea of Perfection*, underlining her international, as well as her national, reputation. Similarly, Nadine Gordimer's *The Pickup* won the 2002 Commonwealth Writers' Prize for the Best Book from Africa, reinforcing her ongoing literary importance as South Africa's most prolific and iconic contemporary woman writer, whose work has followed the trajectory of South Africa's cultural, social and political changes. Indeed, she is the only South African writer to have been awarded the Nobel Prize for Literature. On the other hand, there are new and emerging women writers, often representing a younger generation of 'post-feminists', included here: Australian writers like Gillian Mears, Jo Dutton and Eva Sallis and emerging South African writers like Anne Landsman. For a number of these writers, the novels discussed here are their first novels. The Australian writers both come from, and represent in their work, a number of different locations, from Astley's native Queensland to Heather Grace's representation of the north of Western Australia where she now lives. Both Kate Jennings and Ann Harries now live outside Australia and South Africa, yet engage with subject-matter and myths of nation that originate in their countries of birth and that resonate with current issues there at this particular historical moment.

What is important, then, about all the texts discussed is their engagement with contemporary dilemmas at a time when both nations are undergoing continuing processes of social and political change. It is in these women writers' texts that many of these current anxieties and desires are textualised, and this study provides a map of their writerly concerns.

Part of the process of reconciliation, it seems to me, is coming to terms with the past (often a violent one) and this involves a re-examination of the history of white privilege. Whiteness is no longer invisible: it is recognised as a cultural construct, an 'unmarked marker'[1] and no longer a neutral identity.[2] Thus, the part played by white women in the settler colonies is an important one to excavate. Through a close examination of the texts of white women writers, and the ways these texts engage with issues of privilege and violence, some understanding can be reached of their double-bind. I am aware of the totalising, and perhaps insulting, nature of the notion of labelling writers as 'white' or 'black' but in the context of the deeply ingrained nature of gendered and racialised subjectivities in Australia and South Africa, in the present as much as in the past, it is almost impossible to avoid such terminology.

There are, then, three main strands running through the readings offered in *Writing Woman, Writing Place* – the theme of violence and the violence of representational practice itself, the revisioning of history that many of the women writers have engaged in, and the consciousness of the privilege of whiteness and the ambivalent subject position of white women in the settler colonies as both colonised and colonising.

Violence as theme

There is, at some level, an engagement with the effects of violence, both physical and psychical, in many of the texts under consideration in *Writing Woman, Writing Place*. The ongoing effects of colonial violence on indigenous peoples in the settler-invader colonies clearly still haunt both Australian and South African national identities and collective memories. Both physical violence and epistemic violence are still legacies of both countries' pasts as well as conditions of their postmodernity. Indeed, both the apartheid state in South Africa and Australia's White Australia and assimilationist policies that led to the Stolen Generations (and only ended in South Africa in the mid-1990s and, officially, in Australia in the 1970s) are examples of the inextricability of the physical and the epistemic. The rhetoric of race, often couched in Social Darwinist terminology, and the concept of racial 'purity' go hand-in-hand with programmed systems of violent and enforced separation of races. Political violence and rhetorical violence perform on the same stage. Terry Goldie has pointed out both the physical and the textual violence in representations of the indigene in Canadian, Australian and New Zealand literatures, reminding us that the 'history of white "settlement" is clearly a history of physical violence because [it is] a violation of physical space' (Goldie 1989: 86) while textual depictions of indigenes as violent, satanic and often sexually dangerous act as 'in some sense apologias for the white conquest' (Goldie 1989: 90). But, like many other theorists of violence, including Fanon, Foucault and Etienne Balibar, Goldie emphasises the ambivalence of such representations, what another commentator has called the 'uncanny and ambiguous relations between ethics and violence' (Glover 1998: v).

Others have pointed out that the 'scene of violence' puts the spectator/writer in a 'position of privilege' (Jolly 1996: xi). Rosemary Jolly's *Colonization, Violence, and Narration in White South African Writing: André Brink, Breyten Breytenbach and J. M. Coetzee* is concerned with the staging of violence in these writers' depictions of violent events and the dangers of spectacle and spectatorship that Coetzee has identified with such representations. I am taking a somewhat different perspective, looking both at the 'violence committed through representation' as a 'form of violence in its own right' (Armstrong and Tennenhouse 1989: 2) as well as at the violence represented in the texts considered. I do, however, share Jolly's concern not to merely 'denounce it [violence] and/or pronounce it inevitable' (Jolly 1996: xiv) but rather to follow Lucia Folena's aim of 'pluralizing violence, qualifiying it, exploring the local and historical constitution of such levels [of violence]' (Folena 1989: 220, cited in Jolly 1996: xiv).

While this violence, both in the past and in the present, often takes the form of interracial conflict, it can also be gender-based. Indeed, Amina Mama reminds us in her analysis of violence against women in Africa that 'colonial penetration was both a violent and a gendered process' (Mama 1997: 48) and that the 'colonization process also transformed African gender relations in complex, diverse, and contradictory ways that we have yet to fully understand' (Mama 1997: 53). Teresa de Lauretis, in her essay in *The Violence of Representation*, insists on the inseparability of the representation of violence from the notion of gender – 'violence is en-gendered in representation' (de Lauretis 1989: 240). She continues:

> The historical fact of gender, the fact that it exists in social reality, that it has concrete existence in cultural forms and actual weight in social relations, makes gender a political issue that cannot be evaded or wished away, much as one would want to, be one male or female.
>
> (de Lauretis 1989: 245)

She draws attention to the male-gendered nature of the discourse of theory (using Foucault and Derrida in particular) that, in itself, becomes a form of violent domination as it presumes 'to speak as if ungendered and for all genders' (Armstrong and Tennenhouse 1989: 3). Many of the women's texts considered in *Writing Woman, Writing Place* are concerned with uncovering such unspoken biases and bringing them out in the open. At the same time, however, it is important to maintain an awareness of the potential violence of all texts. As the editors of *The Violence of Representation* remind us in their Introduction to the volume, 'feminist theory sometimes resembles the very thing it hates and suppresses differences of class, age, and ethnicity, among others' (Armstrong and Tennenhouse 1989: 25).

Linked with both actual violence and with epistemic violence is the issue of cultural identity. Stuart Hall has emphasised that 'cultural identities come from somewhere, have histories'. He continues:

But, like everything which is historical, they undergo constant transformation. Far from being eternally fixed in some essentialised past,
they are subject to the continuous 'play' of history, culture and power.
Far from being grounded in a mere 'recovery' of the past ... identities are the names we give to the different ways we are positioned by,
and position ourselves within, the narratives of the past.

(Hall 1993: 394)

The constant interplay between the construction of cultural identities and
the control of historical discourse can, itself, be seen as a kind of violence.
Exclusions from discourses of national belonging, for example, can have
material effects on those excluded. As Hodge and Mishra point out, it was
only as recently as 1967 that Aborigines were classified as citizens of Australia
– up till then, Aboriginal history was marginalised and Aboriginal voices
silenced, 'acting in parallel to the repressive government policies that
attempted to "eliminate" the "Aboriginal problem" ' (Hodge and Mishra
1990: xiv). A number of the women's texts discussed in *Writing Woman,
Writing Place* interrogate these exclusionary practices in historical discourse
and in literary formations, particularly in relation to those discourses of
nationalism that have been prominent in both Australian and South African
cultural production. Their texts do not just rewrite history but interrogate the
very discourses and processes by which such history has been constructed,
revisioning history.

An important part of the transformative process of such post-colonial
and feminist 'writings back' to the seemingly fixed and entrenched
discourses of nation and history is the rewriting of stereotypes. The traditional ways in which women and those 'othered' by the colonial process
have been represented in nationalist discourses as either 'beyond the pale'
or, in the case of women, as merely symbolic of the nation rather than
its agents, have been refigured in a number of the texts under consideration. Thus, the literary type of the Australian 'drover's wife', for example,
came to represent for Australians the tough but vulnerable woman in the
bush who was both mother to the nation and to her own family. The
South African equivalent was the *boervrou*, the farmer's wife, and the farm
novel has provided a popular vehicle for women writers who wish to
subvert and rewrite the stereotypes of South African settlement, just as
novels and short stories set in 'the bush' (or country towns) have provided
Australian women writers with a springboard for re/presenting women
and place. The close links, then, between violence, identity-formation,
gender and race are crucial issues for all the women writers discussed here.

Revisioning history

Canadian writer Daphne Marlatt has written of the ongoing nature of the
'macho culture of frontier heroism' bequeathed to British Columbians by

their pioneer forefathers. 'In this culture,' she continues, 'art of any kind
has little value because it doesn't contribute in an obvious way to survival'
(Marlatt 1998: 86). Despite this deep-seated anti-intellectualism that makes
it particularly difficult for women writers who have 'never figured as cultural
heroes in the macho scheme of things', she asserts the paradox of the
flowering of an 'alternative feminist vision which is not only rewriting
the old heroic script but changing our cultural values as it challenges the
language in which the old values are embedded' (Marlatt 1998: 87),
reversing inscribed gender roles and reinstating women's place in what
she calls the 'great diorama' of history. By subverting ideas of rugged indi-
vidualism and 'the cult of the hero', such women's writing 'foregrounds
relatedness and community' instead (Marlatt 1998: 99).

Much contemporary Australian women's writing, like that of its
Canadian counterparts, similarly subverts and/or ironically engages with
such deeply imbedded notions of history and power. Thea Astley, Kate
Grenville, Eva Sallis and Gillian Mears each, in her own particular way,
engages with these issues. Contemporary South African women writers
have had a somewhat different trajectory, having to deal with the ongoing
effects of apartheid on their society so that issues of race have often eclipsed
issues of gender. In post-apartheid South Africa, though, there is a more
urgent revisioning of historical 'certainties' involving the retelling of histories that show the much more complex intertwining of cultural and racial
strands than the simplistic 'black or white' version allowed.

An important element in this rewriting of history is the recuperation
particularly of women's stories along with a redefinition of the heroic. The
control of the historical record was of particular importance in apartheid
South Africa where misinformation and inaccurate versions of history
shored up the shaky moral ground on which apartheid philosophy was
constructed. Thus, unlike the contemporary Australian women writers, the
revisioning of history for South African women writers was not just a
reversal of the idea of the grand male narrative, or part of the construction of national identity, but also a rewriting and replacing of an obviously
flawed, simplistic and incomplete version of history with a more complex
one. Elleke Boehmer's novel, *Bloodlines*, for example, uncovers the links
between Irish Nationalist resistance and the Anglo-Boer War and the
mixing of blood across races and nations that was for so long suppressed
and outlawed in apartheid South Africa. Such excavation of the hidden
past is an important part of contemporary South African women writers'
revisioning of history, a move that uncovers and destabilises the very
process of Afrikaner nationalist historiography. Ann Harries' novel, *Manly
Pursuits*, similarly disrupts the received version of British imperialism and
its masculinist ideals. Boehmer's novel also explores the links between
women that connect them across time and racial boundaries, as does Anne
Landsman's *The Devil's Chimney* which explores the parallels between the
life of a contemporary white woman living near the Cango Caves in the

Little Karoo and that of Beatrice Chapman, an Englishwoman who came to live there at the turn of the twentieth century. In finding connections, there emerges a deeper understanding of the continuities between women rather than the differences. Sarah Nuttall has commented on the 'current engagement with the past' in South Africa that has emerged out of its 'politically charged society' (Nuttall 1997: 66) and that is contributing to the regenerative processes of personal and political reconciliation. But she warns against its reprising the very structures it 'ostensibly opposes' (Nuttall 1997: 66). It is important, she suggests, for South African literature to engage in the 'rendering of versions of the past as complex and contingent, overwrought by fabrication and frame' (Nuttall 1997: 66) that she encountered in an Australian exhibition whose historical engagement was seen as 'modifying and reinterpreting inherited codes and (nationalist) identifications' (Nuttall 1997: 66). As Ann Curthoys, an Australian feminist historian, has summarised: 'As a cultural practice, history is tied to questions of belonging, kinship, betrayal, inheritance, attachment, fear, and danger' (Curthoys 1993: 167). As such, this engagement with history forms either an overt or subtextual layer of many of the texts to be discussed.

White women's words

Maternal imperialist, pioneer woman, colonising woman, settler-invader woman, white woman: the terminology proliferates without entirely capturing the complexity and instability of her identity. Perhaps the more problematic notion of an 'unsettled woman' or 'unsettling woman' approximates more closely the complicated axes of power and position, of opposition and complicity occupied by white women within the colonies of Australia and South Africa and, more specifically, such women *writers*, with whom this study is concerned. In theorising these writers' texts, the discourses of feminism and post-coloniality are inevitably referenced; and the notion of a 'Second-World' identity that is unstable and contradictory, is evoked.

This complicated positionality of the 'Second-World' writer, whether male or female, has been described by Brennan as 'segregated privilege',[3] a problematic speaking position that embodies a complex post-colonial resistance. Stephen Slemon argues that this mixture of oppositionality and complicity makes the Second-World writer a necessary part of post-colonial studies:

> For in the white literatures of Australia, or New Zealand, or Canada, anti-colonialist resistance has never been directed at an object or discursive structure which can be seen as purely external to the self. The Second-world writer, the second-world text, that is, have always been complicit in colonialism's territorial appropriation of land, and voice, and agency, and this has been their inescapable condition even at

those moments when they have promulgated their most strident and
most spectacular figures of post-colonial resistance.

(Slemon 1990: 38)

One of the points that Slemon emphasises here that is crucial to a reading
of all the settler literatures is the notion of complicity, and the *textualising*
of this 'inescapable condition' of *both* complicity and resistance. It can be
argued that this messy involvement of the narrating voice in the very structures it is seeking to subvert is a useful paradigm for any postcolonial
discourse. Both J. M. Coetzee and Nadine Gordimer provide us with
examples of white women narrators who are crucially and strategically
aware of this ambivalence. Two examples will suffice: Coetzee's white
woman narrator in *Age of Iron* is fully aware of her own marginality
describing her narratorial voice as 'the words of a woman, therefore negligible; of an old woman, therefore doubly negligible; but above all of a
white' (Coetzee 1990b: 72). She is also aware of the demand for her to
commit herself to the either/or of political resistance and her own
complicity and guilt (figured in the text as her cancer) which preclude her
from the revolutionary activities of the 'children of iron', the black children who are resisting apartheid. She says to John, one of these children,
as she evaluates the weakness of her own voice against the power of their
resistance:

> 'It is like being on trial for your life and being allowed only two words,
> Yes and No . . .'

> 'You do not believe in words . . . But listen to me: can't you hear that
> the words I speak are real? Listen! They may only be air but they
> come from my heart, from my womb. They are not Yes, they are not
> No. What is living inside me is something else, another word. And I
> am fighting for it, in my manner, fighting for it not to be stifled.'

(Coetzee 1990b: 133–134)

While Elizabeth's narration shows her as a distinctly unreliable narrator,
this plea of hers for a word that is neither *yes* nor *no* may also be read as
symptomatic of the voice of the white writer. This sense of her own lack of
authority is articulated, too, by one of Gordimer's women narrators. In
Burger's Daughter, Rosa, in describing the ineffectual nature of her own voice,
says: 'What I say will not be understood. Once it passes from me, it becomes
apologia or accusation. I am talking about neither . . . but you will use my
words to make your own meaning' (Gordimer 1979: 171). There is a
remarkable similarity here between these two white women's voices and
Slemon's assessment of the settler writer's voice. Caught as she is between
her role as coloniser and colonised, and unable to escape from her words
being read neither as apologia or accusation but inevitably as a combi-

nation of both, Rosa here speaks from a Second-World space of both complicity and resistance.[4] As Christy Collis suggests, 'the Second World, then, is both a subject position and a reading strategy which moves in the space between polemics' (Collis 1994: 1). It is significant that both Coetzee and Gordimer choose the white woman's voice to suggest the 'mediality and instability of [settler/Second-World] identity' (Collis 1994: 3).

Helen Tiffin has suggested in an article in which she discusses Australian and Canadian texts by two 'settler-invader' women writers, that, unlike the more clear-cut positionality of opposition to colonialism undertaken by a writer like Jamaica Kincaid in *A Small Place*, the 'crime' of colonialism is more complex in the colonies, and so the settler-invader woman's opposition to, or complicity with, such a crime is itself more unstable. She writes:

> But the Jane Doe I began with – the overdetermined yet unidentifiable settler-invader woman – cannot so neatly classify murderer, victim and murder weapon. Nor is *she* easily identified. For in this imperial murder story she is both killer and victim; writer, reader, pupil and teacher; accessory to murder, yet often a (complicit) victim herself. Consequently settler-colony contestation of imperial textual interpellation proceeds from a deeply compromised and ambiguous position.
>
> (Tiffin 1997: 215)

It is the aim of this study to undertake a close literary analysis of such a set of ambiguities and tensions, in order to analyse the ways in which such women writers themselves have expressed them.

While feminist historians, sociologists and cultural studies' theorists have started to identify some of the elements of these 'settler women', there has not been any sustained and theorised *literary* analysis of such representations across the settler literatures, which also makes connections between the historical representations of such colonising women and the contemporary interactions between white women and 'place'. I use the word 'place' deliberately, to suggest not just 'space' but also 'positionality'. Thus, my approach will attempt to take into account the 'extraordinarily complex and simultaneous interaction of gender, class, race and sexuality (to name just four of the most frequently mentioned axes of identity, oppression, and resistance) that create differences between women' (Blunt and Rose 1994: 6). Dorothy Driver, for example, has pointed out the 'mediatory role' of white South African women writers whose 'sympathy for the oppressed and simultaneous entrapment within the oppressive group on whose behalf they may desire to mediate complicates their narrative stance' (Driver 1988: 13). Similarly, Robin Visel emphasises the complicity of the white woman coloniser in that 'although she [the woman coloniser] too is oppressed by white men and patriarchal structures, she shares in the power and guilt of the colonists' (Visel 1988: 39). Thus, Visel describes her position as 'half-colonized' rather than 'doubly colonized'.

That this theoretical position is applicable, too, to Australian women's writing is emphasised in Gillian Whitlock's reminder of the 'complex cultural context' of Australian women's writing, the analysis of which, she believes, should take into account 'the female subject as a site of difference . . . the ongoing effects of a masculinist nationalist mythology, the legacy of a settler colonialism, the dispossession of the indigene, and, most recently, the effects of post war immigration . . .'. Like the South African women critics, she reminds us, too, that 'women at different moments in history have been both oppressed and oppressive, submissive and subversive, victim and agent, allies and enemies both of men and of one another' (Whitlock 1985: 242).

In this study, I will also examine the complex intersections between complicity and resistance in representation itself. Like Blunt and Rose, I locate a complex ambivalence at the heart of such representations and instability as a determining factor in such subject positions. Colonising women, rather than occupying a fixed or 'settled' position within the politics of colonialism, place and nationalism, are both 'unsettled' and 'unsettling' because, as Ella Shohat has pointed out, 'the intersection of colonial and gender discourses involves a shifting, contradictory subject positioning, whereby Western women can simultaneously constitute "centre" and "periphery", identity and alterity' (Shohat 1991: 11). Laura Donaldson reinforces this emphasis on the contradictoriness and complexity of these women's positionality, when she writes: 'Precisely *because* of their contradictory social positioning, the differences within themselves, the women of colonial Australia illuminate some of the most complex historical and theoretical issues of the imperialist project' (Donaldson 1992: 70). It is these 'complex historical and theoretical issues' that this study will seek to unravel. The links between land, gender, identity and indigeneity are of increasing significance in settler cultures, particularly in contemporary Australia and in post-apartheid South Africa, as the processes of national reconciliation become increasingly urgent. This study will be firmly placed within such issues, as it investigates the problematic relationship between settler/white woman, land, indigeneity and identity by examining texts written by women at 'the margins of Empire'.[5]

Comparative studies of Australian and South African literatures

It has most often been the differences rather than the similarities that have been stressed between Australian and South African literatures, particularly in light of the need of each to establish national traditions that distinguish their literary formations from those of their 'mother country', Britain. These assertions of difference have, of course, also partly resulted from white Australians' assertion of their distance from the apartheid system that made South Africa an international pariah for so long. As Gillian Whitlock has suggested:

That colonial view of the connections across southern spaces, between the Southern African and Australian settler colonies in particular, has been contradicted and suppressed most vehemently during the decade of apartheid in South Africa, treated as apparently another moral universe.

(Whitlock 1999: 160)

Sometimes, this assertion of difference is the result of a much broader comparison between Australian and African literatures, between two continents rather than between two settler colonies. So, for example, it is not uncommon to suggest that one of the main literary differences is that 'Australian literature is not often [as] political [as African literature]' (Goodwin 1986: 41). On the other hand, post-colonial theory has encouraged us to look at transnational connections and shared experiences of colonialism. Bill Ashcroft has suggested that a shared aspect of the colonial constructions of Africa and Australia has been the concept of *terra nullius* and that of the 'dark continent' respectively, whereby each place was constructed paradoxically as both fearful and as holding out the promise of a new beginning (Ashcroft 1994: 162). A further point of comparison that is relevant to this study is the 'idea of a discrete world . . . held together by stereotype – the stereotype of "race" – negritude on the one hand, the "typical Australian" on the other – and the historically very recent concept of "nation" ' (Ashcroft 1994: 168).

Also drawing on post-colonial theory, in their Introduction to *Text, Theory, Space: Land, Literature and History in South Africa and Australia*, the editors outline the links between these two 'southern spaces' with shared 'settler myths' and racist policies yet have different histories of colonisation and nationhood (Darian-Smith *et al.* 1996: 1–20). They end their piece with the hope that their collection of essays on 'land, literature and history' in South Africa and Australia will produce a 'rich new body of comparative work'. Such comparative work is risky, though, and it is important to recognise that some comparisons are over-simplistic and that cultural and historical specificity needs to be maintained. It is for this reason that I have kept separate the Australian and South African sections of this study, while hoping that the reader will be encouraged to draw parallels and make contrasts across the two sections that will perform some of this cross-cultural and transnational reading.

One of the striking issues of comparison between the new South Africa and Australia at the end of the twentieth century and the beginning of the twenty-first is the renewed sense in each nation of coming to terms with the past. The more obvious need to effect a transition from apartheid to post-apartheid state by means of the healing process of the Truth and Reconciliation Commission was echoed in Australia's long-overdue release of voices and breaking of silence in the stories of the Stolen Generations published as the *Bringing them Home* report, as well as the 1992 Native Title Act that finally refuted the concept of *terra nullius*. What both these national narratives of past suffering performed was an attempt to heal past wounds by recounting the violence and personal loss that had been unheard or actively buried and hidden. Both have had profound effects on their societies – hopefully, leading to an awareness of reconciliation and redress of past and present injustices – but also on literary production which has had, too, to come to terms. Both literatures, for example, have seen a marked increase in the number of autobiographical works by indigenous writers that flesh out the shorter narratives of the *Report of the Truth and Reconciliation Commission* and the *Bringing them Home* document. But fiction, too, has shown a significant engagement with the process of reconciliation by exploring issues of memory, history and recovery.

Some historical background – text, theory, space

The editors of *Text, Theory, Space* provide an excellent summary of the historical connections, from colonial times onward, between Australia and South Africa which I shall briefly reprise here. Both were settled to guard the 'margins of Empire' – Cape Town established by the Dutch East India Company in the eighteenth century to provide a stop-off for Dutch ships en route to the East Indies; Botany Bay established in 1788 as a penal colony and outpost from which the British could guard their 'imperial interests in India and Asia' (Darian-Smith *et al.* 1996: 6). The nineteenth century and the industrial revolution led to a huge increase in international trade which 'provided a stimulus to agricultural, pastoral and manufacturing production' (Darian-Smith *et al.* 1996: 6) in both South Africa and Australia, making them into thriving settler economies with growing numbers of migrants. While in South Africa, the greater number of African peoples meant that there was overt competition for land, in Australia, the Aboriginal people's claim to land was easily overlooked as they were seen as nomadic peoples who did not farm the land productively and there were fewer of them to resist.

Yet, the settlers of both lands shared an anxiety about their belonging to the 'dark continent' of Africa or the 'land of lost children' of Australia. The Australian bush, like the South African veld, was a harsh and unforgiving environment for European settlers and 'taming' it was always a battle, most often seen as needing to be fought by a strong man and a home-making wife. As the editors of *Text, Theory, Space* point out, there were actual colonial exchanges between the two colonies as imperial officials served time in both places, often bringing ideas about how to deal, for example, with the 'native problem' from one place to the other. Other exchanges involved indentured labourers, white settlers following gold rushes, and involvement in imperial wars. This constituted a 'dispersal' (Darian-Smith *et al.* 1996: 10) of people across these southern lands. With the twentieth century, though, different nationalisms and responses to settler identities emerged.

Jim Davidson has pointed out that in the many interchanges between the two settler colonies, Australia was 'often . . . a source of radical ideas for South Africa' (Davidson 1997: 72) but that each 'occasionally provided a direct precedent for a new measure in the other' (Davidson 1997: 71). Using the Anglo-Boer War and Australian troops' involvement in it as an example, Davidson suggests that the 'complexities of South Africa' (where many Australian troops found themselves sympathising with the Boers rather than the British) exposed Australians to uncomfortable issues about British imperialism that they 'would rather not have known about' (Davidson 1997: 73).

In both Australia and South Africa, the issue of race has been central, linked as it has been to concepts of ownership of land and ideas of nation. The establishment of the Union of South Africa in 1910 constituted the notion of a unified white race with monopoly political representation and a homogenous black race but, as Elaine Unterhalter points out, both these constructions were intensely contradictory and not based on reality, for both white and black populations were divided by class, gender, religious and regional differences (Unterhalter 1995: 226). With the Afrikaner Nationalist government of 1948, the racist segregationalist policies of apartheid were institutionalised and the withdrawal from the Commonwealth to become a Republic in 1961 completed the sense of national self-sufficiency and coming-of-age. With this came the segregation of races in the form of pass laws that maintained African workers as migrant labour in their own country and the various acts that forced urban Africans to 'return' to their 'homelands' (also known as 'Bantustans') even though they may never have lived there. This enforced tribalism or ethnicisation was also a deliberate policy of divide and rule. While Australia had no official apartheid legislation (though the White Australia policy could be seen as its surrogate), unofficial apartheid operated to ensure that 'the indigenous minority were subjected to policies of racial exclusion, segregation and control' (Darian-Smith *et al.* 1996: 13). The forced separation of 'mixed race' children from their Aboriginal mothers so that they could be brought up as 'white' and the Social Darwinist discourses that reinforced the notion of Aborigines as a 'dying race' were part of this process of violent dispossession that continued well into the mid-twentieth century. The equivalent of Bantustans were the missions and Aboriginal reserves where indigenous peoples were subject to the control and surveillance of white authorities, the most obvious example of which was the designation of so-called Protectors of Aborigines. These government officials were, in fact, policing and administering eugenic policies of racial control associated with assimilation. South African Africans had to wait until 1994 to be 'granted' the right to vote; Australian Aborigines and Torres Strait Islanders till 1967. Thus, a shared history of indigenous dispossession and violent repression, despite the difference in numbers, links the two settler societies, in which both Africans and Aborigines are reclaiming land that was taken away from them, at the same time as they are reclaiming a sense of pride in their cultural identities. Similarly, both societies are now embracing their cultural heterogeneity: South Africa as the 'rainbow nation' and Australia as a multicultural society.

But Gillian Whitlock reminds us, in her groundbreaking comparative study of women's autobiographical writing, that while the legacies of settler colonisation make Australia and South Africa similar, there are 'funda-mental differences' (Whitlock 2000: 143). While there are links between the politics of reconciliation in the late 1990s, Whitlock points out that 'Australian "land rights" and "Aboriginality"' are not equivalent to South African "homelands" and "Black Consciousness" ' (Whitlock 2000: 143) even though they share 'settler myths' and legacies of Empire in the *terra nullius* notion and white domination. She calls for a 'space of translation' in the recognition and understanding of politics and literature in contem-porary South Africa and Australia.

As Anne McClintock and an increasing number of other post-colonial and feminist theorists have pointed out, imperial place was not only racialised but also gendered. Imperial masculinist discourses often gendered the land as feminine and nationalist discourse co-opts women as wombs of the nation or as icons of suffering and self-sacrifice. These stereotypes are remarkably similar in both Australian and South African narratives: whereas the drover's wife in Australia represents many of these qualities, it is the Afrikaner *volksmoeder* (Mother of the Nation) who provides a South African parallel. Additionally, the often complicit and ambiguous position of the white woman, particularly in her role as 'maternal imperialist' in relation to indigenous people in these settler colonies, has similar reso-nances in both literatures: she is the 'good fella Missus' in Australia and the 'madam' in South Africa. These representations are explored in detail in the chapters that follow.

Connecting Australian and South African literatures

Apart from *Text, Theory, Space*, there has been remarkably little work done on the connections between Australian and South African literatures: indeed, Gillian Whitlock and Sarah Nuttall, each of whom has researched both lit-eratures, are among the few to have begun to explore these literary links.

Sarah Nuttall's article, 'Nationalism, Literature and Identity in South Africa and Australia', considers how, while Australia chose not to admit to commonalities with South Africa during the apartheid years, in post-apartheid South Africa the relationship between these two places has shifted 'to a different register of recognitions and differences' (Nuttall 1997: 59). She makes reference, as does Whitlock, to Mamphela Ramphele's autobio-graphical account of her visit to Australia in 1990 in which Ramphele cri-tiques Aboriginal calls for a 'homeland policy' and what Ramphele saw as the embracing of victimhood and the 'glorification of indigenous culture'

(Nuttall 1997: 58–59). Reviewing the competing approaches of post-colonial and postmodern theories in South Africa, Nuttall characterises South African literature's preoccupation with 'History and with inheritance' as opposed to Australian literary activity's concern with 'romanticism and renewal' (Nuttall 1997: 62). In both, she suggests, there is a tendency towards a closing down of contradictions and a construction of the past as knowable, raising the problem of how to respond to the new energies of political and social change without reprising or oversimplifying. In the end, the focus is on her own critical practice as someone who is now practising literary criticism in a 'much freer political and cultural space' (Nuttall 1997: 67).

Whitlock's piece, 'Australian Literature: Points for Departure', written partly in response to Susan Sheridan's 1995 'germinal study' of sex, race and nation in Australia, *Along the Faultlines*, emphasises the need to respond to Australian reconciliation and the rethinking of the politics of race by moving 'beyond the boundaries of the nation' and pursuing a 'comparative approach' (Whitlock 1999: 157). In doing this, she argues, one may retrieve 'connections and affinities that have been fundamental to notions of race, settlement and identity' in Australia (Whitlock 1999: 157). She quotes David Carter's comment that the parallels between Australia and South Africa will 'become less and less resistible', (Carter, cited in Whitlock 1999: 157) particularly in relation to the 'expression of Aboriginal resistance and autonomy' as Aboriginal activists look to the new South Africa for inspiration (Whitlock 1999: 161). She urges examination of connections in the 'politics of race and reconciliation' in order to 'consider the national from an inter-cultural perspective' (Whitlock 1999: 161). Whitlock's own comparative work performs this productive interchange and it is in the spirit of her comments here that I have attempted such a comparative approach to contemporary women's writing in Australia and South Africa.

The structure of this book, *Writing Woman, Writing Place*, seeks to make connections, then, between and across these two cultures without oversimplifying or essentialising either by suggesting possible threads that stretch across them and between them. It is only in the final section, 'Beyond the national', that I discuss two texts, one by Australian writer Eve Sallis and the other by South African Nadine Gordimer, in the same chapter. Each of these texts strikingly looks outside its national boundaries at the beginning of the twenty-first century to the Middle East (as a place of real and/or imagined desire) for a new way of engaging with the issue of national identities. Points of comparison are encoded in the chapter headings which show, as outlined above, the ways in which women in these settler colonies shared so much of the experience of displacement, settlement, belonging and alienation in relation to place, whether the bush or the veld, as well as the problematic relations with indigenous people and, indeed, with the notion of nationhood itself. It is in their contemporary writing of self and place by these white women writers that many of these ambiguities, anxieties and dilemmas are articulated.

Part 1

Contemporary Australian fiction

Introduction

Post-bicentennial perspectives

As South Africa in the last decade of the twentieth century has had to come to terms with reinventing itself as a non-racist, post-apartheid nation, so too Australia, perhaps more sharply after the bicentenary of white settlement or invasion in 1988, has had to come to terms with its history of colonisation. The exclusions from the bicentennial's 'unified constructions of national identity' led to 'renewed interrogation' (Magarey *et al.* 1993: xv) of Australian history and cultural practices, and to an increased sense of urgency to find a more inclusive way of defining the nation, taking into account its indigenous people, its immigrant population and its women. Susan Sheridan speaks for many when she comments on her having to confront 'the question of what exactly we were to be celebrating in 1988, and who this "we" were' (Sheridan 1995: 166). One of the important challenges that emerged from this national self-examination was, as Jan Pettman suggests, the challenge 'to move beyond the binaries' and:

> to analyse the particular claims and constructions of Aboriginal politics, and the implications for all Australians of ongoing colonial relations; and to analyse 'the migrant experience' and the significance of racialized difference and of whiteness in Australia.
>
> (Pettman 1995: 90)[1]

The subsequent and ongoing process of reconciliation between indigenous and non-indigenous Australians, with its successes and its losses, has had far-reaching implications for ideas of nation. Similarly, the important work done by feminist and post-colonial scholars in analysing the uneasy and ever-changing relationship between Australian nationhood, nationalism and women as subjects has had a major impact on all humanities disciplines. While much of this work has been done outside the discipline of literary studies, as Leigh Dale points out, in 'those many local works in cultural studies, history, Australian studies, sociology and geography which are so often cited by Australian literary critics as to be foundational' (Dale 1999: 131), the number of new literary histories being written also suggests what Gillian Whitlock has described as 'the turbulence and complexity of

these issues of authority and continuity in Australia in recent years' (Whitlock 1999: 161).

The discipline of Australian literary studies is, as Dale points out, a fairly recent one and one that emerged fully only in the 1970s in oppositionality to the 'cultural cringe', the sense of inferiority to the culture of the mother-country, Britain. Thus, for Dale, the argument 'for the distinctiveness of Australian literary culture' that was part of a 'broader strategy of cultural assertion' was appropriate to its time (Dale 1999: 134), but represents an 'isolationism' that is no longer useful. She pinpoints the need 'to think about Australian literature not in terms of its exclusivity and difference, but (also) in terms of its connections to other literatures' (Dale 1999: 133). David Carter agrees with this double strategy:

> The idea of cultural transfer and transformation is critical in renewing ways of thinking about the nation and national cultures. On the one hand it suggests how and why Australian culture *shares* many aspects in common with other multicultural settler cultures . . . But it will also suggest the relative distinctiveness that cultural forms have taken within this national space.
>
> (Carter 1999: 149)

It is particularly the politics of race and reconciliation, and the influence of theories of gender, race and post-colonialism, that have led to this renewed questioning of the 'place' of Australian literary studies. Theories of white-ness, for example, have reminded us that whiteness, too, is a construct and that its assumed neutrality needs to be uncovered, just as studies of masculinities as well as of feminism have reminded us of the effacement of gender politics in history and culture in favour of a notion of 'universality' (Magarey *et al.* 1993: xvii). Similarly, awareness of Australia's productive multiculturalism has enabled a less Anglocentric viewpoint of Australian cultural formations, to such an extent that historian Miriam Dixson has felt the need to explore the 'sense of uprootedness' and 'grief' of the 'host culture' (Dixson 1999: 43), that of Anglo-Celtic Australians in light of Australia's 'urgent need to think about the sources of belonging' and the 'obsession with identity' (Dixson 1999: 17). While much of this debate has been conducted in the familiar terms of 'Australian-ness' and Australian identity politics, it has also become more possible to take up the 'challenge' that Dale has identified, of 'retain[ing] a space for talking about "nation" in relation to the literary, without becom[ing] *institutionally* captive to the cultural space of the national' (Dale 1999: 135).

While these general trends apply across the range of Australian literary production, it is, of course, with women's writing that this study is concerned, with a focus on how Australian feminist theorists and writers have responded to these challenges. Collections of essays on feminist issues such as *Contemporary Australian Feminism 2* (first published in 1994 and reprinted in 1997 and 1998, its publication history attesting to its ongoing relevance and importance) cover a wide range of cultural, social and political questions. Cross-disciplinary studies like those collected in *Debutante Nation: Feminism Contests the 1890s,* have used feminist theory to show 'how very much more varied, and contested' (Magarey *et al.* 1993: xv) were the social, sexual and political relations than the 'Legend of the Nineties' suggested. Kay Ferres agrees that feminism has refigured and contested the myths of the 1890s:

> The legend of the 1890s has cast a long shadow. The Australian national character it celebrated was specifically masculine: nomadic, independent, anti-authoritarian and fiercely loyal to mates. Those values were explicitly set against the dismal experience of urban life and domesticity. The careworn wives of Lawson's stories are idealised: longsuffering and resigned to neglect. Idealisation is one side of the coin; the other is outright hostility [to women].
>
> (Ferres 1993b: 1)

Feminist historians Patricia Grimshaw, Marilyn Lake, Ann McGrath and Marian Quartly reinforce this view of Australian representations, adding:

> Nationalist mythologies have always been gendered: in Australia the self-conscious elaboration of the national identity has involved the celebration of a particular style of white masculinity embodied in the Australian bushman and updated in such films as . . . *Crocodile Dundee* – a style that was often explicitly defined in opposition to a feminine domesticity and forms of masculine behaviour that were similarly stigmatised and stereotyped . . .
>
> (Grimshaw *et al.* 1996: 2)

This refiguring and re/presentation of women in the bush in contemporary Australian women's writing is addressed in a number of chapters that follow in *Writing Woman, Writing Place.* The specificity of colonial women's experience is emphasised, too, by Dorothy Jones who suggests that women writers in 'newly settled countries' may:

> find themselves mapping two territories simultaneously – the new land, and the nature of female experiences within it. While helping form the unformed places, they must also seek to define and establish within national myth the area of their own experience as women.
>
> (Jones 1996: 194)

Other studies of specific periods and genres in Australian literature in which feminist and post-colonial perspectives are applied include Susan

Sheridan's *Along the Faultlines: Sex, Race and Nation in Australian Women's Writing: 1880s–1930s* (1995) and Fiona Giles' *Too Far Everywhere: The Romantic Heroine in Nineteenth Century Australia* (1998). Increasingly, Aboriginal women are expressing their own perspectives as in Aileen Moreton-Robinson's *Talkin' Up to the White Woman: Indigenous Women and Feminism* and, as previously mentioned, there have been numerous ground-breaking studies in the field of Australian feminist history, of which *Creating a Nation* (1994) is one example, and multicultural studies, a field in which Sneja Gunew's *Framing Marginalities* broke early ground.[2]

With contemporary theorising about whiteness and about colonial and post-colonial racial identities, there has been an accompanying rethinking of the relationships among and between women in feminist theory. Early feminist analysis, quite rightly, focused on the ways in which early twentieth-century Australian women writers 'offered alternatives to the negative male cultural stereotypes which expressed . . . fear and loathing [of the bush]' (Thomson 1993: 35) and stressed their 'sympathetic representations of Aboriginal culture' and their 'sense of sisterhood with black women . . . pressed through a shared, benign relationship with the natural world, in contrast to the exploitative violence of men' (Thomson 1993: 35–36). Judith Wright, in similar vein, while decrying the dispossession of indigenous lands by white settlers and the ongoing wrongs and inequalities, also suggests that women have been more sympathetic to indigenous people and to issues of racial inequality than men. She recounts:

> In 1992 I was asked by an interviewer . . . whether I thought Australian women were fitted for the role of 'emotional custodians' which they seemed sometimes to have taken on . . . referring to the special situation as between the indigenous peoples and their invaders, I was at least able to instance a few well-known peacemakers like Daisy Bates, . . . Olive Pink, and a few others I knew of who had been able to act as shields, helpers and interpreters between the two antagonists – 'Western civilisation' and the 'primitive rural pests' whom they had displaced.
>
> I still think that, in spite of many and saddening exceptions, this has been true of more women than men.
>
> (Wright 1994: 181)

However, with the intervention of indigenous feminist commentators like Jackie Huggins and Aileen Moreton-Robinson, and non-indigenous theorists like Susan Sheridan and Gillian Whitlock, it is the *complicity* of white women rather than their resistance to such forms of racial and colonial violence and dispossession that is emphasised. Gillian Whitlock, writing about Sheridan's *Along the Faultlines*, for example, sees her work as questioning:

the feminist thesis that women have been routinely or consistently excluded from hegemonic definitions of Australianness by recognising that
white women have been accommodated by these definitions, and [that]
they have often accepted the terms and conditions of this exclusion.

(Whitlock 1999: 152)

Similarly, from the perspective of an Aboriginal woman feminist, Aileen
Moreton-Robinson sees the appropriation of 'white masculine values of
separation and independence' by white middle-class women as making
them 'complicit with the colonial project' (Moreton-Robinson 2000: 180).
It is, she suggests, indigenous women's life writings that 'reveal white
women's involvement in gendered racial oppression as unconscious and
conscious subjects' (Moreton-Robinson 2000: 180). Thus it is that, even
in contemporary Australia, issues of complicity and resistance continue to
be explored and problematised. Margaret Jolly, for example, writing of a
more general problem in feminist theory, has drawn attention to the
'disconcerting maternalism' that still 'persists both in the contexts of academic theory and the practical politics of forging international [feminist]
alliances' (Jolly 1993: 104). She goes on to propose that 'colonizing [white]
women' may not yet have 'relinquished our embrace of the maternal
body even if the Empire has receded from our grasp' (Jolly 1993: 104).
The chapter entitled 'Learning to Belong' that ends the Australian section
of *Writing Woman, Writing Place* examines in greater detail this interaction between indigenous and non-indigenous women as imaged in two
contemporary Australian women's texts.

   In the chapters that follow, then, there are three intersecting strands of
analysis: first, the feminist and post-colonial one that recognises the
gendered terms of Australian historical and literary production and the
inequalities between women that destabilise a homogenous category
'woman'; second, the revisioning of history that this recognition engenders; and, third, an emphasis on the different kinds of violence, whether
direct or indirect, that have attended the process of settlement, what Miriam
Dixson has called the 'physical and psychical violence' (Dixson 1999: 118)
that accompanied convictism and that was an inescapable part of race
relations – the 'reality of violence as an *overall early cultural presence*' (Dixson
1999: 121, emphases in the text). In the process, while attending to the
cultural specificities that are embedded in the contemporary texts, I hope,
as well, to draw attention to comparisons with similar issues that are
addressed within the South African texts that make up the second part of
this book.

1 The violence of representation

Rewriting 'The Drover's Wife'

One of the striking aspects of contemporary Australian women's writing is its ongoing preoccupation with contesting stereotypical gender roles that gathered momentum in the 1890s when discourses of new nationhood constructed a legend of Australian national character that was 'specifically masculine: nomadic, independent, anti-authoritarian and fiercely loyal to mates' (Ferres 1993b: 1). As Kay Ferres points out, 'these values were explicitly set against the dismal experience of urban life and domesticity' (Ferres 1993b: 1) resulting in the entrapment of women, so often associated with these 'dismal experience[s]' and therefore 'out of place' in the bush or outback (both ideologically loaded terms still associated with non-urban Australia), in negative representations. While often idealised as the 'Australian Bushwoman' or the 'Bush Mum', more often women were characterised as 'drovers' wives' – 'longsuffering and resigned to neglect' (Ferres 1993b: 1). Such characterisation and confinement to the realm of the domestic rather than the public sphere profoundly alienated women from discourses of nation. As Marilyn Lake suggests, despite their early enfranchisement (white Australian women were given the vote in 1902), they felt 'oppressed by national mythologies and histories, by a national culture that insulted and trivialised them' with the 'nation' and 'women' seemingly 'mutually exclusive categories' (Lake 1997: 48). From the beginning of such emergent discourses, however, Australian colonial and post-colonial women writers, although excluded, silenced and marginalised, 'still found ways to insert a feminised response to Australian landscapes into their writing' (Thomson 1993: 19). They did this by resisting the gender politics entrenched in such representations, often, in the process, subverting the very terms of these notions of nation and destabilising the foundations of the narrative of nationalism and its inequalities that were integral to 'that vision of common nationhood, egalitarianism, and the passionate brotherhood of mateship' (Ferres 1993b: 7).

This chapter examines the ways in which such subversions and challenges to these prescribed gender roles and attitudes towards the bush emerged in the 1890s, at the time of the 'Legend of the Nineties', and have continued within contemporary Australian women's writing. I will examine, first, the ways in which Henry Lawson's short story, 'The Drover's Wife', was 'written back to' at the time of its publication and in late twentieth-century Australian women's writing; and will then go on to examine Kate Jennings' 1996 novel, *Snake*, which, while never announcing itself as a rewriting of 'The Drover's Wife', nevertheless contains enough implied references to the original Lawson story to justify its being read as a contemporary reworking of some of its underlying assumptions about gender politics and bush life. In their ongoing responses to the stereotype, successive generations of Australian women writers have articulated changing attitudes to the issues embedded in the politics of this representation.

Early literary versions of the drover's wife

In theorising representations of Australian women, the 1890s are an inevitable focus, being the decade that led to what is seen as a defining moment in Australian cultural and political history, a time of debate about nation, nationhood, self-definitions and mythologising, leading up to Federation in 1901. 'The Legend of the Nineties' (the title of a book by Vance Palmer that describes the growth of the 'Australian legend' and the 'Australian type') established what have become commonplace stereo types of Australian identity: in particular, the roles assigned, mainly by white male writers, to 'bushmen' and 'bushwomen', those white pioneers and settlers who braved the dangers of the bush to establish the colony of Australia. One of the seminal texts of this time is Henry Lawson's short story, 'The Drover's Wife' (1892) in which, unusually, the narration is focused on the responses of a *woman* in the bush, the nameless 'drover's wife'. She has become an essential part of Australian national mythology, an icon described by a reviewer in 1896 as 'typical of the trials, tribulations, and troubles of the woman doomed by matrimony to work, weep, and wither in the dreadful loneliness of the unfruitful, unpromising bush' ('P.M.' in Roderick 1972: 60).[1] More recently, though, feminist critics in particular have read the story as enacting the kinds of exclusionary practices which nationalist discourse inevitably sets up: excluding, in particular, indigenous Australians, and setting up roles for women which domesticate and 'tame' them in much the same way that the often feminised land was domesticated and tamed. So, as more recent critical perspectives suggest, this kind of bush myth does not just express a realistic and seamless view of the 'separate spheres' assigned to men and women in the bush, to public and private roles, but, rather, can be seen to express the deep anxieties about identity, settlement and belonging to the land that is characteristic of settler-invader colonies. Kay Schaffer, for example, has examined the considerable number of twentieth-century rewritings and revisionings of the 'drover's wife' story as a way of analysing changing attitudes towards Australian womanhood:

> By studying the critical reputation of the drover's wife as a story, as a female character, and as a representative of the nationalist tradition through the twentieth century, we can trace shifting ideological perspectives on Australian culture and woman's place within them.
>
> (Schaffer 1993: 201)

In this way, Australian women can be seen to have been 'caged' not simply by their physical isolation and privations, as in Annie Baxter's memorable phrase about being 'caged in the bush' (Frost 1984: 105), but also by masculinist representations that confined them to captivity in the domestic sphere, in marriage and in nationalist discourse.

In fact, as has been pointed out by a number of commentators, even in Lawson's own time this version of the 'settler woman' was being challenged, most notably in an earlier version published in 1889 entitled, 'The Australian Bush-woman' by Henry's mother, Louisa Lawson. Louisa makes it clear that, for turn-of-the-century feminists, the danger of violence to the bushwoman was not much from outside the bark hut, in the form of prowling 'swaggies', deceitful Aborigines and dangerous snakes, as in Henry's version, but from within the domestic space of the hut itself, in the form of violent and abusive bush-husbands. Similarly, Barbara Baynton in her short stories collected as *Bush Studies* (1902) offers a woman's perspective on women in the bush which sees them as victims of white men, and of the stereotypical notions of womanhood held by such men. This is both actual and 'epistemic' violence (to use Spivak's term): violence that is both physical and institutional. Through a reading of these texts, that is, Louisa and Henry Lawson's versions of the Australian 'bush-woman', and two Barbara Baynton short stories, 'The Chosen Vessel' and 'Squeaker's Mate', some of the characteristics of these early Australian representations of the bush-woman should emerge, illustrating not just the differences between male and female versions but also the ways in which such discourses have enacted the epistemic violence against which contemporary versions are reacting.

It is timely to point out here that it is with literary representations that I am concerned, representations that have not always been attentive to particular historical, sociological and political specificities but that have functioned more as cultural and national stereotypes. Marilyn Lake has argued against such an homogenising term as 'pioneer women' to 'group women as diverse as landowners' wives, squatters' sisters, selectors' wives and daughters and the *de facto* wives of timber workers together simply because they lived close to the bush' (Lake 1981: 9).[2] Rather than 'proximity to the bush', she suggests, it is 'political and economic factors, or structural factors relating to sex and class' (Lake 1981: 18) which determined the specific nature of different women's experience of the bush. While this is certainly true, and Lake provides convincing historical data and evidence to problematise any seamless concept of 'pioneer women settlers' as a conceptual category within the 'pioneer legend', the *literary* representations of such women and the theme of violence with which this study is concerned function more on a metaphorical than a realistic histor-ical level, as tropes for national and social constructions of identity, as this section will outline.

It has been pointed out, for example, by Sue Rowley, an art historian and academic, that the very act of writing these national constructions of gender identities was an integral part of the anxieties of an emerging Australian nationhood which still have purchase one hundred years later, as Australia ponders a possible republican future in the new millennium. She writes of these texts of the 1890s:

> Significantly, this problematic representation of gender relations is embedded in texts which bear witness to the emergence of Australia-as-nation, and articulate a *national* cultural identity. Because the writers and artists saw themselves as laying the foundations of national art and literature, and because they sought to shape locations, stories and characters which were distinctively Australian, their work has occu pied a significant place in our arts and culture. Consequently, their construction of gender has continued to reverberate through Australian culture throughout this century.
>
> (Rowley 1993: 186)

If, as Rowley and others such as Kay Schaffer have suggested, gender roles have been an essential element within the discourse of nation itself, then these representations of women and men in the bush have ongoing and profound significance, not just as literary constructs but as expres-sions of social and political ideals.

One of the most potent of such ideals is that of the family unit itself and, with it, the concept of motherhood. Rowley, for example, points out the paradox of (British) Victorian notions of the family as 'intact and virtuous' pitted against the Australian settler reality of families necessarily separated by physical conditions in which the men had to travel as itinerant labourers or drovers in order to 'tame' the bush, leaving the women and children to fend for themselves (Rowley 1993: 189). With discourses of social order emphasising the need for stability and order within the family unit, as within the nation itself, this 'disordered family' was the cause of anxiety and ambivalence, much of it centred on the figure of the 'bush mum' herself. Caught between impossible demands, impoverished and often alone, she becomes an ambivalent and unsettling figure as 'mother of the nation'. Rowley points out this double-bind: 'In the context of nationalist mythology, underlying the sympathy for the plight of the woman is the deep concern about the ability of such women to nurture and rear the nation's "human capital", their children' (Rowley 1993: 194).

There is one scene in Henry Lawson's story that can be read as encapsulating such ambivalence. In recalling her past battles with the hostile bush and its elements, the drover's wife remembers her attempt to fight a fierce bushfire which threatened the family hut:

> She put on an old pair of her husband's trousers and beat out the flames with a green bough, till great drops of sooty perspiration stood out on her forehead and ran in streaks down her blackened arms. The sight of his mother in trousers greatly amused Tommy, who worked like a little hero by her side, but the terrified baby howled lustily for his 'mummy'. The fire would have mastered her but for four excited bushmen who arrived in the nick of time. It was a mixed-up affair all round; when she went to take up the baby he screamed and struggled convulsively, thinking it was a 'blackman'; and Alligator [the dog] . . . did not in his excitement at first recognise his mistress's voice . . . It was a glorious day for the boys; a day to look back to, and talk about, and laugh over for many years.
>
> (Lawson 1892 in Thieme 1996: 165)

A careful reading of this extract illustrates a number of interesting implications. To fight the fire, the drover's wife has to abandon her 'feminine' clothing and put on her absent husband's more practical moleskins. This, combined with her soot-blackened skin, transforms her from white woman to 'blackman', alienated by such transgression of her maternal role from her own baby who cannot recognise her and cries for his 'mummy'. That a 'blackman' should be an object of such fear even to a baby that he 'screamed and struggled convulsively' says much for culturally inherited notions of race as well as for cultural constructions of gender roles. The older son, Tommy, who stands in for his father, sees her as an object of ridicule because she is, literally, wearing the trousers, already mimicking those fixed notions of gender behaviour imprinted on him by a masculinist society and, presumably, his father. Even the dog is confused by his mistress' apparent change in role. In the end, however, it is Tommy and not his mother who is the 'little hero', and *she* has to be rescued by the 'four excited bushmen' arriving, as in a fairytale, 'in the nick of time'. The fire would have 'mastered' her otherwise: a word that reminds the reader that she is 'just a woman' and that there are, as Lawson points out in the story, 'things that a bushwoman cannot do'. So, despite being able to take on the appearance of a man, she is still too weak, both physically and emotionally, to do a 'man's work' and, if she attempts to do so, she is seen to be neglecting her role as mother. This seems to clearly encapsulate the double-bind that Rowley suggests: if she tries to take on the role as both mother and father, she becomes an object of fear and ridicule. Safer, after all, it seems, for her to remain simply the 'drover's wife'. The ironic tone of the narration, while seemingly presenting a woman's point of view, maintains a sense of amused distance, particularly in its 'summing up' at the end: the incident was memorable not for her bravery but for being, tellingly, a 'glorious day for the boys'.[3]

Louisa Lawson's more sociological account, 'The Australian Bush-Woman' (Lawson 1982: 500–503),[4] provides a somewhat different perspective on the type of the bushwoman. Unlike Henry's representation which, as Delys Bird points out, establishes her as 'resourceful, undemonstratively nurturant, and fiercely protective of her home and family . . . as a new woman for a new society . . . as an Australian pioneer . . . [with] her uncomplaining acceptance of her role and function as a mother' (Bird 1989: 42), Louisa stresses her *equality* with men rather than her more particularly 'feminine' qualities as home-maker, mother, nurturer. For Louisa, she is measured against her 'soft' city sisters and takes on more 'masculine' traits in the bush: 'she is independent, taciturn . . . If the cattle were lost, she would be all day long in the saddle, working as well as any of the men' (Lawson 1982: 500); and she is someone who can 'share almost on equal terms with men the rough life and the isolation which belong to civilisation's utmost fringe' (Lawson 1982: 500). While Henry describes her as 'gaunt' and 'sunbrowned', Louisa's bushwoman is more bluntly androgynous: 'thin, wiry, flat-chested and sunburned' (Lawson 1982: 500); and 'lank, yet wiry, sun-cured while alive, but able to do, and almost always doing, the work of a strong man' (Lawson 1982: 501). Whereas Henry's narrative suggests, as in the extract above, that the woman tries but fails to stand in for the man, Louisa sees no such failure: 'She works harder than a man. You may see her with her sons putting up a fence, or with the shearers, whistling and working as well as any' (Lawson 1982: 501). What these differences illustrate, then, are the differing ideological purposes to which the figure of the 'Australian bushwoman' is being co-opted: while Henry is perpetuating the notion of the bushwoman as the mother of the nation, guardian of the family unit and as tough, often-heroic but still the 'little woman', Louisa is representing her as so self-contained and self-repressed with her 'iron strength of character, patience and endurance' that she will never escape from being 'caged in the bush': 'She is a slave, bound hand and foot to her daily life.' Instead, Louisa, with a strongly feminist agenda, suggests that the next generation, 'Australia's daughters', will be the ones to build on their pioneer mothers' qualities to achieve women's rights: 'Tough, healthy and alert, they can cook or sew, do fancy-work or farm-work, dance, ride, tend cattle, keep a garden, break in a colt. They are the stuff that a fine race is made of – these daughters of bushwomen' (Lawson 1982: 503).

Similarly, Barbara Baynton in her story 'Squeaker's Mate' from *Bush Studies* interrogates the stereotype of the tough Aussie bloke as well as the all-male notion of mateship through her representation of the pipe-smoking, hard-working woman known as 'Squeaker's Mate'. By assigning her the usually male epithet of 'mate', Baynton is challenging the representation of the woman as chattel, as in Henry's 'The Drover's Wife', by suggesting that she is both Squeaker's marriage partner but also his work-mate, while still acknowledging the gender power imbalance in not assigning her an individual identity and name. The opening description illustrates this challenge to gender stereotyping:

> The woman carried the bag with the axe and maul and wedges; the man had the billy and the clean tucker-bags; the cross-cut saw linked them. She was taller than the man, and the equability of her body, contrasting with his indolent slouch, accentuated the difference. 'Squeaker's mate', the men called her, and these agreed that she was the best long-haired mate that ever stepped in petticoats. The selectors' wives pretended to challenge her right to womanly garments, but . . . it neither turned nor troubled Squeaker's mate.
>
> (Baynton 1993: 54)

Here, it is the woman who is the hard worker, carrying the heavier tools; the man who is lazy and weak. While still dressed in 'womanly garments' and 'petticoats' and with long hair, she defies the cultural constructions of such exterior displays of 'femininity' by her physical strength and stature (indeed, her height directly challenges her status as the 'little missus' of Jeannie Gunn's text that is discussed in a later chapter), as well as by her 'masculine' qualities. It is she who displays all the qualities of 'mateship' usually assigned to Australian men, a quality acknowledged by other men, if not by women (who are shown here to be complicit in their own gender stereotyping), while he, Squeaker, shows no such loyalty to her after she is crippled by the tree-felling accident. The accident itself is attributed to his tardiness which leads her to begin the tree-felling on her own. Tellingly, the metaphor Baynton uses of 'a worm [that] had been busy in the heart [of the tree]' (Baynton 1993: 55) 'long and steadily and in secret' can be seen as a trope for the unseen damage done by such entrapping representations of women, for it is an unexpected worm-eaten branch that falls on her, traps her and cripples her. Yet even in her physical dependence, Mary, the woman, retains her strength, seeing off Squeaker's 'new mate' (the word 'mate' here used ironically) and Squeaker himself at the end, with the help of her faithful dog.

One of the crucial aspects of these representations of bushwomen that has been most suppressed and denied is that of their attitude towards Aboriginal men and women. Susan Sheridan highlights the significance of (white) Australian women writers' representations of Aboriginal people:

> for they manifest not only the ambivalence characteristic of all colonial discourse but also, contradictorily, some recognition of women's shared position with these Others. In particular, Aboriginal women as represented in their writing are occasions of momentary affirmation of the potential affinity of women in a culture that is also patriarchal.
>
> (Sheridan 1988: 77)

Sheridan points out that the ambiguities of their position as colonial women who also share the effects of patriarchy with Aboriginal women are encapsulated in Louisa Lawson's statement that Aboriginal women are 'wives and mothers like ourselves' but also 'poor remnants of a dying race' to whom feminists should 'show consideration and kindness . . . sympathizing in their troubles, alleviating, as far as possible, their hardships, and honoring their womanhood as we honor our own' (Lawson 1887, cited in Sheridan 1988: 77). This statement, while unusual in its acknowledgement of 'sisterhood' with Aboriginal women, retains the hallmarks of the 'maternal imperialist' who, while claiming common humanity, is also asserting superior social and racial power, what Sheridan calls the 'simultaneous invocation of this shared gender *identity* and of racial *difference* in its most extreme form' (Sheridan 1988: 77, emphases in text). This issue is discussed in greater detail in a later chapter.

Although she writes of the relationship between settler and indigenous women in the above-mentioned 1887 editorial, Louisa's account of the life of the Australian bushwoman does not mention Aborigines at all. This is an interesting tactical move, as her focus is on women's rights, so it would not be politic to complicate the white woman's positionality by pointing out her complicity in the colonial equation. Henry Lawson's drover's wife, though, displays a typically ambivalent attitude towards Aborigines in his story: she is pleased to have the assistance of ' "Black Mary" – the whitest "gin" in all the land' to help her in her childbirth, but the paradoxical reminder of Mary's *moral* 'whiteness' despite her name that emphasises her *physical* 'blackness' reinforces the connection between dirt, immorality and 'blackness' that colonial discourse promulgated.[5] Less ambivalent is her response to the 'stray blackfellow' who helps her to stock her woodpile. The narration describes her view of him as 'the last of his tribe and a King' and adds, 'but he had built that woodheap hollow'. From her perspective, despite his nobility within his own tribal hierarchy, doomed as it is in its imminent demise (the 'dying race' notion based on evolutionist race discourse and Social Darwinism), he is, apparently, conforming to the colonial stereotype of the 'lazy native' who is also deceitful. He himself is as hollow as the woodpile, because he lacks the moral fibre of the Europeans. The insertion of the word 'but' after 'King' (with a capital 'K') emphasises the hollowness, too, of his title and any claim to nobility. His deception and betrayal of her trust cause 'tears [to] spring in her eyes': she is represented as the innocent and helpless victim of native cunning. Thus, Lawson's representation of the white woman's ambivalent attitude towards Aborigines is remarkably accurate. As Jackie Huggins reminds us: 'In fact, white racialist imperialism granted to all white women, however victimised by sexist oppression, the role of oppressor in relationship to Black women and Black men' (Huggins 1987: 78).

All three of these writers, Henry and Louisa Lawson and Barbara Baynton, agree that one of the main dangers, apart from harsh weather and living conditions, faced by the woman alone in the bush is that of men. For Louisa Lawson, as E. J. Zinkhan points out, the human menace comes not so much from outside the hut as from within it in the form of 'domestic' violence: 'The bush-woman in [Henry Lawson's] 'A Drover's Wife' fears the outsider . . . [t]he bush-woman in Louisa's article fears her own husband' (Zinkhan 1982: 499). Louisa writes of the differences between Australian and European-born bush-husbands, the former merely neglectful and somewhat lazy, like Baynton's Squeaker, content to 'sit with others, talking, while she, a thin rag of a woman, drags two big buckets of water from the creek'; while the latter mete out 'the vilest treatment' to their wives: 'some are worked to death and some are bullied to death; but the women are so scattered and so reticent that the world hears nothing of it at all' (Lawson 1982: 502).

Interestingly, in facing another such danger, when the over-enthusiastic swagman invades her domestic space, wanting more than just his dinner provided, it is Henry Lawson's drover's wife's determination and the dog's 'yellow eyes' that repel him. But, in leaving, he says, 'All right, mum' in a 'cringing tone'. The word 'mum' suggests that his seeing her in her 'rightful' role as bush *mother* reminds him of his own obligations towards her. No such sense of social pressure impedes the men in Barbara Baynton's 'The Chosen Vessel' in *Bush Studies* (1902). The unnamed narrator's husband is represented at the beginning of the story as a bully, who forces her to face a recalcitrant cow, protesting at the penning up of its calf, despite her fear of it, by 'uttering threatening words till the enemy turned and ran' (Baynton 1993: 132). In considering her husband, the woman ruminates that 'in many things he was worse than the cow', and wonders if 'the same rule would apply to the man' (Baynton 1993: 132). Despite this uneasy relationship with her husband, she is restless for his company when he is away shearing. Like Henry Lawson's drover's wife, she is disturbed and frightened by swagmen, and by one in particular who had called that day to ask for tucker. Past experience had taught her that her husband would 'taunt' and 'sneer at her' if she 'dared to speak of the dangers to which her loneliness exposed her' (Baynton 1993: 134), so she remains caged within the hut with her baby, as the swagman seeks to penetrate the cracks in the hut's defences. This is a potent symbol for her entrapment and helplessness, with the swagman, described as having 'cruel eyes, lascivious mouth, and gleaming knife' (Baynton 1993: 136), paralleling Henry Lawson's snake as a phallic and predatory intruder, and exacting his inevitable revenge by raping and murdering her as she attempts to flee. But it is not just the murderer who is guilty in Baynton's story: the man who passes her by without coming to her aid is equally guilty, not for his sexual predatoriness, as with the swagman, but for his idealising of the mother and child whom he sees as a religious image rather than as actual people. Peter Hennessy's superstition is blamed for his attributing the woman's cries for help to his mother's prayers for his salvation. Instead of helping her, he sees the 'white-robed figure with a babe clasped to her bosom' not as 'flesh and blood, but for the Virgin and Child of his mother's prayers' (Baynton 1993: 138). In a deeply ironic comment, the narrator adds: 'Then, good Catholic that once more he was, he put spurs to his horse's sides and galloped madly away' (Baynton 1993: 149). This is a complex scenario, for Hennessy, in response to seeing this 'vision' changes his vote to support the priest's candidate in the election, thereby fulfilling his devout mother's wishes. One (young) mother is sacrificed in order to submit to another (old) mother's moral and religious authority. For, as Kay Schaffer points out, in her 're-reading' of this story, the story's title refers to the 'appellation for Mary, the Mother of God' (Schaffer 1988: 163) and this problematises the idea of the 'maternal' in the story 'in its fusion of literal and figurative levels of textuality' (Schaffer 1988: 163). She draws attention to Baynton's irony, something that critics have not attended to: 'what confers the power of the maternal as a concept, also demands the denial of the mother as a person' (Schaffer 1988: 163).

On another more figurative level, I would suggest that this ending to the story could be seen to enact the stark choices available for the 'settler woman': as a mother, she is bound (tethered, like the cow in the story to her calf) to her child (the young mother of the story dies clinging to her still-live baby whose gown has to be cut from her dead hand); yet as a woman she is subject to, and victim of, masculine stereotyping. She is 'fair game' for the swagman, a woman alone in the bush available for sex (the story suggests that if she had 'ceased to struggle and cry for help' (Baynton 1993: 136) he would have 'merely' raped and not murdered her as well). Yet, at the other end of the scale, being represented as a 'Madonna' figure, too, has its drawbacks, as Hennessy ignores her cries for help, seeing her as an embodiment of his own mother's moral authority. So the story is not reinforcing the nobility and sacrificial qualities of the maternal role (as it has so often been read), but rather, as Schaffer suggests, in its textual subversion of such idealised and romanticised roles for Australian *men and women* in the bush, 'functions to deconstruct the "place" of women in the (male) imaginary . . . by pointing to it from the stance of a dissident, speaking to a tradition from its dangerous margins' (Schaffer 1988: 168). By suggesting that the restrictive roles offered to women, that their being confined to being seen as either 'damned whores' or 'god's police', are equally destructive, Baynton is pointing to the cracks in the 'chosen vessel' of cultural and national signifying practice named 'Australian woman'.

The trope of such cracks in the walls of the bush hut that represents enclosed domestic space is one that is used both in Henry Lawson's 'The Drover's Wife' and in Baynton's two stories, providing both writers with a potent and yet ambiguous image of both fracture and penetration. Sue Rowley has written a fascinating analysis of both visual and literary representations of space in Australian painting and literature, pointing out that 'the cracks between the timber slabs of the walls convey a powerful impression of restricted vision, inadequate protection and entrapment' (Rowley 1989: 80). While Rowley is focusing on constructions of motherhood, her analysis can be usefully applied to representations of settler women more generally. She comments both on representations of domestic space in Lawson's 'The Drover's Wife' and the Baynton stories, pointing out that not only does the hut trap the woman inside, offering her only incomplete and obscured vision and sound in relation to the outside threat in order to build up suspense; but that the man on the outside is similarly impaired: 'Meaning must be constructed within discursive frameworks which allow only partial and fragmented access to the interior' (Rowley 1989: 81). For example, in 'The Chosen Vessel', Baynton describes both man and woman as trying to track each other through cracks: 'He [the swaggie] had walked round and round the house, and there were cracks in some places' while 'she [was] watching through the cracks' (Baynton 1993: 133). Similarly, in 'The Drover's Wife', danger is perceived and let in to domestic space through cracks in the structure: the snake 'sticks his head in through the crack' and the woman watches the lightning through 'the cracks between the slabs'. For Rowley, these tropes of 'thresholds, doors and cracks in the walls, through which men gain access to the interior' are potent symbols of men's limited understanding of 'domestic space and activity' (Rowley 1989: 83). Indeed, this idea could well be extended to suggest that the cracks are fractures or fissures in the monolithic construction of male and female identities in bush mythology, each not only partial, misleading and limiting but also, particularly for the woman, caged within, as dangerous.

Still 'caged in the bush?': contemporary literary versions of 'The Drover's Wife'

Like the genre of the farm novel in South African literature, to be discussed later, that has had an ongoing significance for South African writers and that has continued to be 'written back' to, the concept of the drover's wife has had enduring cultural purchase for contemporary Australian writers. While Kay Schaffer suggests that the figure of the drover's wife has become 'something of a national joke' (Schaffer 1993: 205) in the rewritings by Australian male writers, there has been a different impetus in the rewritings of these representations of place, nation and gender in the contemporary versions of the story by Australian women writers. A notable feature of women's rewritings of the story is their emphasis on its textualisation of disempowerment and their alertness to its gaps and omissions, while, paradoxically, their own stories often reinforce the power of the myth itself and the roles it prescribes for men and women within the nation by reiterating its basic premises.

The short stories

There are four transformative versions of the story by Australian women writers in the short story genre of the original – Barbara Jefferis' 'The Drover's Wife' (1980), Anne Gambling's 'The Drover's De Facto' (1986), Olga Masters' 'A Henry Lawson Story' (1988) and Mandy Sayer's 'The Drover's Wife' (1996).[6] While a number of commentators have already drawn attention to rewritings of 'The Drover's Wife' by both men and women writers, I shall briefly survey only the four women writers' refigurings of the story and the stereotype in the light of the issues already outlined in the previous versions.[7]

Both Barbara Jefferis' 'The Drover's Wife' (1980) and Mandy Sayer's 'The Drover's Wife' (1996), as their titles would suggest, recycle and incorporate aspects of the drover's wife character from previous male-authored versions and thus, as Schaffer points out, by using 'the composite drover's wife of the masculine imagination' could be seen to reconstitute rather than resist such representations (Schaffer 1993: 207).

Jefferis' was the first contemporary feminist rewriting of the story, though there had, of course, been a number of largely postmodernist male reworkings.[8] While the rewritings by male authors tend to contest the 'myth of "Australian bush realism"' (Carrera-Suarez 1991: 140), the rewritings by women authors tend to focus on issues of the silencing of the woman character by the male authorial voice and inequalities of power implied by the discourses of nation and gender. Barbara Jefferis' narratorial voice immediately announces its project in the story's opening words: 'It ought to be set straight'. The first-person narrator is clearly the drover's wife herself, unmediated by a male authorial voice, who refutes all the previous literary versions of herself as 'yarns' and 'jokes', claiming a more 'authentic' knowledge. While she refers to the fact that she has never been given a name except in Murray Bail's version (and then 'he got it wrong'), and that the women are referred to as someone's wife or 'the missus', the story ironically remains equally silent about her name. By rehearsing each version of the story, the narrator attempts to answer them back, retelling aspects of her own life that have been distorted by the male writers. In refuting Henry Lawson's version, for example, she asserts that childbirth was far more 'terrible' than the incident with the snake. It is interesting that this woman narrator (and author, of course) is far more alert to the racial politics than was Lawson: here, Black Mary is initially seen as frightening ('her ugly face came in the doorway. I screamed' – (Jefferis 1980 in Thieme 1996: 266)), but as she helps the narrator in her difficult childbirth, there is gratitude for her knowledge – 'It made me feel a bit different about the blacks' (Jefferis 1980 in Thieme 1996: 266). By suggesting that she had only told Lawson 'the parts of it that were all right to tell to a man' (Jefferis 1980 in Thieme 1996: 267), the narrator suggests a partial version that is distorted by Lawson's own personal inadequacies. Thus, they (male writers) are said to be 'wrong . . . when they write about us' as they 'don't understand the strength women have got . . . because they think it takes away from them' (Jefferis 1980 in Thieme 1996: 267). Ultimately, Jefferis' first-wave feminist rebuttal of the male versions of the Drover's Wife stories aims to show 'how women have a history, too', and that it is a 'different history' (Jefferis 1980 in Thieme 1996: 272) than the one that has been written by men and that 'someone ought to write it down' (Jefferis 1980 in Thieme 1996: 272). However, as Kay Schaffer has pointed out, by remaining within the 'realist' genre and by simply reversing the gender bias, 'the story naturalises rather than problematises the myth as construction' and is therefore not deconstructive of the myth itself (Schaffer 1993: 208).

Mandy Sayer's version of this story draws on Murray Bail's version (re-using Gordon, the dentist, as her husband and the name Hazel for the woman) which in turn refers to the Russell Drysdale painting, and on Barbara Jefferis' rewriting of it. Thus, following Jefferis, she has her narrator declare that as she is now 84 years old, she wants to 'set the record straight' before she is made as silent 'as that woman in the painting' (Sayer, 'The Drover's Wife': 66), drawing attention to the link between representation and the silencing of women's voices. Direct reference is made to the Bail story when the first-person woman narrator reprises Gordon's accusation that his wife, Hazel, has a 'silly streak'. Their son, Trevor, has inherited his father's old-fashioned notions of women as 'merely' wives, emphasising the ongoing nature of the stereotype: the narrator tells us that he persists in addressing letters to her as 'Mrs Gordon D. Brown' long after she has left his father. The woman narrator's affinity with nature and the bush, her love of chopping wood and her encounter with the black-headed python belonging to the snake-charmer Liam, who stands in for the drover, are all picked up from the original story. This time, though, the snake becomes a sexual object in a bizarre dance asserting Hazel's sexuality that Gordon, the dentist, has always ignored in preference for 'long, phallic instruments' (66) used in his dentistry practice. Significantly, she is wearing the black lace nightie that Gordon had pronounced a waste of money.

In suggesting that Gordon is a 'joker' who produces fake identity cards to take on different personae, Sayer is perhaps also implying the chameleon-like nature of the drover's wife herself, so easily made malleable to fit different cultural purposes at different times. This story participates in the process of transforming this image by refiguring the drover's wife so that she responds to the romance and desire of the side-show man rather than remaining with the boring man she had married. By suggesting that the representations of her both in the painting (which she assures the reader is not by Drysdale at all but by her husband, Gordon) and the stories (which are also apparently authored by Gordon – 'all the stories [he] has been spreading about me over the years') are her husband's form of revenge, the narrator is pointing out how he has deliberately made her seem fat and dull, like the 'brown brushstrokes of the desert' (68), rather

than a sexually active and responsive woman, in order to cover up his
own inadequacy. The element that Sayer's version adds is that of the
woman's eroticism: she has sexual agency, resisting her representations as
an asexual or masculinised mother-figure in the earlier male versions.

The other two rewritings of the story both attend more particularly to
the elements of its cultural production and the material effects of such
representations for women and for men. By updating her version of the
story from a wife to a 'de facto', Anne Gambling's story, 'The Drover's
De Facto' (1986), signals a contemporary rewriting of the elements of the
original, partly to demonstrate the enduring circulation of these cultural
and national constructions even in the late twentieth century. Her woman
protagonist is a city girl and an intellectual, writing her MA thesis, who
is attracted to her modern-day drover, a truck-driver, by the appeal of a
'real' man rather than the 'emaciated city boys' (Gambling, 'The Drover's
De Facto': 150) she has previously encountered. Part of this attraction is
the woman's seduction by the *literary* stereotype of the 'romance of the
bush' induced by the late nineteenth-century bush literature of 'Paterson
and Lawson'. Despite the hundred-year gap between these representations, she, like Lawson's original, is 'uneducated and unprepared' for the
life she decides to share with the unnamed 'drover' who, of course, is
'away so much' (151). An added aspect – though this is there by implication certainly in Louisa Lawson's version of the story – is Gambling's
emphasis on the sexual exploitation within their relationship. His demand
for sex whenever he arrives home becomes a 'physical torture' for her
(152) and while she is trapped at home, he boasts of having a girl in every
port on his trips away. Desperately trying to please him and be the 'portrait
of feminine perfection' (155), she becomes the target of his violence as he
accuses her of being unfaithful. She leaves him despite his protestations
that he 'didn't mean it' and the story ends with her decision to 'change
the topic of her thesis' (159), a phrase that can be seen as ironically
suggesting the need for her to revise her romanticised preconceptions of
the bush and of a 'real man', both of which entrapped her in their corollary:
an unchanged version in the late twentieth century of a late nineteenth-
century woman's role as 'drover's wife'. Unlike Lawson's and Baynton's
women, this unnamed woman is able to assert her agency by deciding to
leave. The irony, though, is that the myths of the Aussie male and the
romance of the bush have endured to the extent that they could affect
even an educated city woman who has only noted the attractive aspects
of the story and not the more subtle warnings of domestic violence, small-
town gossip and malice, and the privations of living in the bush.

In Olga Masters' 'A Henry Lawson Story' (1988), the drover's wife is
not mentioned until late in the narrative. Indeed, the woman in this story,
Lil Warwick, at first glance, is the opposite of the drover's wife: she is
excessively timid, has no romantic notions and is obsessed with staying at
home, refusing to go out even to do her shopping. Her only venture into

the outside world takes the form of her walks with her many successive babies in their pram along a road in the bush with 'more than a mile of walking with little risk of meeting anyone' (Masters, 'A Henry Lawson Story': 102). Glad when a fast car belonging to the neighbouring Fisher brothers passes her, so that she does not have to stop and greet them, she smiles one day at the fast-travelling car belonging to Councillor Fisher that has passed her in a hurry and, to her terror, he reverses to greet her. She reminds him, he thinks later, of the drover's wife (his 'favourite story'), a woman he would have liked 'for a mother'. Instead, his own mother was 'a different kind of woman' who worked all her life and did not provide the nurturing bosom he imagines the drover's wife would have had. He himself has remained unmarried and the implication is that he has never found the idealised version of womanhood that the Henry Lawson story seemed to offer. Thus, the title of the story itself – 'A Henry Lawson Story' – takes on the implication that it is just a story, a fantasy of womanhood thought up by men whose real effect is to keep women like Lil too frightened to escape from the domestic sphere, ill-equipped to interact with the wider world, and one that simultaneously traps men into romanticised notions of nurturing women who will mother them. By contrasting the notion of 'story' with the materiality of the lives of the two contrasting characters – the woman psychologically damaged by her prescribed social role that limits her influence to being 'her indoors' as opposed to the successful Councillor who operates confidently in the public sphere – Olga Masters, like Gambling, is reiterating the continuing impact of such representations. The rewritings by these four contemporary women writers, then, recontextualise Lawson's 'The Drover's Wife' thereby providing an index of changing feminist responses to the representation of women from objectification to agency, from the early feminist goal of 'setting the record straight' to Sayer's more contemporary assertion of women's erotic subjectivity.

Kate Jennings, Snake (1996)

Kate Jennings has described her fiction as 'short, grim and subversive'[9] and *Snake*, her first novel (she is a well-known and widely-published poet), displays all these characteristics with its brief chapters that have often ironic and sometimes poetic titles. Its grimness lies in its evocation of rural life for a couple, Rex and Irene, who marry in post-war Australia – she a city woman from a well-to-do family from Sydney's North Shore ('snobs', as Rex characterises them) and he just out of the army 'with a modest row of medals' (Jennings, *Snake*: 15), a country boy who had grown up on a farm and left school early. Rex's parents epitomise the 'battler' breed of Australian farmers: taciturn, practical and stoical. The narration suggests that their wordlessness was a precaution against 'admitting the inadmissable', namely that 'their way of life – tilling a blighted soil under a punishing sun – was intolerable' (9). It is back to this way of life that the newlywed couple returns, to a farm and farmhouse that belongs to Irene's father, with Rex as a share farmer, a position he considers 'ignominious' but at least a 'new start' (31) in an area where his grandfather had once worked, ironically named Progress.

Both grim and subversive is Jennings' portrait of the entrapment of both Rex and Irene in a loveless marriage. From the beginning of her experience of motherhood, Irene is shown to be a rebel, refusing to 'mother' her baby girl at the breast, instead recalling the image of a cat whose maternal instincts, like her own, were 'wrong' and who, having given birth to a kitten, proceeded to eat it (33). For a time, after the birth of her son, Irene was happy in her role as wife and mother, with her 1950s' trophy domestic appliances of 'Hoover twin-tub washing machines' and 'Singer sewing machine' (37) to facilitate her housewifely duties. Additionally, like a good farmer's wife, she bottles fruit and establishes a garden. Unlike the traditional colonial bush wife, however, whose garden was, in opposition to the wildness of the bush, a place of cultivated plants and flowers, Irene is 'ahead of her time' in growing native plants. Irises, though, become her passion. Yet Irene is not happy in her role as farmer's wife, instead desiring to 'be someone else . . . to be somewhere else' (39). Rex's inability to escape her moods, which, despite the open horizons of the bush that 'stretched to the back of beyond' (40), suffocated him, reinforces his lack of understanding of the 'female sex' (41). His needs, he assures her, are simple. 'to harvest his crops, care for his animals, share it all with a good woman' (42). But Irene refuses to be a 'good woman', looking for excitement outside the confines of the marriage in a series of infidelities, seeking to escape the boredom of the domestic sphere by working. Her image of her own entrapment is that of a 'penned heifer' in the peak of physical health but displaying all the signs of unhappiness (69). Her 'dogsbody position' (70) with Freddie Garlick at the radio station does not offer Irene the possibility of seduction she had hoped for, but instead puts her in touch with 'culture' – music, poetry, literature. Instead of liberating her spirit, though, this education makes Irene even more aware of the 'dull, mean and ordinary existence' (72) to which she has been unjustly consigned by being a farmer's wife. After a series of extra-marital adventures, she leaves Rex for 'someone new' and 'following the migratory pattern of Australian adulterers', they go north (144), with Irene identifying her own situation with Oscar Wilde's exile and marginalisation, and the sense of having had the best years of her life stolen from her in her role as farmer's wife. Rex's symbolic gesture in response to Irene's flight from him is to release two hundred pigs on the farm, allowing them to invade Irene's garden which is soon destroyed. His suicide by drowning seems the inevitable conclusion to the destructive relationship.

The fixity of gender roles in the 1950s, as in the 1890s, in Australia is highlighted by the novel's characterisation of gender politics. Echoing the way the drover's wife is known not by her own name but only by her gender and social role, Irene's daughter is known only as 'Girlie', though we are told that she was named after her grandmother whose name is never revealed. Similarly, Girlie's brother is called 'Boy'. While Irene is irritated by Girlie, she has a close relationship with Boy, finding him 'sturdily masculine, with a winning manner' (58). Girlie's refusal to conform to the social parameters drawn up for 'good girls' is illustrated in her subversive dancing when dressing up in the skirt Irene has made her from an old evening gown. She dances 'not to the music, but to a manic rhythm suggested by her own hot blood' (57) and it is this, the narrative suggests, that irks Irene more than anything else. Girlie similarly refuses the stereotypical literary roles for girls, writing epic compositions about a *'fearless* girl' having 'improbable adventures' (60) in foreign places, while Boy has more predictably 'boyish' fantasies about the Battle of Britain. In identifying herself with the virtues attributed to the Anzacs in her prize-winning composition on the iconic figure of Simpson and his donkey at Gallipoli, she is participating in nationalistic discourse at the same time as registering her distance from its masculinist ethos. Thus, she 'used words like "intrepid", "tenacious", and "selfless", and *imagined herself* to have some of these virtues' (67, my emphases). Yet Rex has expectations of Girlie that return us to notions of the drover's wife: he believes a country woman 'should be able to do everything her husband could and more' (61), forcing Girlie to participate in killing a rooster, and punishing her for her 'rebelliousness' (in the form of her refusal) with a dose of Epsom salts. The town's first lesbian couple, Hildegarde and Audrey, who arrive in Progress on a Harley Davidson in 1959, do 'not attract comment' at first, simply because they are beyond the 'ken' of the locals, who wonder why they do not try to make themselves look 'more attractive to men' (81). Hildegarde's friendship with Irene is at first encouraged by Rex but when he sees them in a moment of closeness, he expels Hildegarde from the house, suddenly suspecting what he had scarcely been able to imagine previously.

The novel's narrative perspective itself engages with the notion of different versions of the drover's wife story. Part 1 encapsulates Rex's point of view by means of a second-person narration – the 'you' is the injured husband emasculated by his wife's contempt and sidelined by his children's indifference. Parts 2 and 3 revert to the seemingly objective third-person narration of Lawson's story but, unlike that version, Part 4 of this novel is Irene's viewpoint, again via a second-person narration. Thus, the different focalisations reproduce the ways in which various perspectives have been used to rewrite either distance from, or closeness to, the drover's wife's point of view. The novel also references a number of the original story's major tropes, most notably, those of the bush itself and the snake. As in Lawson's story, the farmer and his wife must face the vicissitudes of life in the bush, narrated in quick successive chapters chronicling the biblical-like 'scourges visited upon the farm' (101) in the form of mice, dust, locusts and hail.

It is, though, the trope of the snake that, evidenced in the novel's title, has most significance. As in Lawson's short story, the snake invites symbolic interpretation. According to Kay Schaffer's Lacanian reading of Lawson's story, the snake is part of a chain of signifiers that 'link the woman to the snake, sin and nature' (Schaffer 1988: 133) at the same time as linking her to Man, as she stands in for her absent husband, as part of the tradition of defining national identity 'against the otherness of the bush' (Schaffer 1988: 136). In addition to the biblical and national associations, the snake also has links with classical mythology. In the Tiresias myth, it was the seer's striking of the snake that turned him into a woman. The snake, then, carries resonances of gender transformations, linking it to the images of androgyny, desexualisation and the refiguring of the feminine in the drover's wife stories.[10] Jennings' version of the story has Irene first encountering a 'long, fast, deadly' (Jennings, *Snake*: 35) brown snake among the asparagus ferns. Its association with the hidden dangers of the bush as one of Australia's 'stealthy, circumspect creatures' (76) is emphasised again in the account of a film watched by the schoolchildren in which a young boy mistakes a snake for a log and is bitten, facing 'certain death' unless able to treat his own bite. Girlie's response to the film is to imagine 'snakes, silent and purposeful, slithering . . . into the house' (77), in an image similar to that in Lawson's story when the snake finds the cracks in the hut in order to invade its hallowed space, reinforcing its fragility as domestic space in the midst of the dangerous bush. Rex's workmanlike approach to snakes, in contrast to Girlie's horrified fascination, is to decapitate them with his shovel, leaving only the flimsy skin to disintegrate with time. Boy, too, on encountering a brown snake (significantly just after his seduction by Irene's friend, Gwyneth) is determined to kill it with an axe, but the snake is too quick for him. Irene, believing snakes to be 'necessary to the balance of nature' (109), calls Girlie a 'scaredy-cat' for being unable to react to a brown snake that was 'promenading' next to her in the vegetable garden. So while it could be suggested that the snake becomes an index of being 'at home' or not in the bush, as well as the inherent dangers of the bush itself, the novel's title both endows and empties the symbol of signifying power. It is not firmly anchored to any one character or event, either symbolic or realistic, but resonates throughout as a reference perhaps to signifying activity itself, with its connotations of Biblical sin, temptation and danger, subject to endless refiguring, like the figure of the drover's wife herself.

Each of these writings-back, then, in the form of the short stories and in Kate Jennings' *Snake*, emphasises a different aspect of the original story that, for each woman author, requires rewriting: whether it be to give voice to and name the woman protagonist, to update the characters to fit contemporary mores, to draw attention to the paralysing influence of such literary representations for women and for men, or to restore a sense of agency and sexuality to the unamed woman. The common thread, though, is the shared sense of the importance of representation itself and its ongoing cultural effects. These women writers are always aware of their simultaneous role in producing and subverting such representations, by 'offering a revision of familiar scripts' (Lionnet 1995: 101). The following chapter extends this notion by examining two versions of contemporary women, both of them perceived as outsiders in relation to mainstream Australia, 'going bush', and, in the process, finding a way of belonging that allows for their 'difference'.

2 'Gone bush'

Refiguring women and the bush

Kate Grenville's The Idea of Perfection *and Eva Sallis'* Hiam

It is clear from its continuing influence on contemporary literature, popular culture and media that the idea of the bush and the images associated with it have ongoing significance for Australian discourses of nation and identity. There has been, since the emergence of the legends of the bush, a contestatory relationship between the city and the bush. Indeed, the inter-dependence of the two that is one of the often noted ironies of the tradition itself is exemplified in Graeme Davidson's suggestion that the myths of the bush were ironically 'born of urban experience' and that the projection of the values associated with the bush – such as the anti-clericalism, nationalism, bush sentiments and racial prejudice identified by Russel Ward – 'must be understood in terms of a concurrent movement to establish the "city" as a symbol of their negation' (Davison 1992: 196–197). But the bush is not a stable signifier: as Whitlock and Carter suggest, it is a cultural symbol 'which has been used by many different individuals and social groups for a wide variety of diverse, sometimes contradictory, purposes' (Whitlock and Carter 1992: 177). It is not surprising, then, that contemporary Australian women writers are still contesting some of these cultural constructions in their fiction. It has already been argued that the discourses of Australian national and cultural identity exclude difference, whether it be that of women in the man's world of the bush, or of its indigenous inhabitants silenced and relegated to the position of 'shadows', or of those from migrant cultures other than Anglo-Celtic. As Patricia Grimshaw *et al.* have suggested, 'The process of creating a nation . . . always involves conflict in the encounter between diversity and the incitement to national uniformity' (Grimshaw *et al.* 1996: 2). Both of the novels discussed in this chapter try to find a space for those excluded from the national imaginary: in Grenville's book, each of her three main characters is in some way trying to live up to an impossible degree of perfection. Much of this pressure emerges from ideas about gender and 'place', both in the sense of location (the setting of a country town or, more generically, the bush) and in the sense of role (within a national mythology that determines roles for men and women). Sallis' novel has a specifically 'multi-cultural' perspective in its central metaphor of an Arabic woman who undertakes the culturally saturated journey from city to country that has become the staple of so many Australian texts of self-discovery. In undertaking and surviving the rigours of this journey, her central character, Hiam, is, for the first time, able to feel 'at home' in Australia. Significantly, in their particular focus on the need of their culturally-marginalised protagonists to find a way of belonging, both these novels are silent about indigenous Australia, though, as a later chapter will show, for some women writers the desire to belong is inextricably linked to notions of indigenous culture.

Kate Grenville, *The Idea of Perfection* (1999)

Like Astley's *Drylands* (to be discussed in the next chapter), Grenville's Orange Prize-winning novel is a wry satire of established myths about the Australian bush – particularly its stultifying effects on gender roles for men and women; the drying up of the old farming economy replaced by the need to attract tourists interested in 'heritage', especially those from the cities; and the pressure of 'belonging' that is tied to the notion of Australian national identity. The 'idea of perfection' is at the heart of the epistemic violence of these stereotypes: trying to be perfect means trying to conform to an impossible role that has been assigned by society. Grenville's novel explores what happens to individuals when performing such a role is an impossible fiction. The three main characters in the novel who each attempt to fulfil the idea of perfection, Felicity Porcelline, Harley Savage and Douglas Cheeseman, either are destroyed by it (in Felicity's case) or ultimately resist it (in the cases of Harley and Douglas) by forming an unlikely relationship, an alliance of misfits. Felicity is tied to the notion of the ideal housewife, obsessively cleaning out dirt from every corner of her house, and by the need to conform to the ideal of the perfect woman who has perfect skin. Her beauty routines, while essentially comic, are also sad: she limits the number of times she has to smile, look up or go out into the sun in order to reduce her chances of getting wrinkles. Harley is obsessed by her 'dangerous streak' which, as she sees it, has made her 'lose' three husbands, the last one to suicide, for which she has always blamed herself. And Douglas sees himself as falling way behind the 'idea of perfection' as an engineer who suffers from vertigo, the far-from-fearless son of a dead war hero (the 'real Douglas Cheeseman') and as a 'duffer' who constantly apologises for just being there and never being good enough. What the idea of perfection does to each of them is to point up their inadequacies and to cause each of them to become dissociated from their own emotions. Each sees themself as performing their own inadequacies. It is only at the end of the novel, when Harley and Douglas begin to communicate outside of verbal language, that Harley feels 'for once' that her looking into Douglas' eyes was 'not a performance' and that 'there did not seem to be a running commentary on it' (Grenville, *The Idea of Perfection*: 389).

Throughout the rest of the novel, each of the protagonists has seen them-self as a character, watched themself perform with words being spoken as if in a script. The use of italics throughout the text signals the lack of sincerity in such dialogue, as if someone else had written the preordained and overused words in order to fit a stereotype. It is such stereotypes, indeed, that Harley and Douglas overcome in the end, in order to become 'themselves', while Felicity succumbs to her obsessiveness which is all that is left to her after her 'affair' (or *awkwardness*, as she euphemistically calls it) with Freddy Chang, the butcher/photographer, allowing her to see herself finally as a 'cruel smiling child' (393).

Grenville's novel has some of the same sense that Astley engenders in *Drylands* of the small-mindedness and petty cruelties of the bush, especially the sense of surveillance the city 'intruders' feel. Harley, for example, 'had forgotten how empty a country town could be, how blank-windowed, how you could feel looked-at and large' (6). Grenville captures, too, Felicity's unthinking almost automatic racism against Chinese people, and, of course, the gender stereotypes are fully embedded. Yet Grenville's is a much less searing portrait of country towns than Astley's or Gillian Mears'; more of a tribute to what she has called the 'wonderful quirky distinctiveness' of country people who have 'a very healthy indifference to matching up to any kind of stereotype'. In *The Idea of Perfection*, it is, according to Grenville, the 'city newcomers' who make complete fools of themselves in the country' rather than the country types being exposed for their xenophobia and lack of intellect, as in Astley's novels. Part of Grenville's sense of what she sees as the more exciting and positive aspects of country towns is her 'sad feeling that a very good and valuable part of Australian culture is dying on its feet' (Sullivan 1999). At the same time, she is aware of the comic aspects of such a nostalgic view of Australian 'bush-types'. In an interview about the novel, she has commented that *The Idea of Perfection* is recognis-ably Australian in that it is 'close enough to the stereotype of Australia – the bronzed Aussie outback thing' but that it is also different in that it's 'a comedy, and a kind of romance, and the setting isn't the heroic parched outback but the sub-culture of the country town' (Ball 2001). She draws an important distinction here between the ordinariness of the country town and its inhabitants and the 'heroic parched outback' which, in its extra-ordinariness, becomes the setting for stereotypes of daring exploits of exploration, survival and 'discovery'. This focus on the stories of everyday people, with its two main protagonists far from heroic figures, challenges the template of the epic Australian novel that has become the literary landmark of contemporary Australian male writers such as David Malouf and Peter Carey.[1] As Grenville has said:

> Australian writers are so lucky – so much about Australia hasn't been written about yet. Our history is full of fantastic stories that haven't been told, our landscape has only been written about in parts, and so

many ways of being Australian haven't been written about up till now. We're a new country, but also we're a country that's changing so fast, there are new ways of being Australian evolving all the time . . . there's still plenty to explore.

(Ball 2001)

This is an alternative anti-heroic view of history as story rather than epic.

There is an important link between the novel's two main tropes, those of patchwork and constructing bridges, and the writing process itself. Grenville has commented on her own writing style as a kind of fabric/ation, an arranging of fragments into a whole that is, she suggests, like the art of quilting: 'It is a question of putting together things which don't necessarily, on the face of it, have any overt relationship, or value, but something happens when you put it all together' (Bennie 1999: 8s). Like patchwork, bridges, too, are structures that require a patient building of sections to make up a whole (Douglas' solution to rebuilding the Bent Bridge is that of modules). In the same interview just quoted, Grenville draws a parallel between writing and building: 'I realised that building a bridge and writing a novel are exactly the same thing . . . having a new problem to solve every day.' All three are linked in her statement that quilting is 'putting shapes together in a structural way'.

In this way, her writing style (that of fragments that the reader puts together to form a whole, with pieces of each character's story gradually emerging into a pattern; using the patchworking principle of the juxtaposition of light and dark triangles) is not just a structural notion but is integral to the novel's major tropes, each of which also stands for its main characters. Douglas is, of course, associated with the scientific discourse of engineering yet he waxes lyrical about the flexible nature of cement as both liquid and solid; while Harley is an unconventional patchworker whose pieces are artworks that reflect the Australian environment. It is their relationship that embodies the novel's epigraph by Leonardo da Vinci – 'an arch is two weaknesses which together make a strength'.

Language itself (with its overused phrases and ideas – ideas that have been 'domesticated by words' (Grenville, *The Idea of Perfection*: 341)), gender stereotypes, stereotypes of place and landscape, myths of city and bush and false expectations about relationships are all implicated in the sense of inadequacy that each of these characters has about 'belonging'. Douglas and Harley particularly (and Felicity, too, to an extent) are outsiders, 'intruders in the bush', city types who find, despite the platitudes, a sense of themselves (and each other) in the bush. While stressing that neither Douglas nor Harley conform to societal gender stereotypes of weak female and strong male (Harley is strong; Douglas is not – it is Harley who has to save Douglas from being stampeded by cows), Grenville also satirises some of the gender stereotypes prevalent in Australian literature. Harley, for example, is seen at first through Douglas' eyes as a typical 'drover's wife' type (and it is surely no coincidence that one of Coralie Henderson's favourite phrases in the novel is 'type of thing'). He mistakes her for a true country type not knowing, of course, that like him she is from the city. On first seeing her, he describes her as a 'big rawboned plain person, tall and unlikely' who 'stood like a man, square-on' (2). He sees her as a *'salt of the earth* type' living 'a proper life anchored solid to the ground' (3). This androgynous description ('it was clear from the way she stood that she'd forgotten about breasts being sexy' (2)) is reinforced in Douglas' later perceptions of her as:

> a real country sort of woman, in her battered old shoes and the baggy tracksuit. Her face was brown from the sun, her cheeks coarsened by years of weather, but the blood flowed vigorously under the skin. Under the old track-pants, he thought she would have powerful legs, getting her along the miles of country back roads and over the paddocks.
>
> (101)

It is hard not to compare this with Lawson's descriptions of the drover's wife outlined earlier. The irony, of course, lies in the reader's prior insight that Harley is not only visiting Karakarook from Sydney (and is not one of the locals or a country woman at all) but also that she has heart trouble and is far from physically fit. In fact, she nearly drowns when swimming in a swimming-hole in the bush. Douglas' instant and mistaken identification of Harley with the drover's wife type demonstrates the gap between stereotype and individual, as well as the persistence of such stereotypes into the twenty-first century. Douglas both admires and seems to fear Harley's perceived strength. He describes her as 'tall and solid, striding through the landscape . . . like an army marching' (384) while he feels himself to be 'a flimsy man alone with his shadow' (328). Throughout the scene where the town's 'gree-nies' including Harley confront Douglas and the men who are to demolish the bridge, Douglas ascribes a kind of primitive Amazon-like quality to Harley. Her African dress, for example, had 'a vigorous barbaric look, the pattern emphatic, bold as a danger sign' (323) and the 'primitive ornament on a strip of leather around her throat' is seen by him as 'possibly a dagger . . . decoration, but . . . also a weapon' (323).

If Douglas sees Harley (whose very name embodies a kind of macho power) as strong and 'masculine', he himself has never been 'one of the blokes'. On meeting Chook Henderson, Douglas wonders 'how you got to be a Chook Henderson . . . It seemed to come naturally to them . . . Whatever it was, it was too late for him now' (52). Similarly, even the most basic of 'Aussie bloke' mateship rituals seems unnatural to Douglas. When greeting the barman with a 'G'day mate', Douglas 'hoped it didn't sound like satire' (48). With his fellow workers at the bridge, he feels excluded from 'the circle of men' (185) whose banter was 'like a foreign language of which he could only catch the odd phrase' (184). Always aware that he does not conform to the stereotype of the Aussie bloke, Douglas has to 'read up on' sports pages, always wishing that he could be 'another sort of man' (5), what he calls a 'normal man' (211). In contrast with Harley's perceived strength, Douglas feels his own inadequacy even more keenly, as in the following: 'Watching Harley Savage stride purposefully, gesture decisively, laugh in that big confident way, he [Douglas] wished he could find it in himself to be a different and less invisible kind of man' (286).

Watching Harley making one of her patchworks from his hidden vantage point outside her window, Douglas sees her as a well-designed mechanism '[o]r a beam of reinforced concrete' (333). Comparing himself with her highlights what he sees as his own weakness, in this extract imaged as contrasting bridge-like structures:

> He was flimsy, trussed about, bolted stiffly together into an ugly rigid muddle of members to disguise the basic weakness of the structure. But she had both the strength of the concrete and the flexibility of the reinforcement. The greater the load, the stronger she would get . . . She would be able to stretch under tension. She was not brittle. She was flesh and bone together, bending without breaking.
>
> (334)

Significantly, it is at this point that Douglas acknowledges his love for Harley, just as she herself realises that her fear of his vulnerability ('as a being far too easy to do violence to' (243)) is part of her fear of her own vulnerability. As she later acknowledges: 'It occurred to her that *being a duffer* might be something he did to protect himself, the way *having a dangerous streak* was what she did' (268, emphases in original).

The 'two weaknesses which together make a strength' is thus their relationship, that, like the Bent Bridge 'looked weak but . . . was not', a structure that had, like Harley and Douglas themselves, been damaged but whose damage was 'the very thing that made it strong' (62).

Like the gender stereotypes, the myths of belonging in the bush and of a notion of shared Australian-ness are shown by Grenville to be alienating and difficult to achieve. Douglas, for example, feels 'small under the big harsh sky' (193), feeling that the country suns, while seeming kindly, had 'something metallic and unforgiving about them' (193). When Douglas goes exploring in the bush, he feels at first that '*Nature* was all around him, expansive, generous, like a hospitable host' (88) but soon becomes lost, 'huge and conspicuous', not exploring but trespassing (91). Unable to work out the solution to the problem of how to escape the cows that pursue him, Douglas suggests that 'being in the country felt like one long intelligence test he was failing' (104). Later, sipping tea with Chook Henderson and the other men working on the bridge, Douglas feels 'stiff and foreign', a profound sense of unbelonging. He muses on the nature of being Australian:

But if you were Australian, you were supposed to feel at home in the country. *The bush*, rather. They seemed to call it that, even when it was just plain old paddocks.

The message had come through loud and clear at school. *An Australian* was a man on the back of a horse . . . So the kids at Kogarah public School, who had never seen a sheep or a cow except at the Show, had had to learn how to be *Australian* off the blackboard . . .

They had sung *Click Go the Shears* . . . They had recited *I Love a Sunburnt Country* and tried to believe they did. Douglas Cheeseman's pale freckled skin did not love a sunburnt country, and for a long time he had thought a *sweeping plain* was something to do with woodwork, but he had sung as sincerely as the rest.

He had thought you could simply apply yourself to it, and learn to be the sort of *Australian* you were supposed to be. He could see now that it would never be that simple.

(191–192, emphases in original)

Douglas is rehearsing here the stereotypical images of Australian identity that tap into a nostalgic notion of the bush and of nationhood that, while clearly outdated, still have cultural purchase. It is the inability of a city person to identify with such images that contributes to Douglas' sense of marginality and inadequacy. But Grenville, of course, is satirising the over-simplification of this notion of nation, this invention of place, that ignores the complexity of contemporary Australian society, which is not 'that simple'.

Part of the exclusionary practices that such simplistic definitions of nation inevitably produce is the 'othering' of those who are seen as not typically Australian. Grenville has Felicity articulate the kind of unthinking racism that has her obsessed with Freddy's difference, his being Chinese. Her repeated protestations that 'she was no racist' inevitably reference Pauline Hanson and her 'One Nation' party whose denials of racism were matched by constant references to minority groups being 'un-Australian'. Felicity is troubled by Freddy's similarity – 'he spoke exactly the way everyone else did' (16) – to the others in the town, desperately seeking some outward sign of difference to confirm her racist preconceptions. Thus, she 'listened for something Chinese in the way he talked, the little foreign something' but 'it was never there' (16). Despite this lack of difference, Felicity clings to her prejudices: 'She was no racist. She was sure of that. But she never thought of Alfred Chang as *Australian* in the way she herself was *Australian*. He was *Chinese*, no matter how long Changs had been in Karakarook' (16).

It is the very instability of the notion of national identity that worries Felicity who would like it to be much more simple: a division into Australian and non-Australian. Her essentialist view of race as innate difference rather

than cultural practice confuses her responses to Freddy whose face she
searches for inscrutability and whose gift of strawberries she initially confuses for dogs' hearts as she remembers that Chinese people '*eat dog*' (24).

Another troubling aspect of such exclusions is the silence in the text
about Aborigines. Apart from the references to Karakarook meaning elbow
in Aboriginal language, the novel itself is silent about Aboriginal history
and ownership of the land. There are no Aboriginal voices in the text and
the idea of history is always that of white history, the history of settlement
or invasion. There are two ways of interpreting such a void: first, that
Grenville is simply echoing her characters' closed-off consciousnesses
(unlike Astley who draws attention to such closed-mindedness); or that she
herself is complicit in the silencing of Aboriginal voices in Australian texts,
whether literary or historical. Perhaps her focus is, instead, on the juxtaposition of notions of epic history with those of everyday lives and, in this
way, she is contesting the grand narratives of the past in a more general
way. Certainly, the text is concerned with the idea of heritage as the
memories and memorabilia of ordinary people. Harley has to discourage
the townsfolk from bringing their 'best' family heirlooms for the Heritage
Museum she is helping them to establish:

> What would put Karakarook on the map were the things that were
> so ordinary that no one had thought of keeping any of them . . . all
> the improvised things made for their houses by people who never had
> enough money to buy one from the shops.
>
> Those things did not survive, because no one thought they were worth
> keeping . . .
>
> (143)

Harley realises that the city tourists want to see the 'improvisation, the
ingenuity, the thrift' of those ordinary people who had to adapt to the
harshness of life in the bush, and that they would then go back to Sydney
'feeling they had been in touch with the real *spirit of the bush*' (144, emphases
in original). While such a collection is seen to celebrate the 'Australian
vernacular', there is also a sense that this, too, is simply another precon-
ceived stereotype. Yet Harley is genuinely moved by the old ladle made
out of a metal file she is given for the museum, feeling it to be a '*labour
of love*' and understanding the implications of this 'corny old phrase' (235).

Set against this history of domesticity and improvised adaptation to the
rigours of the bush is the kind of epic history that is symbolised by the town's
street names with their classical Eurocentrism. The main road is 'Parnassus
Road' which meets 'Virgil Street', the names showing off the classical education of the town's founding fathers (212). It is while exploring these streets
that Douglas comes upon the town's Anzac memorial with its epigraph '*To
Our Glorious Dead*' in gold leaf (212) commemorating the names of the local
war heroes. Douglas, always consumed with guilt and inadequacy over his

own father's death in the war, 'had never liked the gold-leaf lists' but he understands that 'you could not admit that to anyone' (212). In memorialising the more ordinary history of domestic life by way of the Heritage Museum, Harley, like Douglas, is contesting the pressure to conform to the heroic status of the past.

Similarly, Harley contests the distinctions between high art and craft in her own patchwork designs. Once dismissed by her sister as 'just craft' (208), Harley's patchworks now attract the critical attention and academic discourse of the art establishment that gives them the status of 'fibre art'(152), 'wittily subvert[ing] the form' (152). Harley's designs are based not on the high art notions of '*Nature*' that Harley's famous artist-father has always believed to be the subject of all Art, but on the landscape she sees around her, and are made out of the ordinary fabric of past lives – old suit material and a favourite dress that has been cut up and used for scraps. In recognising the landscape around her as the very material of her art, Harley, unlike her father whose artwork depends on 'flowers arranged nicely in a vase' (200), finds a way of imaging place. The patterning of the patchwork depends on contrast between light and dark and Harley is aware of the landscape itself as 'sunlight and shadow . . . together in big simple shapes. *Light, dark*' (37), unlike her father who sees his 'in law's shabby farm, everything grey and blistered in the dry and the heat' as 'not the *Nature* he was thinking of' (200).

Like writing, then, patchwork is a 'kind of magic' and 'part of a pattern' that can illuminate the relationship between dull and jewel-like pieces of fabric (207), changing the one into the other. Perhaps it is unfair to suggest that this novel participates in the kind of exclusions it images when it is clearly meant to be, in Grenville's words quoted earlier, 'a comedy, and a kind of romance' set in the 'sub-culture of the country town'. But in her insistence on the positive as well as the negative aspects of country life ('You took the whole lot, the good and the bad' (179)), it could be argued that Grenville *is* complicit in the suppressing of dark secrets about the past, namely Aboriginal dispossession. Additionally, in her desire to show country folk as both good and bad, she seems to fall into the kind of stereotypes she is also satirising. In the end, her country folk *are* salt-of-the-earth types and it becomes difficult to separate the clichés from the satire, the complicity from the resistance.

Eva Sallis, *Hiam* (1998)

Eva Sallis' Vogel Award-winning novel, like Grenville's *The Idea of Perfection*, involves the literal and metaphorical journey of a city woman to the Australian bush, and charts her encounter with the landscape that becomes an index of her sense of belonging and alienation. The difference in Sallis' novel is that her protagonist, Hiam Sharif, is a migrant Australian. Born in Yemen and educated in Jordan, she has lived in Adelaide with her husband, Masoud, and daughter, Zena, until Masoud's suicide, brought on it seems by his inability to adapt to Australian culture and life, leads her on this journey from Adelaide to the 'green North' in her late husband's taxi. As in Grenville's novel, Hiam discovers aspects of her self during this journey, which is a kaleidoscope of memories, nightmares and often-violent encounters with wildlife with her travelling interspersed with flashbacks. It is a journey that, Hiam comes to recognise, is proof of the regaining of her spiritual and physical strength and the fact that she does it as a woman travelling alone is significant. Like Grenville's novel, the Australian culture Hiam encounters is entirely Anglo – there is no reference to indigenous culture or any sense of her intrusion on Aboriginal land.

Despite the sense of linearity that the journey genre imposes, Sallis' narrative structure works against any such directionality. She has suggested about the novel's structure that:

> It is the thin thread of the road itself which creates the illusion that there is a story. In fact the fragments of Hiam's self which are strung on this road might not have appeared to belong together without it. It is more than a trick: to me the structure itself is symbolic.
>
> (Hunn 1999)

There is an awareness throughout the narrative that Hiam is not simply leaving the past behind in her flight from 'people, family, pain' (Sallis, *Hiam*: 3) but that she is living through it as part of the journey. There is a consciousness of an anti-teleological pull against the directedness of the road image in the narration itself, evidenced in a section of the novel which self-consciously regards its own implication in this genre:

> What could it signify? The road was the protagonist's straitjacket, the car her prison, or her skull; her self on the thread of life. Too clumsy . . . She laughed. Academic theories of long roads. She felt suddenly cheerful and accelerated into a daydream of road meanings.
>
> (64)

In the end, Hiam is frustrated with her 'stilted ideas' about the meaning of roads and the road's obliging readiness to 'be anything' (65) but the idea remains that the road has spiritual, physical and symbolic meaning that the reader constructs.

Throughout the novel, the alienness of the land and Hiam's paradoxical responses to it are emphasised. As an outsider to Australian culture, Hiam's negative perceptions provide interesting parallels with those of the earlier settlers. Thus, as she sets out on her journey, she describes the 'vast, monochromatic land' around her as not 'empty enough to be desolate' but 'new and . . . ugly' (1). As in Lawson's 'The Drover's Wife', the vegetation is 'dull' and the leaves of the 'exhausted trees seemed brown' (1). She does, however, register the changes in landscape as she drives so that when she nears the 'red centre', she reports it in a telephone call to her brother-in-law as somewhere 'famous; it's where Australia is red' (36). But her initial delight at the redness of the land as 'stark and impressive', a 'profound and richly tapestried monotony' (34), transforms into a nightmare image, as in her dreams, of blood and violence:

> The terrible, red and lonely land had taken her up and pushed her on without mercy. She couldn't stop and drove on hating everything she saw. There was blood on the road, on the roadsides, on the battered heads of stiffening black cattle . . .
>
> (36)

Finding the place 'intolerable', she is unable to see 'the point of having seen this or having been here' (37), in a response that opposes the sense of spiritual connection with land that the 'red centre' often induces. Instead, this place reinforces her own sense of alienation and inability to adapt: 'Hiam with the University Education was strangely inadequate out in the red' (65). Additionally, this literal and metaphorical expanding of her horizons reminds her of the enclosed space of the migrant Muslim cultural world she has previously inhabited in the suburbs of Adelaide, a world that was cut off from the larger sense of Australia by its circulation of stereotypes of Australia and Australians. As she comes to realise on her journey:

> She had never understood Australia. She had never understood Australians. She had never known that there was so much outside of herself and her world. It was frightening to know that this road had waited through the years of her incomprehension. It had been here the whole time.
>
> (49)

The sense of cultural alienation and mistranslations that mark relationships between Australians (meaning Anglo-Australians) and migrant Australians (Hiam and Masoud have lived in Adelaide for fifteen years) is emphasised throughout the text. Institutions, in particular, like schools and doctors create fear in Hiam because of the 'constant feeling of something unsaid' and 'of meaning not granted by the understanding of words' (15). While the three migrant women who meet for tea at Hiam's house discuss Australians' stereotypical notions of Arabs ('they think you have money', 'guns' and 'good sex' (18)), the women also betray their own prejudices about 'the Australians' who, they suggest, have 'no heart and no morals' (18). Hiam, on the other hand, feels 'rather sorry for Australians' for their lack of pride and self-respect (19). For her part, she has become familiar with Australians asking her what it was like to grow up as an Islamic woman, with their pity implied, and their preconceptions powerfully in place – 'being Muslim is not highly thought of and Australia itself is' (21). That such cultural mistranslations are not new but are part of a colonial system of classifying that which is unknown, is reinforced in the text by the explanation of their village's name, Man Yadre. The name was given in response to an Englishman's asking the name of that place and being told, 'Man Yadre' which in English means 'who knows?'. This is the name he wrote on the map and it is this name that appeared on all European maps from then onwards, replacing the village's true name, Ain al-Alim, The Well of God, and accepted by the local people as a joke (30).

However, Hiam's adventure in the Australian bush on her journey of discovery is not seen as a colonising activity but as a therapeutic form of self-reliance. As if to emphasise this affinity with the drover's wife and, perhaps, the early explorers, Hiam finds, off a side-road, a deserted bush hut, the description of which echoes that in Lawson's short story:

> It was made of stunted, uneven trunks . . . thatched and patched with
> brushwood tied in clumsy bundles . . . This was the destination and
> here she was stopping. It was bleak and deserted but what else was
> she looking for?
>
> (90)

In addition, it is significantly described as having 'enough cracks and gaps letting in the light to give it a skeletal feel, if not appearance' (91). It is while she is camped inside the hut that Hiam experiences her feverish dreams and hallucinations, reliving and renarrating the 'bitter and violent stories' that Masoud had started telling (94) as Zena grows further apart from her family and her people and marries a non-Muslim Australian ('well, South African', as the text says, signalling the homogenising tendency to elide ethnic differences among Anglo-Australians). While Zena was a child, Hiam was proud she could speak English like an Australian, thus becoming Hiam's 'buttress against being thought foreign' (42), but Zena's teenage abandonment of her cultural cocoon proves unbearable for Masoud and Hiam. Hiam blames her daughter's changed behaviour on Australia, 'the land of damage and imprisonment' that 'forces the mother to become the hunter, setting the snares' and transforming 'the living into heartless stone' (71). She blames her 'very terrible daughter' (80) on the 'terrible country, Australia' (81). For his part, Masoud simply falls apart and ultimately commits suicide.

Hiam's reawakening after this nightmarish reliving of these painful memories is signalled by a reconnection with her physical and spiritual selves. Both these are linked in the image of her awakening to the smell of the earth which in turn reminds her of the Muslim call to prayer which she obeys, her face to the 'spicy earth, smelling the wet soil' (125). Her subsequent vision of the Prophet Mohammad enables her to understand that 'maybe she was going somewhere and it didn't matter that she didn't know' (127). This contrasts with her earlier fear that she was 'travelling with all the purpose of a pilgrimage for no reason and with no knowledge' (59). Her experience of being utterly alone and able to rehearse the past has also reconnected her with the present, so that she is, after this experience, able to stop at a service station and, on the suggestion of the attendant there, remove the taxi sign that had remained on Masoud's car. By removing 'that little slavish cap' she signals her ownership of it as well as a renewed subjectivity. Like the car, she is 'renewed, nobler, more fitting' (128) and less 'out of place' (128). Thus she is able to make a 'grand entrance' onto the highway, with the car finally under her management, as it were.

Her reconnection with earth and spirit enables Hiam to reconnect with people, even those who are not Muslim. With this renewed sense of self she is able to befriend Noah and Annie, two locals, having mistaken Noah for someone Sudanese. It is significant that Noah (named, as Hiam says later, after a 'prophet') can return her Arabic greeting having been taught it by an 'old fella' (128) as a child. It is equally significant that Hiam is able, at this moment, to speak her own name, Hiam Sherif, spelt in the Arabic way though still pronounced in the English way. During this encounter with Australians, the cultural gap is mutual and surmountable rather than one-sided and alienating. While Noah had not heard of Islam but knew of oil and camels, Hiam has never heard of the 'Gagadju or the great storms of the Top-end' but had heard of crocodiles (130). With her arrival in Darwin and the Green North, she realises the extent of her great accomplishment in crossing Australia. Her search for meaning has been replaced by a sense of self and achievement: 'I am Hiam who crossed Australia alone' (135). The trope of the map re-emerges in the text to suggest a renewed sense of place and space. Hiam describes her journey as mapping out of her story 'in blood' (134) and responds to the 'perfect grace' of the petrol station attendant who shows her 'the intricate traceries of the land she had entered' (136) in her search for a Gagadju crocodile. In following his instructions to the South Alligator River, she is given a 'hero's farewell' and names him Ibrahim even though his name-tag tells her he was called Dave (138). In doing this, she is reconciling notions of cultural division within herself and in the larger world around her, so that the prayer at the end of the novel addressed to 'Lord of the Worlds' and 'Lord of the two Easts . . . and two Wests' is a prayer of connection rather than division. By the end of her journey, Hiam has come to terms not just with her self and with Masoud's death and Zena's marriage but also with Australia itself, as a place where East and West can co-exist rather than be antagonistic.

In (re)writing the narrative of a migrant woman and her problematic engagement with 'the bush' in the form of a journey of discovery, Sallis is challenging and resisting stereotypical preconceptions that have trapped both Muslims and Australians into separate cultural and discursive spheres and is, instead, opening up a discourse of shared cultural understanding and a space for belonging.

3   Another country

The 'terrible darkness' of country towns

Thea Astley's *Drylands* and Gillian Mears' *Fineflour* and *The Mint Lawn*

For a number of women writers, as the last chapter has shown, the narrative of the city-woman who has to survive in the bush is a story of endurance, suffering and exclusion as well as a testing-ground for ways of belonging. For other women writers, the bush became a place of freedom, a place where city women could escape the conventions and restrictions of confinement to domesticity and society's rules. In the harshness of life in the bush, it was suggested, such limitations for women could not apply, as they were expected to work 'like men'. An early model for articulating these often contradictory responses of women to the bush is provided in Miles Franklin's *My Brilliant Career* (1901) which exemplifies both the positive and negative aspects of bush life. But, whereas both Grenville and Sallis, in their novels discussed in the previous chapter, find some of these redemptive qualities in 'going bush', even for those excluded from discourses of belonging, Thea Astley and Gillian Mears focus in their texts on the destructive and often physical violence that they associate with country towns.

Thea Astley, for example, as in her earlier novels, *A Kindness Cup* (1974), *An Item from the Late News* (1982) and *It's Raining in Mango* (1987), exposes not just the exploitative cruelty of men towards women, and the petty cruelties involved in daily interactions, but also the suppressed and silenced history of violence between indigenous and non-indigenous inhabitants. In *A Kindness Cup*, she links the self-justifying and smug moral hypocrisy of the town's most respected men and their almost casual acts of violence with a 'horrible boil-up of masculinity' (Astley 1974: 63). Mears similarly emphasises the inequalities in gender and race relations and, like her protagonist, Clementine, in her novel, *The Mint Lawn*, resists the 'familiar and erroneous assumption that country towns are the site of all things wholesome' (Mears 1991: 277). As Clementine's sister, Sky, comments on life for girls in country towns, 'nothing changes' and there is 'nothing to do in them except be horsey. Or Christian' (1991: 200).

This chapter, then, explores two writers' exposure of that hidden underside of 'bush' towns, the 'terrible darkness', as Mears has called it, that lies beneath the surface of those rural values that have been said to epitomise the Australian national character. Part of this underside is the racism and xenophobia on which White Australia was built, part of it the sexism and anti-intellectualism on which the myth of the bush depended. Both writers suggest that alongside these values, or perhaps as a consequence of them, there are always victims.

Thea Astley, *Drylands* (1999)

Thea Astley's novel, *Drylands*, is subtitled 'a book for the world's last reader' and, according to Astley herself, is also her own last novel. It is in many ways a *fin-de-siècle* work, personally, politically and culturally. 'At the age of 74,' she said in an ABC radio interview after being jointly awarded the Miles Franklin Award for 2000, 'it is time to put the biro down.' Her deliberate and rather quaint eschewing of the computer or word processor in favour of the more traditional biro is significant in itself, signalling an attitude towards the writing process that is consciously 'old-fashioned'. Indeed, the death of the reader at the turn of the millennium is an ongoing thematic concern in this novel. The cultural and political landscape of Australia with which she engages is the philistine world of Pauline Hanson's brief 'One Nation' era: a world in which bigotry, inarticulateness and prejudice speak louder than any cultural text. It is a world that Astley fiercely critiques in this novel with its focus on a 'back country' Queensland town suffering from drought, dwindling community and services, and the small-mindedness that Astley has made a trademark of her literary texts (most of which are set, unlike this one, in lush coastal locations). As in these other texts, Astley is exposing the subterranean violence in country towns that undermines notions of mateship, rural values and collective enterprise encapsulated in myths of the bush. In Astley's text, the hypocrisy of the seeming inclusiveness of any nationalistic idea of 'one nation' is exposed to reveal cruel exclusions and bullying tactics designed to silence and subjugate all who are deemed different. By focalising this critique through the persona of a writer, Janet Deakin, who is both an insider as a resident of the town, and an outsider, having come to live there only fairly recently, Astley combines searing satire with a certain (albeit limited) amount of reluctant admiration, acknowledging the need for toughness in a drought-stricken land while simultaneously mourning the loss of innocence. The drought is thus a trope for a cultural, political and psychological aridity.

The mouthpiece for Astley's critique of Australian culture, or rather, its lack of culture, is the 'past fifty' (Astley, *Drylands*: 3) writer, Janet Deakin, whose third-person narration, under the heading 'Meanwhile . . .', alternates in the text with the focalised narration of the other characters in the town. The ellipsis is significant: it both suggests and invites the reader to complete the cliché gleaned from American popular culture, 'back at the ranch', and, at the same time, refuses to engage with it. Additionally, it points to Janet's role in the text as the narrating presence whose voice links the disparate characters of the town but is ultimately unable to orchestrate any overall sense of unity or community. She presents herself as a detached observer, spatially positioned above the town in her 'upstairs flat' (3) above her newsagency, with a view of the entire 'dead town' (11) below. This sense of visual and moral superiority suffuses the text, but, it is suggested, her position of detached surveillance is precarious, as, a number of times in the narration, she is caught in the act of 'spying' by those in the street below. This deliberate undermining of Janet's own sense of place or position even applies to her narration. While the reader assumes that Janet's is the controlling narrative voice of the text, even this certainty is shaken when Evie, the visiting creative writing tutor, writes at the end of her narration: 'She [Evie] would write a story, she decided, about a woman in an upstairs room above a main street in a country town, writing a story about a woman writing a story' (99).

The postmodern sense here of ever-receding meta-narratives suggests that even the watcher is being watched (a sense of paranoia in a number of characters about surveillance is ultimately shown to be well-founded); and implies, too, that Janet does not have complete control over 'point of view'. Perhaps the suggestion is also being made that, despite her constant distancing of herself from the townsfolk, Janet is more complicit and implicated in the community she critiques than she cares to admit. As in all Astley's novels, such ironic layering complicates the too-easy elision of Janet's narrative voice with that of Astley herself, maintaining the 'pervasive ironic perspective of all her works' (Adelaide 1997: 186) as well as what one reviewer has called Astley's concern with 'the politics of narrative, the power inherent in the position of storyteller' (Goldsworthy 1996: 13).

Other aspects of narrative are similarly self-consciously addressed in the text, as when Janet is trying to decide how to begin: 'Thinks: I could begin *onceupona* or *manyyearsago* or *inadistantcountry*. It's been done. I don't like it' (Astley, *Drylands*: 4, emphases in original).

Janet's conscious avoidance of such hackneyed beginnings signals her desire to 'achieve the voice of the times' (10) despite her 'convention-riddled past' (10). Janet's awareness of postmodern fictional techniques[1] and her simultaneous commitment to 'high culture' suggests Astley's ironic positioning of Janet as a *fin-de-siècle* writer, who, while wishing to 'write a book that embraced the themes a lifetime of reading had informed her readers might expect' (10), also wishes to 'achieve the voice of the times'. This need to record the changing times 'with the irony still running in her veins' (10) and 'angry ideas' (3) sets the cynical tone of the text, with Janet as the voice of doom. Towards the end of this first section of her narration, she decides to 'use the place' (16), that is, the town Drylands in which she is living, as the material for her book, making 'the vulgarities . . . part of the scheme' (12). That she has earlier described the town as 'a God-forgotten tree-stump of a town halfway to nowhere whose population . . . was tucked for leisure either in the bar of the Legless Lizard or in front of the television screens, videos, Internet adult movies or

PlayStation games for the kiddies' (4–5) draws attention to her satirical imaging of contemporary outback life. Here, the name of the pub (the Legless Lizard) signifies a commercialisation and vulgarisation of the desert creature as the word 'legless' takes on its vernacular connotation of 'drunk'. Similarly, the very concept of being 'halfway to nowhere' that underpins outback isolation is undermined and distorted by the global and cyber communications to which the townsfolk turn for leisure. Two conflicting concepts of place are being deliberately and ironically juxtaposed, and this is evident in the language of this sentence: the old image of the outback retains its familiar clichés ('God-forgotten', 'halfway to nowhere') while the new sense of global place is couched in the terminology of popular culture ('Internet adult movies', 'PlayStation games', 'kiddies'). This uneasy tug between ideas of 'Australianness' inherited from the 1890s and the obvious and dramatic changes that technology has wrought on traditional notions of distance and space provide a context for Janet's end-of-century anxiety to retain some of these old values.

Part of Janet's misgivings about late twentieth-century Australian culture throughout the text is that 'no one was reading any more' (5). Her early attempts, on first taking over the newsagency, to stock literary journals and books had been met with complaints from the locals as she ran out of 'men's magazines, the bosom-thigh buskers, the car and gun monthlies' (7). Hers is an old-fashioned approach to reading and writing that echoes Astley's comment quoted earlier about putting down the 'biro': Janet decries the way that 'everything [is] dominated by smart-arse technology, a blurred world of technobuzz' (9), reminding her readers that it is 'so hard to read in bed with a weighty computer on your chest' (9). In contrast to this technological world, is the 'miracle' of the book – 'flyspecks on white that can change ideologies or governments, induce wars, starvations or rare blessings' (6). In a polemical section towards the end of the text (239–245), Janet rails against the end of a reading culture, citing Marshall McLuhan's notion of a global village to savage what she sees as the 'dumbing down' of society:

> out there all over the wide brown land was a new generation of kids with telly niblets shoved into their mental gobs from the moment they could sit up in a playpen and gawk at the screen, starved of all those tactile experiences with paper, the smell of printer's ink, the magic discovery that black symbols on white spelled out pleasures of other distances.
>
> (240)

Astley's juxtaposition, in this one sentence, of 'low-culture' colloquialisms (like 'kids', 'telly niblets', 'gobs' and 'gawk') associated with this new cyber-generation with the more poetic vocabulary Janet attaches to the 'tactile experiences' of reading, emphasises the importance of language itself as constitutive of cultural values (as was evident, too, in her description of changing concepts of the outback quoted above).

Janet's critique of globalisation is most savage when she ponders its impact on Australian culture. While debunking the 'stereotyped myths' attached to country people which had them all as 'salt of the earth . . . [l]aconic . . . given to the tall yarn' (241) and the 'claptrap patterns' (241) which make people attach similarly mythical attributes to city folk ('fast movers and talkers'), Janet also seems to be mourning the loss of the traditional bush/city rivalry:

> Townies. Bushies. For a long time they'd been like different races but now, as the world shrank, they were being driven uneasily together by the dominating culture of the screen.
>
> Perhaps that talk about the global village was doomfully right.
>
> (241)

Yet, this book paints a far from flattering picture of country life, dramatising at all levels its physical, intellectual and emotional isolation and desiccation. Drylands is described by Janet as a 'town to escape to, rot in, vanish in . . . or run from!' (16). No longer a pastoral escape, 'the town . . . was being out-manoevred by the weather' (287), 'was vanishing before her eyes' (285) with banks reclaiming properties. Perhaps the most noticeable drying-up, though, is of the 'robust goodwill' that Win Briceland, like Janet, complains has disappeared from country life (290).

Yet, again, Astley undercuts this nostalgic notion of a community united by such country values in her imaging of a town in which outsiders are relentlessly excluded. Franzi Massig, the identity assumed by an accountant on the run from a Sydney law-firm after blowing the whistle on their corporate corruption (and the only name we have for him), ponders his precarious acceptance by the people of Drylands:

> Why do people come to places like this?
>
> . . . Is it the belief that in such a small town they will find the corrosive for their solipsist attitudes, that they'll be taken in all warm-kissy-huggy? Drinking mates? The best of old buggers?
>
> No way.
>
> (52)

Far from finding the mateship and sense of community that is linked with the legends of the Bush, Franzi meets with suspicion and distrust, 'still a newcomer' even after four years (43). His assumed 'foreignness' and a wayward order in the pub of a pina colada are enough to label him an outsider. He learns to 'keep a low profile. Agree. Melt in. Be dull, conservative and so orthodox the town forgets you are there' (42).

Similarly, Evie, the creative writing tutor from Brisbane sent 'to take this culture kick to the underprivileged outback' (70), feels like 'an intruder' (80) in the bush. For her, it is both the town itself and the surrounding bushland that induce 'unidentifiable terror'. She immediately senses the menace behind the town's façade: 'Although there was hard sunlight eye-blinkingly bright in the dry air, there was a darkness about the town, an ingrown self-sufficiency of secrets' (80).

It is in the course of this writing class that Evie and the 'bored house-wives' (as she characterises them) who attend her class, encounter this subterranean violence, 'that underlay of resentment' (87) that erupts to the surface. What is interesting about Astley's (or is it Evie's?) portrayal of these 'small-town bush wives' (85), these contemporary drovers' wives, is that she shows them as both intellectually and physically abject. They find it hard to break through 'those sanctions imposed by the conventions of thinking acceptable' (85) for women like them; and Ro accepts her husband's verbal and physical bullying 'like a willing saint, enduring abuse as a terrible balm' (89). This paradoxical compliancy, entrapment and victimage is vividly encapsulated in that oxymoronic phrase, 'terrible balm'. It is at this point in the text, too, that a particular kind of male solidarity emerges – not the sort of mateship that has been seen as being immor-talised in Lawson's stories (which, significantly, are among the first pieces of reading matter that Janet gives to her husband Ted as she teaches him to read) but a ganging-up: 'The police always took the husband's side in these matters. The police drank with them. They wouldn't do anything to upset a mate' (93).

It is not just the seemingly compliant women, though, who become victims and targets of male violence in the text. Evie herself is 'stalked' by a man who had attempted to befriend her on the train; and Joss (the wife of the publican of the Legless Lizard) is cold-bloodedly terrorised by two locals (whose initial advances were curtailed when they found out she was married to Clem) who hunt her down even when she attempts to escape from Drylands.

This entrapment of women in the roles invented for them by partic-ular masculinist discourses is vividly evoked in Lannie Cunneen's narrative, 'Taking Five'. Watching flies which 'buzzed and hurtled to death against the purple circle of light above the counter bar' (223), she identifies herself with them, deciding that she wants 'just a bit of a life outside kitchen and the wash-house' (224). Her husband Fred displays typically masculinist responses to her rebellion (she obsessively counts the number of school lunches she has made) labelling her mad, disgusting and unreasonable in her desire to become an independent wage-earner, to gain 'another iden-tity than that of slave' (223). She does escape, finding work at the local radio station, leaving Fred to feel 'his mind breaking apart' (234), an abject figure at the end, 'stammering and dribbling his guilt into a dead [phone]line' (236). This reversal emphasises the precarious nature of Fred's bullying which Lannie has earlier attributed as a 'simple fallacy all men make' – that physical strength signals intellectual power.

Astley brilliantly draws the casual cruelty and offhand savagery, particularly perpetrated by men, that relentlessly hunts down anyone who is perceived as being different. It is a cruelty that is passed down from generation to generation, not one that has been invented by the young. This is heartbreakingly evoked in Jim Randler's narrative, 'Letting the Lave go by', in the violent clash between generations. Toff Briceland, the teenage son of Councillor Howie Briceland, has learned from his father 'the finer points of rorting and living well' (140). Toff's initial interest in Jim Randler's boat-building project and his dream of escaping 'from Drylands to waterlands' (139) turns to envy and destructive power. Astley chillingly links Toff's violence and the 'tiny fuse of hatred' in him to his frustrated sexuality, his inability to 'have' a girl or to masturbate. It is this 'manic puritanism' and 'vile sterility' (143) that lead him to set fire to Jim's painstakingly-constructed 'old-fashioned' boat, made not of fibreglass but of timber; a construction that, like Jim himself, is perceived to be past its 'use-by-date' (138). Toff's final words, accompanied by a grin, as he leaves the scene of his crime – 'Sorry, mate' – are a knowing and cynical travesty of the creed of mateship and a reversal of intergenerational respect.

A further image of this lack of respect is provided towards the end of Janet's narration. Objecting to the 'meaningless' thudding of the local teenagers playing basketball outside her window at midnight, she asks them to stop:

> The kids had laughed in her face then danced about her chucking the ball from one to the other . . . Not one of them spoke, answered her protests; just silently, viciously played arrow-fast around her, herding her away like dogs a sheep.
>
> (287)

The wordless power wielded by the youths is more terrifying to Janet than any ensuing argument would have been. The cold-bloodedness of their 'herding her away' reminds the reader of the country skills this generation has inherited but has decided to put to destructive use, ganging up against the vulnerable, playing a game whose rules they all know but from which she is excluded.

This male predatoriness which is part of the 'blokeship club' with its 'unwritten codes' (158) is shared by Toff's father, Howie Briceland, for whom 'hunting gave purpose' (189). It is, ironically as it turns out (Howie and Benny share a common grandfather), on Benny Shoforth that Howie's hatred settles. As a part-Aboriginal, Benny unsettles the townsfolk who are not sure how to classify him: 'Was he one of them, the skin-privileged, or did he deserve dismissive contempt? The very unsureness gave offence'

(158). It is this classic settler insecurity that leads Howie to hunt Benny down in his cave 'way off the beaten track' (180) where he goes to escape eviction. Astley sets Benny's awareness of his Aboriginal relationship with the land against the 'settler fright' and 'scrub-scare' of the whites, to whom the bush is 'alien, spiky, unwelcoming' (182). Even as a schoolboy at an Aboriginal 'reserve school', Benny is aware of this settler anxiety about belonging and writes on the blackboard a parody of the words of Dorothea MacKellar's iconic patriotic poem 'My Country' (1908) – often misnamed 'I love a sunburnt country', one of its most famous lines – substituting the words 'The land belongs to me' for 'The wide brown land for me' (169). Thus, at the heart of both Briceland men's violent assertion of power over those more vulnerable than themselves is their own insecurity – Toff's insecurity about his sexuality, and Howie's about his right to belong and the secrets of his family's mixed ancestry. As Roslynn Haynes suggests in her article on Astley's *An Item from the Late News*, 'Astley does not merely ascribe violence to the males *per se*. She traces the connection between aggression and frustration or insecurity' (Haynes 1988a: 140).

What Astley is engaging with here is no less than the anxious nature of settler identity on the cusp of the twenty-first century. She seems to be interrogating constructions of Australian nationalism that have persisted since the 1890s: mateship, prescribed roles for men and women, and myths of the bush. Recognising the complicity of literary texts in these constructions, she refers to iconic texts already mentioned – MacKellar's poem, Henry Lawson's short stories – and has Franzi misquote 'our dear old anthem' by substituting the words 'our land is rort by sea' (Astley, *Drylands*: 36) for the original's 'our land is girt by sea'. In a passage that savagely attacks the image of Australia as a nation of sports-lovers, Janet describes the obsession with watching sport, symbolised by Clem's installation of a satellite sports channel in the pub, as 'a symbol of male religion . . . League mass, [the men] quaffing their communion Tooheys, joining in the votive prayers of groan, chiack, cheer' (201). That this 'male religion' is linked with other masculinist notions is made clear in her description of the shire clerk who 'used phrases like "the lady wife" and "the little woman" and believed in football codes as if they were the Mosaic Law' (201).

But, through Janet's narration, Astley seems to be attacking more than stale stereotypes of Australianness. It is, after all, the satellite dish itself that enables this global worship, and the paranoia that runs like a thread throughout the text, undermining any sense of pastoral idyll, begins to affect Janet's own thinking. She senses 'some corrupt and deliberate policy . . . behind the system that produced school leavers and even university graduates barely literate in their own tongue' (201–202), leading to a 'kind of feudalism in which the minority wealthy had control of a population . . . serf-style' (202). Janet, like Marshall McLuhan, has become 'a sardonic observer of doom' (240), a doomsayer at the end of the century. Like Paddy Locke, another country woman who 'tries to interest "the ladies" in culture' (251) and fails, Janet, too, overcomes that 'peculiar sense of belonging' (153) that has kept her in Drylands, and decides to leave.

The trashing of the newsagency in Janet's absence and the message scrawled on her type-written manuscript by the unknown intruder in felt-tip pen – 'GET A LIFE!' – force Janet to search for the 'ultimate reply'. Although the text suggests that she would never find it, she considers writing the words 'TOO LATE'. The text comes to its close with Janet abandoning her 'search for the ultimate Eden' (294), sensing the 'pointlessness of it all'. Ending, Beckett-like, in mid-sentence, refusing the full stop, the text is 'a kind of victory, a kind of defeat' (293). While this may be a book for the world's last reader, it is no swansong. For while Janet may decry a society which is becoming increasingly boorish and ignorant, this book exists and is being read. The word still holds its power. Janet, at one point, divides the world into travellers and stayers, readers and non-readers and wonders if there is any congruence between the two groups. If, as Janet opines at the very end of the text, 'the victory would be in leaving' (293), then this book is part of that victory. It is a refusal to be bullied into silence, into mediocrity, into illiteracy. For, as Janet's mother has always told her, 'being unable to read is being crippled for life' (107). Despite the pressure from an anti-intellectual society that values 'getting a life' over 'writing a life', the passion for writing and communicating is clear in Janet's narration and Astley's text. Perhaps it is no coincidence that for many of Astley's generation the first learning-to-read books they would have encountered were the 'Janet and John' series. There is some poetic justice that a book for the world's 'last reader' is being narrated by another Janet who is emphasising not just the importance of reading and writing, but also the need to correct stereotypical representations that have become 'a matiness of tired old catchwords' (83).

If the novel's title refers also to the drying up of a writer's creative juices, the book itself, with its acerbic observations about contemporary Australian society and culture, and its cleverly ironic and ambivalent meta-narrative techniques that interrogate the efficacy of writing and reading in a 'time of disintegration' (Matthews 1973: 173),[2] clearly propounds the opposite. As suggested in the final incomplete sentence of the text – whose meaning and typography reinforce this lack of closure – '[t]here were no endings no endings no'. Despite Janet's apocalyptic voice of doom, the finality is undermined: there is no full stop, the reading process maintains its primacy, and for Astley herself, as the writer behind Janet's narrating voice, books will always matter and there will always be another page to turn.

Gillian Mears, *Fineflour* (1990) and *The Mint Lawn* (1991)

Gillian Mears has commented of her own writing that it engages with the 'covert and overt violence against women' especially in country towns and of the 'overwhelming darkness' that is the underside of life in an Australian country town. Born in the New South Wales town of Grafton, Mears uses this location as the basis for much of her writing. Speaking of her own experience growing up in Grafton, Mears has said: 'You can look at Grafton and think it's quite beautiful and lovely . . . calm and peaceful but I think country towns create their own particular oppressions' (Sorensen 2000: 80).

In another interview, she suggests that growing up in the country gave 'both a sense of freedom and a sense of being stultified' (Hawley 2002: 32). An important aspect of the oppression she identifies that makes country towns the opposite of the pastoral idyll is the 'unbalanced relationship between women and men' and the 'often unacknowledged plights that confront Australian women in small country towns: the trap-like nature of unequal marriage and desire' (Mears 1994: 45). This is particularly evident in her picture of the repressed sexuality and entrapment in a loveless marriage of Clementine, the protagonist of *The Mint Lawn* (1991). But whereas this emphasis on the dark side of the dream (as Hodge and Mishra have described the unacknowledged Aboriginal presence in Australian history and literature) can seem entirely negative, Mears also explores the healing quality of storytelling itself. Like Grenville in *The Idea of Perfection*, her focus is on ordinary people and their alternative histories that make their everyday battles, 'their own sort of gritty ways of surviving', into heroic struggles. Again, as in Grenville, there seems to be an unspoken offering of these more mundane stories in opposition to the epic Aussie heroes like Ned Kelly and the 'explorers'. Like Grenville's comparison of her writing process to making a quilt or patchwork, Mears talks, too, of writing as 'the piecing together of minute shards', emphasising her 'profound preoccupation with the past' in a metaphor of archaeological digging, identifying and fitting together.

Mears' collection of short stories, *Fineflour*, illustrates both these thematic and writerly concerns, exploring the lives of girls and women in two neighbouring fictional Australian country towns called Fineflour and Little Fineflour, and the particular oppressions they encounter which are metonymic of wider oppressions in a still-patriarchal society. There is a town called Fine Flower north-west of Grafton on the upper reaches of the Clarence River in country New South Wales and one possible reason for her use of the name in this collection is given in one of the stories: '1963 seems a cruel year in Fineflour, my town with the gentle and pretty name' (Mears, *Fineflour*: 26). By juxtaposing the apparent peacefulness and picturesqueness of the town's name with the subterranean violence and the 'terrible injustices' (Sorensen 2000: 93) she locates there, Mears is drawing attention to the established patterns of oppression, suffered particularly by girls and women and by Aborigines who have been omitted from history, in such little towns 'with their pockets of terrible darkness' (Sorensen 2000: 93).

The genre of the short story cycle is particularly appropriate for Mears' gradual acculturation of the reader into the people and society of the two towns, and the private and the public lives that each story reveals. Each story has a different narrator (some used more than once); some are first-person narrations; others third-person narrations, and characters from one story appear in another, sometimes as the first-person narrator. Levels of detail emerge gradually between and among the stories themselves, which are also interconnected spatially by the river Fineflour which runs through them all 'linking time and place, character and event' as the dust-jacket notes suggest. Additionally, the stories unfold in time. The collection starts in the 1950s with a tragic event (given an exact date of 1954 in the story 'The 100th Island' on page 37 where the mysterious Busker character of the first story is identified as Jake) and ends with the child-narrator of the first story (Judy Mann) revisiting the town and the graveyard as an adult. Mears thus establishes a contrast between the child's first-person perspective on the domestic tragedy in which she lost her best friend, Gracie (unnamed in the first story, 'The Burial and the Busker') in a murder suicide – something that is only really made clear in subsequent stories – and the adult Judy's first-person perspective on those events in which she considers the 'bitter Joy' of Gracie's mother so ironically named Joy.

So, in the cycle of stories, the town's changes are recorded, with expectations met or dashed, over time. For example, in the first story, the new highway, for which the graveyard has to be destroyed, is expected to bring business to the town (Mears, *Fineflour*: 10), but in the final story, on her return to Fineflour as an adult, Judy confirms that the town, far from flourishing, is decaying (as in Grenville's *The Idea of Perfection* and Astley's *Drylands*):

> It is a strange thing to return to the area you grew up in, grew sad in, discovered death in and find that some of the smaller towns are dying . . . I reach the town late one Sunday afternoon. It has a deathly feel but that river light makes all the dilapidation beautiful. The old buildings peel gold in the sunset.
>
> (178)

The ambivalent nostalgic glow of the golden sunset that recalls Judy's childhood memory is juxtaposed with the signs of present dilapidation, the peeling buildings.

One of the important themes of the collection is the distorting effect of time on memory. In the final story, Judy takes photographs to remember the town she grew up in, to match her childhood memories, just as the stories themselves capture memories in snapshots for the reader to piece together. In trying to find a caption for her photograph of local character, Merv, Judy muses:

> I think I will frame his face and his undies side by side with a suitable caption. Fineflour fragments. No, too corny. Fragments of Fineflour? Worse still! That is a difficulty of any past. It has a way of eluding description. Of defying the truth.
>
> (189)

This self-reflexive comment on the structure and method of the short-story collection we have been reading emphasises the fragmentary nature of memory and history as records of the past. Like any historical, fictional or photographic record, each of the stories is just a fragment or a snapshot in an album – there are elements that will always be outside the frame, or will remain uncaptured both in words and pictures. Like Grenville's anti-heroic alternative history of the everyday, Mears here contests the notion of any history arriving at 'the truth'. Indeed, for Mears it appears that individual stories rather than the historical record provide an archaeology of memory. Jim Placid is a keeper of the town's stories, which he passes down to Lily, listing for her 'all the drownings of the district over the past half-century': 'Jim Placid stacked stories inside Lily the same way he lodged the roots of his old Moreton Bay fig with carefully accumulated bits of tin or timber that could one day prove useful' (98). It is this oral record, rather than official history, that preserves the collective memory that would otherwise be lost. Lily is an eager recipient of these stories, which run 'wild in her head' and whose details she had 'off by heart' (98).

The River Fineflour itself is a trope of memory, a repository of the town's past, particularly as a place of death for many of its inhabitants whose stories appear in the collection, and whose violent drownings are listed by Jim. A place of violence and death, the river is also an integral part of childhood and adolescence in the town, a site of innocence and seduction. That it becomes a kind of bodily presence is illustrated in Judy's description of her summer holidays spent at home at the river: 'My skin went the colour of flood silt . . . the faintly sulphuric, mud flavoured odour of all the other kids who'd stayed at home' (6). The river is witness, too, to the loss of childhood innocence, vividly portrayed in 'Pipedream' when the Pipe family's second son 'seduces' and has sex with Margot on the boat, ironically called 'Pipedream', with the same careless violence with which he drowns a bag-ful of puppies in the river. Both Margot and the puppies are helpless and abject victims of his cruel and mindless behaviour. Mears has commented on the ambivalent nature of Margot's experience in the story that it is both 'a universal tale of girlhood within this kind of atmosphere of powerless-ness', and yet shows Margot as 'somehow finding her power even within the horrible circumstances' (Sorensen 2000: 94). For Mears, the river rep-resents a place where young girls such as Margot while 'doing desperate things . . . cloudy masochistic acts, . . . are working out some kind of a res-olution to whatever is going on in their life or distressing them' (Sorensen 2000: 93). So the river is not just a place of tragic death and violence but also a place of release and return, as when the Mann children, grown up now, scatter their father's ashes on the river (Mears, *Fineflour*: 173) where, as children, they escaped from their father's authority.

The theme of violence and violation, often imaged in Mears' writing through tropes of disease and corporeality, can make for uncomfortable and confronting reading. She has been accused of having an 'obsessive preoccupation with bizarre physical details, sexual behaviour, coarse, abusive language and violence' (Larriera 1997: 3). Her detailing of bodily fluids, for example, can be seen as another way of imaging the 'subterranean things' that she is drawing attention to in her stories, the dark side of the façade of ordinariness and respectability that characterises country towns particularly in the 1950s when the collection begins. This covert violence associated with ideas of masculinity and bullying is linked with the hidden history of violence against Aborigines in the town, a history which, like the bodily fluids, must in time come to the surface of the body politic.

The story 'Fineflour' makes an explicit link between the repression of such stories and the history of settlement of the area. In this story, the specific date (1963), which marks the beginning of Aboriginal activism and the 'freedom rides', is contrasted with the small-minded racism that persists towards local Aborigines in Fineflour. Narrated by one of the Duff boys, whose secret Aboriginal girlfriend, Roo, is one of those victimised by the headmaster of the local school, the story enacts the difficulties of such a relationship across the 'colour bar' – 'She and her family aren't allowed into the memorial baths' (Mears, *Fineflour*: 29) – in the light of segregation. The headmaster's racist rantings against the so-called half-castes typify the town's attitudes towards Aborigines of mixed blood: 'the trouble with them is that they've got the white fella's brain and the black fella's skin. That's why they reckon they're so cunning' (25). The narrator's father's opinions about Aborigines echo those of the headmaster: 'The only answer, Dad says, is to scrag them white but he better never catch me doing the scraggin'. Or give them a patch of dirt out the back of Woop Woop' (27). The history of dispossession and violence on which the town is founded is exposed in this story, imaged as a kind of disease that is emerging despite attempts to cover it up (in an echo of Nadine Gordimer's buried corpse in *The Conservationist* discussed later). This sense of dis/ease permeates the stories. This ineffectual attempt to negate the past is imaged in the memorial tree planted for Gracie which was 'not doing well' as 'some spindling disease seems to have taken hold' (26). Similarly, there is a disease killing the gum-trees of the district which results in trees losing their shape and dying 'with their branches splayed in curious contortions . . . From a distance they could look like crosses' (18). This becomes a physical manifestation of the town's inability to escape its violent past. In this story, 'Fineflour', the narrator's job at his father's butcher shop adds to the sense of death and violence – 'there's an excess of blood' (26). The narrator's attempt to undo some of this racism, and its memorialisation in historical records, by writing 'me 4 Roo' in the girls' toilets is ineffective: 'the damp sick smell of chlorine makes my writing small and stupid' (28).

Even the genteel Miss Andersons disagree over the past and how to interpret or remember it. Jibby tells Ada stories about the past 'to make her less alone' (75) and reminds her of the antics of the young Aboriginal servant, Poddy, they had as children, but Ada's memory is resistant:

> But Ada will not remember. She bowed her head when Jibby told the Poddy-tries-to dive story. Some days she goes silly over the blacks, what happened to them, and calls dear Mumma and Dadda killers. Jibby has to sit her in the Silent Room then.
>
> (76)

Ada's refusal to be complicit in this selective and sanitised version of the past results in her being silenced and infantilised by the stronger-minded Jibby.

The complex process of reconstructing memory and recording the past is reinforced throughout the stories, particularly with references to photographs. Photographs seem to be reliable windows to the past (and windows are another important recurring image in these stories with the narrators and readers often taking the position of voyeur, staring into someone's house and seeing things that are supposed to be hidden, intimate, secret as in Stacey Coope's glimpse into the Mann's kitchen where 'the open fridge looked naked and vulnerable' (61)). However, the ultimately unreliable nature of memory is emphasised in the story, 'Another Country' when Judy hears from her childhood friend, Nadia, who sends her a cassette and a slide. Judy, in her first-person narration, 'remembers' the slide as being an image of Nadia but questions its reliability: 'The hat is too large. The brim obscures so much. What is she looking at?' (107). The questions beyond the frame are unanswered; the blurred outlines are unable to be fully or clearly drawn so that 'the whole picture' eludes the reader or viewer. It is only at the end of the story that Judy reads the caption to the photograph that Nadia has written on a slip of paper: 'October 1971. You in the old garden' (113). That there can be such a fundamental misreading of the identity of the photograph's subject reinforces the way that memory can be obscured as well as captured by photography. The disappointment of the eventual meeting between Nadia and her two boys and Judy in which a 'lack of recognition persisted' (187) echoes the disappointment of Rhys' return from Paris, both 'returns' emphasising the way memory can distort and colour (in rose).

Yet, despite this emphasis on the unreliability of encapsulating moments and memories, it is storytelling itself that proves mesmerising for all the characters. At the end, when Judy goes back to Fineflour, she stays because of the 'intricate, humorous abilities [of Merv] as a storyteller' (187). Merv keeps asking Judy why she has come back, warning her not to 'dally with the past':

> It's hard to explain. All week I try to make him see, in the hope that I might see myself. And all week, I try to persuade him to let me take some photos of him but he won't be in that. So I take some black

and whites of his underwear instead, knowing they will make funny, disgusting enlargements. The brown stains would give the prints a sepia toning and the pub veranda, with the Fineflour behind, is old and graceful enough to provide a successful contrast . . .

While Merv listens to the race results, . . . I try to write down anything at all about memory and the nature of childhood friends who die. And those who live . . .

I look to the river for inspiration.

(187–188)

This can, of course, be read as a description of the book itself and makes you turn to the beginning with a sense of recognition.

Like the *Fineflour* collection, *The Mint Lawn* is set in a New South Wales country town with the River Fineflour running through it, and in imaging this town, Mears particularly emphasises the restrictive lives it allows for girls. Its protagonist and part-narrator, Clementine Young, ultimately rebels against being an obedient child, a 'goody-goody' as she calls herself, both in her school career and her marriage to the much-older Hugh Eastern, her music teacher who, even after their marriage, she still calls 'Mr Eastern'. Clementine's sexuality, graphically described by Mears throughout the novel, is ultimately what traps her into an abusive marriage with Hugh as the result of a teenage pregnancy but is also the source of her freedom via her affair with Thomas Flight. While she protests to Thomas that Hugh has never been deliberately cruel to her, Hugh's crude homophobia and sexism are apparent to Clementine even when she is still in the early stages of her marriage, when 'some part of her already turns from the ideas and scraps of malice and innuendo passing from his mouth' (Mears, *The Mint Lawn*: 256). The only thing that keeps Clementine with Hugh (until her decision to leave him at the end of the novel) is what she calls 'an addictive martyrdom as well as an insistence on being needed' (205). She realises that her marriage is based on Hugh's need for her 'to remain childlike, dependent, obedient and voiceless' (33). The repetition of the phrase 'in my husband's house' (in her first-person narration in the section of that title) emphasises her lack of agency and subjectivity in her role as Hugh's 'living treasure' (32) and 'possession' (183). Clementine recognises in her own rebellion against 'normality' that of her mother, Cairo, whose flirtations outside her marriage and need to be more creative than her 'domestic martyrdom' (99) allows, she used to criticise. As Cairo's friend Patrick tells Clementine: 'At least she is trying. Which is more than you can say for most of the women in this town. Tennis and tipple – she's not one of those ladies. Not entirely anyway' (161). Whenever she returns from Sydney to the bush, Cairo cries because of 'having to return to the hot, landlocked country town where she really lived' (29) and leaving behind the excitement of the city.

Clementine links her entrapment in these 'peculiar patterns of passivity' (50) with the limited choices for girls growing up in country towns – 'marching, sex, horses, Christian youth groups' (50). She resists the 'familiar and erroneous assumption that country towns are the site of all things wholesome' and that she will follow 'the old patterns' (Mears 1991: 277) of domesticity and motherhood, despite being the only one of the three Young girls to remain in her childhood town. Although 'horsey', her sister, Alexandra, is one of those whom Clementine envies for escaping both the town and the narrow choices it allows. Clementine believes that Alex's life in the country 'even as a child . . . has always been more masculine than feminine' (146) enabling her to escape its prescriptions.

The dark underside of the town is expressed in its underlying violence towards women and Aborigines. Springer Street is described as a 'vaguely frightening street, no matter what time of the day' where 'girls are raped in the paddock behind the hotel', girls whom Hugh calls 'hound bitches' (26). Hugh's abusive language is extended to those he calls '*Abos*', a word Clementine 'has always hated' but is unable to resist as she is 'locked into an inarticulate pattern' (26). The small town racism represented in Hugh is expressed by his fear that the town will become 'Bloody Vegemite Village' if the 'rezoning of Moree blacks' goes ahead (27), and is endorsed by his friend Trev. This undercurrent of violence and racism beneath the veneer of a peaceful country town is imaged in the Australia Hotel whose seeming grace, Clementine notes, is an illusion: 'It always smells of vomit, and the beetroot and grease of counter lunches' (27). Similarly, the underlying violence of Hugh's infantalising relationship with Clementine ('He calls me Baby Doll like we're living in 1950,' she tells Thomas (31)) is imaged in his lopping of the gum-trees around his house, significantly poisoned to avoid regrowth (286–287) and his disfiguring of photographs he has taken of her: 'There is a drawerful of chopped pictures. My brown legs have been chopped off at the knee. He has severed the rainbow near when it meets the side of my left ankle' (288).

This potential violence prefigures Hugh's rape of Clementine at the end of the novel and her realisation that their lovemaking 'has always been something not pleasant' (292). This 'diabolic passivity' (292) that Clementine believes has led them to this low-point in their relationship emphasises her own complicity in Hugh's abuse. The 'disease in the air' (292) that she notices in the morning, with the peach trees that have 'glistened overnight with a diseased sort of jelly' (292), reflects the 'continuation of patterns of secrecy' (293) that have led her to remain in this abusive relationship.

As in the *Fineflour* stories and in *Drylands*, the town itself is subject to change over time, as 'progress' encroaches on its so-called old-fashioned values. Thus, the Young girls' childhood home, 'Come to Good', is sold to McDonalds when their father decides to leave it after their mother's death. But, in an ironic turn, the house would become 'a heritage McDonalds'

(a nicely oxymoronic phrase) with 'pictures . . . of the town at the turn of
the century' (142). As in *The Idea of Perfection*, the notion of heritage becomes
a way of exploiting a new commercialism in dying country towns. Thus, the
bobblenut palms remain on the site, retained because of their heritage value
and even Hugh is waiting for his shop to become part of a 'heritage street'
– 'A bit of history, he thinks, would pull in the tourists who surge past along
the highway on the hill' (26). Ironically, of course, the Young's house itself
was never really part of the town's mainstream culture. Situated on the
'dingy side of town . . . the Aboriginal side' (11), it was named by
Clementine's eccentric mother, Cairo, to try to escape the ordinariness of
the place. As Clementine suggests about Cairo's unusual naming of the
house and her daughters:

> Like the mint lawn she tried to make flourish, the name [of the house]
> was an attempt to transform the great and stretching tedium of a
> country-town wife: to eroticise the ordinary. Eventually her attempts
> failed, as I feel we have all failed. I sometimes think she named us to
> be exceptional, to stand apart, but, instead, two of us are married and
> I have never left this town.
>
> (11)

Cairo's mint lawn returns to being an 'ordinary' lawn after her death in
a motor accident and her brief resistance to the norm is swallowed up
and erased.

Clementine's own escape at the end of the novel is from her loveless
marriage and its entrapping domesticity and from the restrictions of the
town. Returning in the final section of the novel entitled 'Husband' to the
first-person narration of the first section, Clementine links her following
of her own desire 'to be free of Hugh' with 'losing the battle against
cobwebs, fleas and moths' (271). The final scene, when she returns to Coal
Stream where her father is camping, is one of reconciliation with her past
and her future. The last image is of her significantly swimming in the sea
in a place that 'is the opposite of being tied up' (a phrase that both suggests
her metaphorical state within her marriage and Hugh's literal tying her
up when he rapes her) where '*everything seems possible*' (298, italics in original). She witnesses a 'rare white rainbow', symbol of hope and escape
from the small-town entrapment in her husband's house.

For both Astley and Mears, then, in these texts, while there is some conso-
lation in the acts of reading and writing narratives that offer an alternative
view, that of the 'dark side of the dream', for both writers, official history
and the circulation of self-justifying myths of the countryside epitomise the
violence of dispossession and the politics of inequality that mark such
places.

4   Learning to belong

Nation and reconciliation

Jo Dutton's *On the Edge of Red* and Heather Grace's
Heart of Light

This chapter explores the moves in contemporary non-indigenous Australian women's writing to begin a dialogue with indigenous issues that can be conducted on a level of greater equality and understanding than that which characterised the position of the 'maternal imperialist'. On the one hand, early twentieth-century white women writers were much more interested than their male counterparts in facing up to issues of Aboriginal dispossession and suffering (as in Katharine Susannah Prichard's novel, *Coonardoo*); on the other, much of their writing was still caught up in the discourses of Social Darwinism that, while bemoaning the fate of the perceived 'dying race' of Aborigines in Australia, simultaneously engaged in the racist discourses that allowed institutional racist practices to go unchallenged. Thus, for example, the 'half-caste' child of Coonardoo and Hugh in Prichard's *Coonardoo* would, in real life, have been forcibly taken from her care under the policies that removed such children to white institutions, yet Prichard does not address this possibility at all in her narrative. Indeed, it is only recently that this issue of the Stolen Generations is being addressed, and these narrative gaps are being filled, as in indigenous writer Doris Pilkington Ganimara's novel/memoir, *Follow the Rabbit-proof Fence*, and the film entitled *Rabbit-proof Fence* that is based on it, both, incidentally, set around the same time as Prichard's novel.[1] Sympathetic identification by white women writers with indigenous peoples, then, has often been silent about the very processes that have enabled the unequal power relations between them to exist, exposing the 'complicity of white women in Indigenous women's oppression' (Moreton-Robinson 2000: 174) and the investment of white women in Australia's racist policies. This chapter will outline the problematic notion of 'indigenisation' before briefly surveying some early twentieth-century women writers' representations of indigeneity as a context for contemporary reworkings of such negotiations, in the form of Jo Dutton's novel, *On the Edge of Red* (1998), and Heather Grace's earlier *Heart of Light* (1992).

Becoming indigenous

Contemporary settler societies share a sense of anxiety about belonging, about being or becoming 'indigenous', alongside a sense of guilt at their dispossession and displacement of indigenous people. Thus, Terry Goldie writes of the process he calls 'indigenization' among the non-indigenous peoples of Canada, New Zealand, and Australia, and of their need to become 'native':

> A peculiar word, it ['indigenization'] suggests the impossible necessity of becoming indigenous. For many writers, the only chance for indigenization seemed to be through writing about the humans who are truly indigenous, the Indians, Inuit, Maori, and Aborigines.
>
> (Goldie 1989: 13)

Similarly, J. M. Coetzee has posed a question that addresses this 'impossible necessity' in relation to South African settler writers who, he suggests, from the beginning of the nineteenth century onwards, have struggled to find 'a language to fit Africa, a language that will be authentically African' (Coetzee 1988: 7). The double-bind of this situation is that no existing African language will do as these are writers of European, not African, descent. Thus, the question becomes: 'Is there a language in which people of European identity, or if not of European identity, then of a highly problematical South African-colonial identity, can speak to Africa and be spoken to by Africa?' (Coetzee 1988: 7–8). Clearly, Coetzee is using 'language' here in a metaphorical as well as a literal sense, as an index of belonging and alienation.

Yet, this process of 'indigenization' is always a complex and often contradictory one, expressing as it does both an anxiety about origins and a need for legitimacy (Hodge and Mishra 1990: 23–24). Hodge and Mishra have no doubt about the source of this tension for non-indigenous Australians – 'the occluded but central and problematic place of Aboriginal Australians in the foundation of the contemporary Australian state and in the construction of national identity' (Hodge and Mishra 1990: 24). They link the ways in which Aboriginal culture has been co-opted by Australian nationalist discourse, in a move that combines a fascination with the culture of the 'other' with a 'suppression of their capacity to speak or truly know it' (Hodge and Mishra 1990: 27), to Said's Orientalism, calling it 'Aboriginalism'. Andrew Lattas analyses the ways in which contemporary Australian discourses, particularly in the media, represent non-indigenous Australians as 'removed from that realm of indigenous truths the land can offer the nation' (Lattas 1990: 52). Thus, as non-indigenous Australians 'emerge as figures who lack a spiritual sense of belonging to and possessing the land', the necessity of 'reconciliation with the spirituality of Aboriginal people is posited as the means for healing the sense of alienation belonging to settler society' (Lattas 1990: 52). In this way, as he and other commentators have noted, Aboriginal Australians are made to bear a heavy symbolic burden within nationalist discourse: not only are they the link to the land and its potential spiritual harmony, but they are also 'expected to provide a common sacred space capable of overcoming the potential ethnic and linguistic divisions created by immigration' (Lattas 1990: 60) within the contemporary nation as a whole.[2]

Alongside this general turn to indigeneity, there has been a particular move in contemporary feminist and environmentalist theory (also known as eco-feminism) to re-turn to 'indigenous knowledges' (Jacobs 1994: 309). As Jane Jacobs points out, while this 'politics of sympathy' does not 'necessarily escape the processes of domination associated with colonialism and patriarchy', it can also 'unsettle or challenge the structures of power normally associated with colonial or settler states' (Jacobs 1994: 309). On the negative side of the equation, Jacobs acknowledges the ways in which, through a discourse of eco-spiritualism, 'all Australians are able to claim Aboriginality by way of an appropriated and re-imagined Dreaming', suggesting, too, following Nicholas Thomas, that this 'ecological discourse requires a primitivist, essentialized Aboriginal' with Aborigines constructed as both 'an otherness and an origin' for settler Australians, as Lattas has outlined (Jacobs 1994: 307). In this way, Jacobs suggests that 'possessing Aboriginal knowledge may be the final step of colonization, the means by which settler Australians are transformed from aliens into indigenes' (Jacobs 1994: 307). Jacobs stresses the central role played by women 'in the pursuit of the indigenously inspired eco nation' (Jacobs 1994: 307) with 'eco-anthropological accounts' replacing 'masculinist' ones, so that women are 'central as nurturers of the feminized planet' (Jacobs 1994: 307–308).

But not all commentators stress the appropriative nature of the relations between non-indigenous and indigenous peoples. Helen Thomson points out that there has always been a predominance of Australian women writers engaging in a degree of 'sympathetic identification with Aborigines, particularly [Aboriginal] women' (Thomson 1993: 31). She suggests that there has, as in the more trendy eco-feminism, always been a link between feminism and environmentalism so that even the early twentieth-century women writers in Australia 'sorrowed at the inevitable destruction of both the physical environment and the black people, as white male settlement pressed on inexorably' (Thomson 1993: 31). According to Thomson, women writers, through 'sympathetic representations of Aboriginal culture were able to challenge the white male antagonism to the bush' and, in this way, 'women wrote themselves back into the forbidden cultural landscape' (Thomson 1993: 35). She, too, links this perceived empathetic response to Aborigines by these early women writers with a way of finding a place: 'Their sense of sisterhood with black women, imperfect though it may be, was expressed most powerfully through a shared, benign relationship with the natural world, in contrast to the exploitative violence of men' (Thomson 1993: 35–36). She cites Dale Spender's view that white women had a different attitude to the enterprise of settlement than men: 'Not only does this make their literature different from that of their male counterparts, but women's writing provides another, often subversive perspective, on the attitudes and values of the country and its development' (Spender 1988: xvii).

Yet, there are clearly problematic aspects of this 'imperfect sisterhood' between non-indigenous and indigenous women. This has been expressed most cogently in indigenous women's critiques of white feminism. Behrendt, for example, strongly criticises white feminism for its own oppressive discourses which she sees as 'white lies', lies that suggest an alignment between white and Aboriginal women in the 'battle against oppression' and the 'lie' that 'white women are as oppressed as we are' (Behrendt 2000: 175). These are debates, of course, that have been taken up more generally with western feminism being accused of colonising activity by a number of indigenous critics. Jacobs quotes Audre Lorde's sense that western appropriations of indigenous culture perform 'a tragic repetition of racist patriarchal thought' and Winona LaDuke's comment that 'it's like mining [our culture]' (cited Jacobs, 306). There are moves, though, to draw attention to such colonising practices, for example, to the privileges of whiteness that have been hidden and the need to remember how, in dominant versions of Australian history, and, indeed, in literary representations such as 'The Drover's Wife', 'white women are mythologised as the brave women who fought against the harsh climate' (Moreton-Robinson 2000: 174). In this way, a conversation can be engaged in between indigenous and non-indigenous women that acknowledges the historical and contemporary inequalities in power relations while at the same time working towards reconciliation. Grimshaw *et al.*, in their *Creating a Nation*, concede that: 'Feminism contains a missionary impulse, but in its bid to forge alliances across racial, ethnic and class barriers feminism also, importantly, opens up the possibility of solidarity between women in common struggles for freedom' (Grimshaw *et al.* 1996: 3). It is both these impulses, the missionary one and the reconciliatory one, that the next two sections of this chapter will explore.

The 'goodfella missus'

The politics of reconciliation, such a vital issue today in contemporary settler-invader colonies, such as Australia, South Africa, Canada and New Zealand, are fraught with complexities. It is notable, for example, that it has been a woman pastoralist in Australia (Camilla Cowley, a Queensland grazier) who has personally made a 'treaty' with the Aboriginal traditional owners of her farmland, despite the Liberal/Coalition Government's refusal to ratify such treaties on a national basis, allowing them their traditional owners' rights to 'her' land. But if there is detectable in the above formulation an element of ambiguity or irony in this gesture of reconciliation that centres on the notion of authority and ownership itself (who has the right to make such allowances? Under what law does the land belong to her to allow this magnanimous gesture to be made?), the relationship between such maternal white figures and indigenous inhabitants of the colonies they settled has *always* been one fraught with such anxieties and contradictions. As Margaret Jolly points out, the term 'maternalism' is not just the substitution of 'soft feminine intimacy' for the 'harsh masculine distance' of paternalism, but suggests, rather, in its symbolic mother–daughter relationship between colonising and colonised women, a 'poignant but strategic expression of the tension between superordination and identification, between detachment and agonized intimacy, between other and self' (Jolly 1993: 115).

The notion of the 'goodfellow missus', like the drover's wife, has become part of the representation of white Australian women from its early twentieth-century beginnings to the mid-twentieth century. Margaret E. McGuire's survey article entitled 'The Legend of the Good Fella Missus' (McGuire 1990) emphasises the 'power and persistence' (McGuire 1990: 124) of this Australian myth, which, she suggests, reached its apogee in the century before the Second World War, and died out with Daisy Bates in the 1940s. McGuire, an art historian, provides a useful definition of the typology of the 'good fella missus':

> The good fella missus is a pioneer outfacing Aboriginal hostility, and bringing succour to their destitution. She is the missionary seeking salvation for her black brethren. She tends the sick, clothes the naked, and soothes the dying. She is also the literary woman enshrining herself in a position of benevolence and authority in race relations. She has sisters in the other colonies in the British Empire such as the memsahibs of India.
>
> (McGuire 1990: 124)

McGuire provides a useful paradigm, too, for the generational nature of this notion of the 'good fella missus', beginning with the pioneer's wife (Mrs Bessie or 'Mumae' in *Coonardoo* is one such example); succeeded by 'Australia's daughter' (as in Phyllis, the native-born granddaughter of Mrs Bessie in *Coonardoo*); and, finally, reinscribed in the 'modern urban woman of the twentieth century who ventures into unknown Australia as writer, artist or anthropologist' (McGuire 1990: 124), a description that could well fit Lara in Jo Dutton's contemporary version of this type in her novel, *The Edge of Red*. The first generation, McGuire suggests, is always represented as a mother because 'motherhood confers authority on the colonial woman, licensing her to speak' (McGuire 1990: 125). In her role as mother to her Aboriginal 'children', she seeks to protect them from their own worst excesses, often, in the process, rescuing Aboriginal women from their abusive and cruel Aboriginal 'husbands'. As McGuire points out, this was something of a distortion of reality, as it was more often the pioneer men who were sexually abusing Aboriginal women, an issue which was decidedly taboo in such 'bush-memoirs'. It was rather more comforting for the colonial woman to see Aboriginal women as having a status 'worse than that of a slave' and Aboriginal men as 'brutes of creation' than to represent Aboriginal society as a 'mirror image of her own sexual and economic repression' (McGuire 1990: 134).

The second generation, 'Australia's daughter' has a more sympathetic and 'natural' relationship to the bush than did her mother, for whom it was often a dangerous and wild place, and to its Aboriginal inhabitants. McGuire suggests: 'She writes herself as the child of culture sympathetic to the children of nature, Aborigines' (McGuire 1990: 137). Phyllis in *Coonardoo* is a good example of this type of young countrywoman who is 'at home' on the land and in sympathy with traditional Aboriginality which has been displaced, thereby destroying the idyllic relationship between the indigenous people and the land which existed before 'contact'.

The third generation, or the 'modern woman' as McGuire calls her, consists of those professional writers, artists and anthropologists of the twentieth century who 'have to make a journey to find Aboriginal subjects in central and northern Australia, and their writings too take on the dimensions of adventure and romance in uncharted territory' (McGuire 1990: 143). It is in this category that McGuire includes Jeannie Gunn and Katharine Susannah Prichard; and it is this 'type of the Good Fella Missus' in its most 'fantastic proportions' that characterises 'the diminutive figure of Daisy Bates' who, McGuire suggests, would 'each day . . . dress formally and cross into the Aboriginal world' (McGuire 1990: 149). Again, while she was the only woman at this time to publicly live alone with 'adult blacks', her writings reflect the ambivalent nature of this relationship. Originally entitled 'My Natives and I' (with a distinct sense of ownership implied), and later to become *The Passing of the Aborigines* (1944), the emphasis is more on herself than on her 'subjects' and on 'those qualities of steadfast endurance, which are characteristic of our race' and on 'their [white women's] influence on the natives' (Bates, quoted in McGuire 1990: 149). The sense of ownership ('my natives') and the strategic importance of the 'dying race' philosophy combine to undermine her own projection of her benevolent maternalism, making her discourse typical of the 'doubleness' of the white woman's tongue.

'The Little Missus': Jeannie Gunn's *We of the Never-Never* (1908) and *The Little Black Princess* (1905)

While there are certainly elements of feminism within Jeannie Gunn's texts (and much of the somewhat limited critical response to her work has been on this aspect), there are also aspects of the texts which problematise her project as 'maternal imperialist', and these contradictions are, of course, immediately apparent in the oxymoronic nature of the term, 'goodfellow Missus' itself. Supposedly used by her Aboriginal servants to describe her, it takes 'pidgin' English to suggest a gender-bending authority mixed with maternalism ('missus' has a more motherly and egalitarian sound than the South African equivalent of 'madam', which seems instead to emphasise a class divide), which equates with the more familiar notion of 'boss'.

Laura Donaldson's feminist reading positions Mrs Gunn's nickname, the 'little Missus', within the same marginalising discourse that Gunn herself applies to the Aboriginal children she indiscriminately terms 'piccaninnies'. According to Donaldson, the term 'little missus' denotes 'one who is dominated and colonized, whose lower/higher relationship to discourse infers nothing less than that of inferior to superior, oppressed to oppressor' (Donaldson 1992: 84). However, Mrs Gunn writes of herself in the third person as follows: 'The mistress had long ceased to be anything but the little missus – something to rule or educate or take care of, according to the nature of her subordinates' (Gunn 1992: 94). The tone of this seems to me to be far more ironic and ambiguous than Donaldson suggests. While appearing to admit to being belittled and bullied, she is simultaneously affirming her ultimate and ironic power over the 'subordinates' who *think* they can 'rule or educate or take care of' her, by retaining her position as 'mistress' and 'missus'.

Mrs Gunn specifically links this ambivalent sense of power and dependency in her role as 'mistress' to her Aboriginal servants. Following her husband's suggestion that she rule them 'with a rod of iron', they all disappear (except for Nellie), and 'there were no lubras to rule with or without a rod of iron' (Gunn, *We of the Never-Never:* 45). In order to 'cultivate' their return, Mrs Gunn tries to endear herself to the 'delightful dusky group, squatting on its haunches' at the Creek, as they try to teach her their language (45). The ambiguity of her position as the 'little missus' is encapsulated in the following narrative comment:

> Undoubtedly I made myself attractive to the blackfellow mind; for, besides having proved unexpected entertainment, I had made everyone feel mightily superior to the missus. That power of inspiring others with a sense of superiority is an excellent trait to possess when dealing with a blackfellow, for there were more than enough helpers next day, and the work was done quickly and well, so as to leave plenty of time for merrymaking.
>
> (46)

While seemingly disparaging her own 'inferior' status, the narrative is actually discursively performing the opposite effect: that is, reinforcing her greater intellectual superiority in being able to manipulate the 'blackfellows' to believe themselves more powerful, while actually harnessing that belief to make them into better *servants*. A similar disjunction is evident in the chapter entitled 'Goodfellow Missus' in *The Little Black Princess*. Mrs Gunn says this of her relationship with her servants: 'You see, I was what white people would call a "bad mistress", but the blacks called me "goodfellow Missus", and would do anything I wanted without a murmur' (Gunn, *The Little Black Princess*: 175). Being a benevolent Missus certainly has its advantages, then, not the least of them being that her wishes are carried out obediently.

Because it is concerned almost entirely with Mrs Gunn's relationship with Aborigines, it is in *The Little Black Princess* that the clearest examples of cultural exchanges occur, illustrating the necessarily ambivalent attitudes of the Missus who is at once both teacher and pupil ('I was the pupil, and they were the teachers, and my lessons were most interesting' (173)). On the one hand, she asserts that she 'never laughed at their strange beliefs' and that she 'found them wonderfully interesting, for I soon saw that, under every silly little bit of nonsense, was a great deal of common sense' (164); on the other, she writes of 'their' ways as 'a perpetual circus and variety show on the premises' (179). While Mickey Dewar believes that Mrs Gunn's 'praise for [the Aborigines] was practically unconditional' (Dewar 1997: 25), her attitude displays rather more of the maternal imperialist than this would suggest. She does, indeed, show unusual sensitivity towards Aboriginal culture, explaining and often justifying local customs to her readers.[3] She approves, for example, of the rule that forbids a man to make any eye contact with his younger female relatives, to prevent temptation to incest, opining to Goggle Eye that 'you blackfellows plenty savey' (Gunn, *The Little Black Princess*: 166). Yet, in describing the way Bett-Bett and Goggle Eye avoid each other in a later episode, she wonders what would happen if they bumped together: 'Perhaps debbil-debbils would have come with a whizz, and would have left nothing but a little smoke!' (174). At the same time as she seems to take Aboriginal knowledge seriously, she undermines it with her sense of the absurdity of this 'superstition' by comparing it with something out of the Arabian Nights.

Similarly, while expressing great interest in corroborees, which she insightfully describes as 'the books of a tribe' (171) in which ancient ways and customs are handed down to the young men, she displays an equally maternalistic response when she is invited to attend a 'debbil-debbil dance'. Her description of this dance again reveals a complex mix of patronising, infantilising and genuine, if somewhat ethnographic, interest. She says, for example, that she agrees to watch the dancers being dressed for the performance as she always 'like[d] to see a blackfellow getting into clothes of any sort' (180). Her tone of voice reflects her somewhat sceptical attitude: 'special magic men . . . went out-bush, and bewitched a tree with all sorts of capers, and prancings, and pointings, and magic' (191). When she plays up by pretending to be frightened by the 'debbil-debbil' dancers, begging them not to carry her off, 'they shouted with delight . . . and tried hard to look fierce in spite of their grins . . . for, if there is one thing a blackfellow likes better than anything else, it is a "play-about" ' (191). While debunking the notion of Aboriginal men threatening to abduct the white woman, she is quick to respond to Goggle Eye's suggestion that it is time to leave as the secret corroboree begins: 'we had our revolvers

with us, but it is always wise to take a blackfellow's hint' (183). Beneath
the veneer of the 'tame Aborigine' is the 'dangerous native', she implies.
This notion is reinforced when she describes the Aborigines' celebration
of the Coronation (of Edward VII):

> [A]ll helped themselves to huge junks [of meat], and began tearing at
> them like wild beasts, dog and master eating from the same joint. I
> called Bett-Bett then, and we went to our camp, leaving our guests
> to their feast; for this part of the entertainment was not pretty.
>
> (206)

The juxtaposition of the celebration of an imperial event with a savage
feast is, of course, ironic, and the clear implication is that the civilising
mission is a fragile one, painting a thin veneer over the 'wildness' beneath.

She takes seriously her role as teacher and missionary, yet she does not
just see this as a one-way cultural exchange. Using pidgin throughout for
Aboriginal dialogue, she acts as a mediator of Aboriginal society when she
translates pidgin phrases for her readers, using her own occasional mis-
understandings to highlight, for example, the different contextual meanings
of the word 'kill' in pidgin (190). She also comes to value the way they
can 'read' in alternative ways by following tracks, for example, by using
sign language, smoke signals and message sticks. Her own inability to learn
the basics of tracking is ridiculed by the Aboriginal women: 'It was the
best joke they had ever heard – a woman who did not know her own
husband's tracks. I felt very small indeed, and, as soon as possible, went
back to the house' (209). Even in her role as teacher, when she is trying
to explain the letters of the alphabet to Bett-Bett, she finds that she is
unable to answer Bett-Bett's questions: 'somehow, she always made me
feel that it was my fault, or my ignorance, that there wasn't [an answer]'
(189). Similarly, she finds it difficult to explain her religious beliefs and
to communicate her own understanding of God: 'It is very, very hard
work to teach any blackfellow the truth of God's goodness and love.
They have no god of any sort themselves, and they cannot imagine one'
(215). While on the one hand acknowledging the shortcomings of her own
culture in its assumptions of superiority, and asserting the equal value of
many Aboriginal cultural practices, she is also committed to teaching and
'civilising' whenever she can.

Bett-Bett's need, at the end of *The Little Black Princess*, to 'go bush' reinforces this sense of essential difference as Mrs Gunn describes her as:

> hungry for her own ways and her own people . . . for anything that
> would make her a little blackfellow girl once more . . . if only she could
> shake off the white man for a little while, and do nothing but live.
>
> (228)

The final words of her narration, though, return to the theme of the mutual interdependence of black and white:

> I walked back to the homestead, feeling strangely lonely, for I had grown accustomed to the little black shadow that was always chattering at my heels; but, when I looked at the little pearl shell [Bett-Bett's most precious treasure, a parting gift], as it lay in my hand, I knew that, in a little while Bett-Bett would need her Missus, and come back bright and happy again.
>
> (229)

So, in shaking off the dust of civilisation and shedding her clothing at the same time, Bett-Bett is going to be 'cured' of her 'bush hunger', but she will inevitably return to 'the white man' on whom she has become dependent. Mrs Gunn sees little irony in having brought about this dependence, but seems to revel in her role as 'her [Bett-Bett's] Missus' who, right at the beginning, 'rescued' Bett-Bett from the 'wild Willeroo blacks'. The ambivalence of this positionality, that is, Mrs Gunn's awareness of Bett-Bett's need for her own people and yet her own complicity in 'domesticating' Bett-Bett that has made her forever dependent on her 'Missus', encapsulates the complexity of the white woman's role in colonialism: she is both sympathetic and 'motherly' towards the indigenous people and yet remains firmly placed within her more authoritative role as 'Missus'.

Katharine Susannah Prichard, *Coonardoo* (1929)

This mixture of authority and sympathy on the part of the white 'missus' towards Aboriginal people and the paradoxical need to find a way of belonging to the land through an understanding of indigeneity is reflected, too, in Katharine Susannah Prichard's novel, *Coonardoo*. Unlike the popular success of Jeannie Gunn's two texts, Prichard's novel was controversial from the start, described by Mary Gilmore in 1928, in a letter to Nettie Palmer, as 'an appalling thing . . . vulgar and dirty'. But it won *The Bulletin* competition jointly in 1928 with one of the judges praising Prichard for making the 'Australian aboriginal a romantic figure'.[4] One of the most controversial aspects of its reception at the time of its publication was the sexual relationship between Hugh and Coonardoo, a white man and an Aboriginal woman, that results in the birth of a 'mixed race' child. It is noticeable, though, that the novel was written and published at a time when the rise of social anthropology, Social Darwinism and the eugenics movement had created a social climate in Australia that was hostile to such interracial relationships. *The Bulletin* (the journal in which *Coonardoo* was first published in 1928 in serial form) had as its banner heading, 'Australia for the White Man'. Prevailing discourses of nationalism, racism and sexism are neatly encapsulated in this catch-phrase. Biological ideas about race predominated at this time in Australia, leading to some rather contradictory ideas. On the one hand, ideas of racial purity led to the notion of Aborigines as a 'dying race'; on the other, ideas about assimilation and 'breeding out' Aboriginality led to the removal of so-called half-caste Aboriginal children from their families, later to be known as the 'Stolen Generations'.

A. O. Neville, Chief Protector for Western Australia in the 1930s, for example, believed that one way of 'solving' the 'race problem' was through 'biological absorption', or what was also called 'miscegenation' between Aboriginal and white people, so that skin colour would be gradually bred out and everyone would eventually become 'white'. Kim Scott's novel, *Benang* (1999), is a haunting account of the material effects of the attempt by some Aboriginal people to be acknowledged as the 'first white man born', the first in the family to appear 'white'. There was widespread public discomfort about Neville's theory as, rather than condoning a kind of apartheid between races, which was the more acceptable view at the time, he was suggesting active inter-marriage or at least interbreeding. Of course, the whole basis behind both assimilation and miscegenation is the discredited eugenicist idea of a hierarchy of races which was to be taken up by the Nazis in order to justify genocide. Anne Brewster points out the links between these national and global assimilationist policies and the 'transnationality of instrumental terror and genocide' (Brewster 2002).

Prichard's going off 'into the interior' in September 1926 (to stay on McGuire's Station in the centre of Western Australia) led to her 'discovery' of the Ngarlawongga (which she transcribes as 'Gnarler') people there. Louis Esson wrote in a letter to Vance Palmer that Prichard would:

> get wonderful material [there]. The station is run by blacks, and I'm sure she will get a fine book out of it. The blacks are so interesting . . . and she's certain to give the spirit of that strange, weird country as it has never been done before.
>
> (quoted in Healy 1978: 140)

Prichard herself wrote in a letter to her friends, the Palmers (quoted in Introduction, p vii): 'And the blacks are most interesting – fair haired – and I find them poetic and naïve. Quite unlike all I've ever been told, or asked to believe about them.' It is statements like these that have led to continued controversy for the novel's reception, with feminist and postcolonial critics pointing out the ways in which, while Prichard's views were clearly sympathetic to Aborigines, she is still caught in the colonising discourse of the time. J. J. Healy praises Prichard for her representation of Aboriginality:

> For the first time in Australian literature a genuine curiosity about Aboriginal life, which was non-anthropological, non-philanthropic,

found its way into the book. Katharine Susannah Prichard placed the Aborigine in modern Australian literature in a manner reminiscent of Russell Drysdale's Aboriginal paintings nearly 30 years later ... [showing] her liberation from preconception and stereotype.

(Healy 1978: 150)

Yet, in her 1929 Foreword, Prichard approvingly quotes Basedown, an anthropologist, with distinctly Social Darwinist views: 'the Australian Aborigine stands somewhere near the bottom rung of the great evolutional ladder we have ascended.' Similarly, Hodge and Mishra point out that Prichard invokes the authority of Mitchell, the Chief Inspector of Aborigines in Western Australia in her Foreword, a man who has been strongly criticised for his attitudes in more recent times. Prichard's representation of Aborigines has also been criticised as caught up in the colonising discourse of the day, so that she is seen to perpetuate the stereotype of Aborigines as representing nature and the feminine principle; and Whites as representing culture and the masculine principle. In addition, she has been criticised by some recent feminist critics for being complicit with masculinist notions of feminising the land.[5]

Apart from Prichard's own ambiguous status in her cross-cultural negotiations with Aboriginal peoples, her characterisation of the white women characters in *Coonardoo*, and, particularly, that of Mrs Bessie Watt, provides another important example of the 'good fella missus' paradigm. While Mrs Bessie, the widow now in charge of managing and working the station, Wytaliba, is gendered in masculine terms (as a 'wiry, restless figure in a pair of trousers, white shirt, and old hat of Ted's [her deceased husband]' (Prichard, *Coonardoo*: 14)), and is obviously the 'right sort' of pioneer woman needed for settling and farming, she is also a mother figure. This doubleness is reflected in the name given to her by the Aborigines, 'Mumae'. While mimicking the sound of 'mummy' in English, the word means 'father' in the Aboriginal dialect Prichard is referencing, so that Mrs Bessie takes on both these roles by standing in for her dead husband's authority as 'master': 'was not Mrs Bessie, father and mother to her son, the woman master of Wytaliba?' (3).

This complex dynamic of survival, mothering and mastery extends to her attitude towards Aborigines. We are told early in the novel that 'Mrs Bessie prided herself on treating her blacks kindly, and having a good working understanding with them. She would stand no nonsense, and refused to be sentimental' (8–9). She seems to exhibit a number of the qualities that Barbara Ramusack ascribes to what she calls 'maternal imperialists', those white women in India who exercised 'a benevolent maternal imperialism ... [who were] frequently referred to as mothers or saw themselves as mothering India and Indians' (133). This ambivalent combination of ownership (Mrs Bessie refers to 'her' blacks) and nurture is exhibited, too, in Prichard's figuring of Mrs Bessie's complex relationship with

Coonardoo, her domestic servant on the station, in particular. While respecting Coonardoo's beliefs, and not trying to 'europeanise' her, as she calls it, she nonetheless draws the line at certain 'native practices'. This contradiction is presented by Prichard in two closely proximate passages narrating Mrs Bessie's attitude to Aboriginality. Mrs Bessie is adamant that she 'would not allow any Christianizing of the aborigines on Wytaliba' and that 'aborigines on Wytaliba should remain aborigines'. It is for this reason, the narration suggests, that Coonardoo who 'all day . . . was Mrs Bessie's shadow, and learned to wait on and do everything for her . . . always at sunset . . . went off with her people and slept with the dogs by her father's campfire' (14). Is it only with hindsight that this passage seems to speak so suggestively of the Robinson Crusoe/Friday paradigm; or did Prichard sense the problematics of this exhibition of maternal imperialism?

The second passage that exhibits a similar ambivalence is just a few paragraphs further on, when Mrs Bessie is told that Coonardoo would be 'Warieda's woman' when she was old enough. Coonardoo herself is 'filled with pride and pleasant anticipation at the thought of being the wife of Warieda'. But Mrs Bessie does not approve despite her carefulness 'not to interfere with her natives in any of their own ways and customs' (16). Again, the text is equivocal about the reasons for her disapproval of this particular custom. She cites Coonardoo's youth as part of her reason, but admits that 'she was not quite sure herself why she was so opposed to Warieda taking the girl' (17): settling in the end for its interfering with her plan 'attaching Coonardoo to herself and Wytaliba' (17). Her motherly protectiveness towards Coonardoo (she tells Warieda that she is 'fond of Coonardoo' and that 'she is my own girl' (16)) is counteracted by her sense of ownership ('I will give her to you'), again, redolent with Crusoe-like attitudes.

For both Mrs Bessie, and for her son, Hugh, Coonardoo represents a link with the land which is only available to, and maybe through, the indigene. It is only through this 'indigenization' that, Terry Goldie suggests, whites in settler-invader colonies can become 'native' and feel a sense of belonging. This 'impossible necessity', which is an appropriation as well as an annexation of indigenous identity, is neatly captured in this passage from *Coonardoo*:

> Mrs Bessie realized that however she might teach and train Coonardoo in the ways of a white woman, teach her to cook and sew, be clean and tidy, she would always be an aborigine of the aborigines. Not that Mrs Bessie wanted to take Coonardoo out of her element. She did not, but she was jealous of an influence on the child greater than her own. She did not wish to lose Coonardoo. Her people did not wish to lose Coonardoo either. She was theirs by blood and bone, and they were weaving her to the earth and to themselves, through all her senses, appetites and instincts.

(26)

The contradictions portrayed here in Mrs Bessie's attitude towards Coonardoo graphically illustrate the settler predicament: the indigenous 'other' is perceived as the settlers' link to the land and to belonging, but the contact between settler and other has already irrevocably changed indigenous culture. Thus, the word 'lose' takes on ironic connotations: Coonardoo is already 'lost' to her own culture because she is bound in service to settler culture.

Prichard's profoundly ambiguous representation of Aboriginality is particularly evident in her representation of Coonardoo herself. While clearly she is meant to be a sympathetic character, a victim of tragic circumstances, there are, nonetheless, still elements of ambiguity, contradiction and stereotyping in her representation. While she is always associated with natural things, like water, the well, the land, suckling the baby, the song of the little kangaroos and so on, she is never really shown to be intelligent or logical, but rather always instinctive. She does not really have a voice or agency in the text: as one commentator has pointed out, her most repeated phrase is the inarticulate and compliant 'eh mmm' and she is often described as a 'shadow', first of Mumae and then of Hugh. It has, therefore, been suggested that Prichard's own attitudes towards Aboriginality are a mixture of sympathy and complicity in the myth of the dying race. The ending of the novel reinforces this idea with the dying Coonardoo returning to Wytaliba to become part of the land in death. Consequently, she becomes a symbol for her entire race in its destructive contact with white settlers, used first on the station and then as a pearler, and in both settings being abused by white men. It has also been suggested that one of the most uncomfortable messages the novel may leave us with is that it is not just the obviously racist whites who have contributed to the suffering of Aboriginal people, but also the so-called enlightened settlers, what Beasley calls 'well meaning exploiters' (Beasley 1993: 88).

Contemporary women's writing of indigenous–non-indigenous relations

Jo Dutton, On the Edge of Red *(1998) and Heather Grace,* Heart of Light *(1992)*

The issue of reconciliation has, as already suggested, been an important one for both Australia in the new millennium and for post-apartheid South Africa. Both these writers, Jo Dutton and Heather Grace, are concerned in their texts with issues of coming to terms with the past, in particular, the past 'dispossession, oppression and degradation'[6] of Aboriginal people. Both are writing with an awareness of contemporary concerns with belonging that take into account both the desire of non-indigenous Australians to find their 'place' and the need to acknowledge the often appropriative nature of claiming such an indigenous identity. Both write of, and from, locations in which relationships between indigenous and non-indigenous Australians have been of crucial social and political importance – Dutton sets her novel in Central Australia, the 'Red Centre', and Grace sets hers in the North of Western Australia, in the same area as Prichard's *Coonardoo* and Pilkington's *Follow the Rabbit-proof Fence*.

Part of the process of reconciliation in Australia between indigenous and non-indigenous Australians, like the Truth and Reconciliation Commission in South Africa, has been to try to heal the wounds of the past by allowing people affected by the violence of past racist policies to tell their stories. In Australia, the Council for Aboriginal Reconciliation was set up in 1990 to try to promote greater understanding between indigenous and non-indigenous Australians and to draw attention to the ongoing inequalities that, for example, have led to much lower life expectancy for Aboriginal Australians. The Australian Human Rights and Equal Opportunities Commission published its report on the Stolen Generations of Aboriginal children, usually those with some non-Aboriginal ancestry, who were forcibly removed from their families by government authorities from the nineteenth century to the 1970s, entitled *Bringing them Home* in 1997. The Report consisted of many of these stories and concluded that such forcible removals were tantamount to genocide. While many ordinary Australians as well as many churches and other institutions have acknowledged and apologised to Aboriginal people for these past injustices, the Federal Government, under Prime Minister John Howard, which had by then replaced the Labor Government that had commissioned the Report, refused to say 'sorry', with Howard criticising what he called the 'black armband' version of Australian history.

Similarly conflicting responses emerged in Australia to the concept of Aboriginal land rights. While the Mabo High Court Decision overturned the colonialist notion of *terra nullius* (the myth that Australia was unoccupied at the time of European colonisation) – a myth that arose because Aboriginal people were not pastoralists and therefore left no visible sign of occupation – the subsequent Wik legislation introduced by the Howard Liberal Government made it very difficult for land claims to succeed in law.

Both these issues lie at the heart of the contested nature of Australian history which, like South African history, has always needed to justify colonisation and settlement and has therefore maintained silence over many incidents that were too difficult or uncomfortable to address. Hodge and Mishra have called this repressed legitimising of colonial history and the relations of domination within it, the 'dark side of the dream', and characterise this darkness not just as the shadow cast by Aboriginal histories and bodies but also by 'an acute anxiety at the core of the national self-image, and an obsession with the issue of legitimacy' (Hodge and Mishra 1990: x). Jo Dutton's novel addresses both the issue of land rights and that of the Stolen Generations as well as the central anxiety of belonging that its white woman protagonist faces. Similarly, Heather Grace's novel explores the ways in which its two non-indigenous women protagonists can negotiate a non-appropriative relationship with place.

Central to both these novels is the issue of cross-cultural relations between indigenous and non-indigenous Australians, in Dutton's novel between white and black women, and in Grace's, between two white women and a landscape they perceive as Aboriginal. Indigenous feminist theory in Australia has emphasised the women's movement as being complicit in the continuing dispossession and disadvantage of indigenous people by not acknowledging its own 'white values, norms and beliefs' (Moreton-Robinson 2000: 173). Sisterhood between white and black women, it is suggested, will be achieved only when white women acknowledge their own advantage (of class and race). Jackie Huggins, for example, draws attention to the white woman 'experts' who wish to co-opt Aboriginal women into the women's movement as continuing to silence and control these indigenous women (Huggins 1994: 75–76, cited in Moreton-Robinson 2000: 173). In Jo Dutton's *On the Edge of Red*, Dorothy, a child of the Stolen Generations, accuses Lara, the anthropologist, of just such complicity: 'You're a strange lot aren't you, you gubbas. First of all you steal the land, then the women, then the kids, and now you're the fucking experts giving it back' (Dutton, *On the Edge of Red*: 90). Dutton's awareness of this uncomfortable relationship between power, privilege and race is set alongside the sense that white women's lack of belonging can be mitigated by means of indigenous knowledge, a problematic notion of 'becoming indigenous' that could be seen to parallel the need for South African whites to feel part of Africa. In a letter to her friend, Celia, Lara admits to this need:

> When you look out over the land and see the [Indigenous] people joined to the landscape a big burp of greed forms in your stomach. You are hungry to belong. Nobody admits this. You keep the jealous thoughts to yourself and pretend that you are doing people a favour by giving them your skills.
>
> (77)

Lara's awareness of this 'greed' to belong and her sensitivity to her own position of privilege as a member of the group of white middle-class women with 'skills' goes some way towards drawing attention to, rather than eliding, the politics of difference that many indigenous feminist theorists have embraced.

Jo Dutton's realist novel has as its protagonist an anthropologist, Lara Haines, whose own personal history as a fostered child seems to emphasise her need to find a way of belonging, not just within a family but also within Australia itself. By travelling from Perth to Alice Springs to work with an Aboriginal Land Claims Council, Lara becomes 'a cartographer of belonging, placing families and sites into records' (72). She is well aware of the irony of her work as part of the 'futile middle-class mission' (36) of white western do-gooders including her friend Celia who travels to the 'third world' as a doctor. She is also tuned in to the ethics of her own use of Aboriginal culture as a way of finding her own belonging, querying the morality of her 'borrowing belongings for a while' (79). The narrative excavates the stories of Aboriginal women, in particular, those of Mabel, whose family history includes children taken away from their parents as part of the 'Stolen Generations'. While some of these are included in the narrative in the form of transcripts, Lara is unsure as to how much she should intervene as 'editor' and explicator of these stories:

> She decided to ask Mabel what sort of directions, if any, she wanted in these stories. So far all she had done was the rather clumsy straightening of the circles of Mabel's language into lines of English. In doing this Lara knew that she had also moved the sense of the story; the rights and wrongs had shifted like a sandbar under the water every time she chose English words. She's the tide, she and her pen.
>
> (143–144)

In her triple role, then, as anthropologist, cartographer and historian, Lara takes on the colonising role of the white woman. However, her sensitivity to the needs of the people whose stories she is recording makes her a different type of anthropologist, one who respects the silences and secrets of Aboriginal culture, particularly as her own sense of being an outsider to mainstream Australian culture makes her identify more with the Aborigines than with the non-Aborigines in Alice Springs.

This sense of fellowship with Aboriginal people originates in her childhood when Lara is unable to understand why 'white kids' thought 'black was inferior' (25). Lara sees Aborigines as 'the strongest people she had ever met' who knew how to stick together (25) and she models her own need to be strong on their ability to outrun the white kids. Indeed, Lara herself is labelled a 'bloody Abo' because she can run barefoot on the netball court (25). In contrast, there is endemic racism in the town, something that is still there when she returns later as an anthropologist. She remembers the local shopkeeper as believing himself to be 'an expert on "the Aborigines"' who had 'three main themes: laziness, dress standards and loose morals' yet who 'only paused for breath to take their money' (26). Years later, racism is still the norm, with the shopkeepers shortchanging Aborigines and a code of apartheid 'not pinned to walls for all the world to read and squirm at like in other countries' but hidden in the dress regulations for entry to places that the locals want to keep 'white' (67). The narrative links such racism with the early settlers' fears of place so that they built towns 'in ordered squares . . . with their backs to the country' with the building code motto the equivalent of 'conquer, deny and desecrate' (67). This paradoxical hunger to belong and simultaneous sense of intruding is intuited by Lara who understands that 'all the things we miss in our own culture we see here, family, sharing, a spiritual reality that's not closed in a building' (78).

The issue of the Stolen Generations comes very close to home for Lara when Mabel, one of the Aboriginal women with whom she is working on the land claim, tells Lara about her granddaughter, Magdaline, who had been taken from her parents because she was partly white and put into a convent. Renamed Dorothy by the Welfare authorities, she had been at school with Lara and was a social and cultural misfit who didn't belong with the white or with the Aboriginal children. Denied her own cultural heritage and family history, Dorothy/Magdaline (whose split subjectivity is signalled in this splitting of her name) eventually finds her way back to her own people and takes a tribal name but 'had no idea how to close the gap caused by so many years away' (89). While Dutton draws attention to Lara's own displacement, marginalisation and lack of a family history (Lara's baby is born with, and dies immediately as a result of, inherited spina bifida but not having contact with her own family, she was unaware of this risk), she never tries to make the two girls' experience equivalent, resisting the move to homogenise the experience of white and Aboriginal foster-children. The difference is made clear: Magdaline is forcibly and cruelly removed from her grandmother's care by the authorities whereas, though the consequences may have been equally severe for Lara, her father had 'given' her to her foster family, unable to look after her because of his alcoholism.

The narrative engages with different versions of history and the problematic engagement in mediating history by white people. As an anthropologist working on a land claim, Lara has to translate and transcribe the 'story of ownership' (103) from the Aboriginal custodians of the land like Mabel. Yet the very process of trying to decide who belonged where was subject to conflict – 'There was unstated disagreement that moved like currents under the surface' (103). As different stories emerged and as Lara tried to establish 'the truth', she found that 'the less clear it all became' (105). Additionally, there was secret business that had to be covered up 'because it wasn't necessary that all the white participants in the Claim Court see everything' (105). In the end, the text itself respects such secrets and Mabel's own version of the stealing of Magdaline, although 'straightened' by Lara into 'lines of English' (143), is left to speak for itself, with Lara respecting Mabel's own decision about whether or not to explain the 'cuts' of mourning that Mabel has made on her body. In a similar move, Lara never explains to the reader how she has been healed by Mabel and the other Aboriginal women after the death of her baby: she returns from their care with cropped hair which she likens to the cuts and scars that are signs of mourning but it is never made clear whether the cutting of her hair is part of an Aboriginal ceremony or is Lara's own equivalent way of 'cutting ties, severing connections' (130) as a material sign of her loss.

Far from trying to avoid the 'black armband' version of history by evading and disavowing any notion of guilt for past injustices, Lara cere-

moniously takes on the guilt of all white Australians on her journey back
to Perth from Alice Springs. In approaching Kadaicha country, she apologises to the country for all the 'sins of the fathers and mothers', offering
a version of colonial history that acknowledges the 'rapes, the beatings,
the chains' and the 'great cruelty' (191) of the colonisers. She makes special
mention of the white women of the time, describing them as 'the great
white fat ones like witchetty grubs, who were cocooned by their men and
not allowed to laugh with their children, or stroke their hair' (191–192).
As 'prisoners in their time' (192), she suggests, too, that they were 'poisoned
with jealousy' (192) of Aboriginal belonging, bound to their clothes and
books but longing for 'love and sharing' (192). In retelling the story of
colonialism in the form of this prayer for reconciliation with the land,
Lara is also showing respect for oral history, and for the telling of stories
such as those of the Stolen Generations represented by Mabel's story in
the narrative, as opposed to the written history of the colonisers that has
covered up the history of oppression.

Yet Lara is aware that there is no easy dispensation and still feels 'like
a tourist: white, stupid and young in this old country' (193). Always aware
of her intruding on the land to which she has no claim, she knows that
there was 'no chance of the country not taking what it was owed or
forgiving her transgressions' (195). Her final act of throwing into the sea
the copies of her taped conversations with her father and her copy of
Margaret Atwood's novel *Surfacing* is, of course, symbolic of her moving
on from the past, and the image she has of Mabel holding her wrist while
telling her story is one of connection, not coercion, of the 'links that can
bind people together' (256). By learning from Mabel and the other
Aboriginal women, and by accepting her father, she has found another
way of belonging, so that she does not have to 'carry her past like weights
in the pockets of a swimmer' (256). Perhaps this is the significance of the
title: she is still aware of her marginality (being 'on the edge') and is not
yet part of the 'red centre' that is regarded as part of Aboriginal belonging
and yet is paradoxically also adopted as a tourist icon (in the form of
Uluru, particularly), yet she returns to the city with a renewed sense of
self and place. The novel has, however, at the same time, attended to the
practices of exclusion, power and dispossession that have been the price
paid by indigenous Australians of her own self-realisation. Thus, while
there is an ongoing sense of tension and awareness of appropriations of
Aboriginal culture, there is also a final note of optimism for such cross-
cultural contact in a space where, in Lara's words, 'her own culture and
theirs crossed and [had] done more than survive' (82).

Heather Grace, Heart of Light (1992)

Dutton's use of Canadian writer, Margaret Atwood's novel, *Surfacing*, as
the book to accompany Lara on her journey inward is significant. Some

critical responses to *Surfacing* have suggested that the (nameless) protagonist's quest for subjectivity is predicated on her (settler) appropriation of
a native American Indian spirituality expressed through the rock art that
her father has been trying, unsuccessfully, to map. Thus, the feminist quest
is linked with the sense of becoming part of the place, with settler identity and an awareness of an indigenous presence that has been displaced
– in other words, with Goldie's notion of indigenization. Heather Grace's
novel, *Heart of Light*, similarly narrates a feminist journey or quest that is
dependent on an awareness of indigenous presence and absence, of uncovering a layer of history that is unwritten but available in the form of rock
art and other remnants. Her two women protagonists, Julie, an artist from
Melbourne (like Grace herself, who was born in Melbourne but lives in
North-Western Australia), working as a temporary cook, and Kass, working
as a governess on the Easton River cattle property in the north of Western
Australia, leave their jobs and set off on a journey with which the novel
begins. Realist sections of the narrative are interspersed with impression-
istic accounts that trace their journey into the bush and away from
'civilisation'. Thus, in Julie's note left on their vehicle as they set off into
the 'heart of light' (not darkness), Julie writes of her being 'excited but a
little scared going off into country possibly never visited by white people'
(Grace, *Heart of Light*: 9). As a city girl, she revels in 'this sense of space'
(17) and the freedom she finds in the bush despite its being 'basic'. Julie's
militant feminism (and implied lesbianism) is expressed (somewhat crudely)
through her reading matter (Anne Summers' *Damned Whores and God's Police*
and a Doris Lessing novel), her boyish appearance (cropped hair and boys'
clothes) and her attempt to wean Kass off her dependence on men and
her desire for marriage. Julie is also politically militant, angry about
inequality in work conditions between male and female workers and about
the unthinking racism she encounters in her trips to Darwin. For Julie,
'the world is a battleground and she is ready for a fight' (72).

   In their journey into the as yet unexplored landscape that is not marked
on the map (42), both women become increasingly aware of the absent
presence or the traces of Aboriginal ownership of the land. Much of this
awareness occurs through their encounters with rock art. Julie's own drawings, described by her at the beginning of the novel as insubstantial with
'no spirit in them' (17) are contrasted with a 'true work of art', the paintings of animals that, according to Julie, have 'simple line' and 'perfect
balance' (17). When she comes across a rock painting of a snake 'outlined
in red and filled with dots' she is struck by the omission of the 'forked
tongue characteristic of European drawings' (45) and is unable to attribute
a meaning to it – wondering whether it was a warning of actual snakes,
a sign of spirits or merely a bored painter 'finding refuge here as she had
done' (45). At other times, the paintings represent the comfort of knowing
that 'others before them' have slept in that place (54). Yet the paintings
can also induce a mystical experience, such as that Julie has in the cave

covered by handprints which 'all speak silently of a continuum of people' who she feels 'press around her' (129). On finding the remains of a skeleton she feels afraid and 'bewitched' (133), and on awakening after a sleep, finds the skeleton and stones have disappeared. In retelling this encounter to Kass, Julie has 'no satisfactory answers' (133) and while Kass attributes it to sunstroke, marijuana or bush magic, she advises Julie not to try to 'work it out' (134).

The idea of an indigenous history that retains its presence and materiality is a strong one in the text. Thus, when Kass finds a stone that seems to be a 'living tool', Julie imagines 'hands which have held it' and is reminded of Phil's warning of a lost 'bush tribe' who may have evaded the fate of other Aboriginal people by hiding from the invaders. As Kass says: 'Imagine! One mob sees what they will lose and refuses to go into the mission. They avoid the leprosy roundups and massacres and all the other invasions. Fantastic!' (135).

Partly ignorant and partly fearful of this perceived presence, whether spiritual or physical, and of their own status as 'intruders in the bush', Julie is never entirely sure if they are indeed intruding on the spirit places of which she had been warned. She is aware that 'perhaps they should not be here at all' but is 'determined to go on' (126). She has, at least, been sensitive enough to Aboriginal custom to have obtained permission to be there from an Aboriginal woman elder, whose country it is, before their journey commenced. Additionally, by contrasting her own grandmother's 'stately old age' with the 'indignity of starvation' (129) suffered by the elder, she shows an awareness of white privilege.

The text still holds out the possibility of 'whitefella' becoming indigenous when, in the final part of the text, such belonging takes on a physical dimension – 'Spreadeagled, she becomes the rock . . . she is the earth' (139). That this absorption into the landscape itself is linked with indigeneity is made clear in the preceding pages when the women come across a white rock that appears to them significant but strange and that 'embodies their fear'. Julie's recognition of her fear as 'not-knowing' suggests that it is based on an ignorance of indigenous culture due to their Eurocentricity. Thus, she realises that: 'this stone, no less than the Great Pyramid of Egypt and the soaring cathedrals of Europe, represents human hope and fear and trust' (138).

For Julie, her experience in the bush and her encounters with natural monuments like the white stone remind her both of her own insignificance and of the need for the preservation of such places where people like her can go 'to find magic and be humble' (143).

In this text, and in Jo Dutton's, then, a conversation between indigenous and non-indigenous cultures is taking place, by means of their white women protagonists, in which there is an acknowledgement of a troubled history of relations between the two. Tentative steps towards reconciliation are being taken in their awareness of white privilege and their representations of indigeneity that attempt to avoid the objectifying and essentialising discourses of the 'maternal imperialists'. It is, though, Dutton's text, with its awareness that it is non-indigenous culture itself that is 'on the *edge* of red', on the margins of Australian identity, and not the 'white centre' that begins to take into account Moreton-Robinson's sense that white feminists all too often leave 'whiteness uninterrogated, centred and invisible' (Moreton-Robinson 2000: 184). In this acknowledgement of marginality and lack of authority by the white woman writer, small steps towards trans-cultural understanding on a basis of equality can begin to be made.

Part 2

Contemporary South African fiction

Introduction

New subjectivities

South African writing over the past decade has provided a fascinating paradigm of a society in transition as it has reflected the changes from a racially divided and repressive apartheid society to a post-apartheid climate of greater tolerance of difference and the non-violent creation of the 'rainbow nation' envisaged by Archbishop Tutu. Many writers whose theme had been the stultifying effects of apartheid on people and place were now able to take up new issues in their texts: issues of memory and history; of a changing society; and of new possibilities for literary forms. In the words of poet Ingrid de Kok, this transitional literature was Janus-faced, 'vigilant of the past, watchful of the future' (de Kok 1996: 5). Albie Sachs' provocative paper 'Preparing Ourselves for Freedom' published in 1990, four years before South Africa's first democratic election, suggested that one-dimensional politically committed works and the concept of the artist as 'cultural worker' could be replaced by art alive to its own 'capacity to expose contradictions and reveal hidden tensions' (Sachs 1991: 118). While there was much controversy in response to this African National Congress 'position paper', the sense that old structures needed to be replaced by a literature of transition was and is a resonant one and it has, indeed, given birth to a number of 'post-apartheid' works that engage with these contradictions and tensions. In the words of Attwell and Harlow:

> South African literature since 1990 has taken upon itself the task of articulating . . . the experiential, ethical and political ambiguities of transition: the tension between memory and amnesia. It emphasizes the imperative of breaking silences necessitated by long years of struggle, the refashioning of identities caught between stasis and change, and the role of culture – or representation – in limiting or enabling new forms of understanding.
>
> (Attwell and Harlow 2000: 3)

Established writers like Nadine Gordimer and J. M. Coetzee have always been alert to such undercurrents and their post-apartheid novels continue to problematise notions of complicity and resistance. Other writers have emerged as new voices in response to the unlocking of the past and the breaking of silences. Not least among these, of course, are the black South African writers like Zakes Mda, Zoë Wicomb, Sindiwe Magona and many others. The focus of this study, though, is on the texts of white woman writers in particular and this section charts the ways in which they in particular have engaged with these challenges over time, especially with regard to their awareness of the ambiguity and complicity of their own textual voices.

The issue of representation and, particularly, that of and by women, has been a central one for South African writing. Dorothy Driver's seminal essay on representations of white (British) women in the South African colonial enterprise (as in Australia) as 'bearers of culture' and 'mediators' articulates their entrapment within patriarchal and imperialist discourses (Driver 1988). Driver points out that 'whatever sympathies may have developed among white women for the indigenous or colonized people' (Driver 1988: 14), white women were 'enjoined or manipulated' into alignment with their own racial group, despite the often-repeated grouping of white women and indigenous peoples as occupying the same space. On the contrary, she suggests, South African white women were specifically 'used to maintain the difference between white and black' (Driver 1988: 14) within imperialist and nationalist discourses. That this symbolic and often idealised role has applied to both English/British colonial women, as addressed by Driver, and to Afrikaner women who took on the mantle of mothers of the nation in their role as Voortrekker Women, is made clear in Yvette Christiansë's analysis of the 'guardian angel' positioning of the 'Voortrekker Mother and Children' statue as part of the Voortrekker Monument and in Jenny de Reuck's work on women in the Anglo-Boer War.[1] Christiansë notes that the representation of the Afrikaner woman in this monument to Afrikaner nationalism 'took place in the larger sphere of the patriarchal political discourse of division' and that such representation 'subjected Afrikaner women to the same gender-based colonisation as other women' (Christiansë 1995: 12). While Voortrekker women were co-opted into the service of the creation of an ethnic identity, often as symbolic of both purity and suffering, they were excluded from the public world of political activity designated for men. According to Elaine Unterhalter, this involved the construction of a concept of 'woman' which was 'organized around domesticity, subordination to male authority, child-bearing and child care' (Unterhalter 1995: 228). Anne McClintock reinforces this interpretation, suggesting that the portrayal of the defeat of the Afrikaners in the Anglo-Boer War symbolically as a weeping woman enabled an overlooking of male defeat in 'images of maternal loss' (McClintock 1995: 378). Thus the figure of the woman, both as Afrikaner *volksmoeder* (Mother of the Nation) and as British 'bearer of culture', is paradoxical, simultaneously evoking the power of women within cultural and national practices and containing them as domestic icons within the private sphere. Unterhalter also, importantly, emphasises the connection between racialised identities and gender by reminding us of the ways in which apartheid legislation controlled 'women's reproduction to ensure the maintenance of race identity' (Unterhalter 1995: 227) by way of the 1950 'Immorality Act' and the 'Prohibition of Mixed Marriages Act' which were notorious for their patrolling and surveillance of interracial relationships. The tension between private and public spheres, then, and the policing of women's bodies are clearly played out in the ways women have been used in these political and national discourses, illustrating too the 'epistemic' violence of representation itself.

Similarly exclusionary practices, as Gordimer has pointed out in a number of her essays, apply to more contemporary writers who have found that the discourses and practices of the apartheid system meant that the experience of 'blackness' was blocked to white writers, and vice versa, resulting in stereotypical representations by each group of writers. Acknowledging the cultural limitations and the 'distorted vision' of her own whiteness, she has commented on the blindness of many whites to black people, drawing attention to the representational practices of apartness and separation that constructed a 'world of strangers', as one of her novel's titles suggests (Gordimer 1988a: 266). More recently, she has written of the dilemma of the white liberal in apartheid South Africa as constituted by a lack of belonging: 'the whites were not my people because everything they lived by ... was the stuff of my refusal' while the 'blacks were not my "people" because all through my childhood and adolescence they had scarcely entered my consciousness. *I had been absent,* Absent from them' (Gordimer 1995: 128). It was, she suggests, only through the imaginative medium of her writing that she could 'bring together what had been deliberately broken and fragmented' (Gordimer 1995: 130) and that only by being a part of this 'transformation of ... place' (Gordimer 1995: 130) could she find a sense of belonging. The first section of the following chapter, 'A white woman's words', looks closely at Gordimer's problematic representations of blackness and of whiteness during the apartheid years, and the uneasy and anxious negotiations between these two 'groups', in two of her novels written during the apartheid era.

A further aspect of white South African women's writing that is crucial to address is its own implication in the structures that it is so often attempting to critique. Thus the issue of complicity emerges in relation to representation. In her discussion of Afrikaner women's complicity in 'deploying the power of motherhood in the exercise and legitimation of white domination' (McClintock 1995: 379), McClintock emphasises the paradox that 'white women are both colonized and colonizers, ambiguously complicit in the history of African dispossession' (McClintock 1995: 379). Eva Hunter, in a feminist analysis of contemporary white women's writing in South Africa, criticises writers like Gordimer and Boehmer whose 'sense of their own inescapable complicity' has led them to 'exhibit as much hatred and contempt as they do for the leisured white woman and for the mother' (Hunter 1999: 44). Hunter accuses these writers of 'blaming' the white woman and denying her agency while failing 'to figure women who are both morally responsible *and* fully sexual beings' (Hunter 1999: 44). She attributes this 'castigating' of those women 'most like the privileged self' (Hunter 1999: 45) to the pressure of apartheid, accusing Gordimer in particular of rendering the white liberal woman 'grotesque and contemptuous' (Hunter 1999: 44) and, in so doing, 'obliterating differences among white women' (Hunter 1999: 45). While there is certainly a sense of guilt that has affected such representations of white women, this seems to me a somewhat simplistic analysis of their texts. Rather, it could be argued, these texts are enacting the ambiguous position of such women, acknowledging complicity as part of their subjectivity and, indeed, of their own texts. Thus, their awareness of their own marginal voices and the lack of authority of their authorship becomes an integral part of the textuality. These nuances are addressed and analysed in more detail in the chapter 'A white woman's words'.

Writing about the work of Zoë Wicomb, Dorothy Driver charts the development of new modes of representation in post-apartheid literature that are breaking away from the binaristic ones that predominated in colonial and apartheid times and that necessitated the use of the terminology of black and white, describing a writing that is at once more subtle and more uncertain, one that is: 'steadfastly insisting on creating more complex subject positions than those of the past, with new subjectivities continually emerging at the critical point between stereotype and representation, and between one discursive subject position and the other' (Driver 1996: 52).

In her 'Afterword' to Zoë Wicomb's novel *David's Story*, Driver links this change in representation to political changes, just as Gordimer connected the stifling nature of representation under apartheid to its own divisive practices. Driver writes:

> Since the official abandonment of apartheid, South Africa has been engaged in debate about the meaning of nation and national belonging. South Africans have been forging new political, cultural and ethnic identities through the opportunities provided by democracy and a new constitution, and also the Truth and Reconciliation Commission and amnesty hearings.
>
> (Driver 2001: 216)

It is, Driver suggests, the very ambiguity, ambivalence and nuances of identity in the new South Africa that have freed writing from the oppressive discursive formations that were imposed by apartheid thinking. The chapter entitled 'Rewriting the farm novel' charts these representations within a specific genre that has been of such importance in South African literary history.

Linked with this change in the nature of representation has been the higher profile given to women's issues in post-apartheid South Africa. The 'first things first' notion, in which political freedom was given priority over women's rights, has been replaced by a strong focus on women's issues and the suspicion with which feminist theory and practice was often regarded by both 'white' and 'black' women in South Africa has diminished. Indeed, women's stories in particular are emerging strongly as part of the release of silenced voices and common issues among women are being found. Driver comments on the ongoing need for 'an awareness of the ways in which women's bodies are used as signs by political or cultural movements that at the same time refuse to hear what women say' (Driver 2001: 239). She also draws attention to the still-hidden layers of violence against women that Wicomb's novel begins to unearth, quoting Joyce Seroke, one of the Truth and Reconciliation Commissioners, as suggesting that the hearings had only 'begun to scratch the surface' of the horror of such violence against women (Driver 2001: 239).

The Truth and Reconciliation Commission has had a significant impact on literature. While the Commission itself was, of course, performing a political and social goal of reconciliation and healing, it was also concerned with narratives of the past and with concepts of 'truth'. Post-apartheid literature, while also uncovering and revisioning history, has, as Ingrid de Kok suggests, a different role, not seeking 'to authorize or resolve'. She continues:

> Its [the literary project's] charge is private, not public. Its bid is to unwrite, retell, and reorganize the nature of the record, investigating the relationships between stories and history, staging the drama of individual and collective experiences and perspectives, examining discontinuities and lacunae.
>
> (de Kok 1996: 5)

Two chapters that follow, 'Revisioning history' and 'A state of violence', both engage with such issues by means of close readings of contemporary texts that deal with these aspects of post-apartheid and apartheid South Africa.

While in the past this mixture of guilt and complicity that has characterised the positionality of the white woman in the apartheid state has provided writers like Gordimer with a productive field of irony and self-reflective textuality, in post-apartheid South Africa it is the increasing fluidity of identity that is resulting in the new subjectivities being explored by contemporary white women writers. In addition to turning to the more experimental modes of writing, including magic realism and fantasy, contemporary white women writers are also interrogating the silences and invisibility of the category of whiteness itself, particularly in relation to the notion of an inclusive feminism. Margaret Daymond has spoken of the need for South African feminists to 'establish a community of purpose within the recognition of 'difference' without 'ignoring how race determines the degrees of power that women may be granted' (Daymond 1996: xix). While it is certainly true that the categories of race have been transformed in the new South Africa, there is still a need to examine and evaluate the ways in which the links between power, oppression and gender have operated in the past, and continue to operate in the present, and this is a project with which the contemporary white South African women writers examined in the next few chapters have been intimately concerned.

5 'A white woman's words'

The politics of representation and commitment

For a number of white South African women writers, political commitment, particularly during the political unrest in South Africa of the 1970s and 1980s, has been an ongoing and fraught issue, both within the world of their texts and, more broadly, regarding the role of literature itself within a repressive regime. Even those 'liberal' minded heroines that Nadine Gordimer has so often portrayed bear within them an ambiguity: while they may commit themselves to political causes, they often retain their inherited white privilege and thus remain outside the experiences of the 'ordinary'. They may journey across the colour bar to 'taste' the life of black South Africans, but usually return to the suburbs and their comfort zones. While often these heroines are feminist in their resistance to patriarchal structures, they can also be seen as marginal, as unable to make a difference. Sarah Nuttall, for example, writing about Elleke Boehmer's heroine in her 1993 novel, *An Immaculate Figure*, suggests that the heroine's story is 'a story about not seeing, not acting, not being, by implication, about being acted upon' (Nuttall 1993). Nuttall goes on to pose the question: 'What *are* the stories that white South African women, encased, ensconced, and often oblivious, are likely to tell?' answering her own question with the statement that 'what might follow on are more ambiguous white South African "heroines" ' (Nuttall 1993). This chapter examines some of these white South African 'heroines' who have engaged in the politics of commitment in the novels of Menán du Plessis and in two novels by Nadine Gordimer, arguing that their subject position is almost always ambiguous. In the work of these writers, the negotiation between feminism and anti-apartheid politics is highlighted as a complex one: South Africa's patriarchal society and its apartheid ideology are often linked as dual systems of oppression in which the white woman activist is always problematically placed.

Additionally, the political implications of literature itself are always under scrutiny in these texts, whether by implication (as in Gordimer's novels) or more overtly, as in du Plessis' work. There has traditionally been, in South African literary debates, an obsession with the political affiliations of the writer as well as the work itself, particularly so during the apartheid years, of course – so that part of the reception of literary work became (and perhaps still becomes) a series of questions about its political import. J. M. Coetzee has suggested that upon publication of a book in apartheid South Africa the question was immediately asked, 'where does this book fit into the political struggle?' (Coetzee, quoted in Penner 1986: 34). Christy Collis points out that the central question for many South African critics and writers has most often been 'not the non-essentialist, post-colonial one of "where is here" . . . but instead the polemical "which side are you on?" ' (Collis 1994: 2). It is, indeed, the 'violent urgencies of the political situation' (Collis 1994: 3) that have taken precedence in much South African writing.

It is often, though, in the texts of white women writers that the links between the politics of race and the politics of gender are made, even though Gordimer often asserted, in the apartheid years, that the issue of gender would always remain secondary to that of racial equality. Her state-ment that 'the woman issue withers in comparison with the issue of the voteless, powerless state of South African blacks, irrespective of sex' (Gordimer 1980b: 918) has led to a great deal of critical debate, particu-larly among feminist scholars, about Gordimer's reluctance to 'think of herself as a feminist writer' (Driver 1983c: 33).[1] However, as Driver points out, Gordimer's more recent acknowledgement of her interest in women's oppression only confirms what has been there throughout her fiction: an interest in what Driver calls 'the debased status of women in society' (Driver 1983c: 33) that runs alongside her critique of apartheid, racism and colonialism.

The following discussion of a 'white woman's words', both in terms of two 'politically committed' white women writers' texts and in terms of their representations of such 'liberal' women, while not dealing with post-apartheid contemporary texts but with those written during the apartheid years, sets the context for the texts that follow by tracing the trajectory of commitment and responsibility that have been such integral aspects of white South African writing. But it is, particularly, the self-consciousness about voice and authority and an awareness of the complicity and marginal status of their own texts that make these white women's texts important.

Gordimer and the paradoxes of privilege

The quotation that forms part of the title of this chapter (quoted earlier in the General Introduction) is adapted from J. M. Coetzee's novel, *Age of Iron*, in which Elizabeth, the white woman narrator, expresses the inad-equacy of her colonisers' language in response to the revolutionary language of the black people in the novel. Describing her words as 'like dead leaves', the gap in comprehension between white and black is thus inscribed within language: 'The words of a woman, therefore negligible; of an old woman, therefore doubly negligible; but above all of a white' (Coetzee 1990b: 72).

Coetzee, through Elizabeth's narration, is addressing the intersecting marginalities that undermine her own speaking position: her gender, her age and her 'whiteness', which 'above all' disqualifies her own voice from being heard. In suggesting the unstable nature of the authority of the white woman's voice, Coetzee is engaging with an issue which Gordimer herself has been concerned: the paradoxical positionality of the white liberal within the apartheid 'body politic', and, for both Coetzee and Gordimer, the figure of the white woman is crucial to this complex positioning of the anti-apartheid author both within and outside the 'infected' state/nation; both complicit and resistant at the same time.[2] This section of the chapter considers the ways in which Gordimer presents her white women characters in *July's People* and *Burger's Daughter*.

Gordimer has described her own writing as a way of finding herself and her 'place' in South African society, a society that had, in her words 'made itself comfortable with injustice' (Gordimer 1995: 115). She writes:

> Only through the writer's explorations could I have begun to discover the human dynamism of the place I was born to and the time in which it was to be enacted . . . I had to be part of the *transformation of my place* in order for it to know me.
>
> (Gordimer 1995. 130, emphases in original)

What is noteworthy here is that in emphasising the notion of 'place' Gordimer is suggesting a transformation not just of physical space but of her role within it. Displaying the 'settler woman's' discomfort with displacement, she is also asserting the need for mutuality, 'for it to know me', a sense of belonging that would make her, in Terry Goldie's terms, 'indigenous' (Goldie 1989). And this process is, not unexpectedly, made possible through contact with 'black experience':

> in mixing more and more with blacks, sharing with them as aspirant writers, painters and actors the sense of *learning how to think* outside the way our society was ordered, I was going through a personal revolution that had no other issue but to lead me into theirs, to find myself, there.
>
> (Gordimer 1995: 130, emphases in original)

But, of course, finding oneself in 'blackness' is a paradoxical and problematic endeavour for a privileged 'white' within apartheid South Africa, as Gordimer recognises, and it has its literary counterpart in the issue of representation itself.

The problem of representation, particularly during the apartheid years, is one about which Nadine Gordimer has agonised. In an early (1976) essay entitled 'English Language Literature and Politics in South Africa', she has this to say about white representations of blackness (and note the irony of the gender-specific language she uses, reinforcing Lockett's point that a study of Gordimer is needed which will 'account for her willingness to recognize racial oppression, the oppression of others, but not to perceive that, in terms of gender politics, it is she herself who is the Other' (Lockett 1996: 15)):

> any writer's attempt to present in South Africa a totality of human experience within his own country is subverted before he sets down a word. As a white man . . . the one thing he cannot experience is blackness . . . As a black man, the one thing he cannot experience is whiteness . . . The white writer . . . is cut by enforced privilege from the greater part of the society in which he lives . . . The black writer is extremely limited in his presentation of white characters . . . because of those large areas of the white experience he is excluded from by law.
>
> (Gordimer 1976: 119)

The implications of this assertion are important, identified by Gordimer as 'the dilemma of a literature in South Africa'. The impact of this cultural apartheid on black and white writers is, as Gordimer asserts, easily discernible in the writing that has emerged from this socio-political situation:

> In the work of white writers, you often get the same gap in experience between black and white lives compensated for by the projection of emotions about blacks into the creation of a black typology. Guilt is the prevailing emotion there; often it produces cardboard and unconscious caricature just as [black] resentment does.
>
> (Gordimer 1976: 119)

The problem is even more acute for white women writers who often try to assume a mediatory role which involves them in a further set of contradictions and ambivalences, as already outlined. As Dorothy Driver points out: 'women's sympathy for the oppressed and their simultaneous entrapment within the oppressive group on whose behalf they may desire to mediate complicates their narrative stance' (Driver 1988: 13). As evidenced in the example from Gordimer's essay quoted above, her linguistic entrapment in the language of patriarchy (Gordimer's use of sexist language) and imperialism (language itself as a form of colonisation) makes bridging the gap between black and white women even more difficult. Driver points out that 'whatever sympathies may have developed among white women for the indigenous/colonised people, then, that white women have historically often either been enjoined or manipulated into aligning politically with their own racial group' (Driver 1988: 14). She gives as an illustrative historical example of this the granting in the late 1920s by Hertzog of the vote to white women and not to black women – a decision to which the suffragettes agreed. Thus, as Driver states: 'The "woman" in "white woman" acts one way, then, and the "white" another' (Driver 1988: 14).

This raises the question of Gordimer's problematic feminism. While there have been some attempts to find feminist patterns in her work (with Stephen Clingman, for example, seeing her as moving towards a 'politicized feminism adapted to the realities of South Africa' (Clingman 1993: 223)), it has more often been the case that Gordimer's own rejection of feminism has confounded attempted feminist readings of her work. Dorothy Driver has argued that Gordimer's novels necessarily relate gender and race issues via an interrogation of power structures, yet there are problems inherent in this position which are summed up by Cecily Lockett, who writes about the invidious position in which she herself is placed as a white feminist in South Africa:

> This makes our position [i.e. white feminists in South Africa] especially difficult, since we may identify with black women but they are more likely to view us as agents of their oppression. It also poses the vexed question of whether we, as white women, have the right to speak for or about black women when we, in our turn, reject the discourses that our oppressors (i.e. male patriarchies) have made about us.
>
> (Lockett 1996: 17)

Dabi Nkululeko has reinforced this from the perspective of a black woman writer:

> As aliens to [black] experience, Euro-settler women have to overcome most of the trappings of their own experience, such as their own class interests and status, and they have to study closely their experience as part of the colonist–settler nation, disassociate themselves from it before they can begin to comprehend the experience of the native women under colonialism . . . In order to extricate themselves from culpability in the oppression of African women, settler women – the 'feminist socialists' – must work among their own people to create conditions for the destruction of such oppression . . .
>
> (Nkululeko 1987: 101)

Gordimer's representations of blackness reflect her own ambivalent role as a white 'liberal' woman writer, 'trapped in whiteness', and trying to find her 'place' in Africa. One African National Congress (ANC) spokesperson for the new South Africa suggested that whites should be called Euro-Africans, which neatly turns the linguistic tables on imperial discourse, but is slightly more accommodating than the term 'Euro-settlers' used by Nkululeko in the quotation above.

These issues become clearer through a reading of the construction and representation of women characters (black and white) in two of Gordimer's more well-known novels of the 'struggle years', at the height of the political struggle against apartheid, *July's People* (1981) and *Burger's Daughter*

(1979). As both novels have been subjected to a great deal of critical attention already, I shall only deal briefly with them, focusing on those aspects
that relate to the issue of the politics of representation and commitment.

One of the subjects that has interested Gordimer in her fiction is the
'heart of darkness' paradigm, that of the 'privileged white woman who
ventures into blackness, seeking to find herself through political action and
personal relationship with the colonized majority of her country' (Visel
1988: 39). As Robin Visel has pointed out in her analysis of the 'half-colonization' of settler women, the efforts of Gordimer's protagonists are
'well-meaning but misdirected', due to their 'lack of historical and self-
understanding – or misconstrued, due to the political stalemate and hostility
between the races in South Africa'. And so, Visel suggests, this 'groping
toward solidarity ends in alienation, exile, imprisonment or violence; there
is, according to Gordimer, no easy identification between the women of
the colonizers and the colonized' (Visel 1988: 40).

This pattern can be clearly seen in *July's People* and Gordimer's representation of its woman protagonist, Maureen Smales, who has rightly been
read as a 'Miranda' figure,[3] that is, caught between her colonising and
colonised selves in the colonial equation. The novel envisages a future
revolution in which members of the Smales family are forced to flee their
comfortable white urban existence in Johannesburg to seek shelter with
their black male servant, July, in his rural village. The inversion of the
colonial situation does not lead to the re-education and self-discovery of
Maureen, the white 'mistress/madam', but rather to her flight from the
overturning of the old hierarchies, both within her marriage and in her
relationship with July. What Gordimer seems to be implying is that both
coloniser and colonised are fixed in their roles. July, in his now-dual role
as servant and host, maintains his old habits of servility, the novel opening
with his bringing of a tea-tray to the Smales in their village hut. The title
of the novel itself is ambiguous – 'July's people' refers to both 'his' white
people, the Smales family, and his own tribal people, who are angry at
the intrusion of the white family from July's 'other life, his other self' of
the city. The encounter between Maureen, the white madam, and Martha,
July's wife, is an interesting representation of the problem of communicating across the margins:

> July presented her to his wife. A small, black-black, closed face, and
> huge hams on which the woman rested on the earth floor among
> cushions, . . . She frowned appealingly under July's chivvying voice,
> swayed, murmured greeting sounds.
>
> – She say, she can be very pleased you are in her house. She can be
> very glad to see you, long time now, July's people –
>
> But she had said nothing.
>
> (Gordimer, *July's People*: 15–16)

The description of Martha is from Maureen's point-of-view, so that the word 'black-black' represents her as doubly different; the word 'closed' represents her as unknowable. Later, the text describes Martha's blackness as 'a closed quality acting upon it from within rather than a matter of pigment' (92) which seems to reinforce the gap as one imposed not just by Maureen's whiteness but as an inherent withdrawing of contact. The fact that July is in fact putting words into Martha's mouth by welcoming Maureen – 'but she had said nothing' – speaking for his wife, serves to underline the mediating position he is in between his rural self (shown in his true name, Mwawate) and his colonised self as shown in the name given him by the colonisers, July, insultingly turning him into a thing, a month. The only common form of language between the two women is Afrikaans, the language of the coloniser, of which Martha knows only a few words. Once again, as in Coetzee's text quoted at the beginning, and encountered again in his novel, *In the Heart of the Country*, the gap which prevents either of them speaking in 'the language of the heart' is inscribed within language itself, the self/other language of the apartheid system and of colonisation. This is pointed up again when the women are going out to gather grass to use for thatch. July's mother tries to show Maureen the purpose of their work:

> She [the grandmother] grinned . . . and pointed a first finger as if to prod the white woman in the chest: You, yes you.

> But the white woman didn't understand she meant the grass was to thatch the house the white woman had taken from her. Martha reproached her mother-in-law in their language; yet it was true; and she could say what she liked, anyway, the woman understood nothing.
> (131)

The limited communication between black and white women is always compromised, even when some sort of maternal female solidarity seems about to be established, as in another part of the novel: 'There was a moment when Maureen could have got on her hunkers beside Martha and helped hold the baby's head while its hair was washed' (146) – but the sentence ends there. This gap is summed up when Maureen thinks of her relationship with Martha that 'it seemed a beginning. Something might have come of it. But not much' (146).

The other seemingly unbreachable gap between black and white women is that of 'place', used to mean both location and role. Maureen's dislocation in July's village is articulated by July himself when he forbids her to work in the fields with the village women: 'You don't need to work for them in their place' (97). This particular use of the word 'place' occurs too in *Burger's Daughter* when the narrator comments on the way '[b]lacks [and here it relates to urban dwellers] don't talk about "my house" or "home" [but] . . . [a] "place"; somewhere to belong but also something that establishes one's lot and sets aside much to which one doesn't belong' (Gordimer, *Burger's Daugther*: 149). Thus, place and role are inextricably intertwined.

It is the ending of the novel which has formed a focus for critical commentary and which is rightly seen as the point at which Gordimer expresses most clearly the ambiguity she associates with the white woman's voice. When a helicopter appears and hovers over the village, Maureen is not sure 'whether it holds saviours or murderers' (Gordimer, *July's People*: 158) and yet, in a climactic ending where the rhythm of the prose increases in speed and tempo, she runs towards the helicopter 'like a solitary animal'. The reader is never sure whether she is running towards friend or foe, but it seems that her running is a kind of liberation. This itself is contradictory, as we are unable to decide finally whether this is a kind of self-sacrifice (anything is better than living in an African village) or a statement of political conversion (is she running towards black revolutionaries to join their cause?) or, as one male critic would have it, as expressing 'powerful presentiments of a female liberation' (Clingman 1993: 199). As Kathrin Wagner says, in trying to find a political and feminist message in the novel, the novel's 'problematic inconclusiveness . . . causes both its political polemic and its tentative feminism to collapse into a confusion which undermines the whole project' (Wagner 1992: 287). It seems to me that this is not just Gordimer opting out of a conclusion: it actually encapsulates the moment of decision for the white woman as both a running towards and a running away from. The white woman is caught in this double-bind in which to turn to any side involves both a betrayal and a commitment, never simply one or the other. Seen in this light, the ending is not disappointing or inconclusive but instead is metonymic of the 'liberal' white woman's position in apartheid South Africa.

This ambiguity is inherent, too, in Gordimer's representation of the woman 'heroine' in *Burger's Daughter*, Rosa Burger. Like Maureen Smales in *July's People*, Rosa sees a form of redemption in blackness, despite being critical of those who seek to exploit this relationship. As the daughter of a Communist martyr, she is more highly politicised and less naïve than many of Gordimer's other ironically constructed white women characters, but she herself is not exempt from ambiguity as a white woman trying to cross the borders towards blackness, what she calls 'the comfort of black' (Gordimer, *Burger's Daughter*: 143). Her father's death in custody and the political mantle of 'liberalism' she inherited as a 'banned person' – 'I have no passport because I am my father's daughter' (62) – leads her to try to define her own position in the political debate in the face of increased black radicalism, whose new credo is less accommodating towards white liberals than in her father's day. As one of the black activists says: 'All collaboration with whites has always ended in exploitation of blacks . . . We must liberate ourselves as blacks, what has a white got to do with that?' (159).[4]

This is most clearly shown in her family's relationship with a young black boy, ironically nicknamed 'Baasie' (meaning little master, the word 'Baas' being obligatory for blacks addressing white men). Rosa's father, Lionel, has taken Baasie into their home while his own father is occupied with political activism, and the two white Burger children grow up with Baasie until he disappears back to his 'homeland' one day. This white paternalism is rejected by Baasie who taunts Rosa with the hypocrisy of her family's treatment of him when they meet as adults in London. It is a shock for Rosa to realise that Baasie has a 'real' name, Zwelinzima Vulindlela, meaning 'suffering land' as it was for Maureen in *July's People* to discover July's tribal name. Like her own name (she was named after Rosa Luxembourg) *his* name has political connotations, which had been denied him by the well-meaning humour or political gesturing of the Burgers (however you read it) when they tried to reverse his role as black servant by calling *him* 'Baasie'. Despite the liberal intentions behind this naming, Zwelinzima recognises its essentially exploitative nature – 'one of Lionel Burger's best tame blacks' (320) is how he describes his father.

The black women in the novel are represented either as exotic and beyond the power even of imprisonment (as in the figure of Marisa Kgosana whom Rosa sees as representing 'the sensuous-redemptive means of perception' of blackness and whose singing in jail shows the unbreakable spirit of revolution) or, like Zwelinzima, rejecting any white involvement in 'the cause', as represented by Tandi, whose reply to a question Rosa asks her is described as 'a forked flicker of the tongue; something that the one to whom it was addressed was not expected to understand, had no right to understand' (166). All political action by whites in the novel is shown to be ineffectual, compromised. As Rosa says of her telephone call to Zwelinzima: 'In one night we succeeded in manoeuvring ourselves into the position their history books back home have had ready for us – him bitter, me guilty. What other meeting-place could there have been for us?' (330).

While not trying to distort the irony with which Gordimer approaches her white woman characters, it seems to me that this lack of common ground, this inability of either black or white to find the words to represent one another, exactly reproduces Gordimer's own sense of the problematic nature of her words and her work as a white 'liberal' woman writer in South Africa. This dilemma is encapsulated in the words with which Gordimer has Rosa describe the ineffectual nature of her own voice. Rosa says: 'What I say will not be understood. Once it passes from me, it becomes apologia or accusation. I am talking about neither . . . but you will use my words to make your own meaning' (171). This accurately reflects the sense Gordimer has of the political impact of her own authorial voice, which, despite her continual reassessing, seems to end up signifying what Coetzee's narrator calls the ultimately 'negligible' nature of a white woman's words, caught as she is between coloniser and colonised, between apologia and accusation. This complex mix of 'apologia' and 'accusation' also neatly encapsulates the mixture of complicity and resistance in which the 'liberal' white woman in apartheid South Africa has inevitably been caught.

Menán du Plessis: 'tussling with freedom'[5]

While, as seen above, Gordimer writes with an ironic perception of the privilege of the white woman in apartheid South Africa, du Plessis claims that she neither perceives herself 'specifically as a woman writer' (Coetzee and Polley 1990: 134) nor that her characters can be classified according to racial labels. She states:

> I refuse to let race be a meaningful category in my texts, in my fiction, in my character's point of view. If race does come into it, it is something that is hurled at people. It is something that comes at them from outside.
>
> (Coetzee and Polley 1990: 135)

It is, rather, she suggests, the notion of class that she emphasises in her novels, and the idea of social and political transition that takes precedence. Her characters are, she asserts, in 'in-between' situations, 'not from a class that is obviously identified as the oppressed, and . . . not from a class that is obviously identified as the oppressors' (Hunter and McKenzie 1993: 75). Yet, she also stresses her own political activism as being linked to her sense of belonging as a South African of Afrikaner heritage (though she writes, of course, in English):

> From the start I was campaigning against [what] was clearly wrong and uncivilised in South African society. It never occurred to me to feel guilty about being here . . . this is my material, this is where I need to be. And if I can do anything in my own small tiny way, then it has to be here.
>
> (Hunter and McKenzie 1993: 64–65)

Her characters are, she suggests, 'marginalised' and this, somewhat contradictorily, clearly reflects what she sees as her own marginal perspective, presumably as a (white), middle-class South African woman. It is, therefore, interesting to compare her two novels of political commitment, both set in Cape Town, *A State of Fear* (1983) and *Longlive!* (1989).

A State of Fear is a complex narrative in the form of a series of letters or diary-entries (we are never sure which, if either) addressed to an unnamed 'you', in which Anna Rossouw, the protagonist, a white teacher in a 'Coloured' school becomes involved in the children's political activism when two students, Felicia and Winston, seek refuge in her house. The complexity of the novel stems from its theoretical musings about literary and historical theories focalised through Anna who admits that 'so much of my world comes out of books' (du Plessis, *A State of Fear.* 71). Another way du Plessis engages with theoretical issues is by means of Anna's reflections on her father's poetry. He is the well-known (fictional) Afrikaans poet Anton Rossouw, whose poetry, Anna suggests, as in his poem *Glas* (Glass) is trying to find 'a system of description more intricate even than the physics that accounts for the ambivalent status of vitreous substances' (175). Similarly, Anna herself is searching for a way of evading the binaries imposed by 'the state' or the system:

> I just wish that our choices weren't broken down into such simple polarities of English or Afrikaans, black or white, liberal or radical . . . For years now I've longed for a politics that would be more profound than revolution itself, yet still simple enough to explain the fate of my own brother to me.
>
> (175)

The linking of private and public relationships and individual theories with global ones complicates the text further, so that Anna's brother, François, for example, holds particular views about human relationships with nature that are both practical but also intensely political and ultimately lead to his breakdown and death. The novel is packed with Marxist notions and formulaic musings by Anna on the class struggle, sounding at times like an academic textbook. Despite this, however, it provides an interesting snapshot of a time, 1980, in South Africa's political history where unrest, boycotts, protests and violence signalled the stirrings of revolution. Quoting Albert Memmi at the beginning of the narrative that the dissenting colonisers will 'inevitably find themselves in one of history's curious impasses', Anna says that she finds it 'almost impossible to accept that' (4). By the end of the narrative, she returns to this notion of Memmi's of the 'coloniser who refuses', refusing the sort of exile that her father has chosen, instead deciding that 'now we have to stay put – to face our historical condition' (171). She continues:

> I've tried so hard to resist – believing, still believing that history cannot be deadlocked, that it's a contradiction in terms, absurd to speak of impasse. I've always felt a fierce, perhaps suspiciously vehement impatience with those English-speakers who lay claim so self-flatteringly to powerlessness . . . No one exists outside of history, I used to think . . . Because we're not aerophagous after all . . . not like those drab-leaved, spiky epiphytes . . . suspended by a piece of grey string from the branches of a tree . . . We're human beings: survivors of floods, catastrophes and even our myths; ja, we're living and responsive; and answerable.
>
> (173)

This affirmation of Anna's seems to be suggesting that political involvement is inevitable, and that no one can claim to live outside the body politic. The need to be 'answerable' is part of the human condition itself.

Yet, like Elizabeth Curren in J. M. Coetzee's novel, *The Age of Iron*, referred to earlier in this chapter, Anna also feels the profoundly marginal nature of her own voice, her own lack of authority. The text keeps returning to a seminal experience of hers during a protest at St George's Cathedral, when the protestors are attacked by riot police with batons, dogs and tear-gas. While Anna significantly describes her own part in the protest as 'only on the very fringe of things . . . teetering insecurely on the bottom-most of the cathedral's patient, stone steps' (67), she acknowledges the experience as 'a tumultuously disintegrating dream of romance' in which she lost, or had ripped from her, 'a dream of the world, or words maybe: some language in which it was still possible to talk about heroes, redemptions, radical transformations' (19). Returning to this experience later in the text, Anna goes further in suggesting that, in contrast to the unrest 'smouldering . . . on the black campuses', this peaceful demonstration had been 'meaningless, historically' and that 'all of it was merely liberal self-indulgence, for white students only. So it meant nothing, they say' (129). Yet she also affirms the reality of the experience – 'But it still happened, didn't it. I know that it really happened' (129). Similarly, Anna's temporary sheltering of Felicia and Winston is seen to be marginal to their real 'mission', of which Anna remains ignorant. Feeding them food and revolutionary textbooks (like Memmi), Anna realises that she 'must only be a small part of their scheme: irrelevant even' and yet is content to be a cypher 'for the time being' (52). Thus, the novel is filled with the angst of the white liberal who realises that her own contribution is marginal but feels that any contribution is better than self-imposed exile or the excuse of powerlessness. While Winston accuses Anna of being a 'liberal white' who makes him sick, Anna argues that she is 'complicit' in his actions by supporting him and Felicia. This blind but adamant support, she suggests, entangles the two of them 'by accident in an odd kind of intimacy' (86).

An important debate that is played out in the text, apart from Anna's personal political commitment, is that of the part played by literature in the revolutionary process. This debate about the role of literature in a 'state of siege' (as André Brink expressed the effect of the apartheid state on writers) is one that has been at the heart of South African cultural life. Menán du Plessis has herself suggested, in a collection of interviews devoted to a discussion of these issues, that she doesn't have any problem with art that is 'dominated by the struggle'. In fact, she asserts that the writers she finds 'interesting and absorbing are those who do grapple with history around them' (Brown and van Dyk 1991: 23). The issue of relevance is clearly present in the text: as a teacher of English, Anna is concerned that her students find their reading relevant to their 'own lives, their current concerns' (du Plessis, *A State of Fear*: 10). Such perceived irrelevance is at the basis of the students' rejection, via a petition to Anna, of any study of Shakespeare (despite the fact that they were studying *Julius Caesar*, a play whose examination of power and corruption would, indeed, have been extremely relevant). Anna attempts to interest them in African novels but shortage of copies of *Things Fall Apart* makes study difficult. Anna's friend and colleague, Marianne, is a staunch supporter of realism in literature, believing that 'committed literature ought to be about the misery of life in a re-settlement camp or in a squatter shanty' (25) while Anna believes such proscriptive limits for literature 'only help to preserve the status quo' (25). Such debates are central to Anna's sense of her own complicity in subscribing to the strictures of the Eurocentric and elitist school syllabus which she sees inevitably resulting in the students' absorbing a sense of their own inferiority (following Fanon):

> I know that I'm not apart from it all. I'm beginning to understand what teaching English literature is about. Why the examination format makes it inevitable . . . If the prescribed literature really has no living meaning for them and yet it's invested with so much apparent [cultural] value – they begin to feel there's something lacking in themselves.
>
> (61)

Education, too, is implicated in the system, and Anna again emphasises her own complicity as an educator who, despite good intentions, still helps to 'instil the values that will keep the ruling classes in power' (62).

This anxiety about the political impact of literature and its value as measured by its political commitment is reflected, too, in Anna's attempts to evaluate her father's poetry about which she remains confused. She describes it as: 'never overtly political; often not even set distinctly in this country. And too private? . . . When I was at university I used to get . . . sick with doubt about Papa's political standpoint . . .' (25).

As part of the Sestigers movement of writers, who turned to what Anna calls Eurocentric models of art, Anton, her father, could be accused of being elitist and, in Anna's terms, 'bourgeois' (41). On the other hand, she suggests that his poetry could also be seen as revolutionary in its attack on 'complacent middle-class values rejecting the stifling cosiness of the family' (42). Set against the imaginative literary world of poetry is that of the news and its reporting. Anna wonders 'whether a scrapbook of newspaper clippings would constitute a genuinely historical account of a period' (24) but dismisses reportage as the panacea of the middle classes – '[t]he fiction they read most avidly each day, to find their own history given an impress of veracity by paper, print, colour photographs, advertisements' (39). Yet, Anna traces her own political conscientization as a thirteen-year-old to reading the newspapers – 'That was when I discovered the word Apartheid . . . Strange that you can know something for so long without knowing that you know it' (43–44).

Anna's own text is also subjected to her sense of doubt about the efficacy of literature and her own writerly appropriation of Felicia's and Winston's stories. Aware of her retrospective imposition of meaning on events that have occurred, Anna can see that she is 'always trying to hold everything together . . . with my dry, uncertain search for words' (28). Unlike Felicia's fierce rejection of 'bourgeois theatre' and 'made-up stories on stages' for 'the real world' (126), Anna's literary world 'seems real enough' to her (16). Yet, even the unnamed and unknown 'you' to whom she is addressing her writing becomes part of what Anna calls 'an epistolary fiction', a one-way conversation that 'keeps winding back on itself' (127). The suggestion that her addressee can't answer her hints that she is writing to her dead brother, Frans, in which case the ending of the novel, in which she longs to return to a natural world of the veld, becomes even more significant, as it is his territory, his preserve. On the other hand, the text may be addressed to her father, whose voice at the end challenges her to admit that the pastoral is dead. The final words of the text, though, are for Winston who, she imagines, has died in prison, implying again that the 'real world' impinges relentlessly on the text itself, always undermining its reaching out for the pastoral, for an ideal, thereby *enacting* the debate between 'real' political action, 'truth' and textuality that has permeated the themes of the novel. Anna's need to 'know, to understand' and to 'believe that if you pursue "truth" for long enough . . . it'll break out all around you one day' (43) is shown to be, indeed, as naïve as she had thought it to be.

Du Plessis' second novel, *Longlive!* (1989) is set during the 1985 political upheavals of township unrest and its violent repression by the police and army. Much less awkwardly written and less formulaic than *A State of Fear*, the novel charts the responses to this 'state of emergency' (in the words of André Brink whose novel of that name also engages with the personal and political crises of these times) of its three main protagonists, André, Desiree and Marisa, as they prepare to farewell the fourth member of their household, Chris, an opera singer who is giving his last concert that afternoon before leaving South Africa to study music in New York. Using third-person focalisation, du Plessis' narrative alternately inhabits each character's consciousness and memories, showing each one's personal journey to the present, significantly beginning with the awakening of each character in the house. It is concerned with showing a spectrum of responses to the political turmoil – from the deliberately non-committed stance of academic David Harvest to the inherited political allegiances of Desiree September, whose family has always supported the Unity Party and been anti-sectarian. As du Plessis herself has commented:

> I think that my preoccupation as a writer, and the kinds of issues that
> I explore, are informed by what I like to call humanism . . . that naturally means that some of the big questions that are going to obsess

me are how to act, what the nature of responsibility is. Those things are obviously going to be coursing through the minds of my characters, it affects the episodes in my novels, in my fiction.

(Coetzee and Polley 1990: 135)

Longlive! clearly shows how her characters debate the nature of responsibility and political commitment, both within their own minds and with one another, and how this course of action can lead, not to solutions, but, 'if anything [to] more problems' (Coetzee and Polley 1990: 135).

André Binneman (whose name significantly translates as 'inner man') is the novel's focus for such debates, as an academic Marxist who is struggling to reconcile theory with practice and to understand humanity's 'unlimited capacity for violence' (du Plessis, *Longlive!*: 4) while preserving his own belief in the innate 'humanness' of society. Like the Marxist slogans on his wall that keep falling off as the putty dries up, his firmly-held ideas are being tested by the need for action that is taking place around him as the University campus is split between those who want to act by joining protest marches, for example, and by boycotting classes, and those who believe that individuals should be free to make their own choices and not be bound by mass decisions. In the face of state and army violence against civilians and the violent suppression of any protests, André feels that: '[s]ome kind of answering action was called for ... In a special sense of the word, it was a question of responsibility. Yet what was a right response? What was right action? The old, evergreen problems obsessed André' (21).

Even when he does make a decision to take action, like joining the protest march to Pollsmoor Prison, André feels a profound sense of anticlimax, particularly when the procession, led by the academic staff, is turned back by armed police: 'This was an instant in history? It felt like nothing' (66). The reversing of the academics' position to the back of the march is emblematic of their lack of relevance. André longs to be able to act without ethical struggle and 'his own pedantry' (71):

> If only he could just go out, take a running jump and land firmly on the far side of all those bristling, self-constructed barricades of words ...
>
> From a wall across the street there was a shout of red paint: *Longlive UDF!*
>
> (71)

At the end, while talking to his brother, Riaan, who is in the South African Defence Force in Namibia (which Riaan insists on calling by its 'colonial name', South West Africa, to André's annoyance), André admits to a serious mistake in his thinking: that instead of theorising about 'the nature of "humanness"', he should have studied 'what was actually there' and asked how people behave 'in reality' (233). Paradoxically, though, when André does take action on a personal level and violently bundles his

racist right-wing father out of their shared house after he's called André a
'*fokken Kommunis*' and Desiree his 'fucking Coloured girl' (251), his father has
a heart attack and the novel's final words are from Riaan, asking him what
they are supposed to do now. The question is left unanswered.

Another character in the text who becomes involved in political activism
is Marisa Siervogel, the dizzy young woman who is a 'failed actress' and
reluctant girlfriend to an abusive partner, Richard. She decides to make
a gesture of political commitment by attending a funeral service in the
black township at which there is likely to be violence. Her own personal
life has been dominated by her lack of agency (she is described most
often as like a 'little doll' and as always acting a part). Even her over-use
of make-up is seen as part of her role-playing, and her breakdown in
Johannesburg while playing Cordelia seems to have been induced by her
inability to recognise the boundaries between her acting and her life. Her
sexual promiscuity is seen as a need to please others, as part of her passivity,
her identity as a 'little toy dancing creature' (105) like the ballerina on
her jewellery box. Even her decision to attend the funeral is hedged about
by doubt. While Richard dismisses her action as guilt and merely 'trying
to shake off the burden of her [Afrikaner] origins' (95), Marisa herself sees
it as a commitment, as a chance to 'change herself' and 'to do the right
thing' (119) even as she acknowledges Richard's cynical assessment of her
marginality: 'What right can you claim to belong in those processions?
Those are not your dead . . . How can you pretend to mourn people you
never knew who . . . belong to a different community?' (135).

Despite Marisa's inability during the funeral 'to shout [slogans] along
with them' (209) and her sense of the 'tastelessness' and 'automatism' of
the mass behaviour at the funeral (209), she does experience a sense of
community when violence breaks out and she is helped by other 'comrades'
to deal with the effects of the tear-gas. Her feeling of 'love' and the 'childish soaring of her heart' that made her long to sing (223) when she is
reunited with her activist friends reinforces the sense that she is going to be
able to manage on her own now. Yet, this brief sense of achievement is
under-cut by Marisa's hysteria at discovering Chris' suicide at the end of
the novel. Even Chris, outwardly the most successful of the housemates
(though the novel deals with him only peripherally), seems too frightened
to contemplate leaving his comfort-zone to go to New York. Thus, political commitment is always problematised in the text.

Indeed, even Desiree September whose family has always been
committed to political action is dissatisfied by her work for the Transport
and Allied Workers Union Advice Bureau. Her colleague there, Vanessa,
voices the sort of doubts affecting them all about the futility of their work
and whether it has any positive effect on society:

> 'this bloody country . . . I used to spout all the clichés about lack of
> commitment and so on . . . You start to think, am I really helping to

change anything? Here we are doing our feeble little bit. But it's a holding operation, isn't it? And maybe we're just prolonging the whole stupid agony.'

(163)

In addition, Desiree feels the weight of André's burdening her with having 'some special, privileged access to truth' (25) because of her being 'Coloured'. Yet she doubts her own father's political efficacy and feels guilt at not being able to help her sickly mother who ignored her own ill-health to support the cause. Thus, the tension between the personal and the political is always unresolved.

The novel *Longlive!* interrogates the seeming ease by which such slogans can be uttered by raising questions about the complex nature of political commitment whether from the point of view of a Marxist academic, a marginal white woman who wants to become an 'amajoini' or an already committed activist like Desiree who is questioning the effects and the toll of such activism on her family's personal lives. Both of Menán du Plessis' novels, then, as well as the two novels by Nadine Gordimer discussed in this chapter, engage with the tangled web of political commitment in apartheid South Africa and, in particular, with the nature and efficacy of inserting a 'white woman's words' into this debate. In so doing, and in their engagement with the ethics of such political resistance, these texts enact the double-bind of the politically committed white woman writer in apartheid South Africa, never fully able to escape from being implicated in the structures they seek to resist.

6 Rewriting the farm novel

Anne Landsman's *The Devils Chimney*

The farm novel and South African pastoral

By setting her novel, *The Devil's Chimney* (1998), in the Oudsthoorn district of the Little Karoo, Anne Landsman is inevitably inserting her text into a traditional South African genre, that of the farm novel (whose Afrikaans equivalent is the *plaasroman*). Like the notion of the bush in Australian literature, the farm in white South African literature has been a trope of embedded ideology, often expressing an ambivalent and contested sense of belonging and alienation. Jennifer Wenzel, following J. M. Coetzee's seminal essay on the farm novel and the *plaasroman*, has summarised the generic features of the *plaasroman* as follows:

> its prominence in a time of profound change, its pastoral response to new modes of agriculture and land ownership, its difficulty with the representation of black labor, and its narrative reliance on the threat of losing the farm as an epiphanic moment of 'lineal consciousness'. . .
>
> (Wenzel 2000: 95)

Wenzel goes on to suggest that these concerns make the genre particularly 'relevant to the current transitional period in South Africa' (Wenzel 2000: 95). Malvern van Wyk Smith also emphasises the underlying 'ambivalence in the iconology of the farm' that makes it both a fetishised and demonised space in South African white writing (van Wyk Smith 2001: 19) – 'Once the epitome of freedom, both in a psychic personal sense and in a national political ideology of self-determination, the farm is now both a trap and a prison' (van Wyk Smith 2001: 19). The instability of this trope 'as both edenic and demonic' (van Wyk Smith 2001: 23) enables Landsman both to draw on past versions of the farm novel and to re-imagine it in terms of a transitional South African identity. Landsman's literary predecessors are among South Africa's most distinguished women writers – Olive Schreiner, Pauline Smith, Doris Lessing and Nadine Gordimer – each of whom, writing in English about South African farms, is also, as J. M. Coetzee points out, simultaneously 'outside the insular patriarchal culture of the Boer farm' because of their gender, their English culture and their free thinking (Coetzee 1988: 63). Like the Australian texts already discussed in which women writers revise and interrogate stereotypical depictions of life in the bush and in country towns, and particularly the restrictive nature of their gender roles, these 'anti-idyll' novels of farming life by English-speaking women writers from the late nineteenth century onwards, according to J. M. Coetzee, 'at the very least . . . provide a foil to the [traditionally Afrikaans] *plaasroman*, throwing its preconceptions into relief' (Coetzee 1988: 64). Like the drover's wife stories in Australian literary and cultural tradition, the farm novel provides a textual space in which the intersections between gender, race and power-relations are inscribed by national mythologies and are therefore open to reinscription over time.

This chapter will briefly survey the genre of the farm novel written in English, paying particular attention to such texts written by women, by way of Schreiner's *Story of an African Farm*, Pauline Smith's *The Beadle* and the stories collected as *The Little Karoo*, Doris Lessing's *The Grass is Singing* and Nadine Gordimer's *The Conservationist*, providing a context for Anne Landsman's contemporary version of this genre in her 1998 novel. J. M. Coetzee's own farm novel, *In the Heart of the Country*, uses an archetypal Karoo sheep farm as setting and also takes up a number of the themes and issues of Schreiner's and Smith's texts, as indeed does his novel *Disgrace* (1999), as van Wyk Smith points out. As there has already been a great deal of critical attention paid to these literary precursors, these texts will not be dealt with in depth but only in the sense of their providing Landsman with a springboard for her later literary response. Landsman's novel both engages with issues raised in these earlier texts and also fills in some of the gaps and silences already noted in these texts, making it a turn-of-the century, post-apartheid text chronicling changing attitudes and currents in South African society while simultaneously, through its engagement with a previous historical era, drawing parallels between past and present.

Set, like Pauline Smith's 1925 short stories of that name, in the Little Karoo, Anne Landsman's novel starts with the disappearance in 1955 of Pauline Cupido, a 'Coloured' woman, who vanishes while visiting the Cango Caves with the white family for whom she works. Forty years later, Connie, the novel's first-person narrator, who runs a kennels near the Cango Caves, is 'trying to remember things'. The Devil's Chimney, one of the series of caves making up the Cango Caves, becomes the place linking Pauline's story with that of Miss Beatrice, an Englishwoman who comes to South Africa to farm with her husband, Mr Henry, in the early twentieth century. Connie tells Miss Beatrice's story to her deaf sister, Gerda, after they view an exhibit containing Miss Beatrice's 'things' from 1910, that remain from her farm, Highlands.[1] The narrative moves between the present day and the early twentieth century, showing via Connie's narration some of the same prejudices and settler anxieties (about Coloured people, fear of black men and the alien landscape), but also an understanding of the displacements and complexities of the past and of contemporary South Africa. The novel's time frame ranges from the late nineteenth century to the present day, ending with the first democratic vote and 'all those Bantu people . . . standing in long lines to vote' (Landsman, *The Devil's Chimney*: 275) and revelations about Robben Island where 'they tortured people and of course we didn't know anything' (275). Connie's own history of alcoholism and physical abuse by her husband, Jack, is retold in a slightly childish way perhaps deliberately echoing the 'faux-naïf' (Coetzee's term) linguistic patterns used by Pauline Smith in her stories collected in *The Little Karoo* and her novel, *The Beadle*. While emphasising Connie's naivety, it also allows for a narrative gap in perspective to emerge as in the words quoted above – 'of course we didn't know anything', where Connie's viewpoint is ironised as national self-justification.

J. M. Coetzee, in his study of South African literature, *White Writing*, has pointed out the centrality of the farm novel as a genre within South African literature. He contrasts Schreiner's use of the farm as metaphor with Smith's. Schreiner's farm is 'indifferent, empty, desolate, barren, wide, vast, monotonous' and situated in 'the midst of one of the topoi of South African literature: the veld as the site of wholesale absence, in this case the absence above all of a personal God'. It is no less than a 'microcosm of colonial South Africa . . . living a closed-minded and self-satisfied existence' (Coetzee 1988: 65). Lyndall's sense of claustrophobia, for example, is summed up in her description of the 'narrow wall that shut me in' (Schreiner, *The Story of an African Farm*: 215). Coetzee continues:

> Schreiner is anticolonial both in her assertion of the alienness of European culture in Africa and in her attribution of unnaturalness to the life of her farm. To accept the farm as home is to accept a living death.
>
> (Coetzee 1988: 66)

While Schreiner's Great Karoo farm is largely a figurative and ahistorical site, Smith's Little Karoo stories, in the form of *The Little Karoo* and *The Beadle*, are much more historically grounded, nostalgic for the Aangenaam Valley (the name itself denoting a welcoming) and for the values it embodies, which, according to Coetzee, 'are those of the womb: closure and fruitfulness' (Coetzee 1988: 67). Additionally, the characters of *The Little Karoo* take on archetypal and almost mythical significance (with story titles like 'The Miller' and 'The Sinner'). Stressing Smith's greater regionalism, Coetzee also emphasises that her nostalgia signals an awareness of 'traditions that have perished everywhere else' (Coetzee 1988: 67), a paradise lost. While this is certainly true, there is also in Smith's stories an undercurrent of a similar epistemic violence to that figured by Schreiner: her characters often suffer pain, disappointment and bitterness. As Geoffrey Haresnape observes in his study of Pauline Smith: 'her austere art, super- ficially so simple . . . explores the mentally claustrophobic limits of the Little Karoo people with fine precision and an accurate penetration to the common humanity that lies beneath their regional and racial peculiari- ties' (Haresnape 1978: 52).

Haresnape goes on to mention 'her ability to present the warping, through a variety of pressures, of human feeling into perverse self-torture and cruelty to others' (Haresnape 1978: 55). Both these writers, then, could be said to be presenting anti-idylls of the farm, representing it as a site of enclosure and entrapment, a place where dreams are shattered on the barren ground of the veld.

Despite this, however, there is a sense of closeness to the land that is particularly noteworthy in Pauline Smith's stories. Despite her leaving South Africa at the age of 12 to return to her parents' home, England, Pauline Smith's unpublished essay, 'Why and How I became an Author', draws attention to the ongoing effects on her psyche of this sense of place, as in the following:

> Much, too, I owe, to the unconscious storing up in my memory, through these impressionable years, of all that was dear and familiar to me, as well as that which was mysterious and strange, in the small world – set in a wide sun-parched plain, bounded north, south, east and west by mountain ranges – which made my universe.
>
> (Smith 1963: 151)

It is noteworthy that, in discussing the narrating consciousness of his own 'South African novel of rural life that *In the Heart of the Country* takes off from' (Attwell 1992: 59–60), J. M. Coetzee points out that the source of Magda's passion (he refuses the term madness often used by others to describe her) is her 'love for South Africa (not just South Africa the rocks and bushes and mountains and plains but the country and its people) of which there has not been enough on the part of the European colonists and their descendants' (Coetzee 1992: 61). This link between love of land and love of people is explicitly made in Landman's novel and it is of particular relevance in terms of black–white relationships, as it is, indeed, in Coetzee's novel.

Tony Voss' earlier survey of farm novels draws attention to the specific setting of Schreiner's *The Story of an African Farm* as one that is '*not* the wilderness, not the veld, or nature, but the farm – a human, social, economic historic unit' whose 'characters are distinguished one from another by their relationship with the farm, and generally the distinction between victims . . . and survivors' (Voss 1977: 111). Jean Marquard, writing about the farm as a 'concept' in South African women's fiction, emphasises, too, the link between the farm novel and the question of 'what it means to be a South African', so that each writer she surveys 'explores ways in which the South African landscape is taken into the psyche of the protagonist' (Marquard 1979: 293). But in downplaying the notion of gender, (she writes that 'self-definition transcends gender but is solidly grounded in location' (Marquard 1979: 293)) it seems to me that she is somewhat underestimating the specifically feminist responses to the farm, and, indeed to the bush/veld, that are so strikingly encountered in all of the texts, despite their differences. In Landsman's contemporary novel, as in the women's texts preceding hers, the emphasis is on black–white relations (colonial and post-colonial), on a sense of belonging or unbelonging to the land, and to the links between gender and authority that South African society places under the microscope. And in each case, whether or not the protagonist is a woman, it is a woman's place within and on the farm that is being interrogated or, at the very least, as in Gordimer's novel, a woman's response to a man's sense of ownership and place that is represented by running a farm. The farm novel, then, has provided a genre for women writers to explore issues that are still relevant, including the links between race, class and gender; the sense of being 'out of place'; the idea of ownership of land; and the privations, for some of the women protagonists, of taking on the role as farmer's wife.

Black–white relations

It is generally acknowledged that while neither Schreiner nor Smith overtly engages with the issue of black–white relationships, the issue is never entirely absent from their texts, whether in their silence or in their articulation. As Dorothy Driver suggests, Smith's work deals with a 'variety of master-servant relations . . . including the relations between landowner and bywoner[2], rich and poor, English and Afrikaans, coloniser and colonised, Christian and Jew, black and white, man and wife, and . . . man and God' (Driver 1983b: 24). It is this awareness of the interconnectedness of different kinds of oppression that marks Smith's work. Smith's story, 'Ludovitje', is an exception in *The Little Karoo* to her 'blindness' to interracial relations, as it deals more than somewhat paternalistically with the religious conversion of the 'Kaffir' Maqwasi who is converted to Christianity by the saintly Dutch boy, Ludovitje. Maqwasi goes back to convert his own people after Ludovitje's death so 'they may also be pearls in his [Ludovitje's] crown' (*The Little Karoo*: 148). This patronising and mostly non-ironic version of black–white relations is Smith's only direct depiction of this interaction in her *Little Karoo* stories, with her focus more fully on the suffering and simplicity of the 'poor whites' she is depicting.

In *The Beadle* (Smith 1976), with its emphasis on the close-knit lives of the farming community at Harmonie, there is only passing reference to black servants. The first is a description of the 'human odour' of two small native children who were 'alert and eager as monkeys' (137); the second, on the same page, a reference to the servants' prayers, repeated at the farmhouse table. Both Spaasie and Klaas, the black servants, pray for obedience, Spaasie to her mistress, and Klaas to his master, so that he may 'run quickly' when his master calls. Whether or not this is meant to be ironic, or 'charged with the force of implied meaning' (Haresnape 1977: 195), as Haresnape suggests, it certainly reinforces the notion of religion, like language, aiding the colonisers' power over their servants. Haresnape suggests that Pauline Smith shows awareness of this tendency, of 'how people can get themselves locked into complex societies' (Haresnape 1977: 195) in which their good intentions sometimes backfire.

Smith certainly shows an understanding of the links between nationalism, religion and race in her perception in *The Beadle* of the Afrikaner's (she uses the term Dutchman) sense of being 'the rightful owner of a country which he, and not the Englishman, had taken from the heathen' (Smith, *The Beadle*: 26). With the Bible as their only book, it was the 'intensity of religious feeling which still makes the Boers a race apart' (25) and that directly contributed to their 'bitter contempt' for 'the heathen'.

Schreiner, on the other hand, while not focusing on the interactions between black farm labourers and their white bosses, is generally felt to reveal an uneasiness about colonial relations that reflects her own split position as colonised and coloniser. Carol Barash, for example, points to Schreiner's 'self-hatred and victimisation, on the one hand, and . . . racist condescension towards black Africans on the other' (Barash 1987: 19). This 'psychosis' in the writer is said to lead to an 'unease' that 'strains every fibre of *The Story of an African Farm*' (van Wyk Smith 1988: 100) confirming Schreiner's awareness of 'a powerful pulse of both sexual and racial exploitation beating throughout the body of Schreiner's work' (van Wyk Smith 1988: 100).

In fact, there are a number of specific references to black–white relations in *The Story of an African Farm*. For example, at an early stage of the narrative, the religiously minded German overseer, Otto Farber, is described as 'explaining to two Kaffir boys[3] the approaching end of the world'. In response, 'the boys . . . winked at each other, and worked as slowly as you possibly could, but the German never saw it' (Schreiner, *The Story of an African Farm*: 38–39). This unseen resistance on the part of the boys shows Schreiner's awareness of a level of response unnoticed by the colonisers. She also draws attention to an undercurrent of history of which most of the colonisers are unaware. While Lyndall and Em as children sit with their backs to the Bushman rock paintings that had been 'preserved through long years from wind and rain by the overhanging ledge' (44), Waldo draws their attention to the paintings and the Bushman who painted them, and has the intuition that the paintings are 'speaking of the old things' and that they are only strange 'to us' – 'to him [the Bushman who created them] they were very beautiful' (49). Waldo's sense of a lost history includes the loss of the Bushmen ('Now the Boers have shot them all'), the wild bucks and 'those days' (50). Like Mehring's lover in Gordimer's *The Conservationist*, Waldo is aware that their ownership of the land is tenuous – 'But we will be gone soon, and only the stones will lie on here' (50). These insights, though, are part of the larger picture of colonial relations in which the shadowy figures of Hottentots and Kaffirs are described through a discourse of Social Darwinism where, for example, Tant' Sanna refuses to allow Kaffir servants to attend the religious service as she 'held they were descended from apes, and needed no salvation' (69). It is important to note, though, that this is Tant' Sanna's viewpoint: Lyndall, on the other hand, looking down from the kopje in conversation with Gregory Rose, perhaps ironically, describes the African below as a 'splendid fellow . . . the most interesting and intelligent thing I can see just now' (227), despite her bitter appraisal of him as a wife-beater who feels justified in his violence because he has bought his wife for two oxen. She goes on to link this man with the notion of a dying race – 'Will his race melt away in the heat of a collision with a higher?' – (as does Katharine Susannah Prichard in *Coonardoo* with regard to Aborigines, as we have seen), calling him 'a vestige of one link that spanned between the dog and the white man' (228). The spatial metaphor of her elevation on top of the kopje and the African man's distance is not, of course, without its own irony and while Gregory is unable to work out whether her remarks were 'of the nature of a joke' or serious, he believes that she 'appeared earnest' (228). While it is easy to attribute these remarks directly to Schreiner herself, it seems safer to suggest that Lyndall is articulating some of the issues and questions regarding race that were prevalent at the time. It is important, too, that her thoughts are couched as questions rather than as statements suggesting that Schreiner was, at the very least, raising some of the complexities of colonial and sexual exploitation.[4]

Doris Lessing's 1950 novel, *The Grass is Singing*, while set in what was then Rhodesia and based on Lessing's own specific memories of that place, incorporates within it experiences that, according to Lessing, 'could have happened in South Africa' (Lessing 1996: 111) and can be considered as part of the South(ern) African farm novel genre, particularly in the light of Lessing's comment that Schreiner's *African Farm* 'really had an enormous impact' on her (Lessing 1996: 113).[5] Lessing's novel is a frightening portrayal of the racist psyche and of its flimsy foundations, imaged through the consciousness of Mary Turner, a reluctant farmer's wife who comes to hate and fear the bush as she hates and fears the African farm labourers and their families. Unlike Pauline Smith's portrait of the dignity of the 'poor whites', Lessing focuses instead on their degradation that leads to cruelty and abuse towards their African workers. By beginning her novel with the fact of Mary's brutal murder at the hands of her 'boy', Moses, Lessing then traces the trajectory of misery and displacement that has led up to this event, showing how she had, once coming to the farm, been 'driven slowly off balance by heat and loneliness and poverty' (Lessing, *The Grass is Singing*: 28). Her phobia of the black farm labourers is ironically linked by Lessing to a sense of belonging. Tony Marston, newly arrived on the farm, has to unlearn his ideas of equality and get used to the settlers' ideas about 'the native', so that he would, like the other settlers, be 'coarsened to suit the hard, arid, sun-drenched country' with a 'new manner to match their thickened sunburnt limbs and toughened bodies' (18). He comes to realise that 'anger, violence, death seemed natural to this vast, harsh country' (19) so that Mary's murder is not so much a surprise as a kind of confirmation of his expectations. By suggesting that this racist attitude is almost a condition of settlement, Lessing is showing how stereotypical ideas about the black man as one who will 'thieve, rape, murder, if given half a chance' (25) are constructed as part of the white settlers' own sense of vulnerability, their awareness of the tenuousness of their place on the land and are, in effect, the price of their sense of belonging. It is significant that Mary 'had never become used to the bush, never felt at home in it' (160). Instead, she feels the bush to be 'hostile' and always ready to engulf and take over the domestic space of the house – 'It [the house] would be killed by the bush, which had always hated it . . . so that nothing remained' (195). This emblem of nature overtaking 'civilisation' is a common colonial trope, expressing the deep anxiety of settlement.

Mary herself, of course, is shown to be a product of this societal attitude that links racism and belonging. Despite not having 'come into contact with natives before, as an employer on her own account' (58), she is afraid of 'natives' as 'every woman in South Africa is brought up to be' (59), being taught by her mother that they 'were nasty and might do horrible things to her' (59). Her responses to the black 'houseboys' on the farm, once she is married to Dick, simply enact these inbred prejudices, so that she is a 'virago' (69) to them. Her violent repugnance extends to the women, too, whom she sees as 'alien and primitive creatures with ugly desires she could not bear to think about' (95). It is her relationship with Moses, though, that encapsulates the combination of fear and fascination of white woman for black man, and the battle of wills between them for authority and power. Her use of the *sjambok* to strike his face to punish him for being 'cheeky' ironically and paradoxically gives him power over her, so that when he becomes her 'houseboy', she is aware of a different attitude towards him. His gradual assumption of an intimacy with her, the 'sacrosanct white woman' (151), that extends to his dressing and undressing her despite her initial nausea at his touch, and her dependence on him ('she felt helplessly in his power' (154)), lead to the final tragedy of her murder. For, as Tony Marston comes to realise:

> 'white civilization' . . . will never, never admit that a white person, and most particularly, a white woman, can have a human relationship,

whether for good or evil, with a black person. For once it admits that, it crashes, and nothing can save it.

(26)

It is inevitable, then, that colonial and racial relations are intertwined, and Lessing's bleak portrait of this dysfunctional society provides a fierce critique of the double-bind for the white woman who, unlike the white men, is unable to become coarsened and immune (in the bodily way already alluded to, whereby 'their thickened sunburnt limbs and toughened bodies' (18) match the hardness of the country). Instead, she falls apart, forced by the rules of racism to take on the role of 'madam' (or 'madame' as Moses calls her) in a dangerous power-game of which she is not in control.

Nadine Gordimer's more contemporary 'dystopian' (Chapman 1996: 393)[6] version of the farm novel, *The Conservationist* (1974), places a similar emphasis on the nexus between race and place. The shallowly buried body of a black man that resurfaces (both literally and figuratively) throughout the novel becomes symbolic of dispossession as well as of the buried history that the contemporary farm has covered over. Thus, as in Schreiner's African farm, Mehring as narrator muses that 'all the earth is a grave-yard, you never know when you're walking over heads – particularly this continent, cradle of man, prehistoric bones' (Gordimer, *The Conservationist*: 148).

Much of the novel is concerned with the vexed issue of ownership of the land, with the farmer, Mehring, a rich city businessman, admitting to a 'hankering to make contact with the land' (22) and determined to make the farm productive. While purporting to be a conservationist, Mehring is also shown to have ulterior motives, such as using the farm as an attractive venue for sexual liaisons. As in Landsman's novel, there is a focus in the novel on relations between farmer and black labourers. Mehring's relationship with his farm labourers is a paternalistic one. He knows when to reward them with cigarettes and other 'bonsellas' (gifts) but is also aware that they 'know everything about him' (57) and that when they complain about him 'in the safety of their own language . . . [they] can say what they like' (75). Thus, the position of power is always somewhat compromised. This is symbolised by Mehring's desire to keep people off his land. While pointing out to his son, Terry, the new sign he has erected in English, Afrikaans and Zulu demanding 'No Thoroughfare', Mehring concedes that nothing will keep out the black people 'trespassing' on his farm. He realises that the sign can be read in two ways, as can his ownership of the farm itself – as a 'hopeful claim that can never be recognized' or, alternatively, not as 'a sense of possession but concern for the land' (141), as proof of his role as conservationist.

Mehring's lover, though, as a white liberal who ultimately has to flee South Africa because of her anti-government activities, has a less romantic view than Mehring does of his role as farmer/conservationist, puncturing his notion of being buried peacefully on his farm. She tells him:

'That bit of paper you bought yourself from the deeds office isn't going to be valid for as long as another generation. It'll be worth about as much as those our grandfathers gave the blacks when they took the land from them. The blacks will tear up your bit of paper. No one'll remember where you're buried.'

(177)

She is similarly ironic about his paternalism towards his labourers: 'You'll even think in time there's something between you and the blacks, mmh?' (178).[7] The ultimate emergence of the black body after the floods on the farm unnerves Mehring as he realises that 'it was never possible to be alone down there' (251). The 'stink to high heaven' (251) that emerges from the mud is the buried violence that has accompanied the pastoral idyll for the white farmers and that can never be covered over. The proper burial of the unknown and unnamed body that ends the novel signifies the return of the land to its rightful 'owners' – 'he had come back. He took possession of this earth, theirs; one of them' (267). Mehring has been unable to conserve the privilege that enabled him to buy the farm in the first place, and the 'coming back' (that echoes the ANC slogan, 'Mayebuye') is an admission of the failure of his pastoral dream of ownership.

In J. M. Coetzee's *In the Heart of the Country* (1978), as in Landsman's *The Devil's Chimney*, the protagonist's consciousness, or the narrating consciousness, is not reliable. Magda's diary-like entries contain contradictions and dreamlike sequences that make it impossible to separate 'fact' from 'fantasy'. Similarly, in Landsman's *The Devil's Chimney*, Connie's retelling of Miss Beatrice's story contains enough fantasy-elements for Coetzee to have hailed the novel as 'South Africa . . . for the first time seen through the lens of magic realism' (dust cover notes). In both texts, then, the sexual encounter between white woman and black farm labourer can be read as wish-fulfilment, fantasy or actuality. Magda's coupling with Hendrik in *In the Heart of the Country* is alternatively described as a 'rape' (acting out the stereotypical fear of the black man by the white woman) and as the fulfilment of Magda's desire to overcome her position of privilege as white 'mies' (mistress) in order to achieve intimacy with the farm servants. In Landman's version, Connie describes Miss Beatrice visiting Nomsa and September, her two 'Coloured' farm servants, in their *pandokkie* (hut) and the ensuing wild sexual threesome which results in her pregnancy. Like Magda, who tries to get close to both Hendrik and Klein-Anna, Miss Beatrice is seen to be using Nomsa and September to assuage her own feelings of guilt, not just at her position of privilege and authority but also at her affair with Mr Jacobs and her betrayal of Mr Henry's trust. The following extract, in which she talks to Nomsa and September, illustrates these mixed motives:

I want you to love me, she said. I am sorry . . .

And how must we do that? Nomsa said this . . .

You know everything, Miss Beatrice said. You hear what's inside my head. September grunted and spat and looked at her. Then he said, *Die mies is verlief.* In love.

(Landsman, *The Devil's Chimney*: 87)

Miss Beatrice's sense that her servants 'know everything' is typical of the white woman's problematic relationship with them: it is at the same time both paranoid and admiring of what she sees as their instinctual knowledge. Similar is her need for both love and forgiveness.

Rewriting gender and authority

While Landman's farm novel includes some of those stereotypical characters to be found in Smith's stories, like the Jewish ostrich baron, Mr Jacobs (whose representation is complicated by its being mediated via Connie as if it were Miss Beatrice's),[8] it also refigures the stereotypical male and female colonisers. In an echo of Gregory Rose in Schreiner's *The Story of an African Farm*, a man who is feminised (as his surname suggests) and takes on the disguise of a woman in order to nurse Lyndall at the end of the novel, Mr Henry, Landsman's Englishman, is no 'butch' empire builder: he is an artist with 'hands that were as soft as a baby's and he always wore white' (Landsman, *The Devil's Chimney*: 16) in contrast to the locals who wore khaki and *veldskoene*. While he is shown to be cowardly and effeminate, Miss Beatrice is imaged as fearless, tall, thin and androgynous, with hair that she cuts shorter and shorter. She is even, as in Lawson's 'The Drover's Wife', said to have killed a *boomslang* with a *knobkierie* – 'she wasn't scared of snakes' (20). Interestingly, Miss Beatrice, in another echo of the Australian drover's wife, is shown to adapt to the land by taking on the characteristics of being male and dressing like a 'klonkie' (a young Coloured boy) – as soon as Mr Henry disappears on his 'long walk', she dresses in men's clothes and her skin seems to darken. Again, as in the Australian stories, this becoming male and becoming indigenous ('I think on the inside she went black, like a kaffir,' says Connie as narrator of Miss Beatrice's story (43)) seems to allow the white woman a sense of belonging, a way of overcoming her displacement in this barren and unfriendly land. Wearing *veldskoene* (18) like an Afrikaner man, Miss Beatrice 'didn't worry anymore about white people . . . she just made Highlands her country' (43).

Mr Henry lacks all authority on the farm which is run by September, a state of affairs that is not appreciated by the rural folk: 'The people in Oudtshoorn said it was a disgrace to watch a Coloured man come into town and order things and drive around as if he was the *baas*' (19).

Indeed, when Henry disappears from the farm and Miss Beatrice is left on her own, despite her initial fears, she takes on the role of farmer with relish:

> She knows that she is the female ostrich, dressed in the colours of the earth, set here, on this piece of land, to belong. In a split-second, everything is different. She cannot live here with Henry. She no longer wants to lick that envelope like a good girl. She will not go back to England. This land is hers. She is the Queen Bee.
>
> (32)

Her desire to 'belong' and to make a success of ostrich-farming allows her to challenge the strictures of accepted gender roles, though the men at the Oudtshoorn bar, where no women are allowed, and where she goes to talk about farming, are 'furious because she was trespassing' (44). That this sexism is ongoing in contemporary South Africa is made explicit by Connie's narration. Her husband, Jack, responds to this aspect of Miss Beatrice's story by asserting that 'no woman knows how to farm, the way a farmer does. It's not in her blood' (46).

Schreiner's farm is imaged as 'undomesticated and undomesticable' (Coetzee 1988: 64), as a place of 'bigotry, hypocrisy, and idleness' redeemable only by its setting in nature (Coetzee 1988: 64), a place that remains alien to both men and women. Landsman, though, shows Miss Beatrice adapting to the land and finding a place within it – even embodying the place – 'She was the wide, open veld, the long earth with its bumps and holes' (Landsman, *The Devil's Chimney*: 85) and becoming indigenous by imaging herself as a 'Knysna loerie . . . the rarest of Cape birds' who would 'live here, and . . . would stay'(161). Mr Henry, on the contrary, remains an outsider in the Little Karoo, 'tired of everything so upside down' (127) and always longing for a return to England, to see familiar buttercups and primroses and 'no more tumbleweeds and baboons' (127). For Mr Henry, it was 'the song of England that beat inside his head' (200) and his death, being kicked by the ostriches, is a fitting metaphor for his ignorance (he should never have approached an ostrich sitting on an egg) and blindness to place.

In rewriting gender, Landsman also engages with and refigures the imperial trope of land as woman, both in Miss Beatrice's identification of her own body with that of the veld as above, and also in her description of the underground caves as metonymic of women's bodies, the Cango Caves representing a place of disappearance and eroticism, like some kind of giant 'shoppie' (Connie's word for 'vagina'). Teresa Dovey suggests that the 'female cavity, the hole' is a 'metaphor for the pastoral mode, a mode which traditionally articulates a sense of loss, or nostalgia' (Dovey 1988: 149), arguing for a reading of Coetzee's *In the Heart of the Country* as an ironic rewriting of *The Story of an African Farm* not only in content and context, but also in structure. The pastoral mode itself, she suggests, represents the 'sterility and stasis of rural life in the colony' (Dovey 1988: 152) and Coetzee's novel highlights the narrative 'hole' that rebuts the notion of linear progress. The link between the phallic hero of exploration narratives and the feminisation of the land has been well made by, among others, Anne McClintock who identifies it as a 'strategy of violent containment' betraying acute 'male anxiety and boundary loss' (McClintock 1995: 24). Landsman's novel both embraces the identification of woman with land and, by imaging the male coloniser in the form of Mr Henry as blind to place, and as himself 'feminised' (he wears white and paints the landscape), refutes the trope of male explorer as active and phallic, thus resisting the 'poetics of ambivalence and [the] politics of violence' that characterise the feminising of the land (McClintock 1995: 28).

Hidden secrets – past and present

As in all the farm novel texts surveyed, Landsman's includes the trope of a hidden violence, buried beneath the surface of civility. Like Gordimer's buried body in *The Conservationist*, this violence is intuited by Connie, the present-day narrator of Miss Beatrice's story: 'Now it is quiet . . . But if you listen very hard, you can hear something underneath all that silence, which is the terrible things people carry around in their heads like the story about Pauline . . .' (273).

An important part of these 'terrible things' is the sense of repressed passion that surfaces in a number of the farm novels surveyed. Pauline Smith's *The Beadle*, for example, makes the point that it is Andrina's very innocence and acceptance of her passive role in farm society that makes her such an easy target for the Englishman's sexual advances. For the Englishman, on the contrary, living at Harmonie was an escape from the 'intolerable moral and social restraints' by which his English relatives 'proved their damned superiority' (Smith, *The Beadle*: 18). The farm allowed him freedom to 'live his life as he pleased among these simple people' (17) and, indeed, he escapes the consequences of his seduction of Andrina by returning to England when he becomes bored. For those left behind, though, there is no such easy escape and Andrina tragically re-enacts her own mother's secret of an illegitimate birth, giving rise to a train of guilty secrets emerging through the Beadle's confession. Aalst Vlokman's guilt has been hidden behind a fierce religiosity which, it seems, is partly the cause as well as the effect of this repression. This theme of repressed passions awakened echoes the illicit sexual liaisons between Miss Beatrice and Mr Jacobs in Landsman's novel, while Miss Beatrice's illegitimate child, Precious, is even more daringly portrayed as the child resulting from her ménage-à-trois with the servants. Thus, while the sexual liaisons themselves may be kept secret, the truth ultimately emerges in the form of a child and the consequences have to be faced.

This hidden violence is also linked with the macho life of the farm where 'there is always something to poison, or shoot, or chase'. Connie imagines that she hears screaming in the night and doesn't know where it's coming from, or 'whether it's animal or human, European or non-European. I try to close my ears, or sometimes I take a *dop* [alcohol] for my dry throat and it puts me to sleep' (Landsman, *The Devil's Chimney*: 42). In this image, it appears that the violence is also the haunting presence of the past, both personal and national, that Connie has to try to forget by drinking. The loss of her baby (while closely linking her to Miss Beatrice's loss of her baby, Precious) is something she has never come to terms with but Landman's novel clearly links male violence in the domestic sphere with interracial violence, past and present. Thus, Mr Henry is imaged as having 'thorns and a poison sac' (106) and as 'the most frightening animal of them all, worse than puffadders and tarantulas and even a *boomslang*' (198), with Connie commenting that her Jack is also 'like that'. Like Mr Henry, Jack is seen as dangerously poisonous, like one of the deadly creatures of the veld:

> You have to be careful. I never let him walk behind me . . . You never know when he [Jack] might *klap* you on the head. Once he bit me . . . I thought a scorpion was stinging me and I almost fainted. He laughed like a drain. I didn't think it was so funny.
>
> (106)

This violence is not just against the women, Miss Beatrice and Connie. It is also directed against black servants. When Mr Henry uses the *sjambok* to teach September a lesson, and ends up snapping his neck and killing him, Connie as narrator links this with a present-day example in which an Afrikaner, Gerrit Potgieter, wanted to 'show the *kaffir* . . . a big lesson' (196). Killing one of the African men, Potgieter was surprised to be arrested – 'He didn't know you can't do that anymore. He didn't know about the Courts' (197). In contrast, Connie asserts that after killing September, Mr Henry just went back to the house and 'there was no policeman knocking at the door the next morning' (197). While the violence hasn't changed, the consequences have. The link between violence, the past and the present is made even more explicit in the reference to the Truth and Reconciliation Commission. Connie's sister, Gerda, wants to tell her the truth about Connie's dead baby and uses a newspaper article on the Truth Commission to make her point. The parallels with both Mr Henry's and Gerrit Potgieter's acts of violence and their consequences are clear: 'It's [the newspaper article] about these policemen who did torture on some Coloureds, and they left them standing there with bags on their heads while they had a nice *braaivleis*' (247).

The national process of remembering and forgiving that took the form of the Truth and Reconciliation Commission is connected by Connie with her own personal tragedy, and her own need to forget that takes the form of alcoholism: 'How can you forget when something terrible happens like my baby with a leaking heart? I drink and it goes away but the next morning it's all back, and I have to start all over again' (252).

Despite the changes that Connie realises are happening in a post-apartheid South Africa, changes that are being barely tolerated by the likes of her husband Jack and Gerrit Potgieter, she also suggests that 'in most ways Oudtshoorn is still the way it always was' (273). Although Connie herself feels somewhat alienated from, and frightened of, the veld – 'I'm not sure if the koppies and bushes are for me anymore. Maybe it's the blood pressure or maybe it's all the changes, I don't know' (276) – the novel ends on a note of hope with Connie asserting that she is going to learn to swim and that she 'doesn't mind seals so much', the seals being the image of 'all the black people lying down in the sun' on the beach. By excavating the past in the form of Miss Beatrice's story, Connie seems to have come to terms with her own past loss and in so doing is also able to look ahead to a new South Africa in which the old racist stereotypes can be re-imagined.

By drawing on the traditional setting and genre of the South African farm novel, then, and by weaving past and present into her narrative, Landsman is able to measure the extent of the changes to society in terms of gender relations, racial relations and sense of belonging to the land. The farm itself, as in the literary predecessors, provides a metaphor for settlement and struggle, for ownership and exploitation. As Connie says, 'When you have a farm, my ma says because she grew up on one, everything always goes wrong' (41). While there are some things that have not changed much in the years between Miss Beatrice's experience of life in the Little Karoo and Connie's contemporary experience, such as women's entrapment in society's expectations, and the sense of place as a threat to settlement, there is also much that is more equitable. Perhaps, though, this sense of new possibilities with which the novel ends comes at a price, for it is Connie's sense of distance from the 'koppies and bushes', as in the quotation above, that accompanies her renewed sense of self. This ambiguous ending fittingly encapsulates the complexities of gender, race and place with which farm novels, particularly those written by women, have always been concerned.

7   Revisioning history

Elleke Boehmer's *Bloodlines* and Ann Harries'
Manly Pursuits

Ever since South Africa's first democratic elections in which all the population, black and white, were able to vote for the first time, it has been
in the process of coming to terms with its often violent and divisive past
in order to move on as a 'rainbow nation'. The 'new' South Africa cannot,
of course, sever its connections with the old South Africa. It is only 'post'
apartheid in the sense of its having to come to terms with the effects of
that period of history, notably through the Truth and Reconciliation
Commission, but also in formulating priorities for the nation and for individuals. Literature, naturally, follows a similar trajectory. As Attridge and
Jolly have noted in their Introduction to *Writing South Africa*: 'the current
South African situation forms a productive arena for the exploration of
the uses and limitations of, as well as alternatives to, judgemental writing'
(Attridge and Jolly 1998: 7).

One of the notable ways in which such alternatives are being explored
is in the rewriting and revisioning of the past. André Brink has written of
the need for post-apartheid literature to articulate the voices that have
been silenced in the past: 'History provides one of the most fertile silences
to be revisited by South African writers: ... because the dominant voice
of white historiography ... has inevitably silenced, for so long, so many
other possibilities' (Brink 1998c: 22).

Clearly, many black South African writers have felt the need to rewrite
aspects of the old version of South African history, that was propagated
by the extremely one-sided history syllabus in schools. Bloke Modisane,
in his autobiographical *Blame Me on History*, has described the way in which
such history was taught to black schoolchildren:

> South African history was amusing, we sat motionless, angelically atten-
> tive, whilst the history teacher recounted – as documented – the wars
> of the Boers against the 'savage and barbaric hordes' for the dark
> interior of Africa; the ancestral heroes of our father, the great chiefs
> which our parents told stories about were in class described as blood-
> thirsty animal brutes ...
>
> (Modisane 1986: 41)

Recent examples of texts that rewrite this 'heart of darkness' version of South African history include Zakes Mda's *The Heart of Redness* (2000) which revisits the story of Nongqawuse and the mid-nineteenth-century cattle slaughtering among the amaXhosa people by means of a more contemporary feud between Believers and Unbelievers over a tourist development at Qolora, and Zoë Wicomb's *David's Story* (2001) in which a political activist, David Dirkse, rediscovers his personal history and that of the 'Coloured' South Africans, revisiting the stories of Eva/Krotoa and of Saartje Baartman, in a postmodern and post-colonial narrative. Both of these novels 'write back' to the past in a deconstructive and non-linear way, restoring and replacing the power of representation while acknowledging the proximity of myth and 'history'.

There has been a great deal of discussion in post-colonial theory of such a revisioning of history, one that attempts to expose the 'dominance of the assumptions and methodologies of the master narrative of History itself' (Ashcroft 2001: 98). In using the term 'revisioning' here, I am following Bill Ashcroft's explanation:

> The remedy [to the problem of responding to the master narrative of history] is not 're-insertion' but 're-vision'; not the re-insertion of the marginalized into representation but the appropriation of a method, the re-vision of the temporality of events. This is interpolation in its fullest sense, and is crucial to the political interpretation of post-colonial experience because it is an attempt to assume control of the processes of representation.
>
> (Ashcroft 2001: 98)

Ashcroft distinguishes between 'interjection' in which a 'contrary narrative, which claims to offer a more immediate or "truer" . . . record of those experiences omitted from imperial history, is inserted into the historical record' (Ashcroft 2001: 101) and 'interpolation' in which the very foundations of history and its processes are written back to in the form of 'counter-discourse' which 'operate from the fractures and contradictions of [historical] discourse itself' (Ashcroft 2001: 102).

Each of the novels discussed in this chapter – Elleke Boehmer's *Bloodlines* (2000) and Ann Harries' *Manly Pursuits* (1999) – uses a form of this revisioning. Both texts focus on the issue of the gendered nature of historical discourse and both use the Anglo-Boer War (1899–1902) as their historical reference point. There are a number of reasons why this war has continuing importance within South African history. It has, as many commentators have already pointed out, been appropriated throughout South African historical discourse for political ends to represent the formation of a distinctive Afrikaner identity that emerged from the clash between British imperialism and Afrikaner nationalism. As Jenny de Reuck has pointed out, the 'cultural appropriation of suffering' (citing Arthur and

Joan Kleinman 1996: 1) by the Afrikaner nationalist version of history has concentrated attention on the victimhood of the Boers in this war, failing to acknowledge the war-time experience of black people (de Reuck 2001: 81). The recovery of these suppressed stories of the 'others' involved in the war has become part of a post-apartheid rewriting of history. Another aspect of the Anglo-Boer War that was notable was the active involvement of women. British women like Millicent Fawcett and Emily Hobhouse established a Ladies' Commission and the Women and Children's Distress Fund to help both Boer and British women and children interned in what have now become known as concentration camps, during the war. On the other hand, Afrikaner women and children were forced off their farms by the British policy of 'slash and burn' and were put into concentration camps, many dying of disease and hunger. Yet, as Anne McClintock points out, the active role of these women was 'purged' and 'replaced' by the image of a 'lamenting mother with babe in arms', inserting in place of an active political and military role that of 'suffering, stoical and self-sacrificing' (McClintock 1995: 378). At the core of this disempowerment of the Afrikaner woman and her iconic reinstallation as *volksmoeder* (Mother of the Nation) is gender politics. To avoid the 'mighty male embarrassment of military defeat' (McClintock 1995: 378), the suffering Afrikaner woman *became* the image of the Afrikaner nation. Thus, the Afrikaners' appropriation of their women's role in the war and their pain and suffering that was memorialised in the Women's Monument (the 'Vrouemonument') in Bloemfontein helped to mould the concept of a 'wounded nation', as de Reuck describes, with the Afrikaners figured as a 'chosen people' in direct opposition to British imperialism (de Reuck 2001: 94). Thus, the Anglo-Boer War provides a potent image of an historical turning-point for the South African nation and one that is subject to much contestatory interpretation, not least because of its gender and racial politics.

Boehmer's novel, set in the period between Nelson Mandela's release from prison and before the first free elections, interweaves present and past not only to suggest the ongoing influence of the past on the present but also to draw attention to the 'intertwined history of resistance' that links resistance movements across national boundaries, as well as across time. Thus, the Irish Brigade that fought with the Boers in the Anglo-Boer War could be seen as historically linked with the modern-day IRA and, in turn, with black resistance movements in South Africa. Ironically, of course, the sides have changed and the IRA supported the fight for freedom of the ANC, not the Afrikaners as did their forefathers. Emphasising the links between women across race and class that began with the work of the Ladies' Committee in the Anglo-Boer War, Boehmer's novel has a present-day white woman journalist, Anthea Hardy, joining forces with an older Coloured woman, Dora, to try to reconcile Dora's son's act of contemporary political violence with her family's convoluted past. Instead of emphasising the separate nature of the races, her text shows their inextricable links, thus writing back to, and resisting, the very basis of the apartheid state's policy of racial separation.

Harries' novel, too, revisions history by destabilising the very certainties upon which imperial historical consciousness was based. Her exposure of the links between imperial history, gender politics and scientific discourses like Social Darwinism undermines the certainties of History, in particular the myth of manliness that accompanied the version of imperial history that consisted of 'Great Heroes' like Cecil John Rhodes.

Elleke Boehmer, *Bloodlines* (2000)

By calling her novel *Bloodlines*, Boehmer inevitably calls to mind the definitive analysis of 'blood, taint, flaw, degeneration' that J. M. Coetzee characterises as defining elements in the work of Sarah Gertrude Millin, whose 1924 novel, *God's Stepchildren*, traces the history of the Flood family back to an act of interracial miscegenation, 'the flaw of *black blood*' (Coetzee 1988: 139, emphasis in original) that is the origin of the 'tragedy of mixed blood' (Coetzee 1988: 140) of their family's secret past. Even in the whitest of family members, this 'original sin' of mixed blood is felt and 'will out'. Boehmer's novel, on the other hand, resists and rewrites this concept of racial purity that formed the basis of the apartheid state, replacing the sense of sorrow and shame at the past with pride and ownership. Thus, Dora Makken overcomes her sense of the past as something to be silenced and hidden (like the wooden chest and Boer hat that have been handed down in her family) and comes to embrace it as part of her mixed identity as Irish and 'black'.

In Boehmer's *Bloodlines*, there is a focus on the 'Coloured' people whose own history so vividly resists the apartheid notion of separateness and racial purity. As Gertie Maritz tells Anthea at a party at Dora's house, it is the Coloured people who, more than most, 'know history isn't straight' and who 'carry this mixed-up country inside us' (Boehmer, *Bloodlines*: 103). He draws Anthea's attention to their lack of tribe and language, and to the 'unlawful mating' between black and white that is 'in our skin' and is betrayed by their names (103). Following Liz Gunner, Zoë Wicomb locates the notion of shame in 'the very word, *Coloured*' which, she reminds us, was a category of race established by the Nationalist Government's 1950 Population Registration Act, where it was 'defined negatively as "not a White person or a Black"' (Wicomb 1998: 101). This link between 'shame and identity' is also explored by Wicomb in her discussion of Saartje Baartman, the so-called Hottentot Venus, who has, in post-apartheid South Africa, become an 'icon of postcoloniality'. Wicomb explains the way that Coloured identity and naming has been a source of shame as a result of miscegenation, a word and a concept that were unspeakable in apartheid South Africa. She writes:

Miscegenation, the origins of which lie within a discourse of 'race', concupiscence, and degeneracy, continues to be bound up with shame, a pervasive shame exploited in apartheid's strategy of the naming of a Coloured race, and recurring in the current attempts by coloureds to establish brownness as a pure category, which is to say a denial of shame.

(Wicomb 1998: 92)

The vexed issue of the use of the term Coloured itself, and the debate in post-apartheid South Africa as to whether to use inverted commas around the term or to preface it with the words 'so-called' illustrate the contested nature of apartheid and post-apartheid discourses and identities. Karen Lazar quotes Alex la Guma as rejecting being called a 'so-called' Coloured for making him feel 'like a "so-called" human, like a humanoid' (Lazar 1999: 46), and also cites Matthew de Bruyn's comments that the use of the term 'so-called' for just one racial group and not for others 'implies that the others are pure' (Lazar 1999: 46, citing de Bruyn 1984: 29).

By emphasising the hybridity of both racial and national identities, Boehmer is resisting the notion of racial purity that emerged after the Anglo-Boer War and that was such a vital part of Afrikaner nationalist discourse. Additionally, as both post-colonial theorist and as novelist, Boehmer has emphasised the 'horizontal contexts' of nationalist movements and the concept of 'cross-border interdiscursivity' (Boehmer 2002: 8) that linked Ireland and the Boers during the Anglo-Boer War. Resisting the notion of centre and margin as a model for international contact, she focuses instead on the ways in which nationalist movements in South Africa, Ireland and India, for example, co-operated to form alliances of anti-imperial opposition. The Anglo-Boer War of 1899–1902 in which the Irish Brigade provided material as well as psychological support for the Boers against the English is an example of this international support network that forms the historical basis for Boehmer's novel, *Bloodlines*. Other commentators have pointed out the necessity for a recovery of silenced voices from this period of South African history, 'particularly given the ideologically saturated historical matrix of the "Anglo-Boer" war' (de Reuck 2001: 85). As Jenny de Reuck points out, although the suffering and victimhood of Afrikaner women and children in English 'concentration camps' was used to forge a national Afrikaner identity, the parallel suffering of the indigenous Black population received little attention in 'official' South African history (de Reuck 2001: 82). Similarly, and presumably partly because of the 'ideological appropriation of that experience' (de Reuck 2001: 82), the Irish involvement in the Anglo-Boer War went largely unnoticed in apartheid versions of history.

Boehmer's novel seeks to revisit this historical event and thereby to reveal a hidden or silenced aspect of its historical import (the equal sacrifice and suffering of black South Africans alongside Afrikaners as well as the Irish connection) and to draw parallels with the contemporary struggle for freedom by black activists in the dying days of the apartheid state. Thus, the novel is set in the period after the release of Nelson Mandela in 1991 and before the country's first democratic elections of 1994. It interweaves historical documents from the time of the Boer War, reconstructing letters and diaries of Kathleen Gort, an Irishwoman who volunteers as a nurse in the Anglo-Boer War on the side of the Boers, and including letters from W. B. Yeats and Maude Gonne, with a violent contemporary bombing by a 'coloured' man, Joseph Makken. The interaction between a young white journalist, Anthea Hardy, and Makken's mother, Dora, forms the basis of the novel's negotiation between present and past as Anthea uncovers Dora's Irish ancestry that might mitigate the circumstances surrounding Joseph's act of violence. While written in the third person, the novel's perspective moves between Anthea and Dora so that the thoughts of each are revealed to the reader, if not to one another. Thus, the narrative focus could be seen to negotiate not just between past and present but also between differing interpretations of both, by means of the different thought-processes of Anthea and Dora. The prefatory section of the novel provides a symbolic representation of this realigning of history: it describes a postcard in the local history museum which shows a photograph of five people at the Jetty Tea Room captioned 'Natal 1899' around the time of the siege of Ladysmith and written by people caught in that siege.[1] The postcard is displayed next to a bullet ostensibly 'stained at the tip "with Boer blood"'. Yet, the writing on the back of the postcard is 'not revealed to the public', that is, the words that suggest it is the 'Irish rebels and not the Dutch who are most successful at lobbing bombs into the town [Ladysmith]'. By suggesting that both Anthea Hardy and Dora Makken know this postcard, the narration is already drawing connections between the two women while also hinting at its gradual revelation of the hidden side of the history.

The unfolding of Dora's history accompanies the developing relationship between Dora and Anthea. Anthea is originally described as the classic white liberal woman, recognisable from Nadine Gordimer's novels, whose commitment to a more equal South African society tends to be theoretical rather than practical. Thus, on initially hearing the news of the Clacton bombing, and unaware that her boyfriend, Duncan, is one of the fatalities, Anthea, as an inexperienced journalist, welcomes it as 'a big Event, the Real Thing' (Boehmer, *Bloodlines*: 7) and as a 'massive swoop of good fortune' (7). Yet, when she comes to write of the event, she is unable to find the words:

> What did she have to say? What did she in fact know? The words were shambling, pallid, so clumsily weak . . . It was the timing, not the violence only but the timing of the thing that hit so hard. The dust of his prison cell had barely been brushed from the Old Man's shoes[2]

... And then ten victims fell at the beach front. Their deaths, now, had an especially harsh quality, like murder.

(10)

She finds it impossible to reconcile this act of violence that on the face of it was striking at the 'troubled heart of the dying white state' (14) with the deaths of innocent local people. Yet she is aware of the justification that could be made for such acts of violence and of the luxury of her own position as a bystander – 'Always easier to print than to carry out those ideals, she thought . . . Easier to shout than to bomb, be bombed' (18). At the same time, though, by committing a 'terrorist' act at the time when there were 'new signs of hope' (18) for a post-apartheid nation, she believes that the bomber has undermined the state's emerging optimism.

It is only when she is touched so personally by Duncan's death at the hands of the bomber, though, that Anthea's liberal values are tested. Speaking to her politically-conservative parents, she uses the word 'terrorist' to describe Joseph Makken, aware as she does so that it was not a word she would have used before – it was a word 'used in police reports'. As a liberal, she would have substituted 'activist, freedom fighter' but now 'that language . . . stopped in her throat' (44). In echoing the language of the state, Anthea is aware of her own betrayal of her liberal beliefs; and by comparing the bomber to an IRA 'fanatic', she is participating in the kind of political double-speak that she had previously condemned: 'The politics she herself had once warmly supported had crashed into her life . . . these petty one-word lunges, *terrorist, IRA fanatic*' (48, emphases in original). On the opposite side of the political and linguistic divide, Joseph Makken, in his trial, prefers to describe his act as 'armed propaganda' (28). It is Anthea's recognition, on seeing a photograph of Joseph's mother, Dora, at the trial that she is 'like any other woman' that Anthea begins to want to 'attach things together: this stricken figure, her own private grief' (51).

Anthea's desire for a relationship with Dora is the key for her of a 'new understanding, a seeing differently' (51). Dora's own initial response to Anthea is that she is 'snatching into her private space' (36) and Dora tries to evade Anthea's probing that accompanies her trying to understand Joseph's motivations and the 'violent transformation of people's lives' (67). At first, Dora's response to Anthea is one of distaste. She believes that the two of them 'couldn't be further apart' and that there was 'no common language between them, nothing to say' (66). While she emphasises their difference, Anthea is looking for a way of bringing things together, of creating 'a pattern' (67). Painfully aware of the separation that difference in colour brings, and of the racial nature of the bomber's crime (as all his victims were white), Anthea finds it impossible to 'see Dora free of race' although 'this was what she believed in' (69). Anthea takes on the role, in her own words, of a 'message-carrier, a go-between – between the past and the present' (193), as she realises that the Makken family history could hold the key to Joseph's life sentence being commuted. Having discovered the story of Dollie Makken, Dora's grandmother, whose sexual relationship with an Irish soldier, Joseph Macken, during the Anglo-Boer War led to the birth of Sam, Dora's father, Anthea is determined to make further connections by reconstructing the story, which she describes as 'the blank space in our hoped-for network of links and connections between Europe and Africa, then and now, between the different warring sides' (193). In other words, not only will the story reconcile past and present but will also provide the means of reconciliation between black and white in the present time by unravelling what Anthea calls 'an intertwined history of resistance' (175).

Dora, however, is well aware of the gap in power between Anthea and herself. She compares Anthea's probing of her family history to the hubris of a colonial explorer, demanding:

> What gives you the right to be part of that *we*? This right to be excited? Approaching my family story with its hidden sorrows and shame like a *discovery* . . . What gives you that right?
>
> (176)

> What gives you the cheek to come here and educate me about my own family?'
>
> (177)

Anthea's response is, again, that of the reconciler who 'wanted to see how we reached where we were . . . to see how we were related, not apart, mixed-up in a shared history . . . helping to piece things together, filling the gaps' (178). Once Dora agrees to co-operate with Anthea, the narrative consists of their collaborative reconstruction of Dollie's story, which in itself is emblematic of the 'confused history' of the Coloured people.

It is important to the novel's message that Dollie's story can only emerge as a result of the collaboration between Dora and Anthea. Dora has to both excavate her own family memory (which is retained in Irish revolutionary songs that have been handed down to her from her Irish grandfather) and has to imaginatively reconstruct Dollie's thoughts. It is Anthea's notebook and computer that transcribe Dora's version of Dollie's story and thus she takes on her role as 'go-between'. Their growing co-operation and relationship echoes that from the past between Kathleen Gort and Dollie. Kathleen takes Dollie under her wing and it is she who gives the pregnant Dollie her wooden chest in which Dora and Anthea later discover her letters addressed to her Aunt Margaret in Ireland but never sent. Other historical items like the Boer hat that Dora has always had take on significance as Dollie's story is pieced together. In place of the 'hidden sorrows and shame' that had characterised her view of her family's history, and her belief that the past is a 'sleeping beast . . . best left undisturbed' (58), Dora comes to see it as something to be proud of.

While all the women in the text oppose violence, each is fighting from within the system. Anthea's motivation is that of reconciliation as well as the more immediate and practical one of having Joseph's sentence commuted. She refutes the notion of the bombing as an isolated incident, seeing it rather as a 'vast network of mixed-up causes and effects . . . the past coming back to haunt us, sort of' (120–121). Similarly, as shown in the historical documents that are reconstructed in the text, the Irish women, including Kathleen Gort, Maud Gonne and Kathleen's Aunt Margaret, are committed to involvement in the war despite their awareness that 'war is a black infamy' (188) and that 'women have always been the pawns in men's wars' (164). For them, it is the Empire that must be resisted, and the Boers who must be supported in their battle for 'land, language and liberty' (149). Their patriotism and nationalistic fervour, as Daughters of Erin, despite their awareness of the futility of war emphasises the complexity of women's alignment with nationalism. Similarly, Anthea's motives in trying to help Joseph and Dora are seen to be complex. As Arthur warns her, her liberal sympathies could 'easily be manipulated' (192) and the question is raised of who is controlling whom and who is holding the pen. Dora's need to 'weave misleading fabrications into what she says about Dollie . . . to plead greater restitution' (194) emphasises the always-subjective nature of historical discourse and the risk of self-justification in historical rewritings.

In the end, though, the re-imagining of the family history has a thera-peutic effect on both Dora and Anthea, and Dora is able to give Anthea Joseph's tee-shirt to wear as a gesture of their reconciliation. In doing so, she accepts Anthea and reconciles herself with the past in language that echoes the title of Desmond Tutu's account of his experiences of the Truth and Reconciliation Commission – *No Future Without Forgiveness* – and his belief that 'the wounds of the past must not be allowed to fester': 'It's like forgiveness must feel, she thinks, the relief of forgiveness . . . the resent-ment's gone, a wound that's closed' (231).

The uncovering and unravelling of the shared history of black and white South Africans brings together the older Coloured and young white woman in the emerging new South Africa, allowing each to gain an understanding of the other. It is this more than the outcome of Joseph's appeal that is important in the novel (we never hear if his defence of Irish ancestry is successful or not) – the shared history of violence and the healing that can occur when the past reveals not so much the divisions of belief and commit-ment but their commonality, their shared bloodlines.

Ann Harries, *Manly Pursuits* (1999)

While Elleke Boehmer's novel, as we have seen, uses the Anglo-Boer War as a reference point for the notion of transnational co-operation in order to undermine the very idea of national and racial purity on which the apartheid state was based, Ann Harries' novel, *Manly Pursuits*, as its ironic title suggests, focuses on the links between imperialism and gender politics in the period leading up to the Anglo-Boer War, just after the Scramble for Africa. Gathering together in Cecil John Rhodes' house, the Great Granary (more commonly known as Groote Schuur), on the slopes of Table Mountain, many of the famous thinkers and politicians of the late nineteenth century who were among Rhodes' friends and acquaintances, she probes and destabilises the seeming certainties of late-Victorian turn-of-the century scientific and political discourses, particularly those of imperialism. This is a reworking of the Boys' Own stories as well as of the 'official' histories that have simplistically elevated these officers of Empire into heroes (Rhodes is referred to throughout as the 'Colossus', thus not only making a verbal pun on one of the seven wonders of the classical world but also alluding to Rhodes' heroic status in imperial history and the possibility of his being 'toppled by an earthquake and sold for scrap' like the original Colossus of Rhodes (Harries, *Manly Pursuits*: 8)) or denigrated them as villains. Using a male narrator – the only character in the novel who is not an historical figure but an imagined one, Professor Francis Wills, an Oxford University ornithologist – Harries interrogates the idea of manliness itself and its links with Empire. In so doing, she uncovers deep insecurities, particularly those related to gender-identity, among the seemingly rugged colonialist male figures who came to stand for the masculinist ideals of Empire itself. Harries draws attention to the metahistorical nature of her text and to the subjective rather than objective tendencies in historical discourse in two ways: by presenting the text itself as a manuscript sent by Wills to Olive Schreiner (as outlined in Wills' letter to Schreiner at the end of the novel), and thereby hinting at the intervention or mediation of a woman author, and by including at the end of the text two newspaper accounts outside its historical period (from the 1950s and 1990s respectively) that highlight the way events are recorded and then become 'history'. Linking this with the binary opposition set up in Victorian discourses between science and art/aesthetics, she is able to engage ironically with icons of South African and British politics, literature and art, re/placing them in history with contemporary hindsight. Thus the cause-and-effect version of imperial history, that which 'orders reality' (Ashcroft 2001: 93) as it narrates events and that is the equivalent of a Social Darwinist notion of progress (including the civilising mission), is undermined by the intrusion of the personal into the political, of the contingent on the planned and by the non-chronological presentation of events. In this way, her literary text, while based on biographies that report 'historical fact', *transforms* imperial history by its interpolation into the discourse of history itself, effecting a revisioning of history that 'disrupts its discursive features and reveals the limitations of the discourse itself' (Ashcroft 2001: 103).

An important part of this transformative process is the novel's emulation and disruption of the genre of historical biography. The structure of the novel is, at first glance, much like that of an historical biography, so that each chapter names a place and a date, or uses a broad descriptive term like 'Voyage' or 'Childhood'. But as one reads, it becomes clear that the usual chronology of the biography or teleological historical timeline is being undermined so that, for example, 'Cape Town 1870' is sandwiched between two other chapters entitled 'Cape Town 1899'. Significantly, too, the clarity of this structure of time and place is interrupted twice by chapters entitled 'Olive Reveals a Secret' and 'Miss Schreiner Tells Another Story', allowing these personal stories (both in the form of oral narratives told to the narrator by the Olive Schreiner character) equal weight with the more traditionally historical discourse. Similarly, the novel makes use of both present and past tense rather than using the more traditional historic past, and refers to Rhodes as 'he' or 'the Colossus' for the first few chapters, relying on the reader's familiarity with the story of Rhodes to be able to identify the subject and, reputedly like Rhodes himself, 'by coming in at an angle' (Harries, *Manly Pursuits*: 3) rather than directly. Finally, by filtering the narrative through a first-person narrator, one who is an Oxford don immediately recognisable as pedantic, self-absorbed and somewhat judgemental (and who snobbishly repeats the rumour, complete with exclamation mark, that Rhodes had 'read his Aristotle and Marcus Aurelius in English!' (3)), the appearance of historical objectivity is deliberately absent as the narrating voice is foregrounded. Characterising himself as 'father confessor to the Southern Hemisphere' (62) who unwillingly finds himself privy to other people's secrets and stories, admirer of Linnaeus' 'sublimely ordered' (74) system of classification and confirmed believer in scientific rationalism, Wills could be seen as the contradictory voice of imperial history itself.

The issue of gender ambivalence is a central one in the novel. While the discourse of imperialism emphasised qualities of manliness and perceptions of a muscular masculinity alongside those of Britishness, Harries' novel exposes the much more fragile aspects of gender construction at this time of the *fin de siécle* and the crisis of masculinity, itself under pressure from the 'New Woman' and the suffragette movement. Rhodes himself in the text, for example, is characterised as having a 'queer soprano' (13) falsetto voice that the narrator at first mistakes for that of a woman. His tendency to surround himself with attractive young men as his secretaries, his distaste for marriage (Joubert suggests that Rhodes believes that 'wives get in the way of Great Ideas', both for himself and for others (134)) and his intimate friendships with men, like Dr Leander Starr Jameson, imply a gender ambivalence that has Rhodes express sympathy for Oscar Wilde and even promise Wills to send Wilde money to help him in his exiled disgrace. Indeed, the Olive Schreiner character goes further, stating that she would lay her head 'on a block that he [Rhodes] never loved a woman. Men, certainly, but he has a horror of being left alone with a woman' (173).

Other men in the text are shown to have exploitative relations with children that are often expressed through the medium of photography. Dodgson's photographs of young girls, for example, which he sentimentally describes to Wills as illustrating his subjects' 'state of innocence', to Wills appear to show them, rather, as '*knowing*', 'world-weary' and 'ambiguous' (155). Wills himself becomes attracted to the child, Maria, in Cape Town and his photographing of her in nude outdoor scenes that seem to border on the pornographic is partly the reason for his being sent back to England in disgrace, with Mrs Kipling branding him a paedophile. The Frank Harris character also professes a sexual preference for very young girls and in the scene at a cross-dressing London Club in a flashback to 1885, Wills, accompanying Wilde and Harris, meets there 'men of Empire, soldiers and explorers, hunters and traders, who have lived for years in colonial outposts' (191). The bizarre decoration of the Club with its trophies of imperial plunder becomes the backdrop for Wills' sexual encounter with one of the 'young creatures' whose gender and racial ambivalence provide an image of the gender politics of Empire itself. The Boys' Own adventures are shown to be exactly that – homosexual encounters, often with the 'natives' as in the poem recited by a young man about his intercourse with young Pathans. Thus, Harries' text makes explicit those unspoken aspects of the imperial project, in the process exposing the 'feet of clay' of those whom History has decreed to be imperial heroes.

Further contradictions are exposed in the text regarding the very nature of the imperialist project itself. The Rhodes character himself, for example, is shown to have been inspired to play out his destiny to 'advance the power of England by land and sea' (42) as exhorted in Ruskin's inaugural 1870 lecture at Oxford. Yet, when Rhodes, on his return from South Africa four years later, with his body now 'grown muscular' (150) after his diamond-mining exploits, attends another lecture by Ruskin, he emerges from it confused, aborting his intention to 'identify himself to his hero' (151). What has confused Rhodes is Ruskin's condemnation of railways as 'Amputation! Penetration! Pollution' (150), slicing through the landscape 'in their abominable straight lines' (151). Ruskin's alternative notion of a more gentle, less interventionist way of building roads as a challenge to rail was also a way of providing 'Useful Muscular Work' for the upper classes. Ironically, of course, Rhodes' dream of a Cape to Cairo railway has emerged as a result of his being inspired by Ruskin's original talk of advancing British power in the colonies. Similarly confused is Rhodes' desire to replace indigenous plants, animals and birds in the surrounds of his Groote Schuur home with others that would 'improve the amenities of the Cape' (5). While Rhodes' request for two hundred British songbirds that has brought Wills to Cape Town represents his desire to hear the sounds of a British dawn chorus, and is metonymic of his imperial project of transplanting British culture to all corners of the earth, it is the very opposite of what Ruskin has advocated – that is, that the 'most moral thing you could do was leave Nature intact' (40). The wrong-headedness of Rhodes' relocating of British birds and animals is illustrated in the text by the survival of only the starlings among Wills' British songbirds, now regarded as a 'pest', as are grey squirrels, similarly introduced to make the alien surrounds seem more British.

The text, indeed, presents the debate between Science on the one hand and Art and Aesthetics on the other as central to the tensions and ambiguities of the time. The text, for example, stages a discussion between Ruskin and Wills regarding photography that has Ruskin condemning Wills for using a 'wagonload of equipment' to record the road-building activities at Hinksey when a 'simple pencil on a plain sheet of paper' (147) would 'convert a work of Labour to a work of Art' (147). Decrying the photographs as 'collodion composition[s]' (147), he refuses to appear in them. Wills, by using photography to immortalise 'this historic venture' (147), has to freeze time and have the road-builders arrange themselves 'into a useful muscular tableau' (148). This emphasises the staged nature of such a record of 'reality'. Like imperial history itself, this seemingly unmediated process of recording events is, of course, an authored and therefore subjective interpretive activity. A further example of the tension between Science and Art is addressed in the text's exploration of the debate about vivisection and the irony of Wills' having to dissect a nightingale in order to find out why and how it sings. By juxtaposing the imaginative narratives of the nightingale (Rhodes' recounting of the Hans Andersen story, and Wills' recalling of Wilde's 'The Rose and the Nightingale') with Wills' scientific activities, the text shows how the Darwinian notion of 'man's superiority over animals' (261) is linked to the same kind of imperial arrogance displayed by Rhodes.

This sense of superiority extends not just to humans' power over animals and nature, but also to other races encountered in the imperial project. Wills immediately renames the two 'small black boys' who guard his birds, as he is unable to pronounce their real names which require 'a mastery of clicks in the throat that would choke my bronchial tubes' (29). By calling them Chamberlain and Salisbury, 'elevating' them to the position of British politicians, he is both belittling them and demonstrating the cultural arrogance of Empire that has based its idealistic notions on the convenient hierarchy of Social Darwinist thought. But the text shows how this mindset leads to misreadings of 'native' cultures. Wills is unable to decipher the boys' designs in the sand around the aviary they are guarding, immediately assuming that they represent some 'tribal art' or have more 'sinister, talismanic properties' related to 'voodoo and black magic' (29). The text later reveals that the boys are playing a game of motorcars. At the same time, Wills realises that the indigenous people are more aware of their own power than seems at first to be the case. Thus, he recognises the 'blatant irony . . . distilled' in the word 'baas' that 'slices through the air like an assegai' (31) rather than expressing the servility of the 'lower orders'.

Similarly, there is a moment of disturbance to the balance of master/servant power during the dinner-table discussion of British justifications, based on Darwinism, for being 'the best race to rule the world' (207), in Rhodes' words. With the recital of Kipling's poem about taking up the 'white man's burden' that characterises colonised peoples as 'half-devil and half-child' (208) and in response to Dr Jameson's racist remarks about 'Kaffirs' running South Africa, Wills becomes aware of the reaction of Orpheus (the black servant) who utters 'a line of tribal dialect' (212) under his breath, heard only by Wills' finely-tuned ears. Wills argues against Rhodes' view that, based on Darwin's theory of Natural Selection, 'the best race wins' (212) in the game of imperialism, but is unable to convince the company. The instability of these views of empire, though, has been signalled, to Wills at least, in the moment of resistance by Orpheus, significantly spoken in his own language.

The gendered nature of both Empire and of Darwinism, with its emphasis on the male of the species as the active participant and the female as 'the maidservant of evolution' (McClintock 1995: 283) with a duty to reproduce, is emphasised in the text by means of the Olive Schreiner character. Famous in real life, of course, for her views on gender and race issues as well as on matters of empire, her warnings in this text about the disastrous future awaiting South Africa should the Anglo-Boer War not be averted are shown to be prescient.[3] Her allegorical book denouncing Rhodes as 'laying the foundations for a national tragedy' (70), *Trooper Peter Halket of Mashonaland*, is described by the Captain of the ship bearing Wills to the Cape as 'the equivalent of two thousand sticks of dynamite' (69–70) because of its exposure of Rhodes' 'native policy' in Matabeleland. Schreiner's writing about women's rights is condemned by Kipling and Joubert, the latter of whom decries her as 'one of those New Women who feel it is their duty to shriek about male domination, sexual inequality, and all that rubbish', accusing her, in the language of both Freud and Darwin, of being 'nothing more than a female hysteric who isn't able to reproduce herself' (104). While initially Schreiner and Rhodes seem to have much in common, including their large-scale obsessions and dreams, their opposing methodologies – Rhodes to possess 'vast tracts of land' for the Queen, Schreiner to write about 'women's role in society and the absolute necessity for a man and woman to be equal' (169) – cause them to become antagonists, each representing a contesting ideology.

There is a telling moment in the text when Wills, developing one of his photographs taken in the grounds of Rhodes' estate, finds an unexpected image of Olive Schreiner in the background. Deciding that she is 'spoiling' his photograph, he decides to remove her image during the development: 'Fortunately it is simple to remove unwanted images: a few movements of my fingers under the light would cause the intruder to fade into the darkness of the interior forest when I redeveloped the negatives' (103).

This simple excision of 'unwanted images' from the record, whether they be of women or other races, is metonymic of the narrative methods of imperial history. The imagery here of light and darkness is no accident: it reproduces the notion of the civilising light of empire dispelling the darkness of the African continent. But, more importantly, this idea of 'redeveloping' the original has ironic connotations regarding the way imperial history purports to report events objectively using scientific methodology while clearly manipulating 'reality' even as it does so. Harries' text, by exposing the fissures and instabilities underlying the processes of the British colonisation of South Africa, revisions this historical discourse.

Both these texts, then, in different ways, cast new light on a period of South African history that was central to its identity-formation as a nation and both interrogate the prevailing one-sided version of history, whether it be that written by Afrikaners to facilitate a national sense of victimhood or that written by the British to justify Empire.

8 A state of violence

The politics of truth and reconciliation

Gillian Slovo's *Red Dust* and Nadine Gordimer's
The House Gun

The Truth and Reconciliation Commission (TRC), presided over by Archbishop Desmond Tutu, was South Africa's 'massive public reckoning with a legacy of political violence' (Sanders 2001: 242) and has had immense repercussions both within South Africa and around the world. It was a crucial process in the transition from apartheid to post-apartheid South Africa and has provided a model of 'coming to terms' that has since been adopted worldwide. In outlining the reasons for its particular approach, Tutu emphasised the dual need to acknowledge the past and deal with it adequately so that it would not 'blight our future' (Tutu 1999: 32). Rejecting the 'notion of national amnesia' (Tutu 1999: 32), the TRC instead would empower victims of apartheid violence to 'tell their stories, [be] allowed to remember and in this public recounting their individuality and inalienable humanity would be acknowledged' (Tutu 1999: 33). The granting of amnesty for full disclosure by perpetrators represented the 'carrot of possible freedom in exchange for truth' (Tutu 1999: 34). Thus, the idea that the truth could set one free was a literal and figurative lynchpin of the TRC. The Truth Commission's hearings gripped South Africa and the world providing both a controversial model for dealing with political violence, flawed in the opinion of some by its failure to deal out justice by instead providing therapy, and, at the same time, a 'beacon of hope' (Tutu 1999: 229) for dealing with reconciliation of past conflict so that South Africans could become a new 'rainbow' nation.

In her personal account of the daily workings of the TRC which she attended as a journalist, Antjie Krog in *Country of my Skull* muses on the choice between truth and justice, suggesting that 'to restore memory and foster a new humanity . . . perhaps . . . is justice in its deepest sense' (Krog 1998: 16). The Publisher's Note to her book describes the effects of the TRC in this way:

> Many voices of this country were long silent, unheard, often unheeded before they spoke, in their own tongues, at the microphones of South Africa's Truth Commission. The voices of ordinary people have entered the public discourse and shaped the passage of history.
>
> (Krog 1998: viii)

The link between the stories of ordinary people and history itself is a crucial one, enabling a release of suppressed voices and a valuing of such stories that was hitherto limited only to 'official' history. There are, of course, compelling parallels between such narratives and those of Australia's Stolen Generations. It is not surprising, then, to find that this process of probing, of release and of uncovering the traumas of past events has had an impact on South African literature. André Brink, for example, has emphasised the necessity for South African writers to respond to the enquiries of the TRC so that its processes are 'extended, complicated and intensified in the imaginings of literature' in order for society to 'come to terms with its past and face the future' (Brink 1998a: 30).

Both the novels discussed in this chapter are such responses to the Truth and Reconciliation Commission and both explore the implications of this national coming to terms with past and present violence and the processes of recovery. Gillian Slovo's *Red Dust* (2000) deals directly and specifically with a TRC amnesty hearing in Smitsrivier, a small South African *dorp* near Port Elizabeth; while Gordimer's *The House Gun* (1998) is more obliquely concerned with issues of violence, retribution and recovery in a transitional South Africa where the old certainties are no longer applicable and the boundaries between public and private worlds are collapsing. Both novels use the setting of a trial, Slovo's in the form of a Truth and Reconciliation Commission hearing, Gordimer's in the form of a criminal trial, to examine what Njabulo Ndebele has called 'the particular nature of our state' and its 'dislocating traumas' (Ndebele 1998: 457–458). In discussing the transition from apartheid to post-apartheid South Africa, Ndebele suggests that by choosing negotiation over revolutionary violence, political activists, and indeed, all South Africans, committed themselves 'to posing questions and researching them for solutions', opting for 'complexity, ambiguity, and nuance' (Ndebele 1998: 458). In a statement that closely fits a central aspect of both Slovo's and Gordimer's text, he writes of 'how the fluid boundaries between state induced behaviour and personal volution so destroyed the sense of both personal and public morality that there was nothing left in the end but self-perpetuating violence without transcendent goals' (Ndebele 1998: 458). This tension between the personal or private and the public, the issue of morality and violence, both interpersonal and state-induced, and the peculiar intimacy that developed between enemies are all explored in the two texts discussed below.

Gillian Slovo, *Red Dust* (2000)

It is not surprising that Gillian Slovo found the Truth and Reconciliation Commission such a rich context for her novel, *Red Dust*. As a daughter of Joe Slovo and Ruth First, both members of the Communist Party and of the African National Congress, her childhood was dominated by their clandestine political activities and the 'secrets' that were never revealed to

her, as well as by their public personae, as chronicled in her autobiographical text, *Every Secret Thing: My Family, My Country*. She, like her
protagonist, Sarah Barcant, lived in exile (but Slovo lived in London not
New York) and she, too, was to find that her seeming escape from South
Africa 'was far from absolute' (Slovo 1997: 108). Her own life was tragically touched by her mother's violent death by letter-bomb and this, too,
would have made the Truth and Reconciliation Commission hearings
more than of merely academic interest to her. The emergence of truth
and the concept of forgiveness are thus both deeply personal and public
at the same time.

Slovo's Shakespearean epigraph for the book – 'Is not the truth the
truth?'– draws attention to the contested nature of 'truth' that will form
the basis for her narrative. The novel focuses on four people whose lives
and experiences are 'on trial' through the TRC hearings – two 'victims',
James Sizela whose son Steve, an ANC activist, was murdered in custody
and who is desperate to find out where his son's body is so he can give
it a dignified burial and Alex Mpondo, who was an associate of Steve's
and who was tortured in custody; and two 'perpetrators', Pieter Muller
and Dirk Hendricks, both members of the Security Branch and Smitsrivier
locals who were implicated in the torture and killings of activists. The lives
of these people from opposing sides are intimately connected, 'like a series
of tripwires radiating out' (Slovo, *Red Dust*: 31) and it is the complex and
often paradoxical nature of these connections that the narrative explores.

Local lawyer Ben Hoffman lures back to Smitsrivier his protegé, Sarah
Barcant, now a successful New York prosecutor, to help him in the Truth
Commission proceedings. Sarah's 'escape' from apartheid South Africa 14
years earlier had remade her: now she must overcome the 'stunning dislocation' (6) and yet the familiarity she feels on returning to her birthplace,
Smitsrivier. All these protagonists are reluctant participators in this process
of uncovering the past, each unwilling to face their demons. The narrative moves among them, showing the ways in which the Truth Commission
impacts on their lives, with both liberating and destructive outcomes. Sarah,
for her part, has made a pact not to 'allow herself to be dragged into a
contemplation of her past' (12), a past that she now rejects. For his part,
Dirk Hendricks, who is applying for amnesty for the torture of Alex
Mpondo among others, wants to forget what was done in the past as 'long
gone' believing that 'all that mattered now was the present' (27). Alex
Mpondo, having taken years to 'recover, even partially, from what
Hendricks had done to him' felt it all 'seeping back' with 'his past . . .
being slowly excavated' (30).

Embedded in the novel's narrative is an ongoing commentary on the
principles behind the Truth Commission dramatised by means of various
characters' responses and attitudes to their participation in the proceedings. It is not only the perpetrators like Pieter Muller but also the victims
who are reluctant to participate in the TRC process. Alex, for example,

as a victim baulks at participation partly because of his trauma associated
with being tortured by Dirk Hendricks, partly because of his guilt at not
knowing if he was implicated in Steve Sizela's death by betraying him.
His motives are therefore mixed – 'He didn't want Hendricks exposed.
Or humiliated. Or forgiven . . . Alex had come to terms with what
happened. All he asked was he be left in peace' (31). Pieter Muller, who
is being sued to 'frighten him into making an amnesty application'
(20), is unrepentant throughout and escapes justice by goading James Sizela
into shooting him, although his wife, Marie, the only other witness to
the killing, insists that Muller committed suicide in order to preserve his
reputation as a 'good man'. From the beginning, Muller sees the Truth
Commission as a confrontational 'set-up' (82), describing it bitterly as
'justice, rainbow-nation style: the new stereotyping where black had become
white and white, black' (94) and as 'so bloody hypocritical' (95). Using
descriptions like 'circus' and 'ritual cleansing' to describe the TRC, Muller
simply refuses to participate.

Even those who do get to tell their stories to the Commission, though,
are shown to have mixed motives and to be able to perform acts of peni-
tence by playing the part they know is required of them (it is no accident
that the hearings take place on a stage). Dirk Hendricks is an example of
this problematic notion of the sincerity of confession (an issue that J. M.
Coetzee has explored in great depth and subtlety in his novel, *Disgrace*).
While Dirk professes that he has to tell the truth 'because this is the Truth
Commission' (86) and that he wishes to 'make a clean breast of things'
(86), Alex, the person who knows Dirk most intimately as his victim, characterises Dirk's evidence as 'a series of ritualised lies to a commission that
had been set up to hear the truth' (132), as a 'practised apology' for getting
himself off the hook. He compares Dirk's saying, 'I'm sorry', to the 'familiar
South African litany' spoken by black servants to their white masters 'out
of fear' not out of 'real regret' (132). In addition to the questioning of
Dirk's sincerity, the narrative has him echoing the familiar excuse that
other perpetrators had already used, that 'terrible things were happening
in our country' (231) – an interesting link with the words with which
Gordimer begins her novel, *The House Gun*, 'something terrible happened'.
By appealing to Alex to meet him 'face to face' in private, not 'here, like
monkeys in a zoo' (233), Dirk wants to justify his actions and emphasises
their common humanity, something he was unable to acknowledge when
he tortured Alex in the 'state of emergency'. But, unlike Pieter Muller,
Dirk really seems to believe that the amnesty hearing was more than a
'pretence at justice' (251) and that he could indeed be set free by telling
the truth. While this involves betraying Muller, with whom he worked so
closely in the Special Branch, by revealing where Steve Sizela's body is
buried and by admitting that there was a farm on which the torture was
perpetrated, Dirk feels little regret. He is concerned that in showing how
things operated then, that he would not be 'shoulder[ing] the blame for

everything that had gone wrong in the past' (254) but rather admitting to his part in a wider political and historical picture.

Thus, the complex motivations behind the 'truth-telling' are integral to the text, with Dirk as an example of a perpetrator who appears to be willing to divulge the truth, while maintaining his own sense of self-justification, believing himself to be as much a victim as a perpetrator, and suffering from similar post-traumatic stress disorder to that suffered by victims like Alex. Far from helping to distinguish truth from lies, victims from perpetrators, Ben points out to Sarah that the bond that links Alex to Dirk, that between tortured and torturer, is 'the same bond that binds this country to its past. None of us are free of it. Not me. Not even you, Sarah' (150). By acknowledging that both Dirk and Alex are 'in their own way, patriots . . . As is Pieter Muller' (151), Ben is emphasising the inter-connectedness of South Africans and their inextricable histories of violence and oppression.

Indeed, it is in the exchanges between the lawyers Ben and Sarah that the narrative offers competing interpretations of the efficacy of the TRC. At the beginning, Ben comments on the TRC as the country's way of healing itself, echoing Archbishop Tutu's own words about healing the wounds of the past. Alex, though, takes up this metaphor, describing the Commission as South Africa's 'very own Band-Aid . . . the Truth Commission as social antiseptic' (239). Sarah's initial reaction to the Commission is that its policy of amnesty lets off the guilty and that the notion of its probing for a 'neutral' truth is an impossible one – 'even the name's a giveaway . . . Whose truth exactly? In your words: the torturer's or the freedom fighter's? The policeman's or the terrorist's?' (38). In their debate about the competing notions of truth and justice, with Ben arguing for the Commission's effectiveness in facilitat-ing society-wide reconciliation, it is Sarah who is sceptical about such reconciliation, citing crime statistics as a way of showing 'how long it's going to take' (318). Ben's acceptance of the Commission's work – 'it is what it is' (318) – echoes his acceptance of Alex's refusal to pursue the case against Dirk Hendricks, and, ultimately, his acceptance of death itself as his own failing health deteriorates further. For Sarah, her involvement in the TRC process has meant an acknowledgement of her own past, and an accep-tance of it. Her relationship with Alex and her admission that 'try as she might to escape it, this country defined her' (338) has her looking at the landscape differently, accepting 'the feeling of home' (338). All who have been involved in the Truth Commission in the narrative, then, have been touched in some way by 'truth' or some version of it, whether at a public or a private level.

The elusiveness of truth and the complexities of the healing process envis-aged in the 'circus' of the TRC lead to outcomes that are more complicated than the simple 'Band-Aid' that Alex originally envisaged. For Alex, the story that Sarah had tried to tell him about his involvement in Steve's death, one 'with a beginning, a middle and its own neat ending' was not one that applied to South Africa – 'There was too much history here, too much bad history, for that kind of completion' (336–337). For him, the 'packaged slogan' of the Commission that the truth 'will set you free' is just that, a slogan, for, as he comes to realise, 'the truth was never so easy to come by' (337). For, although Steve's body had been exhumed and Muller's part in his death confirmed, there remained many questions about responsibility, and Alex's own sense of guilt would never be assuaged by Sarah's reassurances. Ultimately, it is the red dust of the landscape in this town 'on the edge of the desert' that both covers up and reveals history. As Alex ponders the distant and the more recent past on his reluctant return to Smitsrivier at the beginning of the novel, he links the history of white settlement with the land around him: 'It was an exacting land, its unending scrub and stunted trees bleached brown and beige and grey in the dazzling light of the midday sun, silent witness to all that butchery' (30).

Like the haunting image of the body buried on Mehring's farm in Gordimer's *The Conservationist*, there is a sense in this narrative that the past can never be completely excavated: only the land itself bears witness to the acts of brutality that accompanied dispossession. As in the drover's wife stories, the 'unending scrub and stunted trees' are symbolic of the settlers' constant battle with the 'exacting' land, a battle that involved ongoing 'butchery' of its indigenous peoples. The suppressed past with its uncomfortable truths can only be 'read' in the landscape. Truth and reconciliation can only be partially reconstructed, partially recovered. As Alex muses: 'The truth: had any of them uncovered it? And if they had – had it made them any better? Sometimes, Alex doubted it' (171). Perhaps in his suggestion that 'all South Africa could aspire to was a general moving on' (337), the narrative is also admitting, through Alex, that the past can never be fully exhumed because individual stories, while empowering, are always incomplete versions of 'truth' and that the 'true' history of violence will remain always buried in the silent landscape.

Nadine Gordimer, *The House Gun* (1998)

Gordimer's 1998 novel, *The House Gun*, begins with the words, 'something terrible happened'. This, like Slovo's epigraph about truth in *Red Dust*, is at the heart of the novel's concerns with issues of guilt, punishment, retribution, confession and violence. As in two other post-apartheid texts – Breyten Breytenbach's *Dogheart* (1999) and J. M. Coetzee's *Disgrace* (1999) – there are two significant metaphors in the text: guns and dogs, emblematic of a society trying in vain to protect itself from the violence within, a violence that has penetrated the razor wire fences and the armed response unit home protection systems and has taken up residence inside the once-hallowed white domestic spaces of the suburban block or the farmhouse. Each of these texts, like Slovo's, holds up a mirror to a society trying to understand itself and, especially in Gordimer's novel, putting itself on trial. Gordimer has written of the legacy of violence that apartheid and racism bequeathed to the new South Africa, suggesting that violence 'has become the South African way of life' and that 'the vocabulary of violence has become the common speech of both black and white' (Gordimer 1999a: 140, 142). Gordimer's text focuses on violence perpetrated not by blacks on whites (as in Breytenbach's and Coetzee's) or on particular cases brought before the TRC (as in Slovo's) but within a household of young, privileged, middle-class people, a Dostoevskyan crime of passion, in a post-apartheid moral climate where, as Gordimer has commented of her novel, 'the climate of violence seems to seep through, like some kind of stain, so that it forms the connection of their lives' (Paul 1998). This paradoxical assertion of violence as a way of linking the individual to the communal so that personal trauma becomes collective experience is a central aspect of the text.

But the novel is not just about a specific crime and its specific punishment (and the Dostoevskyan parallels are signalled throughout in quotations from *The Idiot* and in the references to Duncan's lover as Natalie/Nastasya): as Gordimer has suggested in another interview about the book:

> It takes place in a particular time, in a particular city . . . There are huge changes in the lives of blacks as well [as whites] and even though one would think this is just release and freedom, it brings its problems.
>
> (Garner 1998)

The unspoken but clearly present backdrop to the narrative is the process whereby the whole society is on trial: the Truth and Reconciliation Commission. André Brink has suggested that '[t]rying to understand the new South Africa without the TRC would be futile' and Archbishop Desmond Tutu described the Commission as 'South Africa's attempt to come to terms with her often horrendous past'.[1] Antjie Krog expresses the effect of the Commission even more vividly in her chilling account of its proceedings entitled *Country of my Skull*: 'When the TRC started last year, I realized instinctively: if you cut yourself off from the process, you will wake up in a foreign country – a country that you don't know and that you will never understand' (Krog 1998: 131). This is echoed in Gordimer's text when the narration describes the law court where Duncan, son of the middle-class professional couple, Claudia and Harald Lindgard, is on trial, as a place smelling of 'a foreign country to which they were deported' (Gordimer, *The House Gun*: 7). In tackling questions about justice, truth, and coming to terms with the past in the more private, intimate and self-contained space of a middle-class white family whose son has been accused of committing a murder, Gordimer is presenting a kind of microcosm of the wider political process of remembering, forgetting and reconciling that was being played out in the Commisson hearings and that Slovo explores in fictional form in *Red Dust*. The violence that was sponsored by the apartheid state infected personal relationships in its aftermath, and moral questions of retribution and punishment affect not just the body politic but individuals therein. Coming to terms with forgiveness, guilt and responsibility is part of the process of 'recovering' from the disease of apartheid, and forging a new state in which black and white can form more equal relationships. What, Gordimer seems to be asking, are the links between these vast, almost inconceivable acts of political violence and the more private acts of violence arising out of personal relationships within families or communities? How can we read the notion of guilt and punishment in a society which is pledged to forgive and forget in order to move on? How does the enormity of the crime of apartheid and other crimes of the past affect the way so-called 'ordinary' crime is viewed? How does post-apartheid South Africa in its attempt to become a more compassionate society face the moral dilemma, for example, of enforcing the death penalty for murder?

But, as in this conversation Antjie Krog records she overheard at the Truth and Reconciliation Commission hearings, even this process of recovering from apartheid is not always an equal one: she heard someone saying:

> What makes me angry is that whites are privatizing their feelings . . . they hide in their suburbs, they hide behind their own court interdicts and legal representatives. The pain of blacks is being dumped into the country more or less like a commodity article . . .
>
> (Krog 1998: 161)

It is no coincidence that Gordimer's couple, the Lindgards, are described as having moved to 'this townhouse complex with . . . security-monitored entrance' (3) and that it is the 'buzz of the intercom' that alerts them to the presence of a visitor. Here, the white middle-class family believes it has been shielded from such violent intrusions, until Duncan's friend brings the message of violence into their carefully-cushioned existence. What happens, Gordimer asks, when a whole society has become used to having guns inside the house as 'protection'. How does this affect relationships and 'crimes of passion'? On a wider level are questions of truth and justice. What happens when your own history comes back to haunt you, when the structures you have put in place for your own protection are shown to be the source of your own destruction? It is what André Brink calls this 'tense interaction between private and public' (Brink 1998b: 87) in Gordimer's work that forms the basis for the complex exploration of private and public crime and punishment in *The House Gun*.

Harald says, as Duncan's trial progresses, that 'Justice is a performance' (Gordimer, *The House Gun*: 240). The need for public confession of a crime, the need to be seen to be cleansing the wounds of the past, to be *performing* forgiveness and repentance, was an aspect of the Truth and Reconciliation Commission that did not meet with universal approval. Breytenbach, for example, in *Dogheart* describes the Commissioners as 'dogs of God' and

refers to 'the inquisition called the TRC . . . so that memory may be excavated, shaped, initiated and corrected where needed to serve as backbone
to the new history of the new nation. Our earth is full of skeletons'
(Breytenbach 1999: 21). On the other hand, the process of excavation and
recovery enacted by the proceedings of the Commission is referred to by
its Chairman, Archbishop Tutu, in the following terms:

> However painful the experience, the wounds of the past must not be
> allowed to fester. They must be opened. They must be cleansed. And
> balm must be poured on them so they can heal . . . There can be no
> healing without truth.[2]

How, though, does an entire society come to terms with a history of
violence (Breytenbach's refrain is that 'This has always been a violent
country') and a present-day reality in which violent crime is so prevalent?
And how are the many competing 'truths' which emerge in the stories
told to the Commission to be reconciled?

Unlike Slovo's novel, where the much wider concepts of guilt, repentance
and truth are explored, Gordimer's emphasis is on the private and public
shame of parents. What is interesting about Gordimer's novel is that it is
precisely this 'outing' of the very private details of their son's relationships
and his homosexuality that the parents have to come to terms with; and
how middle-class politeness and their need to allow him his privacy has, in
fact, created a gap between them. As Gordimer has said of the novel: 'It's
about how children know their parents and how parents know their children' (Garner 1998: 3). The whole idea of family relationships changes:
what one felt one knew, one doesn't. This gap affects the relationship
between Claudia and Harald, too: if one doesn't know the son, how can
one know the husband/wife? After the initial pages of the text where the
husband and wife's dialogue is indicated by 'he, she' as if there is no
real difference between them, this sense of distance between them immediately asserts itself during their first experience of the Court at Duncan's
hearing. Harald stands back for Claudia 'with the politeness of a stranger'
and, in turn, '[s]he gave the stiff smile with which one greets somebody
one isn't sure one knows' (Gordimer, *The House Gun*: 7). Uncertainty
and the need to rethink what had been taken for granted uncover hidden
streams of violence and desire beneath the veneer of the ordinariness
of suburbia: they are 'two creatures caught in the headlights of catastrophe'
(128).

The other aspect of this catastrophe is the need to take responsibility
for it. Each of the parents wishes to assume or escape culpability by looking
back at Duncan's childhood to trace which of them may be blamed: 'something vulnerable, incriminating to either, might be revealed. Someone must
be to blame' (66). Each, in turn, reacts differently: for Harald, this event
suddenly links him to other violent events in the world, 'his own life no

longer outside but within the parameters of disaster. The news was his news' (28) whereas for Claudia, 'private disaster means to drop out of the world' (28). Each, too, is forced to reassess his/her habitual frameworks for making sense of the world: Harald his religion; Claudia her humanism linked with scientific rationalism; he as a company director, she as a doctor. For once, they are ill-equipped to fix things (early on in the narration, it has been suggested of Claudia that 'if something's broken she can gauge whether it ever can be put together again' (4)) and both must open 'a new calendar' (5) with which to measure time, as the need for them to re-identify their own son forces them to reassess their entire past to make sense of their present trauma. It is no great leap of imagination to see this couple, then, while they are clearly represented as specific individuals in a realistically drawn environment, as also being emblematic of an entire society faced with coming to terms with hidden crimes and exposures, a process that involves a re-examination of the most basic of moral and ethical principles.

There is clearly a political aspect of the text which, with Gordimer's customary irony and self-irony, draws attention to the ease with which certain South Africans could, like the Lindgards, claim ignorance of such crimes and try to segregate themselves from danger. In the disruption of their middle-class white suburban existence, their comfort zone, Harald observes that they now belonged 'to the other side of privilege' (127) comparing their changed status to the 'forced removals of the old regime, no chance of remaining where they had been' (127). What is important about this spatial metaphor of placelessness is that it draws attention to the ways in which their previous privilege had, in fact, cushioned them from being part of the wider society which had enacted 'such cruelty . . . in the name of that State they had lived in' (126). While the capitalisation of the word 'State' implies a national identity, there is also the suggestion that it is a state of mind, indeed, a state of oblivious ignorance. The violence and violations had been no concern of theirs, 'none of it had anything to do with them' (126). Their forced personal experience of crime and violence has forced them into acknowledging common humanity with those from whose lives they had always been able to maintain distance. As Claudia realises when treating a black woman whose son is in jail:

> Claudia is not the only woman with a son in prison. Since this afternoon she has understood that. She is no longer the one who doles out comfort or its placebos for others' disasters, herself safe, untouchable, in another class.
>
> (17)

Linked with this loss of security of tenure is their increasing dependence on those from 'the Other Side' of privilege, in particular, Hamilton

Motsamai, the black Advocate who is defending Duncan. This reversal of power is expressed in the narration as an ironic failure of the old structures of discourse in these 'changed times': 'The black man will act, speak for them. They have become those who cannot speak, act, for themselves' (89). Like the familiar 'institutional domain' of Claudia's clinic with its 'steaming sterilizer [and] with its battery of precise instruments for every task' (12) in which black nurses have to translate for her the patients' words not available in English 'to express what they felt disordered within them' (12), she and Harald now need a translator to grant them access to 'justice'.

The trope of disease is an important one in the text. In addition to its more obvious link with Claudia's profession, it provides a sense of the body politic needing to be cured as in Archbishop Tutu's previously quoted metaphor of 'no healing without truth'. It is no coincidence that the seat of the Constitutional Court which is, just prior to Duncan's trial, to decide on the abolition or retention of the Death Penalty is the Old Fever Hospital. Gordimer draws attention to this imagery of disease by suggesting that the Hospital 'will house the antithesis of the confusion and disorientation of the fevered mind' (131) in its decision to choose 'health not sickness, life not death' (132) by abolishing the death penalty. When Harald wonders 'where people with infectious diseases go now', Claudia replies that inoculation prevents such epidemics. She continues: 'What we have to worry about medically is only communicated intimately, as you know; so it wouldn't be right to isolate the carriers from ordinary contacts, moving about among us. Yet that's another thing people fear' (141).

Obviously on one level a reference to HIV/AIDS, this should also be read as a trope which links disease and violence: both are spread by contact, via the personal, the intimate, the 'private' act which becomes public. Thus, Claudia and Harald have been 'infected' by the violent act committed by their son, and consequently implicated in the societal violence around them. The personal is linked with the political in an *intimacy* brought on by an act of violence. This is reinforced by the immediate juxtaposition of the above quotation about the spreading of disease with the image of a 'labyrinth of violence' (141) in the city in which they are now caught up 'through intimate contact with a carrier of a nature other than the ones Claudia cited' (141).

While rejecting the 'collective phenonemon' of violence (143) as an excuse for Duncan's act, Harald also recognises the 'common hell of all who are associated with it' (143). In trying to understand this personal act, both Harald and Claudia connect it to wider political and societal violence, State violence which 'under the old, past regime had habituated its victims to it . . . People had forgotten there was any other way' (50). Similarly, in trying to retrace any possible source for Duncan's violent act, Claudia connects it with the 'brutalizing experience' of his army training where he was 'taught to kill' by firing at targets which, Clauda reminds

Harald, were 'in the shape of human beings' (67). Harald wonders whether the present-day violence (listing car hijackings, taxi wars and Duncan's own crime of passion) is the aftermath of the 'inhumanity of the old regime's assault upon body and mind', a habit of dehumanisation and cruelty that is the present legacy of a violent past. Perhaps, he suggests, quoting from Herman Broch's *The Sleepwalkers*, this is a neccesary transition for the new generation to 'the rising glare of freedom' (142), Gordimer's familiar 'interregnum'.

The trope of the house gun itself must be read in the light of this idea of communal or collective violence and communal responsibility: a culture of violence which filters down to the individual. Like a house pet, the house gun is described by Duncan (when we briefly get a view of his version of events about halfway through the novel) as 'always somewhere about' (151). The judge, too, in his summing-up at Duncan's murder trial, implicates the wider responsibility of a violent society when he says:

> The gun happened to be there . . . that is the tragedy of our present time, a tragedy repeated daily, nightly, in this city, in our country. Part of the furnishings in homes, carried in pockets along with car keys, even in the school-bags of children, constantly ready to hand in situations which lead to tragedy, the guns *happen to be there*.
>
> (267, emphases in original)

In such a chain of linked causalities, the attribution of blame and responsibility is complex: to what extent can individual responsibility be separated from collective responsibility? Again, it is tempting to read this metaphorically as a necessary part of the process within a society, in which something terrible has happened, trying to assign or escape blame.

But while this novel does not suggest any easy answers or moral certainties, it seems that Gordimer tries hard to construct an upbeat ending. For both Harald and Claudia 'out of something terrible something new' (279) has emerged and they find a new way of living in the new South Africa, no longer cocooned in their own ignorance, and agreeing to take some responsibility for Natalie's baby, even though the father is not necessarily Duncan. Duncan is given the final words of the novel: his seven years in prison giving him time to read Homer's *The Odyssey* and to muse on the idea of violence as a 'repetition we don't seem able to break' (294), yet concludes with the words: 'I've had to find a way to bring life and death together' (294). What the reader is inevitably left with, though, is a reminder of J. M. Coetzee's uncharacteristically unambivalent assessment of apartheid: 'The whites of South Africa participated, in various degrees, actively or passively, in an audacious and well-planned crime against Africa' (Coetzee, quoted in Attwell 1992: 342). While, as Harald declares, it is 'not a detective story' (16), in its exploration of crime and punishment Gordimer's *The House Gun* links the issues of violence, guilt and responsibility to turn the spotlight on those 'liberal-minded' whites who were not racist but had stood by while the crime of apartheid was perpetrated, not wishing to risk losing their privileged place within that society. That there is the possibility of recovery is suggested in the cautious optimism of the ending; and by the novel's figuring of complex new relationships and moral dilemmas in a society trying to simultaneously come to terms with the past, deal with present trauma and construct a positive moral and ethical climate for its future. By having Claudia as the (metaphorical) diagnostician of disease who is unable to use the age-old methods for curing such disease, Gordimer is emphasising the complex role of the white woman in the new South Africa. Both Claudia and Sarah, in Slovo's novel, are, by the end of the texts, able to find tentative ways of feeling at home, both in the context of their own private worlds and in the wider world of the state itself, the new South Africa.

Part 3
Beyond the national

9 Exile and belonging

Nadine Gordimer's *The Pickup* and Eva Sallis'
The City of Sealions

It is a striking coincidence that both a South African and an Australian
woman writer should write, at the beginning of the twenty-first century,
about the issue of national belonging by setting their novels outside their
own countries, in the Middle East. So differently placed in terms of generational and national identities – Gordimer an internationally regarded
writer born in South Africa in 1923, and Sallis an emerging young
Australian writer – both writers have ended up at a similar point in these
novels, exploring issues of global and national belonging. In both Nadine
Gordimer's and Eva Sallis' novels, the protagonist, a young woman from
a privileged Western background, travels to an Arabic village and 'finds'
herself in that remote place by means of a relationship with a Muslim
man. Both deal with Orientalist stereotypes as well as with images of global
culture and cultural imperialism, though Gordimer's text is more ironic
about its protagonist's cultural and material South African heritage and
the choices and advantages that it confers, while Sallis' protagonist, Lian,
is haunted throughout by her mother's untold story as a Vietnamese refugee
who survived as a 'boat person' and has not unlocked her painful past.
This inability of Phi-Van, Lian's mother, to come to terms with her past
has resulted in her violence towards Lian which in turn has caused Lian
to dissociate from her own body. It is only when she becomes pregnant
by Ibrahim, her Yemeni lover, that Lian is able to think about her own
mother and motherhood itself as something other than the cruel posses-
siveness she has learnt it to be through her destructive relationship with
Phi-Van. Both these Australian and South African women's physical jour-
neys are also inner ones of self-discovery: Julie, Gordimer's protagonist,
finds a peace in the desert itself, and a relief from her guilt at her material
privilege (though there are underlying ironies in this process), while Lian
paradoxically learns about belonging and home by experiencing both the
positive and the negative effects of entering a different culture. For both
authors, the cultural, religious and linguistic effects of Arabic culture impact
on their women characters, changing their perspectives and their sense of
belonging in the world. For both women, this is a painful process at times
but both end up finding an equilibrium, Lian by returning to Australia

and Julie, on the contrary, by deciding to stay in the Arabic village. Coincidentally, both women have relationships with men named Ibrahim and both have to adapt to the roles for women that accompany Muslim cultural life.

Nadine Gordimer, *The Pickup* (2001)

Nadine Gordimer's most recent novel, *The Pickup* (2001), is unusual for her in its use of two locations: not just the South Africa we have come to expect to see represented in her novels, but also an Arab village in the desert in an unnamed country. This is a significant change in Gordimer's work which has always been specifically South African-based, and it is no accident that this move has coincided with a new South Africa, one that has emerged, in Gordimer's words, from 'the epitome of cultural isolation . . . cut off not only from Europe and the Americas, but also from the continent to which we belong, even countries of some of our closest neighbours' (Gordimer 1999b: 212). In addition to the excitement of cross-cultural exchanges whereby South Africans are now welcomed abroad after the period of cultural boycott, the new South Africa also opened its borders to a wide range of peoples, many of them settling as so-called 'illegal immigrants' in the big cities like Johannesburg. This influx of people has, according to Gordimer, given rise to reactions of xenophobia and resentment among local people, despite the fact that, as Gordimer has pointed out, 'apart from South African Africans themselves . . . we are all immigrants here' (Kossew 2001: 56). The issues of displacement, economic exile and migration that form the major themes of this novel are both age-old and recent ones that lie at the heart of a South African sense of national belonging.

Gordimer has stated that if she wishes to make political comments, she does so in the form of non-fiction essays or articles rather than in her fiction. She is addressing here the problem of South African fiction, particularly during the apartheid years, being seen as 'too political' and too polemical. Yet, of course, her own fiction is deeply political and often polemical. It is interesting, then, to compare her recent non-fiction essays, in her role as a Goodwill Ambassador for the United Nations Development Program, on globalisation with the similar issues addressed in this novel. Whereas her non-fiction comments on globalisation seek, as in the work of some post-colonial theorists,[1] to interpret globalisation as a positive force for transformation and equality, *The Pickup* is far more ambiguous. Its narrative could be read as implying that globalisation, rather than leading to more choice for those from 'underdeveloped' nations, reduces such choices, while enabling only the already privileged to participate in the interchange of ideas that she sees as part of the 'frontierless land' of cultural globalisation. In the essay entitled 'Cultural Globalization: Living on a Frontierless Land' already referred to above, she emphasises the circulatory nature of globalisation, suggesting that 'globalization is a circular, not a linear concept; the very root of the word implies this shape of whole-ness, at once a setting forth and receiving in one continuous movement' (Gordimer 1999b: 213). In another address on the issue, she envisages globalisation 'with a human face' as a way of eradicating world poverty, illiteracy, and lack of technological skills, all of which she sees as 'the basic qualifications for benefiting from the concept of globalization' through what she terms a 'just consumerism'.[2] Despite these idealistic aims, she concedes, in an interview, that globalisation 'doesn't really redress the problem on the ground floor where the people are' and that it has, indeed, led to the proliferation of 'economic refugees' who flee 'the countries where they can't find work'.[3] These problems relate to South Africa, too, she suggests, where the influx of people from other African countries has led to high unemployment and increased poverty. It is against this background that her novel explores the tensions between privilege and poverty, between exile and belonging, between the national and the global, between choice and compulsion.

The two main characters in the novel, Julie Summers, who comes from a well-off white family, and 'Abdu' (the false name taken by Ibrahim Ibn Musa), an illegal immigrant in Johannesburg from 'some unnamed Arabian country' (Kossew 2001: 61), ultimately reverse roles. Julie is a quintes-sential Gordimer character, a privileged woman from a sheltered and materially rich background, who uncovers through her interaction with 'the Other' via a journey of discovery, in this case, to another country, aspects of herself and her place that her claustrophobic and protected lifestyle had masked. In Johannesburg, Julie is the one with contacts, money and power, no matter how strenuously she may try to evade them. But when Abdu's application for permission to stay on in South Africa is refused (despite the best efforts of Julie's family connections to overcome his illegal status) and Julie decides that they will both return to his home-land, it is she who has to adapt and learn how to be a migrant in an Islamic Arab society. Paradoxically, this experience is an empowering one for Julie, despite having to forgo her scepticism about marriage and become Abdu's wife – according to Abdu's cultural norms, they must be married if they are to return to his family. In Abdu's village, she finds a 'place' for herself that she has never experienced in her own place, Johannesburg, where she has led an emotionally sterile and unproductive existence in the field of Public Relations.

In Ibrahim's desert village, she rejects this Public Relations exterior and travels inwards, discovering aspects of herself as teacher, as 'sister' and as a member of Ibrahim's extended family, that she was unaware of previ-ously in her cold, middle-class blended family from 'The Suburbs'. The desert that adjoins the village becomes a place of spiritual growth for Julie: deprived of the material privileges to which she has been accustomed, she finds a spiritual element within herself that is, for her, far more fulfilling. Even this rudimentary description of the novel's plot can be seen to link with Gordimer's ideas of what she calls 'the ethic of mutual enrichment' of cultural globalisation: to quote again from her essay regarding cultural exchanges via art: 'their "rate of exchange" is the expansion of ideas . . . as coming from the life and spirit of the Other, the unknown country and society' (Gordimer 1999b: 209). Paradoxically, of course, while Julie is keen to expand her own cultural horizons through her immersion in Ibrahim's Arabic culture, Ibrahim's only desire is to escape the poverty and limitations of his own village by emigrating to 'the West' so the idea of such mutuality is problematised. Warned by both Ibrahim that his country is 'not for you' and her father who cautions Julie that it is a place where women are 'treated like slaves', Julie is nonetheless determined to experience to the full a culture of which she knows nothing. Ibrahim remains desperate to leave what he sees as his backward village for the wider world – trying to get to Australia, Canada and the United States. He is unable to understand how or why Julie, who has so many choices about where to live, would choose the very place from which he is trying to escape. And one is always aware that Julie still has the power to choose to leave whenever she wants to, while Ibrahim does not. The idea of the world as a global village is still an extremely one-sided one: only those from privileged countries are really free to 'pick up' other cultures and to drop them, too, when they wish to. Maybe this is another layer in the meaning of the title. The phrase that Ibrahim uses for Julie's careless acceptance everywhere is that 'the freedom of the world was hers' (Gordimer, *The Pickup*: 115).

Gordimer is fascinated by the kinds of power shifts that occur when people become displaced from their comfort zones (a theme she has, of course, already minutely explored in a number of novels, notably *July's People*) and have to adapt to new ways of thinking and being. Much of this adaptation occurs through language – what initially seems to be a barrier to communication can become a means for productive cross-cultural exchange. On first meeting Ibrahim's sister, Maryam, there is a 'phrase-book exchange' (121) during which Julie decides to overcome their mutual incomprehensibility, 'each unable to imagine the life of the other' (121) by learning their language. This she does in exchange for teaching them English so that she would not 'sit among his people as a deaf-mute' (143), to overcome what Maryam has sensitively picked up as Julie's being 'lonely without our language' (151). But Ibrahim is aware that it is English that is needed if he is to get 'a decent job anywhere' (152) and he resists teaching Julie even the 'love words' in his language that she asks him for.

Gordimer sets up a number of contrasts in the novel between notions of home, belonging and exile, particularly in relation to the notion of the global and the local. It has been suggested that globalisation produces not necessarily homogenised culture but rather the 'energies for interchange, circulation and transformation' (Ashcroft *et al.* 2002: 217). This cultural circulation is illustrated early on in the novel in the name of Julie's favourite haunt in her multicultural 'hip' neighbourhood in Johannesburg – the L.A. Café. While this would seem to be a signal, indeed a symbol, of homogenising American culture, the text assures us that 'most people . . . didn't know the capitals stood for Los Angeles' (Gordimer, *The Pickup*: 5) and the café is referred to throughout the rest of the novel as the EL-AY Café, a transformative spelling that seems to recall an Arabic or Middle Eastern derivation. Thus, the specificities of the national reference point are lost and the seemingly unbreachable division between West and East is undermined. The Café itself and indeed The Table (in capital letters) where Julie and her friends meet are emblematic of the social freedom and mobility of the new South Africa. She and her friends 'have distanced themselves from the ways of the past, their families, whether these are black ones still living in the old ghettoes or white ones in The Suburbs' (23). But there is still a strong sense of a politics of place. While Julie's cottage is 'sufficiently removed from The Suburbs' ostentation' (18) to assert its difference from her father's luxurious home, its studied shabbiness gives away a lifestyle in which 'luxuries [are] taken for granted as necessities' (18). It is also, the narration suggests, the 'quarters of someone not used to looking after herself' (18). For Julie, this lifestyle and its location away from The Suburbs (also significantly capitalised) is a construction (she later describes it as 'playing at reality, a doll's house, a game' (164)), a deliberate choice, just as it is her choice to drive a second-hand car. But when it breaks down, she is able to borrow her wealthy father's Rover, embarrassed as she is by it. For Abdu, in contrast, there are only two kinds of people – those with choice, and those without (21). As an illegal immigrant, of course, he is among the latter.

Abdu's forced migration from poverty and politics is strongly contrasted with the 'relocation' of Julie's father's friends who are emigrating from South Africa to Australia, to 'an even more privileged life, safe from the pitchforks and AK-47s of the rebellious poor' (48). The emigrating couple are described as 'her father's kind of people', those who 'may move about the world welcome everywhere' (49), he, significantly, the executive director of a world-wide website network. Abdu, on the other hand, has to live 'disguised as a grease-monkey without a name' (49) despite his university degree, until forced to leave by the South African authorities. Julie's decision to go with him as his wife marks the change of physical location in the novel, but also the change in self that Gordimer links with the word 'locate'. This is expressed in Julie's sense that 'her crowd, Mates, Brothers and Sisters . . . are the strangers and he [Abdu] is the known' (92). So we have this constant shifting play upon notions of exile and belonging.

Yet, in previously trying to imagine Abdu's place, Julie is aware that to her he is a 'cutout from a background that she surely imagines only wrongly' (25) with stereotypical preconceptions of palm trees, camels, and alleys hung with carpets. When she does arrive in his country, it is she who has to 'relocate', she who is the outsider, described in Ibrahim's consciousness as 'one of those elaborate gifts brought home that are not what is needed' (174). (It is at that point that Abdu becomes Ibrahim, taking on his own name in his own country.) Her desire to 'see the place' (125) is deflected by Ibrahim who says, 'What is there to see in a place like ours . . . Tourists don't come here, what for' (125). When Ibrahim tries to satisfy her need to know by taking her to the local market, she is upset by the 'hideous things' (plastic utensils . . . and kettles decorated with flower patterns of 'organic ostentation that seemed tactless in a desert village' (126)) that the world dumps there. When she asks why they don't make these things themselves locally, Ibrahim replies that: 'These [plastic ones] don't break so soon' (126). Further evidence of this global interchange and circulation is the 'Easternised American pop' playing on the car radio in contrast with the amulets and illuminated Arabic texts hanging there, too. When visiting the capital city to go to yet another Consulate in Ibrahim's attempt to gain acceptance in the West, they encounter a similar juxta-position of cultures: mosques side-by-side with 'the even more familiar international choice of Nike boots, cellphones, TV consoles, hi-fi and video equipment' (203). When Ibrahim's group of friends, all young men like himself who are looking to emigrate, get together, they discuss the need for change and the desire to 'catch up' with the West. They want a voice 'over the Internet not from the minaret' (176). At the same time, though, they make it clear that they don't want to be taken over by the modern world. There is a disjunction between Julie's privileged rejection of glob-alised culture and their thirst to embrace it.

It is against this background of the ongoing tension between local and global, between the old/traditional and the new, that Julie encounters the desert 'where the street ended' and, with it, the end of 'this everyday life' (131). Julie's somewhat romanticised response to the desert as 'eternity', as a place with 'no measure of space . . . no demarcation from land to air' (172) is contrasted with Ibrahim's description of the village as 'this dusty hell of my place' (173). While he shuns the desert as 'the denial of everything he yearns for', Julie seeks it out as a place that doesn't change, but just exists (229). It is, perhaps predictably, while she is in the desert whose sands 'dis-solve conflict' (231) that she makes her decision to remain in the village rather than going with Ibrahim to America, to where he has finally obtained permission to emigrate, thanks to Julie's mother's connections. But Julie's sense of newfound freedom and belonging to a family that she paradoxi-cally finds here is, for Ibrahim, a place of constriction, a 'cursed village', that was 'not his place' despite the fact that the rest of the world tried to confine him there. Both Julie and Ibrahim reject 'home' to find a sense of belonging in exile. As Ibrahim muses of Julie's decision to stay: 'Like me, like me, she won't go back where she belongs' (262).

There are, though, a number of underlying ironies – as we expect in a Gordimer text – built into this seemingly neat scenario of exchange.

Julie's ability to ask for money from her uncle in South Africa shields her, and Ibrahim's family, from the desperate poverty around them and raises the question of whether she would really have been so keen to stay and commune with the desert if she had had to live 'authentically' without the benefit of her privilege which she has never really left behind. The ease with which she can call on her contacts from outside the confines of the village is emphasised again when she orders a copy of the Koran in translation as she wants to familiarise herself with both language and religion. The book is ordered by her mother in California 'through one of those wonderful Internet book warehouses' and arrives by a door-to-door courier service (143–144).

A further irony is the notion of freedom itself, particularly the vexed question of women's freedom in Islamic society. Julie finds out early on that, as she had been warned, she is not able to move freely in the village – she has to be accompanied: 'that's how it is in the place he thought he had left behind' (122). Similarly, 'even she who may go everywhere in the world, do as she likes' is forbidden from entering the mosque (132). It is significant that these anxieties about the contrasting notions of a woman's place are focalised through Ibrahim and not through Julie, through the contrast between 'his place' and what she's used to. It is, after all, he who has to mediate between the cultural expectations of both Julie and his family, between the different sets of rules that apply. Yet, this is an aspect of Julie's experience that seems glossed over in the text, and always, Julie is seen to have a way out, choices open to her, that are not available to the other women in Ibrahim's family. Like her mother before her, Maryam is not given the chance to study further but has to submit to an arranged marriage. Julie, on the other hand, can decide whether or not to dress like the local women (Maryam 'kits' her out for the *rih* wind in a protective robe) and which religious practices she will follow. Thus, Ibrahim describes her decision to fast at Ramadan as 'another adventure' (153).

There is also some evidence in the novel of the kind of fetishistic Orientalism (this is, of course, a pre-September 11 text) that images Ibrahim as an 'oriental prince'. Their mutual 'picking-up' raises a number of questions: is he simply using her as a ticket to stay in South Africa at the start of the novel; is she using him as an exotic other to create some excitement in her somewhat mundane existence? How this mutual exploitation leads to the more profound loving relationship we are expected to believe has evolved during the course of the novel is never fully articulated. There is always a sense of impermanence in the relationship, a fragility that seems to me to originate in this initial sense that each is imposing an identity on the other for their own selfish purposes. Indeed, their relationship is never fleshed out enough to be convincing, being imaged mainly through their sexual activities and their exploration of each other's bodies, 'that unspoken knowledge they can share; that country to which they can resort' (130). However, it could be argued that the frequent shifts in perspective

and the awareness within the narration of this spectrum of attitudes antic-
ipates these kinds of criticisms. This is especially focused in Julie's final
decision to refuse to emigrate with Ibrahim to America, one that she
believes is brought on by the desert itself. Ibrahim's reaction to this pre-
empts that of the reader – 'for him . . . her decision was a typical piece of
sheltered middleclass Western romanticism. Like picking up a grease-
monkey' (262). But, at the same time, he recognises within her the same
spirit that moves him to try to escape from the place he belongs. She is
attempting to escape her inherited privilege, both in South Africa where
her father belongs, and in America, where her mother lives the privileged
Californian lifestyle. He, of course, on the other hand, is attempting to
escape the opposite of privilege, the poverty, the hopelessness, the sense
of entrapment. In the end, she chooses the solidarity of his family's women,
those whom Ibrahim suspects she has taught not just English but also
communicated 'her rich girl's Café ideas of female independence' (256).
Ultimately, Julie is able to form an unspoken and unlikely alliance with
Ibrahim's steely mother who understands that Julie is the one who will
'bring him home at last' (259).

There has often been a coldness and detachment in Gordimer's novels
that has made the reading process seem somewhat formulaic. This novel,
though, like its predecessor, *The House Gun*, (from which, incidentally, the
black attorney, Hamilton Motsamai, makes an appearance again in this
novel), has a spareness of prose and a more intimate sense of character
that marks it as one of Gordimer's more 'mellow' works. There is, though,
still an overall sense of the novel as a chess-game, with a central thesis
that the characters are playing out. Both Julie and Ibrahim retain elements
of stereotypes – the rich spoilt South African white woman and the exotic
Arabic man. But there is also an underlying sense that Gordimer as novelist
is tuned in to this fixity in representation and that it is indeed part of the
text's irony that these stereotypes are so hard to resist or overcome, even
in a global world where cross-cultural understanding is promoted. After
all, if you are trying to emigrate, it is where you come from not who you
are that is the main criterion for acceptance or rejection. You are, thus,
literally and figuratively, confined to your place in a world that is far from
'frontierless' but, instead, is erecting fences and boundaries to keep unde-
sirable aliens out while allowing the privileged to move freely and
unhindered. It is fitting, then, that the novel ends ambiguously, with questions unanswered, and with a sense of readerly unease rather than in a
formulaic neat ending. Both Julie and Ibrahim face a perverse kind of
freedom: she in his 'backward' village, he in the 'advanced' United States.
The irony of the outcome of their relationship is its sacrifice – that their
different needs can only be satisfied by being apart, at opposite ends of
the world. Will Julie stay in the desert village and, if so, what sort of life
will it be for her on a long-term basis? Will Ibrahim come back? Will he
even go to America or change his mind at the last moment?

Like the paradoxical quality of muteness yet 'infinite articulacy' (211) that Julie finds in the desert itself, these final questions raised in the mind of the reader are met with silence.

Eva Sallis, *The City of Sealions* (2002)

Sallis' novel, like Gordimer's, juxtaposes two contrasting and often conflicting worlds – those of South Australia and the Yemen – and the protagonist's movement between them. The narrative structure of this novel, with its interlocking stories of Lian's childhood and escape from home, the Arabic story of the two Abdallahs, one of the land and one of the sea, and fragments of the unspoken and untold story of Lian's mother, Phi-Van's traumatic escape from Vietnam to Australia as a refugee, like its central tropes of the sea and islands, all emphasise the notion of borders and thresholds, of movements between different surfaces and spaces, of exile and belonging. The fragmented nature of the narrative and the idea of healing and repair are echoed early on in Lian's dream of the beach on her first night in Yemen, in which she dreams of a sea 'belching up rotten ships and repairing them' (Sallis, *The City of Sealions*: 2) in images of famous shipwrecks and disasters not all of whose 'parts and components could be found' (2). It is only towards the end of the novel that italicised fragments that appear in short dissociated phrases like 'slap slap slap' and 'three big green leaves' coalesce to form a more coherent part of Phi-Van's Vietnamese story. Simultaneously, the reader is 'fed' snippets from the Arabic story of the Abdallahs in which Abdallah of the Land (called a Lacktail by the sea people) visits Abdallah of the Sea (a Merman) thereby entering a completely different medium, that of water, and having to adapt to different physical, cultural and even religious practices (despite their shared Islam). These fragmented stories parallel the experiences of Lian in her escape from 'home' (Kangaroo Island off the coast of South Australia) to the village of Sanaa in Yemen as she, too, has to adapt to a completely different culture and language and still retain her sense of self.

The theme of belonging and yet being an outsider at the same time that Gordimer sketches in Julie's rejection of her white privilege in Johannesburg is echoed in Sallis' novel by Lian's split sense of self. While Nev, her father, and his brother, Mal, are fiercely proud of being Islanders and Australians and wish to inculcate this sense of belonging in Lian, she is aware of her mother's strangeness, not only in her identity as a 'slope' but also in her inability to be a mother to Lian. From an early age, Lian is aware of Phi-Van's 'tainted mother-love' (14) which is compared with a life raft to which Phi-Van clung 'with a suffocating and insatiable desperation' while at the same time driving Lian from her 'with a strange cruelty' (14). This inability to love her daughter is linked with her own lack of a mother and the loss of her Vietnamese family that forms the dark shadow of her past. This 'cold war' between mother and daughter is waged on the 'territory' of Lian's body which her mother wants to control and silence, expressing itself in physical and emotional violence in which Phi-Van denigrates Lian's physical self. This brings about Lian's becoming an emotional island herself, enclosed within a 'magic circle' (14) of dissociated feelings. Lian's awareness that 'something in her was broken, or not connected, and had been so from her earliest years' (26) leads her to collect other people's stories and to a sense of separation from her own life which she always narrates rather than experiences. Thus, to protect herself from Phi-Van's suppressed story, Lian 'armoured herself in stories' (28), becoming 'the master of carrion introspection' (27).

It is, indeed, a search for a 'foster mother tongue' and a refusal to even think of learning her mother's tongue, Vietnamese, that leads Lian to study Arabic, first at University and then in Yemen. This escape, though, is only partial: she 'carried Phi-Van's story curled and growing beneath her ribs' (35) in an image echoing the pregnancy that makes Lian return to Australia, her mother country. Her utter incomprehension of the Arabic she hears on her arrival in Yemen contrasts Arabic 'in its natural habitat' as a 'wild and slippery thing' as opposed to the 'domesticated, even crippled Arabic' she had learned in Australia (53). Her attempts to write the elusive language are compared to sculpting with water as Lian is unable to 'make a phrase of her own' (73).

Clothes, as in Gordimer's text, become an index of belonging and of blending in, a kind of freedom rather than the restriction that Western interpretations of veiling often suggest. Lian adopts the *balto* and the *hijab* not out of cultural respect like her friend Helena but because it gives her the freedom to escape from being stared at and classified as a European or American woman. Whereas previously her appearance was the cause of comments and the assigning of labels ('The Australian, The Chinese, A Muslim. A Christian' (97)) causing 'an impediment in the flow of passers by' (52), with her veiled appearance 'she floated easily through the streets' (99) in what she believes to be anonymity. Yet Helena warns her that her misplaced sense of belonging is an illusion: 'You will never fit in here. None of us will . . . The trick is to enjoy the privilege of being an outsider who knows her way round' (54). Lian becomes aware that despite the outer covering of belonging, she remains an outsider incomprehensible to others – 'unread, unopened, you cease to mean anything beyond your skin and fabric covers' (96). This awareness of her own loneliness in entering another culture connects her to her mother's alienation in Australia and ultimately brings her home.

Lian is aware, too, that this classifying of her self as other is a two-way form of cultural mistranslation of which she too has been guilty. On first arriving in Yemen, she writes letters home that are filled with 'disconcerting clichés' about 'exotic others, the mystery of the East, the Orient, Arabia Felix' (46) and she is alert, too, to the tendency to generalise about Arabs. On the other hand, she too takes on the stereotypical identity of the 'demo Australian' (135) and performs as 'the uncouth antipodean' (135) she thinks the English students in particular expect. She becomes acutely conscious that 'nothing had a history with her in it' (66) and of intercultural misreadings that leave her feeling helpless and sometimes violated. In an interesting echo of J. M. Coetzee's *Disgrace*, it is via the ethics of how different cultures treat dogs that Lian queries her responsibility to either intervene in what could be seen as cruelty to dogs, or try to remain dispassionate, remembering her status as an outsider who has no right to judge another culture's practices. Indeed, the novel includes a range of responses to intercultural encounters, from the cultural imperialism of American students who 'gave a picture of Yemeni culture and people as the incarnation of cruelty, bigotry, misogyny' (122) and then return to America as 'scholars' and those who compare 'souvenir atrocities' (181) within Arabic culture, to those who, like Helena, try hard to 'fit in' and remain sensitive to local customs. Lian's 'hopeless' desire for acceptance merely returns her to thoughts of her mother, Phi-Van, whose own cultural dislocation and 'terrible history' (86) have led to her fits of violence, depression and attempted suicide.

Lian's relationship with Ibrahim, like her responses to Yemeni culture itself, is one of alternating attraction and repulsion. Indeed, it is Lian's own dislocation that enables her to see Ibrahim as her double, a 'misplaced man' whose sense of imprisonment in his family after his father's death has led him to look to the outside world for 'something to shake him to pieces' (133). While initially Lian feels her heart lurch in Ibrahim's company, she is described as fighting against their deepening relationship, leading to her emotional withdrawal that is linked to her mother's hold over her body and her locked emotions. The moment of their sexual encounter, that significantly takes place at the coast after Lian has been diving in the Red Sea in a return to the medium where she most feels at home, is 'her one free moment' (173). But the after-effects of her losing her virginity are to further emphasise her disconnectedness from women close to her: according to Ibrahim, it is her mother she needs while Lian, on the contrary, feels her mother's destructive pull even more powerfully. In fleeing from Ibrahim, Lian is seen to be drawn closer to her mother and the shadow of her mother's haunting story.

Unlike Gordimer's Julie in *The Pickup*, who, according to her Ibrahim sees its observance as 'another adventure', evidenced by her breaking of the taboo of abstaining from sex, Lian takes Ramadan much more seriously, and uses it as a time to withdraw completely from society so that her 'body and mind were starved to stillness' (184). She is described as 'beautifully entombed in Yemen' (184) and yet finds her observance of this religious time through abstinence enables her to connect with 'every soul in the city . . . all hungry, all anticipating, all calm' (185). She sees this as a way of participating in a harmonious cultural dance. It is during the hallucinogenic 'madness' induced by the fasting that Lian encounters

Abdallah the Merman, imagining that she is swimming with him. It is at this point, after telling him of Phi-Van's story devouring her, that he offers to release her from it. The snippet of her story that appears in italics describes Phi-Van keeping watch over the body of her sister, Mei-Ling, and amplifies the phrase that has been repeated previously – 'three green leaves slap slapped against a bamboo pole' (193). Lian's emergence from Ramadan and her re-entry into Ibrahim's family is described as a resurfacing (195), and while more at peace than before, she is still disconnected.

Finally, it is letting go of the need to belong that enables Lian to return to Australia. Unlike Gordimer's Julie, whose experience of the muteness of the desert and the simplicity of village life frees her from the guilt of privilege and prevents her from leaving with Ibrahim to go to America, Lian reconnects with her mother's story. This is partly through her discovery of her own pregnancy and the pressure on her from Ibrahim's mother and family, but also partly her response to the depressing ending of the Abdallah story when the distance between Abdallah the Merman and Abdallah of the Land is emphasised, rather than their commonalities. The grief of Abdallah of the Land's loss of his friend and his banishment from the water is imaged in the blankness of the reflective water and the emptiness of the horizon. Lian simultaneously recognises that she would never belong in Yemen and yet that she can never 'unlearn the unravelling she had learned' (217). Like Abdallah, who keeps returning to look for his friend in the water, she realises that there is no easy return home because there is 'no forgetting' (217). Her pregnancy is both wonder and disaster (224) and with the imagery of the sea and Phi-Van's journey intertwined, Lian feels powerful enough to 'wrestle her mother to life' (227). One assumes that this will take the form of telling her mother's story and that in doing this Lian herself will be washed back home.

It is this ultimate return to the mother and to the mother-country that releases Lian's voice and subjectivity in a narrative that focuses on the personal aspects of exile and return, rather than the more globalised political issues that are at stake in Gordimer's novel. Whereas Gordimer's Julie is ostensibly trying to find a more simple, communal and 'authentic' way of life outside of her own sense of national belonging, which involves a rejection of her family and her inherited privilege, Sallis' Lian comes to terms with her hyphenated identity as partly Vietnamese and partly Australian by tuning in to her mother's story and in so doing embracing the three-way relationship inscribed in Phi-Van's last letter to her – *Phi-Van Lian Neville*. Accepting her position between these two identities allows Lian to return home.

These differing ways of interpreting 'home' and 'place', with Gordimer's Julie finding her place outside her own physical home with another family, and Sallis' Lian needing to return home to find her place within her family, both show continuing engagement and fascination with issues of subjectivity and belonging in contemporary women's fiction in South Africa and Australia that have been there in all the texts analysed. *Writing Woman, Writing Place* has traced some of these fictional engagements and the complex intersections of gender, race and place that make the texts work at so many levels of signification.

Notes

Introduction: place, space and gender

1 Ruth Frankenberg uses this term in her 'Introduction: Local Whitenesses, Localizing Whiteness' in Ruth Frankenberg (ed.) (1997): 1–33, 1. See also Ruth Frankenberg's *White Women, Race Matters: The Social Construction of Whiteness* (Minneapolis: University of Minnesota Press, and London: Routledge, 1993).
2 For more detailed discussion of this, see Richard Dyer, *White* (London and New York: Routledge, 1997), especially his Introduction and the chapter entitled 'The Matter of Whiteness'.
3 Timothy Brennan in *Salman Rushdie and the Third World: Myths of Nation*, New York: St. Martin's Press, 1989: 35.
4 For a more detailed account of this argument, see Sue Kossew, 'Resistance, Complicity and Post-colonial Politics' in *Critical Survey* 11.2 (1999): 18–30.
5 This term is used by Louise Yelin in the title of her book, *From the Margins of Empire: Christina Stead, Doris Lessing, Nadine Gordimer* (Ithaca and London: Cornell University Press, 1998). The theoretical basis of *Writing Woman, Writing Place* rests on the inter-sections between feminist and post-colonial literary theories. Gayatri Spivak's theorising of the native 'subaltern' woman has in turn led to a substantial amount of work being done on the complex issues of race and gender, particularly in considering the differences between so-called Third- and First-world approaches. Vron Ware's *Beyond the Pale: White Women, Racism and History* (1992) is an example of the application of these theoretical issues to a reading of racism in British culture and the complex position of the white woman coloniser, which extends some of the other feminist studies of imperialism like those of Sara Mills' *Discourses of Difference: An Analysis of Women's Travel Writing and Colonialism* (1991); Mary Louise Pratt's *Imperial Eyes: Travel Writing and Transculturation* (1992); Moira Ferguson's *Subject to Others: British Women Writers and Colonial Slavery 1670-1834* (1992); and Anne McClintock's *Imperial Leather: Race, Gender and Sexuality in the Colonial Contest* (1995). Publications such as *Writing Women and Space: Colonial and Postcolonial Geographies* (Alison Blunt and Gillian Rose (eds) 1994) and *Space, Gender, Knowledge: Feminist Readings* (Linda McDowell and Joanne P. Sharp (eds) 1997) have provided me with useful theories of feminist geography, and the 'spatial politics of difference' with which inter-disciplinary feminist analysis of power relations has engaged. These works, and others too numerous to list here, all provide a useful foundation for the theoretical and critical issues with which this study will engage.

Part I Introduction: post-bicentennial perspectives

1 This chapter provides a detailed review and critique of the history of Australian nationalism.

2 This is in no way intended to be an inclusive list but merely to suggest a range of issues that have been addressed in the 1990s and beyond.

1 The violence of representation

1 'P.M.', 'Henry Lawson's Prose' from the Melbourne *Champion*, 5 September 1896 in Roderick, Colin (ed.) (1972), *Henry Lawson Criticism 1894-1971* (Sydney: Angus and Robertson): 58–61, 60.
2 Lake mentions studies such as Miriam Dixson's *The Real Matilda*, Anne Summers' *Damned Whores and God's Police*, Eve Pownall's *Australian Pioneer Women*, Judith Godden's (1979) 'A New Look at Pioneer Women', *Hecate* 5.2, and Patricia Grimshaw's 'Women and the Family in Australian History: A reply to *The Real Matilda*', *Historical Studies* 18.72 as examples of such tendencies.
3 Kay Schaffer provides a detailed re-reading of 'The Drover's Wife' in *Women and the Bush* (Schaffer 1988: 132–137) to which I am indebted. Similarly, I have responded to a number of issues she raises in her analysis of Barbara Baynton's *Bush Studies*.
4 The editor's note provides details of the article's publication history: it was published in two parts in the *Englishwoman's Review* of 15 August 1889 and 15 October 1889, although an earlier publication appeared in the 1889 Boston *Women's Journal*, 27 July.
5 Mary Douglas' (1966) study, *Purity and Danger. An Analysis of Concepts of Pollution and Taboo*, London: Routledge & Kegan Paul, suggests that ideas of pollution and dirt are used to regulate transgressions of perceived and agreed social barriers. Extending this argument to her study of Empire, Anne McClintock (1995) points to the importance of the idea of cleanliness in the British Empire: 'Soap and cleansing rituals became central to the demarcation of body boundaries and the policing of social hierarchies' (*Imperial Leather: Race, Gender and Sexuality in the Colonial Contest*, London: Routledge, 33).
6 All references are to the editions as listed in the Bibliography and appear in the text.
7 Previous analyses of the original stories and rewritings have been published by the following: Werner Arens (1986) 'The Ironical Fate of "The Drover's Wife": Four versions from Henry Lawson (1892) to Barbara Jefferis (1980)' in P. O. Stummer (ed.) *The Story Must be Told. Short Narrative Prose in the New Literatures in English*, Würtzburg: Königshausen & Neumann; John Thieme (1989) 'Drover's Wives' in J. Bardolph (ed.) *Short Fiction in the New Literatures in English*, Nice: Faculté des Lettres; Kay Schaffer, 'Henry Lawson, the drover's wife and the critics' in Magarey *et al.* (eds) (1993) *Debutante Nation: Feminism Contests the 1890s*, Sydney: Allen & Unwin; and Isabel Carrera-Suarez (1991) 'A Gendered Bush: Mansfield and Australian Drover's Wives', *Australian Literary Studies*, 15.2: 140–148.
8 Murray Bail (1984) 'The Drover's Wife' in *The Drover's Wife and Other Stories*, St. Lucia: Queensland University Press; Damien Broderick (1991) 'The Drover's Wife's Dog' in *The Dark Between the Stars*, Melbourne: Mandarin Press; and Frank Moorhouse (1980) 'The Drover's Wife', *The Bulletin*, 29 January 1980: 160–162. All of these are collected in John Thieme (ed.) (1996) *The Arnold Anthology of Postcolonial Literatures in English*.
9 Kate Jennings, 'Interview of the Month: Kate Jennings: Q & A', *The Australian Women's Weekly Online Book Club* http://aww.ninemsn.com.au/aww/Books/articles/Feature/article413.asp (Accessed: 2 December 2002).
10 I am indebted to Elizabeth McMahon for drawing this to my attention.

2   Gone bush

1   I am thinking here particularly of novels like David Malouf's *The Great World* and Peter Carey's *True History of the Kelly Gang*.

3   Another country

1   At the end of the text, when her manuscript has been 'shuffled out of sequence', Janet is reminded of the term 'deconstruction' (293). Astley's attributing this awareness of contemporary literary issues to Janet makes her more than just a conservative voice in the wilderness of popular culture.
2   This phrase is used by Brian Matthews in his Review Article (1973) 'Life in the Eye of the Hurricane: The Novels of Thea Astley', *Southern Review*, 6.2 June: 173.

4   Learning to belong

1   For a fuller discussion of this connection, see Brewster 2002.
2   There have been a number of books exploring contemporary Australia's need to 'belong' and a related turn to spirituality. These include: David J. Tacey (1995) *Edge of the Sacred: Transformation in Australia*, Blackburn, Victoria: HarperCollins; Roslynn D. Haynes (1998) *Seeking the Centre: The Australian Desert in Literature, Art and Film*, Cambridge: Cambridge University Press; Ken Gelder and Jane M. Jacobs (1998) *Uncanny Australia: Sacredness and Identity in a Postcolonial Nation*, Melbourne: Melbourne University Press; and Peter Read (2000) *Belonging: Australians, Place and Aboriginal Ownership*, Cambridge: Cambridge University Press.
3   It is noteworthy that she occasionally addresses her readers as 'you' and that her intended readership appears to be other white women, as in her words, describing the way a 'blackfellow can . . . make hard work into play' and, more particularly, make washing day into fun: 'if you like real fun, it's a pity you were not there' (Gunn, *The Little Black Princess*: 176).
4   *The Bulletin*, established in 1880 and still published in contemporary Australia, was instrumental in the nationalist push that led up to Federation in 1901, under the editorship of J. F. Archibald. It has been described as 'the most influential exponent of the separatist model of masculinity which lay at the heart of the eulogies to the Bushman' (Magarey *et al.* 1993: 3).
5   See Kay Schaffer's (1988) *Women and the Bush* and Drusilla Modjeska's Introduction to *Coonardoo*, Sydney: Angus & Robertson (1990 edition) as examples.
6   These words are used by Sir William Deane, past Governor-General of Australia, in a pamphlet entitled *The Stolen Generations*. The pamphlet was compiled by Senator Trish Crossin and published by the Senate Printing Unit, Canberra in September 2000.

Part II Introduction: new subjectivities

1   Jenny de Reuck's 'Social Suffering and the Politics of Pain: Observations on the Concentration Camps in the Anglo Boer War 1899–1902' in Sue Kossew and Dianne Schwerdt (eds) (2001) *Re-Imagining Africa: New Critical Perspectives*, New York: Nova Science, discusses the ideological appropriation of Afrikaner suffering for the purposes of 'forging a national identity . . . that consists in part of victim-hood' (82) while simultaneously erasing from history the parallel suffering of black men and women.

5 'A white woman's words'

1   See also Karen Lazar's articles on Gordimer, particularly 'Feminism as "Piffling"? Ambiguities in Nadine Gordimer's Short Stories' in Bruce King (ed.) (1993) *The Later Fiction of Nadine Gordimer*, London: Macmillan, 213–227.

2   Coetzee's criticism of André Brink's stated position as a dissident Afrikaner writer who can diagnose the ills of the apartheid society is couched in these terms:

> The paradox implied in Brink's major metaphor of the writers as the *diagnostic organ* of the body politic lays bare the problem even more cruelly. Is diagnosis carried out from inside or outside the body? . . . If from inside, how does . . . the diagnostic organ escape corruption by the sick body? If from outside, how did the organ find its way out of the body?
>
> (Coetzee 1990a)

This article is revised and reprinted as 'The Politics of Dissent: André Brink' in Coetzee's (1996) *Giving Offense: Essays on Censorship*, Chicago: University of Chicago Press: 204–214.

3   Such as those by Susan M. Greenstein, 'Miranda's Story: Nadine Gordimer and the Literature of Empire', *Novel*, 18 (Spring, 1985) and Kathrin M. Wagner, '"Both as a Citizen and as a Woman"? Women and Politics in Some Gordimer Novels' in Anna Rutherford (ed.) (1992) *From Commonwealth to Post-Colonial*, Mundelstrup: Dangaroo Press, 276–291.

4   This phrase is echoed in Gordimer's (1988c) essay entitled 'Where Do Whites Fit in?' in Stephen Clingman (ed.) *The Essential Gesture: Writing, Politics and Places*, London: Penguin.

5   Menán du Plessis, *Between the Lines II: NELM Interviews* eds. Eva Hunter and Craig Mackenzie (1993): 75. In this interview with Eva Hunter, Cape Town November 1989, du Plessis talks of her characters as having 'a certain degree of freedom' and continues, 'I suppose this is really what I explore in my work. It's that tussling with that freedom that you've been given' (75).

6   Rewriting the farm novel

1   There is a sense in which the 'magic realism' of the text could be seen to apply to telling a story to a deaf person. But the text also explains that Gerda 'listens' by placing her hand at Connie's throat to feel the sounds she is speaking.

2   Bywoner is an Afrikaans word meaning 'a person who lives on another's farm under certain conditions of service'.

3   Like others of her time, Schreiner uses now-unacceptable terminology to distinguish different black 'races' – using the word 'Kaffir' to suggest Bantu, 'Bushman' for San and 'Hottentot' for Khoikhoi. Whether in this quotation she is using the word 'boy' to denote any age-group of 'Kaffir', or whether they really were young, is not clear, but this was, of course, widely used until fairly recently in South African racist discourse.

4   Joyce Avrech Berkman (1989) has suggested in her study, *The Healing Imagination of Olive Schreiner: Beyond South African Colonialism*, Amherst: University of Massachusetts Press, that 'Schreiner was unique [among her contemporaries] in the comprehensiveness of her critique of Social Darwinism. She alone faulted Social Darwinism for its rationale in defending race, gender, and class inequality, and she alone realised in its logic the interconnectedness of all three modes of domination' (Berkman 1989: 77). For further discussion of this aspect of Schreiner's writing in texts other than *The Story of an African Farm*, see Laura

Chrisman, 'Colonialism and Feminism in Olive Schreiner's 1890s Fiction', *English in Africa*, 20.1 May: 25–38.

5   While set in Southern Rhodesia, Lessing constantly refers to the farm and its owners as being 'South African', so I am, following Jean Marquard's example, including *The Grass is Singing* as part of the South African farm novel genre.

6   Michael Chapman uses this term in his chapter (1996) 'The Truth of Fiction and the Fiction of Truth: Writing Novels in the Interregnum' in *Southern African Literatures*, London and New York: Longman: 393.

7   Robin Visel emphasises the 'privileged claustrophobia' of Gordimer's white women characters whose 'identification with this symbol [the buried black body] is always problematic' (Visel 1990: 121).

8   There is a brief discussion of this stereotypical anti-semitism in Jochen Petzold's chapter on *The Devil's Chimney* in his 2002 book, *Re-imagining White Identity by Exploring the Past: History in South African Novels of the 1990s*, Studies in English Literary and Cultural History 5, Trier: Wissenschaftlicher Verlag Trier, 123–124.

7   Revisioning history

1   The town of Ladysmith in the British colony of Natal was besieged by the Boer forces during the Anglo-Boer War for 118 days. Its inhabitants including local civilians and British garrisons suffered from starvation and disease, resulting in many deaths.

2   This is a reference to Nelson Mandela's release from prison.

3   See Anne McClintock's chapter on Schreiner entitled 'Olive Schreiner: The Limits of Colonial Feminism' in McClintock (1995) for a comprehensive discussion of these issues.

8   A state of violence

1   Both these quotations appear on the dust jacket of Antjie Krog's *Country of my Skull* (1998).

2   Archbishop Desmond Tutu, *The Truth and Reconciliation Commission of South African Report*. A similar metaphor is to be found in Tutu's *No Future Without Forgiveness* where he writes of the TRC process of reparation: 'But as a nation we are saying, we are sorry, we have opened the wounds of your suffering and sought to cleanse them; this reparation is as balm, an ointment, being poured over the wounds to assist in their healing' (Tutu 1999: 57).

9   Exile and belonging

1   See particularly Bill Ashcroft (2001) *Post-colonial Transformation*, London and New York: Routledge; and the new edition of Ashcroft, Griffiths and Tiffin's (2002) *The Empire Writes Back*, London and New York: Routledge.

2   Nadine Gordimer, 'Letters to Future Generations', Online. Available: http://www.unesco.org/opi2/lettres/TextAnglais/GordimerE.html (accessed: 18 September 2002).

3   Yamauchi, Tadashi, 'Literature Offers Insights into Changing World', Interview with Nadine Gordimer, *The Daily Yomiuri Shimbun Online* (no date), Online. Available: http://www.yomiuri.co.jp/dy/civil/civil006.htm (accessed: 25 September 2002).

Bibliography

Adam, Ian and Tiffin, Helen (eds) (1991) *Past the Last Post: Theorizing Post-colonialism and Post-Modernism*, New York and London: Harvester Wheatsheaf.

Adelaide, Debra (1997) 'Thea Astley – "Completely Neutered": Gender, Reception and Reputation', *Southerly*, 57.3: 182–190.

Alexander, M. Jacqui and Mohanty, Chandra Talpade (eds) (1997) *Feminist Genealogies, Colonial Legacies, Democratic Futures*, London and New York: Routledge

Arens, Werner (1986) 'The Ironical Fate of "The Drover's Wife": Four Versions from Henry Lawson (1892) to Barbara Jefferis (1980)' in P. O. Stummer (ed.) *The Story Must be Told. Short Narrative Prose in the New Literatures in English*, Würtzburg: Königshausen & Neumann.

Armstrong, Nancy and Tennenhouse, Leonard (1989) *The Violence of Representation: Literature and the History of Violence*, London and New York: Routledge.

Ashcroft, Bill (1994) 'Africa and Australia: The Post-colonial Connection', *Research in African Literatures*, 25.3: 161–170.

Ashcroft, Bill (2001) *Post-colonial Transformation*, London & New York: Routledge.

Ashcroft, Bill, Griffiths, Gareth and Tiffin, Helen (2002) *The Empire Writes Back*, London & New York: Routledge; first published 1989.

Astley, Thea (1982) *An Item from the Late News*, St Lucia: University of Queensland Press.

Astley, Thea (1987) *It's Raining in Mango*, New York, G. P. Putnam's Sons; also published by Penguin, 1989.

Astley, Thea (1989) *A Kindness Cup*, Ringwood, Victoria: Penguin; first published by Thomas Nelson, 1974.

Astley, Thea (1999) *Drylands: A Book for the World's Last Reader*, Ringwood, Victoria and Harmondsworth: Viking, Penguin

Attridge, Derek and Jolly, Rosemary (eds) (1998) *Writing South Africa: Literature, Apartheid and Democracy, 1970–1995*, Cambridge: Cambridge University Press.

Attwell, David (ed.) (1992) *Doubling the Point: Essays and Interviews*, Cambridge, MA and London: Harvard University Press.

Attwell, David and Harlow, Barbara (2000) 'Introduction: South African Fiction after Apartheid', *Modern Fiction Studies*, 46.1: 1–9.

Bail, Murray (1984) 'The Drover's Wife' in *The Drover's Wife and Other Stories*, St Lucia: Queensland University Press; also collected in John Thieme (ed.), *The Arnold Anthology of Post-colonial Literatures in English*.

Ball, Maggie (2001) 'Interview with Kate Grenville: 27 February 2001', online. Available: http://www.suite101.com/mybulletin.cfm/authors/5643 (accessed 20 June 2002). No page numbers.

Barash, Carol. L. (ed.) (1987) *An Olive Schreiner Reader*, London: Routledge and Kegan Paul.

Bardolph, J. (ed.) (1989) *Short Fiction in the New Literatures in English*, Nice: Faculté des Lettres.

Bartlett, Alison (1999) *Jamming the Machinery: Contemporary Australian Women's Writing*, Canberra: ASAL (Association for the Study of Australian Literature) Publication.

Baynton, Barbara (1993) 'Squeaker's Mate', *Bush Studies*, Sydney: Angus & Robertson, 54–71; first published 1902.

Beasley, Jack (1993) *A Gallop of Fire: Katharine Susannah Prichard: On Guard for Humanity*, Earlwood, Australia: Wedgetail Press.

Behrendt, Larissa (2000) 'Aboriginal Women and the White Lies of the Feminist Movement: Implications for Aboriginal Women in Rights Discourse', *The Australian Feminist Law Journal*, 1: 27–44, 37–43; also cited in Aileen Moreton-Robinson, *Talkin' Up to the White Woman: Indigenous Women and Feminism*, St Lucia: Queensland University Press.

Bell, Linda A. and Blumenfeld, David (eds) (1995) *Overcoming Racism and Sexism*, Maryland: Rowman and Littlefield.

Bennett, Bruce and Strauss, Jennifer (eds) (1998) *The Oxford Literary History of Australia*, Melbourne: Oxford University Press.

Bennie, Angela (1999) Review of *The Idea of Perfection*, 'Nobody's Perfect', *Sydney Morning Herald*, Spectrum 31 July: 8s. Also available online. Available: http:www.uscis.bigpond.com/kgrenville/fic/idea/reading-resources.html (accessed 20 June 2002).

Berkman, Joyce Avrech (1989) *The Healing Imagination of Olive Schreiner: Beyond South African Colonialism*, Amherst, MA: University of Massachusetts Press.

Bird, Delys (1989) ' "Mother, I won't never go drovin'"': Motherhood in Australian Narrative', *Westerly*, 4 (December): 41–50.

Blunt, Alison and Rose, Gillian (eds) (1994) *Writing Women and Space: Colonial and Postcolonial Geographies*, New York, London: The Guilford Press.

Boehmer, Elleke (1993) *An Immaculate Figure*, London: Bloomsbury.

Boehmer, Elleke (2000) *Bloodlines*, Claremont: David Philip.

Boehmer, Elleke (2002) *Empire, The National, and the Postcolonial 1890–1920: Resistance in Interaction*, Oxford: Oxford University Press.

Brewster, Anne (2002) 'Aboriginal Life Writing and Globalisation: Doris Pilkington's *Follow the Rabbit-proof Fence*', *Australian Humanities Review*, online. Available: http://www.lib.latrobe.edu.au/AHR/archive/Issue-March-2002/brewster.html (accessed 6 January 2003).

Breytenbach, Breyten (1999) *Dogheart: A Memoir*, New York, San Diego and London: Harcourt Brace & Company.

Brink, André (1998a) 'Stories of History: Reimagining the Past in Post-apartheid Narrative' in Sarah Nuttall and Carli Coetzee (eds) *Negotiating the Past: The Making of Memory in South Africa*, Oxford: Oxford University Press: 29–42.

Brink, André (1998b) 'The Heart of the Novel', *Leadership*, 17.2: 84–88.

Brink, André (1998c) 'Interrogating Silence: New Possibilities Faced by South African Literature' in Derek Attridge and Rosemary Jolly (eds) *Writing South Africa: Literature*,

Apartheid and Democracy, 1970–1995, Cambridge: Cambridge University Press: 14–28.

Broderick, Damien (1991) 'The Drover's Wife's Dog' in *The Dark Between the Stars*, Melbourne: Mandarin Press; also collected in John Thieme (ed.) *The Arnold Anthology of Post-colonial Literatures in English*.

Brown, Duncan and van Dyk, Bruno (eds) (1991) *Exchanges: South African Writing in Transition*, Pietermaritzburg: University of Natal Press.

Brydon, Diana (1991) 'The White Inuit Speaks: Contamination as Literary Strategy' in Ian Adam and Helen Tiffin (eds) *Past the Last Post: Theorizing Post-Colonialism and Post-Modernism*, New York and London: Harvester Wheatsheaf: 192–203.

Brydon, Diana (1996) 'Trousered Women: Cross-dressing in Some Contemporary Australian and Canadian Texts' in Hena Maes-Jelinek, Gordon Collier and Geoffrey V. Davis (eds) *A Talent(ed) Digger: Creations, Cameos, and Essays in Honour of Anna Rutherford*, Amsterdam and Atlanta: Rodopi: 184–202.

Carrera-Suarez, Isabel (1991) 'A Gendered Bush: Mansfield and Australian Drover's Wives', *Australian Literary Studies*, 15.2: 140–148.

Carroll, Peter (ed.) (1982) *Intruders in the Bush: The Australian Quest for Identity*, Melbourne: Oxford University Press.

Carter, David (1999) 'Good Readers and Good Citizens: Literature, Media and the Nation', *Australian Literary Studies*, 19.2: 136–151.

Chapman, Michael (1996) *Southern African Literatures*, London and New York: Longman.

Chapman, Michael, Gardner, Colin and Mphahlele, Es'kia (eds) (1992) *Perspectives on South African Literature*, Parklands: Ad. Donker.

Chaudhuri, Nupur and Strobel, Margaret (eds) (1992) *Western Women and Imperialism: Complicity and Resistance*, Bloomington and Indianapolis: Indiana University Press.

Chrisman, Laura (1993) 'Colonialism and Feminism in Olive Schreiner's 1890s Fiction', *English in Africa*, 20.1: 25–38.

Christiansë, Yvette (1995) 'Sculpted into History: The Voortrekker Mother and the Gaze of the Invisible Servant', *New Literatures Review*, 30 Winter: 1–16.

Clayton, Cherry (1990) 'Women Writers and the Law of the Father: Race and Gender in the Fiction of Olive Schreiner, Pauline Smith, and Sarah Gertrude Millin', *The English Academy Review*, 7 December: 99–117.

Clingman, Stephen (ed.) (1988) *The Essential Gesture*, London: Jonathan Cape.

Clingman, Stephen (1993) *The Novels of Nadine Gordimer: History from the Inside*, London: Bloomsbury.

Coetzee, Ampie and Polley, James (eds) (1990) *Crossing Borders: Writers Meet the ANC*, Bramley: Taurus.

Coetzee, J. M. (1988) *White Writing: On the Culture of Letters in South Africa*, New Haven and London: Radix, Yale University Press.

Coetzee, J. M. (1990a) 'André Brink and the Censor', *Research in African Literatures*, 21.3 Fall: 59–74.

Coetzee, J. M. (1990b) *Age of Iron*, London: Secker & Warburg.

Coetzee, J. M. (1992) in David Attwell (ed.) *Doubling the Point: Essays and Interviews*, Cambridge, MA and London: Harvard University Press.

Coetzee, J. M. (1999) *Disgrace*, London: Secker & Warburg.

Collis, Christy (1994) 'Siting the Second World in South African Literary Culture', *New Literatures Review*, 27 Summer: 1–15.

Crossin, Trish (2000) *The Stolen Generations*, Canberra: The Senate Printing Unit.

Curthoys, Ann (1993) 'Identity Crisis: Colonialism, Nation, and Gender in Australian History', *Gender & History*, 5.2: 165–176.

Dale, Leigh (1999) 'New Directions: Introduction', *Australian Literary Studies*, 19.2: 131–135.

Dale, Leigh and Ryan, Simon (eds) (1998) *The Body in the Library*, Atlanta and Amsterdam: Rodopi.

Darian-Smith, Kate, Gunner, Liz and Nuttall, Sarah (1996) *Text, Theory, Space: Land, Literature and History in South Africa and Australia*, London and New York: Routledge.

Davidson, Jim (1997) 'Sisters of the South: South African Connections and Comparison', *Australian Studies*, 12.2: 69–77.

Davis, Geoffrey V. (ed.) (1994) *Southern African Writing: Voyages and Explorations*, Amsterdam and Atlanta: Rodopi.

Davison, Graeme (1992) 'Sydney and the Bush: An Urban Context for the Australian Legend' in Gillian Whitlock and David Carter (eds) *Images of Australia: An Introductory Reader in Australian Studies*, St Lucia: University of Queensland Press, 191–204.

Daymond, Margaret (ed.) (1996) *South African Feminisms: Writing, Theory, and Criticism, 1990–1994*, New York and London: Garland Publishing.

de Bruyn, Matthew (1984) 'Coloured Rule in the National Democratic Revolution', *African Communist*, 97: 28–38.

de Kok, Ingrid (1996) 'Standing in the Doorway: A Preface', *World Literature Today*, 70.1 Winter: 5–8.

de Lauretis, Teresa (1989) 'The Violence of Rhetoric: Considerations on Representation and Gender' in Nancy Armstrong and Leonard Tennenhouse (eds) *The Violence of Representation: Literature and the History of Violence*, 239–258.

de Lepervanche, Marie and Bottomley, Gillian (eds) (1988) *The Cultural Construction of Race*, Sydney: University of Sydney Studies in Society and Culture, No. 4.

Denoon, Donald (1979) 'Understanding Settler Societies', *Historical Studies*, 18.73 October: 511–527.

de Reuck, Jenny (2001) 'Social Suffering and the Politics of Pain: Observations on the Concentration Camps in the Anglo Boer War 1899–1902', in Sue Kossew and Dianne Schwerdt (eds) *Re-Imagining Africa: New Critical Perspectives*, New York: Nova Science, 81–100.

Dewar, Mickey (1997) *In Search of the 'Never-Never': Looking for Australia in Northern Territory Writing*, Darwin: Northern Territory University Press.

Dixson, Miriam (1999) *The Imaginary Australian: Anglo-Celts and Identity – 1788 to the Present*, Sydney: UNSW Press.

Donaldson, Laura E. (1992) *Decolonizing Feminisms: Race, Gender & Empire-building*, Chapel Hill & London: The University of North Carolina Press.

Douglas, Mary (1966) *Purity and Danger: An Analysis of Concepts of Pollution and Taboo*, London: Routledge and Kegan Paul.

Dovey, Teresa (1988) *The Novels of J. M. Coetzee: Lacanian Allegories*, Craighall: Ad. Donker.

Driver, Dorothy (ed.) (1983a) *Pauline Smith*, Johannesburg: McGraw-Hill.

Driver, Dorothy (1983b) 'Introduction' in Dorothy Driver (ed.) *Pauline Smith*, Johannesburg: McGraw-Hill, 21–31.

Driver, Dorothy (1983c) 'Nadine Gordimer: The Politicisation of Women', *English in Africa*, 10.2: 29–54.

Driver, Dorothy (1988) ' "Woman" as Sign in the South African Colonial Enterprise', *Journal of Literary Studies*, 4.1: 3–20.

Driver, Dorothy (1992) 'Women and Nature, Women as Objects of Exchange: Towards a Feminist Analysis of South African Literature' in Michael Chapman, Colin Gardner and Es'kia Mphahlele (eds) *Perspectives on South African Literature*, Parklands: Ad. Donker, 454–474.

Driver, Dorothy (1996) 'Transformation through Art: Writing, Representation and Subjectivity in South African Fiction', *World Literature Today*, 70.1 Winter: 45–52.

Driver, Dorothy (2001) 'Afterword', in Zoë Wicomb, *David's Story*, New York: The Feminist Press, 215–271.

du Plessis, Menán (1987) *A State of Fear*, London: Pandora; originally published by David Philip, 1983.

du Plessis, Menán (1989) *Longlive!*, Claremont: David Philip.

du Plessis, Menán (1991) 'Menán du Plessis [Interview]', in Duncan Brown and Bruno van Dyk (eds) *Exchanges: South African Writing in Transition*, Pietermaritzburg: University of Natal Press.

du Plessis, Menán (1993) 'Interview with Eva Hunter' in Eva Hunter and Craig Mackenzie (eds) *Between the Lines II: NELM Interviews*, Grahamstown: NELM.

Dutton, Jo (1998) *On the Edge of Red*, New South Wales: Anchor Books (Transworld Publishers).

Dyer, Richard (1997) *White*, London and New York: Routledge.

Eaden, P. R. and Mares, F. H. (eds) (1986) *Mapped but not Known: The Australian Landscape of the Imagination*, Nestley, South Australia: Wakefield Press.

Ferguson, Moira (1992) *Subject to Others: British Women Writers and Colonial Slavery 1670–1834*, London and New York: Routledge.

Ferres, Kay (ed.) (1993a) *The Time to Write: Australian Women Writers: 1890–1930*, Ringwood: Penguin Books.

Ferres, Kay (1993b) 'Introduction: In the Shadow of the Nineties: Women Writing in Australia, 1890–1930' in Kay Ferres (ed.) *The Time to Write: Australian Women Writers 1890–1930*, Ringwood: Penguin.

Folena, Lucia (1989) 'Figures of Violence: Philologists, Witches, and Stalinistas' in Nancy Armstrong and Leonard Tennenhouse (eds) *The Violence of Representation: Literature and the History of Violence*, 219–238.

Foley, Timothy, Pilkington, Lionel, Ryder, Sean and Tilley, Elizabeth (eds) (1995) *Gender and Colonialism*, Galway: Galway University Press.

Frankenberg, Ruth (1993) *White Women, Race Matters: The Social Construction of Whiteness*, Minneapolis: University of Minnesota Press, and London: Routledge.

Frankenberg, Ruth (ed.) (1997) *Displacing Whiteness: Essays in Social and Cultural Criticism*, Durham and London: Duke University Press.

Frankenberg, Ruth (1997) 'Introduction: Local Whitenesses, Localizing Whiteness' in Ruth Frankenberg (ed.) *Displacing Whiteness: Essays in Social and Cultural Criticism*, Durham and London: Duke University Press, 1–33.

Frost, Lucy (1984) *No Place for a Nervous Lady: Voices from the Australian Bush*, Victoria: McPhee Dribble/Penguin Books.

Frow, John (1998) 'The Politics of Stolen Time', *Australian Humanities Review*, 9, February–April, online. Available: http://www.lib.latrobe.edu.au/AHR/archive/Issue–February–1998/frow1.html (accessed: 29 January 1999).

Frye, Marilyn (1995) 'White Woman Feminist' in Linda A. Bell and David Blumenfeld (eds) *Overcoming Racism and Sexism*, Maryland: Rowman and Littlefield, 113–134.

Gambling, Anne (1986) 'The Drover's De Facto' in Susan Johnson and Mary Roberts (eds) *Latitudes: New Writing from the North*, St Lucia: University of Queensland Press, 150–159.

Gardiner, Michael (1983) 'Critical Responses and the Fiction of Pauline Smith', *Theoria* LX May: 1–12.

Garner, Dwight (1998) *Salon* Interview with Nadine Gordimer on 'Table Talk', online. Available: http://www.salonmagazine.com/books/int/1998/03/c0v_si_09int.html (accessed 6 August 1999).

Glover, D. (1998) 'The Ethics of Violence: Introduction', *New Formations: A Journal of Culture/Theory/Politics*, 35 Autumn: v–vi.

Goldie, Terry (1989) *Fear and Temptation: The Image of the Indigene in Canadian, Australian and New Zealand Literatures*, Kingston, Montreal, London: McGill-Queen's University Press.

Goldsworthy, Kerryn (1996) Review of *The Multiple Effects of Rainshadow*, *Australian Book Review*, 13.

Goodwin, K. L. (1986) 'The Land and its People in African and Australian Fiction' in Peggy Nightingale (ed.) *A Sense of Place in the New Literatures in English*, St Lucia: University of Queensland Press, 37–46.

Gordimer, Nadine (1976) 'English Language Literature and Politics in South Africa' in Christopher Heywood (ed.) *Aspects of South African Literature*, London: Heinemann, 99–120.

Gordimer, Nadine (1978) *The Conservationist*, Harmondsworth: Penguin; first published Jonathan Cape, 1974.

Gordimer, Nadine (1980) *Burger's Daughter*, Harmondsworth: Penguin; first published Jonathan Cape, 1979.

Gordimer, Nadine (1980) 'The Prison-House of Colonialism', Review of *Olive Schreiner: A Biography* by Ruth First and Ann Scott, *The Times Literary Supplement*, 15 August, 918.

Gordimer, Nadine (1982) *July's People*, Harmondsworth: Penguin; first published Jonathan Cape, 1981.

Gordimer, Nadine (1988a) 'Living in the Interregnum' in Stephen Clingman (ed.) *The Essential Gesture*, London: Jonathan Cape, 261–284.

Gordimer, Nadine (1988b) 'Where Do Whites Fit in?' in Stephen Clingman (ed.) *The Essential Gesture: Writing, Politics and Places*, London: Jonathan Cape, 31–37.

Gordimer, Nadine (1995) 'That Other World that Was the World' in *Writing and Being: The Charles Eliot Norton Lectures, 1994*, Cambridge, MA: Harvard University Press, 114–134.

Gordimer, Nadine (1998) *The House Gun*, London: Bloomsbury.

Gordimer, Nadine (1999a) *Living in Hope and History: Notes from our Century*, New York: Farrar, Strauss and Giroux.

Gordimer, Nadine (1999b) 'Living on a Frontierless Land: Cultural Globalization' in *Living in Hope and History: Notes from our Century*, New York: Farrar, Straus and Giroux; also published as 'Cultural Globalization: Living on a Frontierless Land' in *Co-Operation South* 2, 1998: 16–21.

Gordimer, Nadine (2001) *The Pickup*, London: Bloomsbury.

Gordimer, Nadine (no date) 'Letters to Future Generations', online. Available: http://www.unesco.org/opi2/lettres/TextAnglais/GordimerE.html (accessed 18 September 2002).

Grace, Heather (1992) *Heart of Light*, Fremantle: Fremantle Arts Centre Press.

Graham, Duncan (ed.) (1994) *Being Whitefella*, Fremantle: Fremantle Arts Centre Press.

Greenstein, Susan M. (1985) 'Miranda's Story: Nadine Gordimer and the Literature of Empire', *Novel*, 18: 227–242.

Grenville, Kate (1999) *The Idea of Perfection*, Sydney: Picador.

Grieve, Norma and Grimshaw, Patricia (1981) *Australian Women: Feminist Perspectives*, Melbourne: Oxford University Press.

Grimshaw, Patricia, Lake, Marilyn, McGrath, Ann and Quartly, Marian (1996) *Creating a Nation*, Ringwood: Penguin; first published by McPhee Gribble, 1994.

Gunew, Sneja and Yeatman, Anna (eds) (1993) *Feminism and the Politics of Difference*, St Leonards: Allen & Unwin.

Gunn, Jeannie (Mrs Aeneas) (1992) *We of the Never-Never and The Little Black Princess*, Pymble: HarperCollins; combined edition first published by Angus & Robertson, 1982; first published 1908 and 1905 respectively.

Haggis, Jane (1990) 'Gendering Colonialism or Colonising Gender? Recent Women's Studies Approaches to White Women and the History of British Colonialism', *Women's Studies International Forum*, 13.1–2: 105–115.

Hall, Stuart (1993) 'Cultural Identities and Diaspora' in Patrick Williams and Laura Chrisman (eds) *Colonial Discourse and Postcolonial Theory: A Reader*, London: Harvest Wheatsheaf, 392–403; originally published in J. Rutherford (ed.) *Identity: Community, Culture, Difference*, London: Lawrence & Wishart, 1990, 222–237.

Haresnape, Geoffrey (1969) *Pauline Smith*, New York: Twayne.

Haresnape, Geoffrey (1977) 'Barriers of Race and Language. Pauline Smith's Critique of a Rural Society' in Dorothy Driver (ed.) *Pauline Smith*, 190–197; originally published in *English in Africa* 4.1, 1977.

Haresnape, Geoffrey (1978) 'Pauline Smith' in Kenneth Parker (ed.) *The South African Novel in English*, London: Macmillan, 46–56.

Harries, Ann (1999; 2nd edn 2000) *Manly Pursuits*, London: Bloomsbury.

Hawley, Janet (2002) 'Runaway Success', *Sydney Morning Herald Good Weekend*, 2 May 2002: 30–33.

Hawley, John (ed.) (1996) *Writing the Nation: Self and Country in the Post-colonial Imagination*, Amsterdam and Atlanta: Rodopi.

Haynes, Roslynn D. (1988a) 'Shelter from the Holocaust: Thea Astley's *An Item from the Late News*', *Southerly*, 2: 138–151.

Haynes, Roslynn D. (1988b) *Seeking the Centre: The Australian Desert in Literature, Art and Film*, Cambridge: Cambridge University Press.

Healy, J. J. (1978; 2nd edn 1989) *Literature and the Aborigine in Australia*, St Lucia: University of Queensland Press.

Heywood, Christopher (ed.) (1976) *Aspects of South African Literature*, London: Heinemann.

Hodge, Bob and Mishra, Vijay (1990) *Dark Side of the Dream: Australian Literature and the Postcolonial Mind*, North Sydney: Allen & Unwin.

Holst Petersen, Kirsten (1991) 'The Search for a Role for White Women in a Liberated South Africa: A Thematic Approach to the Novels of Nadine Gordimer', *Kunapipi*, 13.1–2: 170–177.

Holst Petersen, K. and Rutherford, A. (1985) *A Double Colonization: Colonial and Post-colonial Women's Writing*, Aarhus, Denmark: Dangaroo.

Hudson, Wayne and Bolton, Geoffrey (eds) (1997) *Creating Australia: Changing Australian History*, St Leonards: Allen & Unwin.

Huggins, Jackie (1987) 'Black Women and Women's Liberation', *Hecate*, 13.1: 77–82.

Hughes, Kate Pritchard (ed.) (1998, 2nd edn; first published 1994), *Contemporary Australian Feminism 2*, South Melbourne: Longman.

Hunn, Deborah (1999) 'Deborah Hunn interviews Eva Sallis', *Outskirts: Feminism along the Edge*, 4, online. Available: http://www.chloe.uwa.edu.au/outskirts/archive/VOL4/article3.html (accessed 25 September 2002).

Hunter, Eva (1999) 'Moms and Moral Midgets: South African Feminisms and Characterisation in Novels in English by White Women', *Current Writing*, 11.1: 36–54.

Hunter, Eva and McKenzie, Craig (eds) (1993) *Between the Lines II, NELM Interviews, Series No 6*, Grahamstown: National English Literary Museum Publication.

Ingersoll, Earl G. (ed.) (1996) *Putting the Questions Differently: Interviews with Doris Lessing 1964–1994*, London: HarperCollins/Flamingo.

Jacobs, Jane M. (1994) 'Earth Honouring: Western Desires and Indigenous Knowledges', *Meanjin*, 53.2: 305–314.

Jacobs, Jane M. and Gelder, Ken (1998) *Uncanny Australia: Sacredness and Identity in a Postcolonial Nation*, Melbourne: Melbourne University Press.

Jefferis, Barbara (1980) 'The Drover's Wife', *The Bulletin*, 23–30 December 1980: 156–160; also in John Thieme (ed.) *Arnold Anthology of Post-colonial Literatures in English*, 265–272.

Jennings, Kate (1996) *Snake*, Port Melbourne: Minerva.

Jennings, Kate (no date) 'Interview of the Month: Kate Jennings: Q & A', online. Available: http://aww.ninemsn.com.au/aww/Books/articles/Feature/article413.asp (accessed 2 December 2002).

Jolly, Margaret (1993) 'Colonizing Women: The Maternal Body and Empire' in Sneja Gunew and Ann Yeatman (eds) *Feminism and the Politics of Difference*, St Leonards: Allen & Unwin, 103–127.

Jolly, Rosemary (1996) *Colonization, Violence, and Narration in White South African Writing: André Brink, Breyten Breytenbach and J. M. Coetzee*, Athens and Johannesburg: Ohio University Press and Witwatersrand University Press.

Jones, Dorothy (1996) 'Women, Place, and Myth-Making: A Post-colonial Perspective' in Hena Maes-Jelinek, Gordon Collier and Geoffrey V. Davis (eds) *A Talent(ed) Digger: Creations, Cameos, and Essays in honour of Anna Rutherford*, Amsterdam and Atlanta: Rodopi, 191–202.

King, Bruce (ed.) (1993) *The Later Fiction of Nadine Gordimer*, London: Macmillan.

Kleinman, Arthur and Joan (1996) 'The Appeal of Experience, The Dismay of Images: Cultural Appropriations of Suffering in our Times', *Daedalus*, 125.1 Winter: 1–24.

Kossew, Sue (1999) 'Resistance, Complicity and Post-colonial Politics', *Critical Survey*, 11.2: 18–30.

Kossew, Sue (2001) ' "Living in Hope": An Interview with Nadine Gordimer', *Commonwealth: Essays and Studies*, 23.2: 55–61.

Kossew, Sue and Schwerdt, Dianne (eds) (2001) *Re-imagining Africa: New Critical Perspectives*, New York: Nova Science.

Krog, Antjie (1998) *Country of My Skull*, London: Jonathan Cape.

Lake, Marilyn (1981) ' "Building Themselves Up With Aspros": Pioneer Women Re-assessed', *Hecate*, 7.2: 7–19.

Lake, Marilyn (1997) 'Women and Nation in Australia: The Politics of Representation', *Australian Journal of Politics and History*, 43.1: 41–52.

Landsman, Anne (1998) *The Devil's Chimney*, Johannesburg: Jonathan Ball Publishers.

Larriera, Alicia (1997) 'HSC Books Row: Kramer's Admission', *Sydney Morning Herald*, 4 April: 3.

Lattas, Andrew (1990) 'Aborigines and Contemporary Australian Nationalism: Primordiality and the Cultural Politics of Otherness', *Social Analysis*, 27: 50–69.

Lawson, Louisa (1887) 'A Word for the Blacks', *The Dawn*, 1 November, 1; cited in Sheridan 1988, 77.

Lawson, Louisa (1889; 2nd edn 1982) 'The Australian Bush-Woman', in 'Notes and Documents', *Australian Literary Studies*, 10.4, October: 500–503; also in *Englishwoman's Review* of 15 August 1889 and 15 October 1889, although an earlier publication occured in the Boston *Women's Journal*, 27 July 1889.

Lazar, Karen (1983) 'Feminism as "Piffling"? Ambiguities in Nadine Gordimer's Short Stories' in Bruce King (ed.) *The Later Fiction of Nadine Gordimer*, London: Macmillan, 213–227.

Lazar, Karen (1999) 'Lemmings, Cats, Pigs: Gordimer's Women during the Interregnum and Beyond' in Andries Walter Oliphant (ed.) *A Writing Life: Celebrating Nadine Gordimer*, London: Viking Penguin, 19–48.

Lessing, Doris (1986) 'Breaking Down these Forms', Interview with Stephen Gray originally published in *Research in African Literatures* 17; and reprinted in Earl G. Ingersoll (ed.) (1996) *Putting the Questions Differently: Interviews with Doris Lessing 1964 1994*, London: HarperCollins/Flamingo.

Lessing, Doris (1994) *The Grass is Singing*, London: HarperCollins, Flamingo; first published 1950, Michael Joseph.

Lever, Susan (2000) *Real Relations: Australian Fiction: Realism, Feminism and Form*, Rushcutters Bay: Halstead Press.

Lionnet, Françoise (1995) *Postcolonial Representations: Women, Literature, Identity*, Ithaca, NY and London: Cornell University Press.

Lockett, Cecily (1996) 'Feminism(s) and Writing in English in South Africa' in Margaret Daymond (ed.) *South African Feminisms: Writing, Theory, and Criticism, 1990–1994*, New York: Garland.

Macaskill, Brian (1990) 'Interrupting the Hegemonic: Textual Critique and Mythological Recuperation from the White Margins of South African Writing', *Novel*, 23.2 Winter: 156–181.

Maes-Jelinek, Hena, Collier, Gordon and Davis, Geoffrey V. (eds) (1996) *A Talent(ed) Digger: Creations, Cameos, and Essays in Honour of Anna Rutherford*, Amsterdam and Atlanta: Rodopi.

Magarey, Susan, Rowley, Sue and Sheridan, Susan (eds) (1993) *Debutante Nation: Feminism Contests the 1890s*, St Leonards: Allen & Unwin.

Mama, Amina (1997) 'Sheroes and Villains: Conceptualizing Colonial and Contemporary Violence against Women in Africa' in M. Jacqui Alexander and Chandra Talpade Mohanty (eds) *Feminist Geneaologies, Colonial Legacies, Democratic Futures*, New York and London: Routledge, 46–62.

Marlatt, Daphne (1998) 'Subverting the Heroic in Feminist Writing of the West Coast' in *Readings from the Labyrinth*, Edmonton: NeWest Press, 86–107.

Marquard, Jean (1979) 'The Farm: A Concept in the Writing of Olive Schreiner, Pauline Smith, Doris Lessing, Nadine Gordimer and Bessie Head', *Dalhousie Review*, 59.2: 293–307.

Martin, Susan (1998) 'National Dress or National Trousers?' in Bruce Bennett and Jennifer Strauss (eds) *The Oxford Literary History of Australia*, Melbourne: Oxford University Press, 89–104.

Masters, Olga (1980) 'A Henry Lawson Short Story', *The Rose Fancier*, St Lucia: University of Queensland Press, 100–105.

Matthews, Brian (1973) 'Life in the Eye of the Hurricane: The Novels of Thea Astley', *Southern Review*, 6.2: 148–173.

McClintock, Anne (1993) 'Family Feuds: Gender, Nationalism and the Family', *Feminist Review*, 44 Summer: 61–80.

McClintock, Anne (1995) *Imperial Leather: Race, Gender and Sexuality in the Colonial Contest*, London and New York: Routledge.

McClintock, Anne (1997) ' "No Longer in a Future Heaven": Gender, Race and Nationalism' in A. McClintock, A. Mufti and E. Shohat (eds) *Dangerous Liaisons: Gender, Nation and Postcolonial Perspectives*, Minneapolis and London: University of Minnesota Press.

McDowell, Linda and Sharp, Joanne P. (eds) (1997) *Space, Gender, Knowledge: Feminist Readings*, London: Arnold.

McGuire, Margaret E. (1990) 'The Legend of the Good Fella Missus', *Aboriginal History*, 14.1–2: 124–150.

Mda, Zakes (2000) *The Heart of Redness*, Oxford: Oxford University Press.

Mears, Gillian (1991) *The Mint Lawn*, Sydney: Allen & Unwin.

Mears, Gillian (1994) 'Why I Write' in Anna Rutherford, Lars Jensen and Shirley Chew (eds) *Into the Nineties: Post-Colonial Women's Writing*, Mandelstrup and Armidale: Dangaroo Press.

Mills, Sara (1991) *Discourses of Difference: An Analysis of Women's Travel Writing and Colonialism*, London and New York: Routledge.

Modisane, Bloke (1986) *Blame Me on History*, Johannesburg: Ad. Donker; first published Thames & Hudson, 1963.

Moore, Catriona (ed.) (1994) *Dissonance: Feminism and the Arts 1970–90*, St Leonards: Allen & Unwin.

Moorhouse, Frank (1980) 'The Drover's Wife', *The Bulletin*, 29 January 1980: 160–162; also collected in John Thieme (ed.) *The Arnold Anthology of Post-colonial Literatures in English*.

Moreton-Robinson, Aileen (2000) *Talkin' Up to the White Woman: Indigenous Women and Feminism*, St Lucia: University of Queensland Press.

Ndebele, Njabulo S. (1998) 'Home for Intimacy' in Andries Walter Oliphant (ed.) *A Writing Life: Celebrating Nadine Gordimer*, London and New York: Penguin Viking, 455–459.

Nightingale, Peggy (ed.) (1986) *A Sense of Place in the New Literatures in English*, St Lucia: University of Queensland Press.

Nkululeko, Dabi (1987) 'The Right to Self-Determination in Research: Azanian Women' in Christine Qunta (ed.) *Women in Southern Africa*, Braamfontein: Skotaville Publishers.

Nuttall, Sarah (1993) Review of *Screens Against the Sky*, *Southern African Review of Books*, Issue 26, July/August, online. Available: http://www.uni–ulm.de/~rturrell/antho2html/Nuttall.html (accessed 13 October 2002). No page numbers.

Nuttall, Sarah (1997) 'Nationalism, Literature and Identity in South Africa and Australia', *Australian Studies*, 12.2: 58–68.

Nuttall, Sarah and Coetzee, Carli (eds) (1998) *Negotiating the Past: The Making of Memory in South Africa*, Oxford: Oxford University Press.

Oliphant, Andries (ed.) (1988) *A Writing Life: Celebrating Nadine Gordimer*, London and New York: Viking.

Olubas, Brigitta and Greenwell, Lisa (1999) 'Re-membering and Taking Up an Ethics of Listening: A Response to Loss and the Maternal in "The Stolen Children"', *Australian Humanities Review*, 15: October–November, online. Available: http://www.lib.latrobe.edu.au/AHR/archive.html#indigenous (accessed 4 February 2001).

Paul, Donald (1998) 'A Conversation with Nadine Gordimer', *Boston Phoenix* 'Weekly Wire', online. Available: http://weeklywire.com/ww/01-05-98/boston_books_3.html (accessed 6 August 1999).

Pearce, Sharyn and Neilsen, Philip (eds) (1996) *Current Tensions: Proceedings of the 18th Annual Conference ASAL 96*, Brisbane: Queensland University of Technology.

Penner, Dick (1986) 'Sight, Blindness and Double-Thought in J. M. Coetzee's *Waiting for the Barbarians*', *World Literature Written in English*, 26.1 Winter: 34–45.

Pettman, Jan Jindy (1995) 'Race, Ethnicity and Gender in Australia' in Daiva Stasiulis and Nira Yuval-Davis (eds) *Unsettling Settler Societies: Articulations of Gender, Race, Ethnicity and Class*, London: Sage, 65–94.

Petzold, Jochen (2002) *Re-imagining White Identity by Exploring the Past: History in South African Novels of the 1990s*, Studies in English Literary and Cultural History 5, Trier: Wissenschaftlicher Verlag Trier.

Pratt, Mary Louise (1992) *Imperial Eyes: Travel Writing and Transculturation*, London and New York: Routledge.

Prichard, Katherine Susannah (1990) *Coonardoo*, North Ryde: Angus & Robertson; first published c. 1929.

Qunta, Christine (ed.) (1987) *Women in Southern Africa*, Braamfontein: Skotaville Publishers.

Rajan, R. S. (1993) *Real and Imagined Women: Gender, Culture and Postcolonialism*, London and New York: Routledge.

Read, Peter (2000) *Belonging: Australians, Place and Aboriginal Ownership*, Cambridge: Cambridge University Press.

Ritchie, Susan (1996) 'Dismantling Privilege, Inventing Self: Postmodern Feminism and South African Post-Colonial Subjectivity' in John Hawley (ed.) *Writing the Nation: Self and Country in the Post-Colonial Imagination*, Amsterdam and Atlanta: Rodopi, 151–160.

Roberts, Sheila (1985) 'A Questionable Future: The Vision of Revolution in White South African Writing', *Journal of Contemporary African Studies*, 4.1–2 October: 215–223.

Roderick, Colin (ed.) (1972) *Henry Lawson Criticism 1894–1971*, Sydney: Angus and Robertson.

Rowley, Sue (1989) 'Inside the Deserted Hut: The Representation of Motherhood in Bush Mythology', *Westerly*, 4: 76–96.

Rowley, Sue (1993) 'Things a Bushwoman Cannot Do' in Susan Magarey, Sue Rowley and Susan Sheridan (eds) *Debutante Nation: Feminism Contests the 1890s*, Sydney: Allen & Unwin, 185–198.

Rowley, Sue (1994) 'Going Public, Getting Personal' in Catriona Moore (ed.) *Dissonance: Feminism and the Arts 1970–90*, St Leonards: Allen & Unwin.

Ruden, Sarah (1999) '*Country of My Skull*: Guilt and Sorrow and the Limits of Forgiveness in the New South Africa', *ARIEL: A Review of International English Literature*, 30.1 January: 165–185.

Rutherford, Anna (ed.) (1988) *Aboriginal Culture Today*, Mundelstrup: Dangaroo, 76–91.

Rutherford, Anna (ed.) (1992) *From Commonwealth to Post-Colonial*, Sydney and Mundelstrup: Dangaroo Press, 276–291.

Rutherford, Anna, Jensen, Lars and Chew, Shirley (eds) (1994) *Into the Nineties: Post-colonial Women's Writing*, Mandelstrup and Armidale: Dangaroo Press.

Rutherford, J. (ed.) (1990) *Identity: Community, Culture, Difference*, London: Lawrence & Wishart.

Sachs, Albie (1991) 'Preparing Ourselves for Freedom' in Duncan Brown and Bruno van Dyk (eds) *Exchanges: South African Writing in Transition*, Pietermaritzburg: University of Natal Press, 117–125.

Sallis, Eva (1998) *Hiam*, St Leonards, Sydney: Allen & Unwin.

Sallis, Eva (2002) *The City of Sealions*, Crows Nest: Allen & Unwin.

Sanders, Mark (2001) 'Extraordinary Violence', Afterword in *Interventions*, 3.2: 242–250.

Saunders, Kay and Evans, Raymond (eds) (1992) *Gender Relations in Australia: Domination and Negotiation*, Sydney: HBJ.

Sayer, Mandy (1996) 'The Drover's Wife', *Australian Book Review*, May: 66–68.

Schaffer, Kay (1988) *Women and the Bush: Forces of Desire in the Australian Cultural Tradition*, Cambridge: Cambridge University Press.

Schaffer, Kay (1993) 'Henry Lawson, The Drover's Wife and the Critics' in Susan Magarey, Sue Rowley, Susan Sheridan (eds) *Debutante Nation: Feminism Contests the 1890s*, Sydney: Allen & Unwin, 199–210.

Schaffer, Kay (2001) 'Manne's Generation: White Nation Responses to the Stolen Generation Report', *Australian Humanities Review*, 22, June–August 2001, on-line. Available: http://www.lib.latrobe.edu.au/AHR/archive/Issue–June–2001/schaffer.html (accessed 8 August 2001).

Scherzinger, Karen (1991) 'The Problem of the Pure Woman: South African Pastoralism and Female Rite of Passage', *UNISA English Studies* XXIX, I: 29–35.

Schreiner, Olive (1980 repr.) *The Story of an African Farm*, Harmondsworth: Penguin, with an Introduction by Dan Jacobson.

Sheridan, Susan (1988) ' "Wives and mothers like ourselves, poor remnants of a dying race": Aborigines in Colonial Women's Writing' in Anna Rutherford (ed.) *Aboriginal Culture Today*, Mundelstrup: Dangaroo, 76–91.

Sheridan, Susan (1995) *Along the Faultlines: Sex, Race and Nation in Australian Women's Writing: 1880s–1930s*, Sydney: Allen & Unwin.

Shohat, Ella (1991) 'Gender and Culture of Empire', *Quarterly Review of Cinema and Video*, 13: 45–84.

Slemon, Stephen (1990) 'Unsettling the Empire: Resistance Theory for the Second World', *World Literature Written in English World*, 30.2: 30–41.

Slovo, Gillian (1997) *Every Secret Thing: My Family, My Country*, London: Virago.

Slovo, Gillian (2000) *Red Dust*, London: Virago.

Smit, Johannes A., van Wyk, Johan and Wade, Jean-Philippe (eds) (1996) *Rethinking South African Literary History*, Durban: Y Press.

Smith, Pauline (1963) 'Why and How I Became an Author' – unpublished. Cf. 'A Note about Pauline Smith's unpublished essay, "Why and How I became an author" ' by Geoffrey Haresnape in *English Studies in Africa*, 6.2 Sept 1963: 149–153.

Smith, Pauline (1976) *The Beadle*, Cape Town: A. A. Balkema; first published 1926.

Smith, Pauline (no date) *The Little Karoo*, with an introduction by Arnold Bennett, London: Jonathan Cape; first published 1925.

Sorensen, Emma (2000) *(Re)Positioning the Gaze: The 'Subterranean' Feminist Themes within Gillian Mears' Novels, The Mint Lawn and the Grass Sister*, unpublished Honours thesis, University of New South Wales. Publication of edited version of Appendix, 'In Conversation with Gillian Mears' pending in *Antipodes*, 17.2: 125–131.

Spender, Dale (1988) Introduction to *Penguin Anthology of Australian Women's Writing*, Harmondsworth: Penguin.

Stanton, Sue (1999) 'Time for Truth: Speaking the Unspeakable – Genocide and Apartheid in the "Lucky" Country', a combined review/article of *The Stolen Children: Their Stories*, ed. Carmel Bird, *Australian Humanities Review*, 14, July–September, online. Available: http://www.lib.latrobe.edu.au/AHR/archive/Issue-July-1999/stanton.html (accessed 13 October 1999).

Stasiulis, Daiva and Yuval-Davis, Nira (eds) (1995) *Unsettling Settler Societies: Articulations of Gender, Race, Ethnicity and Class*, London: Sage, 207–240.

Stummer, P. O. (ed.) (1986) *The Story Must be Told. Short Narrative Prose in the New Literatures in English*, Würtzburg: Königshausen & Neumann.

Sullivan, Jane (1999) 'Out of the Dark', *The Age*, Saturday 14 August, online. Available: http:www.uscis.bigpond.com/kgrenville/fic/idea/reading-resources.html (accessed 20 June 2002). No page numbers.

Tacey, David J. (1995) *Edge of the Sacred: Transformation in Australia*, Blackburn, Victoria: Harper Collins.

Thieme, John (1989) 'Drovers' Wives' in J. Bardolph (ed.) *Short Fiction in the New Literatures in English*, Nice: Faculté des Lettres.

Thieme, John (ed.) (1996) *The Arnold Anthology of Post-colonial Literatures in English*, London and New York: Arnold.

Thomson, Helen (1993) 'Gardening in the Never-Never: Women Writers and the Bush' in Kay Ferres (ed.) *The Time to Write: Australian Women Writers 1890–1930*, Ringwood: Penguin Books, 19–37.

Tiffin, Helen (1997) 'The Body in the Library: Identity, Opposition and the Settler-Invader Woman' in Marc Delrez and Bénédicte Ledent (eds) *The Contact and the Culminiation: Essays in Honour of Hena Maes-Jelinek*, Liége, Belgium: Liége Language and Literature, 213–228.

Turner, Graeme (1994) *Making it National: Nationalism and Australian Popular Culture*, St Leonards: Allen & Unwin.

Tutu, Desmond (1999) *No Future without Forgiveness*, London: Rider.

Unterhalter, Elaine (1995) 'Constructing Race, Class, Gender and Ethnicity: State and Opposition Strategies in South Africa' in Daiva Stasiulis and Nira Yuval-Davis (eds) *Unsettling Settler Societies: Articulations of Gender, Race, Ethnicity and Class*, London: Sage, 207–240.

van der Merwe, C. N. (ed.) (2001) *Strangely Familiar: South African Narratives on Town and Countryside*, Parow: Contentlot.com (www.contentlot.com).

van Wyk Smith, Malvern (1988) Review Article: Olive Schreiner, *English in Africa*, 15.2: 93–100.

van Wyk Smith, Malvern (ed.) (2001) 'From "Boereplaas" to Vlakplaas: The Farm from Thomas Pringle to J. M. Coetzee' in C. N. van der Merwe (ed.) *Strangely Familiar: South African Narratives on Town and Countryside*, Parow: Contentlot.com (www.contentlot.com), 17–36.

Visel, Robin (1988) 'A Half-Colonization: The Problem of the White Colonial Woman Writer', *Kunapipi*, x.3: 39–44.

Visel, Robin (1990) ' "We Bear the World and We Make it": Bessie Head and Olive Schreiner', *Research in African Literatures*, 21.3: 115–124.

Voss, A. E. (1977) 'A Generic Approach to the South African Novel in English', *UCT Studies in English*, 7: 110–119.

Wagner, Kathrin M. (1992) ' "Both as a Citizen and as a Woman"? Women and Politics in Some Gordimer Novels' in Anna Rutherford (ed.) *From Commonwealth to Post-colonial*, Sydney and Mundelstrup: Dangaroo Press, 276–291.

Wagner, Kathrin M. (1990) ' "History from the Inside"? Text and Subtext in Some Gordimer Novels' in Geoffrey V. Davis (ed.) *Crisis and Conflict: Essays on Southern African Literature*, Essen: Die Blaue Eule Press, 89–107.

Walker, Cherryl (ed.) (1990) *Women and Gender in Southern Africa to 1945*, Cape Town and London: David Philip and James Currey.

Ward, Russel (1958) *The Australian Legend* Melbourne: Oxford University Press.

Ware, Vron (1992) *Beyond the Pale: White Women, Racism and History*, London and New York: Verso.

Wenzel, Jennifer (2000) 'The Pastoral Promise and the Political Imperative: The Plaasroman Tradition in an Era of Land Reform', *Modern Fiction Studies*, 46.1: 90–113.

Whitlock, Gillian (1985) 'Graftworks: Australian Women's Writing 1970–90' in Carole Ferrier (ed.) *Gender, Politics and Fiction: Twentieth Century Australian Women's Novels*, St Lucia: University of Queensland Press, 236–258.

Whitlock, Gillian (1993) 'White Women, Racism, and History', *ARIEL: A Review of International English Literature*, 24.3 July: 117–123.

Whitlock, Gillian (1999) 'Australian Literature: Points for Departure', *Australian Literary Studies*, 19.2 October: 152–162.

Whitlock, Gillian (2000) *The Intimate Empire: Reading Women's Autobiography*, London: Cassell.

Whitlock, Gillian and Carter, David (eds) (1992) *Images of Australia: An Introductory Reader in Australian Studies*, St Lucia: University of Queensland Press.

Wicomb, Zoë (1998) 'Shame and Identity: The Case of the Coloured in South Africa' in Derek Attridge and Rosemary Jolly (eds) *Writing South Africa: Literature, Apartheid, and Democracy: 1970–1995*, Cambridge: Cambridge University Press, 91–107.

Wicomb, Zoë (2001) *David's Story*, New York: The Feminist Press.

Williams, Patrick and Chrisman, Laura (eds) (1993) *Colonial Discourse and Postcolonial Theory: A Reader*, London: Harvest Wheatsheaf.

Wright, Judith (1994) 'Being White Woman' in Duncan Graham (ed.) *Being Whitefella*, Fremantle: Fremantle Arts Centre Press, 177–181.

Yamauchi, Tadashi (no date) 'Literature Offers Insights into Changing World', interview with Nadine Gordimer, *The Daily Yomiuri Shimbun Online*, online. Available: http://www.yomiuri.co.jp/dy/civil/civil006.htm (accessed 25 September 2002).

Yelin, Louise (1998) *From the Margins of Empire: Christina Stead, Doris Lessing, Nadine Gordimer*, Ithaca and London: Cornell University Press.

Zinkhan, E. J. (1982) 'Louisa Lawson's "The Australian Bush-Woman" – A Source for "The Drover's Wife" and "Water them Geraniums"?', *Australian Literary Studies*, 10.4: 495–499.

Index

Where references are given to notes, the chapter number precedes the note number